Dreaming Pachinko

Also by Isaac Adamson

Hokkaido Popsicle

Tokyo Suckerpunch

Dreaming Pachinko

Isaac Adamson

Perennial

An Imprint of HarperCollins*Publishers*

A portion of Mitsutaka's poem taken from *Listen to the Voices from the Sea*. Copyright © 2000 by Midori Yamanouchi. Published by University of Scranton Press. Reprinted with the permission of University of Scranton Press.

A portion of "The Boatman's Song" taken from *Low City, High City: Tokyo from Edo to the Earthquake*. Copyright © 1983 by Edward Seidensticker. Published by Alfred A. Knopf.

HarperCollins books may be purchased for educational, business, or sales promotional use. For information please write: Special Markets Department, Harper-Collins Publishers Inc., 10 East 53rd Street, New York, NY 10022.

FIRST EDITION

Designed by Jamie Kerner-Scott

Library of Congress Cataloging-in-Publication Data
    Adamson, Isaac.
        Dreaming pachinko / Isaac Adamson.—1st ed.
          p. cm.
    ISBN 0-06-051623-2
     1. Chaka, Billy (Fictitious character)—Fiction.
    2. American—Japan—Fiction. 3. Tokyo (Japan)—
    Fiction. 4. Journalists—Fiction. I. Title.

    PS3551.D39538 D7 2003
    813'.6—dc21

                        2002038736

03 04 05 06 07 ❖ /RRD 10 9 8 7 6 5 4 3 2 1

This is a work of fiction.

Mr. Nakodo is based on no actual functionary within the esteemed Ministry of Construction, nor any other person in any other ministry in Japan, the United States, or any other territory, excluding Canada. Similarly, Inspector Arajiro is not modeled after an actual member of the Tokyo Metropolitan Police Department, nor is he based on the vice principal of the author's junior high or anything like that.

The Man in White doesn't exist. Should he appear in your hotel room one morning, immediately contact a mental health care professional. As to the existence of the Seven Lucky Gods, well, it's really nobody's business what gods you believe in.

Sadly, all the events surrounding World War II actually occurred, save for one. The author wishes he just made them all up, but, unfortunately, he did not.

Finally, any similarities between the fish depicted in this book and any real-life fish, whether living or dead, is purely coincidental.

To my wife, Chee-Soo Kim, for her patience and understanding

PART ONE

"We wake from the deep sleep of a long night.
How sweet the sound of waves beneath us."
—from "The Takarabune" (folk song)

1

Lucky Benten Pachinko

They were the first words he'd spoken in almost an hour and I missed them. They were drowned in the pachinko drone, an endless babble layered with ringing bells and whistling whistles and jingling jingles and every noise game designers could think of to keep you from thinking. Hyper-speed electronic dance tunes blasted from the surrounding speakers at brainwash volume but no one was dancing. No one looked like they'd danced in years.

"Could you repeat that?" I said.

A fresh stream of pachinko balls tumbled down the face of the machine—an assemblage of plastic and metal that tried to utilize every color in the visible spectrum. Gombei hunched forward, neck giraffing, eyes protruding from his skull as if the game was literally pulling him in. When the balls had all run their course he glanced back at me over his shoulder, face frozen in a rigid half smile. "Life is just like pachinko," he said. Then he twisted the knob to send more balls cascading through the maze of obstacles.

Pachinko, in case you're lucky enough never to have seen it played for hours on end, is like a combination pinball and slot machine. Playing consists of turning a knob and watching hundreds of steel balls stream down a vertical board studded with metal pins. Players hope some of their balls bounce into special holes on the board, which earns them more balls. The balls can then be cashed in for prizes, the prizes traded for money. That's all there is to it. Serious players will argue there's all kinds of strategy and skill involved, but the game ain't exactly *shogi*.

And I didn't know how life was like pachinko, but at this point I had to take what I could get from Gombei. I wrote the quote in my notebook, figuring it might make a good lead-in for his segment in "Fallen Stars"—a series of where-are-they-now articles *Youth in Asia* was running about yesteryear celebrities.

I'd been against the idea from the start. Our demographic couldn't care less about forgotten stars—we were a teen magazine, I argued. We should be reveling in the present, glorifying the now with the latest pimply hyperbole—not unearthing fossilized celebs felled by bad luck, bad decisions and the passage of time. Kids, I protested, aren't interested in the ways life can go wrong, and tough-luck stories had as much business in the pages of *Youth in Asia* as advertisements for life insurance or funeral plots.

It was one of the better rants I'd gone on at a *Youth in Asia* editorial meeting and it made absolutely no difference. Roughly four hours later I was thirteen thousand feet above the earth in a 747 bound for Narita Airport, on my way to interview one-hit wonder Gombei Fukugawa, whose story was about as tough luck as they came.

I finally found him hiding from the sweltering July sun in a smoke-choked basement at the Lucky Benten Pachinko—a second-rate pachinko parlor in the freewheeling Ameyayoko-cho shopping arcade near Tokyo's Ueno station. Gombei looked a lot different than he had in his old press-kit photos. Hair hanging in uncombed tangles, skin gone pasty from spending every waking hour under fluorescent lights. His signature outfit used to be a ridiculous lemon-yellow jumpsuit, but now he was dressed in a tatty gray raincoat and his shoes looked like they'd been buffed in a cement mixer. About an hour ago, his prepaid pachinko card had run out, but he conned me into buying him another one thousand yen worth of balls. I suppose it's no wonder he'd become a pachinko junkie. He'd taken so many knocks since his duo Lemon Lime were topping the J-POP charts that the guy probably identified with pachinko balls.

About the only thing I'd learned during the last two hours about Gombei Fukugawa was that he took his pachinko very, very seriously. Seriously enough to build a whole fatalistic philosophy around. I'd given up on getting any of my questions answered hours ago, resigning myself to just sitting in the tiny chair next to him, writing down the pachinko aphorisms he occasionally muttered and watching the smoke from countless cigarettes fog under the mirrored ceiling. When that got boring, I busied myself untying and retying my wing tips. Once I got the laces just the way I like them, I killed time counting how many people in the arcade were wearing eyeglasses.

That's when I spotted the young woman seated at a machine down our row. Her head was drooping forward, her hair falling over her bare shoulders. She wore a sleeveless white dress meant for better places than a pachinko dive, and the look on her face said she knew it. And no, she wasn't wearing eyeglasses.

What I noticed first was her mole. It was tough to miss. The thing was half the size of a jelly bean, and clung barnacle-like to the outer rim of her left nostril. All her physical flaws must've been concentrated into that protruding growth, because otherwise she was calendar material, the type that made you wish there were fifteen months in a year.

Used to be one look at a woman like her and I'd be wrecking my life as fast as possible. But I was older now, maybe a little wiser. I'd learned slower ways to wreck my life, and she probably had younger lives to wreck.

So I took a second look.

A green plastic basket of steel balls rested on the ledge in front of her as she sat staring at the machine like she was lost. She was the only woman in the room, and as far as I could tell, she wasn't actually playing the game. It looked more like she was meditating, trying to achieve pachinko mind. Something about her presence unsettled me. Seeing her there gave me the same feeling you get when the phone rings in the middle of the night then stops just as you reach for the receiver.

"Life is like pachinko," Gombei resumed, each word emerging like a separate thought. "Because life is a game of chance. Which means it's mostly a game of loss. Of dimin-

ished returns. Pachinko has its very origins in defeat. In surrender to the inevitable."

"Yeah," I said. "How so?"

"Pachinko was invented in the wake of the Fifteen Years
War. What you call World War Two."

I started to ask him another question but he held up a
hand to silence me then turned the knob again. One of the
balls landed in the V-zone, opening the two Magic Tulips of
Magic and sending a digital slot-machine-style display spinning at the center of the machine. It came up lemon, lemon,
mackerel. The machine spit five or ten balls into Gombei's
tray and he spoke again.

"During the war, Japan was producing a fantastic number
of ball bearings. To be put in planes and battleships and submarines and whatever. Then one day, Japan surrenders. Suddenly the war is over. Tanks are dismantled, weapons are
destroyed. Everything of value is either stolen and sold on
the black market or confiscated by the Americans. But all
these metal balls remain. Thousands of them, maybe even
millions, in factories and warehouses. Just sitting there.
Nobody knew what to do with them. But this guy, this inven-
tor type, he worked in one of these warehouses. Day after day
he looked at these crates of worthless metal balls, struggling
to find some use for them. Until one day, out of the blue . . ."

Just then I became aware of a faint noise to my right. A
sound like steady rain on a tin roof. Gombei kept talking. It
was the most he'd talked all day, but my pen had stopped.
The sound grew louder. I turned around and glanced over my
shoulder.

Thousands of pachinko balls were spreading over the
floor, careening against machines, bouncing and rolling with
a mad jailbreak energy as they glinted under the fluorescent

lights, celebrating their escape in a frenzy of motion at once hypnotic and strangely beautiful.

Suddenly the young woman in front of the mad cascade toppled sideways from her chair. She hit the floor twitching and jerking, her slender legs knocking against the upended plastic basket and scattering the few steel balls still trapped inside. More balls poured from the machine she'd been playing. The jackpot collection tray was already overflowing, sending a torrent of balls ricocheting against the floor.

Nobody else in the pachinko hall even noticed.

I pried myself out of my seat, dropped my notebook and moved toward the fallen woman. I had to shuffle, keeping my soles against the floor to prevent the balls from rolling underfoot as they beat and roiled by the hundreds against my wing tips. Time unfurled with the elastic rhythm of a dream, sound receded into a low, distant pulse, and for a moment I felt like I was walking on the bottom of the ocean.

The woman had thrust her pelvis into the air and her back was frozen in a stiff arch. Blood rushed to her cheeks, her eyes clamped shut and thin foam gathered at the corners of her mouth.

I finally reached the woman and turned her onto her side. Not having a jacket to use, I ended up kicking off my wing tips and placing them under her head so she wouldn't bang it on the floor. As an afterthought, I tried pulling the hem of her dress down to a less-revealing level when her underwear caught my eye. I wondered if I should feel guilty about it, then wondered if the wondering was the same thing as feeling guilty. The sounds of the arcade now came rushing back with a vengeance. Between the incessant bass throb of the dance music and my own idiotic thoughts, I felt like my skull was going to crack open any second.

Suddenly Gombei pushed me aside. He reached into his raincoat and shoved a cell phone in my face. I was so amazed he'd torn himself from his game I just gave him a blank look.

"Call an ambulance!" he yelled.

"But she's just having—"

"Do it. Hurry!"

The phone was so tiny the numbers were like samizdats, but I managed to dial. I pressed the phone against one ear and my hand against the other, trying to block out the relentless techno madness and all the pachinko cacophony. By then two arcade attendants in black-and-yellow-striped vests had strolled over to check out the situation. A dispatcher answered and I gave her my name and told her what had happened. She asked if the young woman had any kind of medical emergency ID, and I told her to hang on a minute.

"Check her for ID!" I yelled to Gombei.

"Shouldn't we stick something in her mouth?"

"Shouldn't we what?"

Something so she doesn't swallow her tongue?"

"It's a myth," I said. "Like free love or trickle-down economics."

"Like tickle what?"

I waved off the question. The woman had fallen right beneath a large speaker mounted on the ceiling and it was nearly impossible to hear anything but the music.

"Check her for ID!" I said again.

"Check her what?"

"Try to find a driver's license or medical ID or something!"

Gombei nodded. He fell to his knees and started going through her Luis Vuitton handbag. The two pachinko worker bees looked at the woman then looked at each other while

row upon row of silent men sat mesmerized by shiny metal
objects, utterly oblivious of anything outside the game.

"The hell is going on down here?"

The gruff voice belonged to the manager. A short guy with
nicotine-stained teeth, rolled shirtsleeves and a failed comb
over. His eyes jumped to his two young drones, to the woman
in the white dress, then over all the spilled pachinko balls,
and finally to Gombei and me.

"The hell is going on here?" he repeated.

The bumblebee kids shrugged. Gombei stopped searching
her purse long enough to shout an answer. "She's having a
fit!"

"She's what?"

"She's having a seizure," I clarified.

The manager nodded and looked at Gombei suspiciously.
Through no fault of his own, Gombei was grinning as if going
through the purses of seizure victims was his ideal way to
spend an afternoon. The manager then shot a look at the bumblebee kids. They bowed hurriedly then buzzed off in different directions, and the manager shifted his gaze back to the
woman on the floor.

"Should I call an ambulance or what?"

I pointed to the phone I still had pressed to my ear. He
grunted and mopped the sweat from his forehead. Gombei
gave up looking for the woman's identification, and just
stood there, hands shoved deep in the pockets of his raincoat.
I tried to tell the dispatcher we couldn't find anything, but
the dispatcher had already hung up. I handed the phone back
to Gombei. Nobody said anything for a while.

It was the manager who finally spoke.

"She's quite the raggle, huh?" he said in a conspiratorial
tone. "Except for that thing on her nose."

I didn't know what a raggle was but I checked my watch, remembering I'd heard somewhere the average seizure lasts between one and two minutes. The knowledge didn't help much, because I had no idea how long ago her seizure had started. We watched as the young woman in the white dress gradually stopped trembling as her muscles relaxed and she sank into a prone position on the floor. She was fast asleep. The insane music grew even louder and faster now, swelling to a crescendo. I noticed Gombei and the manager were not just watching, but unabashedly staring now. I followed Gombei's sight line and realized my efforts at preserving the woman's modesty had been in vain, which explained the intensity of their gazes.

Suddenly four guys in pale green uniforms pushed their way into the picture. It was the ambulance crew. They asked me what had happened and I told them. The lead guy said she'd be fine, and there was nothing to do but let her sleep. She'd likely wake in a few moments. So we all let her sleep. I found myself staring at her mole. I tried not to, but no matter where else I sent my eyes, they always came back to the mole.

Twenty minutes passed.

The medics started getting nervous. Two of them snapped on latex gloves and began checking her vitals. The other two disappeared and returned a few moments later with a gurney, but the wheelbase was too wide to fit through the rows of pachinko machines. Another ten minutes hobbled by. Finally, they decided they'd better take her to a hospital. They carefully rolled her limp body onto a stretcher, strapped her and her Luis Vuitton handbag down and carried her away. It took all four of them to get her out of the pachinko parlor and they had to hoist the stretcher above their heads as they squeezed between the machines. Four men in green carrying a body in white through the haze of cigarette smoke as the music droned. It was like a funeral procession from some parallel universe.

The pachinko players didn't notice any of it. They just went right on twisting knobs as if nothing was happening. Once the ambulance crew had gone, Gombei, the manager and I all looked at each other again then turned our attention to the spot where she'd lain. A few shiny pachinko balls wandered aimlessly across the space she'd vacated. Other than that, there was nothing there but my empty shoes.

"You think she'll be all right?" said Gombei.

"Sure," I said. "She'll be fine."

But I wasn't sure. I didn't know much about seizures, but it seemed she should have woken up before they carried her out. The song ended and for a fraction of a second the room fell silent save for the tinny murmur of the machines. Then another synth assault filled the air, a tune that sounded identical to the last one, only this one had pings instead of beeps. Probably qualified as a completely different musical genre these days.

The manager lit a cigarette and continued staring down at the floor. "I guess I'd better get the ball jockeys to clean up this mess," he said. With that he turned and trundled off to find the bumblebee kids.

He was gone about two seconds before Gombei hit the floor and began scooping up the loose pachinko balls. At first I thought he was just trying to help the manager clean up. But then I noticed he wasn't putting the balls back into the woman's basket. He was putting them into the pockets of his tattered raincoat.

As Gombei glanced up at me from the floor, I thought I

detected a flicker of sadness in his expression. A distant realization that pilfering spilled pachinko balls was pretty damn
low. But trapped as he was in a face that suggested mildly
pleasant thoughts forever looping through his brain, it was
tough to tell.

2

The Hotel Cerulean

All of eastern Japan was experiencing a record-melting heat wave and, like everything else, the heat was magnified in greater Tokyo. Factory effluvium, traffic emissions, miles of sun-absorbent blacktop, exhaust from countless air-conditioning units, and body heat from some twenty million people conspired to do the sun a few degrees better. Early July was supposed to be the rainy season, 100 percent humidity, 90 percent chance of torrential downpour every day. Since I'd arrived there'd been plenty of humidity but somehow the moisture had refused to coalesce. My sweat glands took the drought as a challenge and were busy trying to soak the city all by themselves when I walked into the lobby of the Hotel Cerulean.

The Hotel Cerulean had nothing to do with the color blue. It was conceived as a marine hotel, and was to be part of the Odaiba Seaside Park project, a man-made island in Tokyo Bay built partially out of trash. The hotel was going to be erected near the Maritime Science Museum, and the investors decided to go all out and turn the hotel into an attraction in its own right, like a mini Sea World with room service. But due to some shady, immensely complicated backroom deal involving an unfinished suburban golf course, bad bank loans, and a vacant office tower hundreds of miles away in Osaka, the Hotel Cerulean investors were forced out of Odaiba.

Problem was, they'd already contracted architects, construction companies, interior decorators, aquarium suppliers, exotic fish dealers and the like. Canceling the contracts would mean disrupting harmony and losing serious face, not to mention lots of capital. The hotel backers decided to go ahead with their plans, and so a new site was selected, one in the Kyobashi district, which is how a marine hotel came to sit near central Tokyo, a good distance from the nearest salt water.

All of this I'd learned yesterday from the Walrus. The Walrus liked to talk.

I wiped the sweat from my brow and pushed the button at the front desk. The first seven notes of "Popeye the Sailor Man" rang through the lobby. Beneath it, the sound of waves. While I listened to the piped-in surf, I watched hundreds of small silvery cuttlefish turn first one way then another inside the massive aquarium behind the front desk. They did each movement in perfect unison, each fish completely synchronized with every other, no stragglers and no showboats. A truly Japanese vision of the ideal underwater society.

"Good evening, Mr. Chaka," said the Walrus, emerging from the back office. The Walrus was the hotel's manager; he wore a custom-designed uniform complete with a stiff high collar, epaulets and rank bars. Like something a closeted Prussian naval officer would've worn on parade day. Nearly lost amid the cheap medals and fancy ribbons was a name tag identifying the wearer as Admiral Hideki.

"Evening, Walrus."

"I'm sorry?"

"Admiral," I corrected. "Evening, Admiral."

A salt-and-pepper mustache the size of a toupee crouched under his nose, almost completely covering his mouth. Admiral or not, as long as he kept that mustache I couldn't think of him as anything but the Walrus.

"I hope you are finding everything to your satisfaction here at the Hotel Cerulean?"

"Yep. Smooth sailing."

"And you are enjoying the Octopus's Garden?"

"The room is perfect."

"Excellent," he said. "Perhaps you'd like the tour now?"

Since I'd checked in last night he'd twice offered the tour. From the crestfallen look on his face when I declined, I got the feeling he'd go on asking. But this time I had a good excuse. I had to call my new boss back in Cleveland. With that, I gave him a respectful bow and made my way to the Octopus's Garden.

● ● ●

THE OCTOPUS'S GARDEN was a hull in the basement decorated with battleship-gray wallpaper and a fish tank where the window should've been. The aquarium was home to a single goldfish about the size of my big toe. Next to the aquarium hung a laminated placard written in English, sort of.

LET'S ABOUT THE CARP

This fish are recognized as the honorable carp.

For Japan, the carp (koi) are dearest for their courage and dedication. They are seen for good fortune, with festivals held to their respect.

This carp are the kohaku *koi, celebrated to their venerable red-and-white patterns. Such as snowflowers and fingerpatterns, no two are corresponding. Carp ripen to sizes nearly two foot of length and they are a peaceful specimen and may perhaps experience profuse longevity.*

Let's enjoy the friendship of the carp!

But it wasn't an honorable carp with venerable patterns, it was just an ordinary goldfish. For that matter, I don't know why they called my room the Octopus's Garden, because the only thing that resembled an octopus was the gaudy chandelier dangling above the bed. Nothing about the Hotel Cerulean made much sense but I wouldn't come to find out how strange a place it truly was until later, until it was too late.

The goldfish swished his tail and puckered at me from across the room. I flipped on the lights, kicked off my wing tips and had a look at my notebook.

"Life is like pachinko. Because life is a game of chance . . . of loss. Pachinko has its origins in defeat . . . in surrender."
(WWII, tanks, ball bearings in warehouses

Before I could even close the parentheses my interview had been interrupted by the strange spectacle of ball bearings spilling all over the floor and the woman having a seizure. Probably just as well—the interview was headed nowhere. The whole piece was headed nowhere, and I suppose it wasn't Gombei's fault that he didn't want to talk about anything but pachinko. Given the way his life had turned out, I couldn't blame him.

Like I said, Gombei used to be in a pop duo, a male-female pair called Lemon Lime. A Donnie and Marie Osmond type of thing. Wholesome lyrics, choreographed song-and-dance routines, more smiles than a toothpaste commercial. Gombei was the lemon half. The lime half, Aiko Shimato, had died when Gombei crashed his motorcycle on the Rainbow Bridge during a rainy night seven years ago. In addition to being a performing duo, they'd been romantically involved.

They had only a single hit under their belts when the accident happened, a number called "Sunshine My Heart" that burst onto the scene after it was used in a commercial for a unisex citrus-scented deodorant called, for reasons that only made sense in Japan, Ophelia. The Japanese music scene is notoriously flavor-of-the-minute, but the Lemon Lime hype machine was just getting cranking when the accident happened. Without the motorcycle crash, they probably could've parlayed interest in their hit song into at least one more chart topper. Those combined five minutes and fifty seconds of music would've earned them at least one year of celebrity, countless television appearances and a few hundred million yen. Depending on how badly their management company was ripping them off, they might've been set for life.

Not that Lemon Lime were especially talented. Their music might as well have been computer generated by some pop-cliché algorithm. Prefab and utterly disposable, it was the kind of stuff marketed to kids who didn't know any better by adults who should've. And as far as Lemon Lime's looks, they were nothing special either. The two of them were good-looking enough in that overly cute way, but every TV pop sensation was good-looking enough in that overly cute way.

What set them apart was their chemistry. Together, Gombei and Aiko, Lemon and Lime, had that indefinable something, that intangible, inexplicable aura of superstardom. Whenever you saw Lemon Lime, it was impossible to take them out of context, to imagine them offstage, as regular human beings engaged in regular human being activities. You couldn't picture either of them slurping noodles or clipping their toenails or getting the flu. And you couldn't ever imagine one without the other. Their talent, their genius, was projecting the illusion that they existed only as a unit, only within that magical, untouchable Lemon Lime universe.

That illusion, indeed that universe itself, was forever shattered with the accident. Aiko snapped her neck and was killed instantly. Gombei survived, but left most of his face smeared down a sixty-meter stretch of the newly completed Rainbow Bridge.

The accident prompted a media frenzy. A few weeklies sniffed for scandals—speculating that Gombei had been drunk at the time, insinuating that there was trouble in the Lemon Lime relationship, or even that yakuza thugs hired by a rival singing duo had somehow caused the fatal accident. But the stories came to nothing. In the end, it was just a guy being careless, driving too fast in the rain, maybe trying to impress his girlfriend just like any of us stupid guys might.

Gombei survived his lapse of judgment, but his career didn't. His handlers should've known it was over, but either blinding greed or an admirable but hopelessly misplaced sense of loyalty dictated they try to reinvent him as a solo act.

Months of reconstructive plastic surgery ensued. The flurry of knife and putty work left Gombei's features almost completely immobile, frozen in the pleasant, neutral expression of a guy smiling at a joke not funny enough to laugh at. Charming enough in still frames, in real time his fixed grin came across as masklike and unsettling. His creepy smile couldn't help but conjure up thoughts of the accident, couldn't help but remind you of his missing other half, now gone forever.

Gombei released a new single one year after the accident but nobody noticed. His agent found him faceless work for a while doing voice-overs for radio commercials and the odd animated TV show, but that dried up after a couple of years. The last time the public had heard anything of Gombei was three years ago, when he made the tabloids after a shoplifting incident at a Family Mart in Komagome. LEMON GETS SQUEEZED, ran the headline. He was smiling in the pictures, but then he couldn't help it.

And now *Youth in Asia*, Cleveland's hottest-selling teen rag, was making Gombei the featured "Fallen Star." I saw it as my duty to make one last plea to stay the exhumation.

I picked up the phone and dialed.

On the other side of the world, Sarah answered.

● ● ●

SHE ASKED IF I WAS calling up to resign again.

Like most of our jokes, it had undertones that weren't so funny. Sarah had come into *Youth in Asia* years ago as a nineteen-year-old with mean looks and a talent to match. I taught her some of the finer points of writing for teens, and we became kind of a team. Then we became quite a bit more than that. We had a good thing going for a while, but when we tried to define what we had it wasn't good anymore.

All these years later, everything suddenly changed.

Ed, my editor of fifteen years, had stepped down for reasons of health and sanity. By the time his doctors finally gave him the ultimatum, he was drinking sixteen cups of coffee a day and sucking down enough coffin nails to keep half America's tobacco lobbyists in Armanis. When Ed left *Youth in Asia*, he'd asked me to become his successor, but I wasn't interested in being glued to a chair in Cleveland. I was best on the beat, mixing with the kids, getting the scoop straight from the streets. Handcuffing me to a desk, I explained, would be like confining Jimi Hendrix to the acoustic guitar. Hell, it'd be like making him play the ukulele.

Ed said he was just a workingman who didn't know his ukuleles from his Yoko Onos but he knew a thing or two about opportunities and what he knew was that they didn't knock hard and they didn't knock twice.

Thanks anyway, I said. First thought, best thought.

But when I had that first thought, I didn't know Ed's next thought was to make the same offer to Sarah. I didn't know that she would stop working for our failing online sister publication, generasiax.com, and come back on board. And I certainly didn't know she would become my boss.

When she did, I threw a few tantrums (You acted like a chihuahua with Tourette's, Sarah told me), threatened to resign and skulked around the office for a couple of weeks rethinking the first-thought principle. The Gombei Fukugawa gig got me thousands of miles out of the office, thank God, but I couldn't help but think it was still some form of retribution.

No, I answered Sarah, I wasn't calling to resign.

I was calling to reiterate that I didn't think this Gombei story was such a great idea. She told me I wasn't paid to reiterate—I was paid to write. The magazine had spent good money to send me to Tokyo, and my job was to find Gombei Fukugawa and get the story.

I explained that I had found him. No mean feat, I added, considering he had no steady job, no known address and even his former agent had trouble putting a name with the face. I'd told her how I'd had to scour every pachinko joint in the Low City, going half deaf in the process and clocking a lot of miles on my wing tips. Now that I had reached him, I felt I owed my shoes an apology.

Tell your shoes that life is a journey, Sarah said, not a destination.

I told Sarah to leave my shoes out of this. And as far as Gombei was concerned, there was no scoop. Just a guy terminally down on his luck, one who didn't need his misery dragged out and splashed all over the magazine.

Sarah smelled blood. What's his problem? she asked. Drinking? Drugs? Glue sniffing? Was he into prostitutes? Had he become a prostitute? Kiddie porn—was it kiddie porn? It had to be kiddie porn. Or a sex change. A botched sex change. Kiddie porn featuring children with botched sex changes! No, a cult. A pedophilic—

"Pachinko," I interrupted. "It's goddamn pachinko, Sarah."

Her end went silent for a moment. I wanted to think she

was considering calling off the story—calling off the whole "Fallen Stars" series—but who knows what was going on in her head. I'd never figure it out, but I couldn't stop trying. The worst habits are always the hardest to break.

Just get the story, Sarah sighed.

Then she hung up.

I stood there holding the phone and listening to the dial tone. It was becoming one of my favorite pastimes.

The Man in White

I awoke to a terrible noise and squinted against the harsh light as an eight-armed glass monster descended from the ceiling. Then I realized the monster was just the chandelier and the noise was just the smoke alarm. My brain kept up the good work for a few more seconds, but finally sent up the white flag. There was no way to explain the man sitting in the chair at the foot of my bed.

He had neatly trimmed whitish hair and skin so waxy and colorless you'd think he spent all summer in a subterranean cave. He sat in the clam-shaped chair, one leg crossed over the other with geometric precision, showing off creases in his slacks sharp enough to cut sashimi. As he took focused drags from his cigarette, the smoke meandered toward the ceiling, gathering in a loose cloud around the complaining smoke alarm. Even with his white pants, white jacket, white shirt and white cravat I still didn't think he was one of the good guys. No good guy in the history of the world has ever worn a cravat.

"I take it you're not here to feed the fish."

He didn't seem to hear me, so I said it again, hollering above the din of the alarm. This time he responded. His thin lips parted and he shook his head about three millimeters to either side. Though he was sitting I could tell he was small. Delicate and perfectly proportioned, like a mannequin from an upscale clothing store for jockeys.

"This room is no smoking," I said. "Hear the alarm going off? No smoking."

The man paid no attention. He just leaned back in his chair and waited, cocooning himself in smoke so thick it was almost liquid. We both sat there listening to the alarm. From the look on his face, you'd think it was "Moonlight Sonata."

"You don't want to talk?" I yelled.

No answer.

"Fine. I'm going to call security."

He blinked slowly and blew another plume of smoke toward the ceiling. It was hard to tell where the smoke ended and he began. I picked up the phone and listened. The line was dead.

Across the room, the goldfish stabbed through the waters of its tank, an orange yellow blur bumping against the glass, twisting, thrashing, looking like he was trying to spit a hook. Minutes went by. Loud and annoying minutes.

I wondered who had sent the guy. I'd made a lot of enemies in Tokyo over the years, an occupational hazard when
you're writing for teenagers. Could be the manager for some
coffeehouse ambient drip-hop group I'd slagged, or someone
upset with my critique of their favorite alien-vampire-as-
crime-fighting-shoe-salesman manga, or maybe a low-level
yakuza jealous that his underage girlfriend had my picture
tacked up on her wall. In any case, I figured there was gonna
be a fight and I figured I was gonna be ready.

But the guy hadn't threatened me yet. He'd hardly even
noticed me. Besides, I just didn't feel like fighting that morning. I felt more like having a cup of coffee and reading about
whichever reform politician had been caught taking bribes
this week. But I wouldn't be doing that either. Not until I
dealt with the strange little man at the foot of my bed.

"OK," I groaned. "Where's the fire?"

The man in white put out his cigarette with a delicacy
usually reserved for the tea ceremony and dropped it in the
waste can next to the dresser. Still not a word. I yawned and
got out of bed.

"I'm going to put some clothes on," I shouted. I felt like an
idiot standing there in my boxers, yelling at the guy, pointing
toward the bathroom. "When I get back, you're going to tell
me what you're doing here."

The man produced a gunmetal lighter the size of a small
hand grenade and lit another cigarette with a flip of his wrist.
I stomped across the room, grabbed a pair of pants and a
white button-down shirt, walked into the bathroom and
closed the door behind me. I splashed some water on my face
and got dressed. A few seconds later, the alarm went dead.
When I came out the man in white was gone. The smoke had
completely vanished, as if he'd never been there.

• • •

I MADE MY WAY OUT of my room, down the stairs, out of the hotel. Traffic was already thick as cars lined Showa-dori Avenue and pedestrians moved noiselessly along the sidewalk. I looked up and down the street, but my guest in white was nowhere to be seen. Instead, I found a gray Aston Martin washed up on the curb. A bearish man in a black suit was standing in front of the car, holding an open umbrella in one hand and a sign with my name on it in the other. It wasn't raining, so he must have been using the umbrella to shield himself from the heat. Fat chance of that working. Even at this hour of the morning the air was hot and sticky, practically congealed.

I strolled up to him and cleared my throat.

He snapped to attention and stared at me blankly for a moment. Then he spoke.

"Are you Mr. Billy Chaka?"

"Depends," I said. "You working for Anna Wong?"

"The movie star Anna Wong?"

"That's right," I said. "Because if you are, you can get back in your car and go tell Miss Lady Wong that my idea of romance doesn't include playing second banana to a chimpanzee in britches. Maybe I'm old-fashioned, maybe even a little green, but I'm no sucker. You go tell her that."

"I'm not Ms. Wong's chauffeur," he said.

"No? You must be the chimp."

He closed the umbrella. "Mr. Chaka, please forgive my haste, but I have been waiting for you for some time. I am under extra special instructions to bring you to visit my employer, the honorable Mr. Nakodo. May I respectfully request, Mr. Chaka, that you please get in the car, please?"

I didn't know any Mr. Nakodo, but I'd never been in an Aston Martin before. Didn't even know they existed outside James Bond movies. Besides, the chauffeur was under extra-special instructions, and they'd even spelled my name right on the sign. Before getting into the car, I took another look around for the man in white, but he was nowhere to be found. Maybe his part of the job had just been to get me awake and out of the hotel. It's a highly specialized workforce running this highly complicated world we live in.

I climbed into the back of the car, an area larger than my hotel room and more tastefully furnished. Lace seat covers over pristine white leather upholstery, a flat-screen TV mounted on the back of the driver's seat, a coconut-scented air freshener that worked a little too well. The driver got in, fired up the engine and away we went. I wasn't in the mood for conversation, so I turned on the TV.

For ten minutes I fiddled with a remote control that had enough buttons to command a Martian space probe before finally settling on a cartoon about a little boy superhero who did good deeds with urine. In the span of one stoplight, he pissed out a fire, shot a trapped kitten out of a tree with his pee and foiled a bank robbery by micturating in the gas tank of the getaway car. And here I'd been unheroically using urinals all these years.

I gave up on the TV and stared out the window. The Aston Martin crawled southwest through a labyrinth of streets canyoned by an endless architectural freakshow in which every conceivable mutation of concrete, glass and steel was fused together into a dense hodgepodge that went on for seemingly ever. Half of the structures looked like they'd been turned inside out. Spindly metal staircases helixed up the buildings' sides, rusted pipes crawled the walls like ivy, tangles of wires and cables went every which way. Above all the clutter, the morning sky a dirty white haze holding a thin promise of rain.

We were soon in the bustling international ghetto of Roppongi. The American embassy was nearby, and I wondered if that's where we were headed. Maybe I was finally getting deported. I hadn't committed any felonies recently, but my foils in the Tokyo Metropolitan Police Department had been trying to get me banned from Japan for years. Thanks to their institutional sluggishness and general ineptitude I'd been living on borrowed time for close to a decade—which only proves even bureaucracy has a good side.

Eventually we wound up in the Ark Hills neighborhood.

The Akasaka-Roppongi Knot—a.k.a. Ark Hills—was a minicity located on some of the most expensive acreage of a city known for having the priciest real estate in the world. Ark Hills was one of those luxury communities built in the prelapsarian eighties when Japanese conglomerates were snapping up property from Honolulu to Helsinki, decorating their corporate offices with van Gogh paintings and doling out expensive golf club memberships as New Year's bonuses. While much of Tokyo's rabbit-hutch housing consisted of squat ferroconcrete blocks with all the charm of your average washing machine, Ark Hills boasted red-brick high-rises and the kind of stunning marble façades you'd expect in a land where putting on a good front is part of the national character.

But the foundation of Ark Hills was about as ugly as they came. Through a practice called *jiyage*, real estate companies had hired yakuza thugs to bully individual landowners into selling out cheap, allowing them to buy up whole blocks that could then be sold at much higher prices to developers. The bullying included hurling bricks through windows, tossing dead cats onto doorsteps and that time-tested technique favored by thugs the world over—the unexpected midnight visit. Yakuza liked to believe they were the modern embodiment of Bushido, the way of the warrior, but I couldn't recall too many dead cat hurlings in Musashi's *Book of Five Rings*.

On the other hand, at least the yakuza made no secret of their criminal nature, unlike the colluding real estate developers, bid-rigging construction companies and kickback-happy politicians that played it off legit. Like in every highly developed capitalist society, the biggest crimes in Tokyo went unpunished because the biggest crimes weren't even called crimes. They were called business-as-usual.

We turned right just before the ANA Hotel and continued up a narrow street. About thirty seconds past the Ark Hills Towers the driver made a right near the Spanish embassy. The car stopped in front of an ornate wrought-iron gate set in a high stone wall. Struck me as more like something you'd see at some manor in the English countryside than in the middle of Tokyo. The gates suddenly lurched open with a horrible grating sound to reveal a driveway lined by two rows of stunted cherry trees.

How Sweet the
Sound of Waves

The trees were perfectly distanced from each other, all the same height, each with the same chalky pesticidal band painted at its base. They even seemed to have the same number of branches reaching up into the morning sky, begging for rain.

In the distance ahead a shimmering mess of prismatic glass and surgical chrome cowered amidst a riot of foliage.

The way the plants spilled over the rolling grassy hill, they
didn't seem to be encircling the house so much as fleeing it.
I couldn't blame them. The house looked almost as obscene
as the price of the land it sat upon—a three-story catastrophe,
all jarring angles and gleaming surfaces. Yesterday's forgotten
vision of tomorrow.

Before I could say a word, the driver opened my door and
pointed up to the house. Like somehow I might not have
noticed it. I looked back toward the wrought-iron gate set in
the stone wall. Tokyo Tower stood in the distance behind it,
rising just above the treetops, the Eiffel knockoff the sole
reminder I was still in a city of millions.

I got out of the car and walked toward the house following a foot path through what might loosely be described as a
garden. Cypress trees tangled with bilbaos and ginkgos butted
up against pines while spiny shrubs waged a ground war
with chrysanthemums and snapdragons and all kinds of
flowers I couldn't name. It was worlds away from your classic Japanese-style landscaping, where every feature is meticulously arranged for maximum harmony and plants are
clipped and pruned and fretted over like sickly children.
This garden didn't invite contemplation so much as it did a
machete.

Sunlight sparkled over the surface of a small pond farther
down the path, off to one side of the house. Two eight-foot-
high Doric columns supporting nothing but air stood by what
I guessed was the front door. Between them stood a guy in an
old-fashioned butler suit, like something you'd see in a man-
nerly British whodunit. He looked like he'd been standing
there for twenty years and wasn't half finished.

"Good day, Mr. Chaka," he said. "I believe you are here to
see Mr. Nakodo, yes?"

"If you say so," I said.

Overhead, the sun drilled a white-hot hole through the haze. I listened to the cicadas and crows and distant car horns and the sound of my wing tips clicking over the flagstones and wondered what the hell I was doing here as I followed the manservant into the house.

I took off my shoes as was customary and the manservant gave me a pair of shiny plastic slippers complete with the Chinese characters for Nakodo printed on the instep. Then he handed me off to a different guy in the same butler suit who guided me through the lavish maze this Mr. Nakodo called home.

The interior designer must have been in cahoots with the landscaper because the place looked like a nightmare you'd have after a long day at a crowded museum. Paintings and sculptures and objets d'wealth were crammed willy-nilly into every nook and cranny. The collection looked as thoughtfully assembled as your average lynch mob and was probably worth more than I'd earn in three or four cycles on the eternal wheel of death and rebirth.

After a disorienting journey I found myself sitting in a small room and sinking into a plush leather chair. The butler said Mr. Nakodo would be with me shortly, asked if I wanted tea or coffee. I declined and he walked away, leaving me in the study. Compared to the other rooms, this one was practically empty. Heavy curtains were drawn over the windows. A large desk dominated the center of the room and the walls were decorated with framed black-and-white photographs.

I sat in the chair, watched the minutes limp by and counted individual dust motes. There weren't many to count. Just when that started to get dull, I heard a whirring noise behind me.

An old man in an electric wheelchair sat three or four feet away. His impossibly fragile body was wrapped in an ornate, multilayered kimono, so that his head almost seemed to be floating on the loose bundle of black and tan fabric. I realized with a start that he'd been sitting there the whole time, ever since I got in the room. The man managed a toothless smile in my direction and I smiled back.

"We wake from the deep sleep of a long night," he said, nodding his head and grinning, his skin a thin parchment drawn taut over his skull.

"Come again?"

"We wake from the deep sleep of a long night."

"We sure do," I said, having no idea what either of us meant. "Are you Mr. Nakodo?"

He didn't answer. All at once his mouth snapped shut and his face went slack. When next he spoke it came out as little more than a groan.

"How sweet the sound of waves beneath us."

Before I could knee-jerk agreement on the sweet sound of the waves he pushed a knob on the chair and whirred across the carpet, driving straight out of the room. I couldn't even see the back of his head as he receded. Just a wheelchair zooming down an empty hall until he veered left and out of sight.

I sat there wondering what to make of it.

Nothing came to mind, so I stood up and decided to take a look at the photographs decorating the walls. They were mostly cheerless group shots of serious men in suits. Big-business types posed in front of big logos of big companies or seated around big tables in anonymous boardrooms. A few of the more playful, outdoorsy shots featured vaguely familiar looking politicians attending groundbreakings and ribbon cuttings, wearing smiles as stiff and ill-fitting as the ceremonial hard hats they posed in.

It took me a while to realize what all the pictures had in common, besides an utter lack of joie de vivre. One guy showed up in every photo. A round-faced, middle-aged man in a gray suit. He was tough to spot at first, until I learned his trick. He was always poised near the edge of the frame, like he was about to sneak out of the picture. And apparently, nobody ever taught him to smile for the camera.

"I'm sorry to keep you waiting," said a voice behind me.

With his hair slicked back to expose his broad forehead, the man looked exactly as he did in the photos, except maybe a little more foregrounded. His gray suit was expensive and tailored and still didn't do much to hide his paunch. As he shuffled into the room and closed the door behind him, I fought the urge to whistle "The Baby Elephant Walk." The man flicked on a light switch, but it didn't do much to brighten the room.

He walked to the large mahogany desk and took a seat. I slouched back into the leather marshmallow recliner. Looking back, I should've been on guard the moment he didn't bow. Alarms should've sounded when he didn't offer me one of his cards, didn't repeat his servant's offer of tea, and didn't apologize that his house was not as big as those in America, even though it was. I should've picked up the phone and called the cops right then, but at the time, I was happy to skip all the etiquette and find out what the hell I was doing there. Little did I know just how long that would take.

"Mr. Chaka," he began. "My name is Mr. Nakodo, and I would like to thank you. I don't know if you have . . ." He paused and his eyes focused on the surface of the empty desk. Then he cleared his throat and began again. "I don't know if you have children of your own, but perhaps you can imagine the difficulties. At any rate, I brought you here to let you know that I am deeply indebted to you for helping Miyuki."

"For helping Miyuki?"

"Yes. My daughter. I'd like to thank you very much."

"You're welcome very much."

"You have a cultivated sense of honor."

"I grew up in Cleveland."

"I regret I am unfamiliar with the city."

"That's OK," I said. "I'm unfamiliar with your daughter. The one I supposedly helped. Don't get me wrong—I appreciate parents being grateful. I get a lot of that because of what I've written. And I'll answer fan mail, sign autographs, give you a nice tour of the office if you're ever in Ohio. But I'm not wild about uninvited guests showing up in my hotel room."

Nakodo sat stiffly in his chair and fixed his gaze on me. After a time, he hunched forward and let out a long sigh. The guy certainly didn't carry himself with the kind of overbearing manner I'd expect from someone in a house like this.

"You speak Japanese quite well," he said.

"That bad, huh?"

"On the contrary. Still, I'm afraid there has been a misunderstanding."

You don't get by in Japanese without learning that "misunderstanding" can mean roughly nine million different things. I didn't want to misunderstand what he meant by misunderstanding, so I just buttoned my lip and waited, returning his stare.

"Mr. Chaka, do you know why you're here?"

"The head of a dead cat?" It was the answer to some koan, but I could never remember which one. I figured if I said it every time I didn't have an answer I'd luck out eventually. Nakodo didn't seem to be amused.

"You really have no idea?" he asked, wrinkling his brow.

I shook my head. He continued peering across the desk, his face the same dour, ashen gray of his suit. Something about the way he looked that moment made me feel sorry for him, though I couldn't think of any special reason why I should.

"Miyuki, my daughter, is in many ways what you might call estranged." Nakodo considered it, his eyes roaming the corners of the room as if looking for a TelePrompTer. "Yes, I think that's the word. Estranged. Against my wishes, she decided not to enter the university, bent as she was on pursuing . . . well, I really can't say. Finding herself, I believe, was the term she used."

He waited for a sign of acknowledgment before continuing. Half of conversational Japanese is knowing exactly when and how to grunt to keep the speaker comfortable, but I just nodded my head. After my rude wake-up call that morning, I wasn't particularly concerned about Nakodo's comfort level.

"Her mother and I certainly didn't grow up with such notions," he eventually continued. "We hardly gave a thought to finding ourselves. Even now, I struggle to understand the precise meaning of 'finding oneself.' But I realize that young people are different today. That the whole world is different. And I remember what it is to be young."

With that he let out another deep sigh. His eyes got a faraway look, and he waited a moment before resuming. "Actually, that's not entirely true. Sometimes, my memories feel as if they are part of someone else's life. Strange, isn't it? Do you remember, Mr. Chaka, how it felt to be young?"

"Sure, I guess. Like it feels now, only more so."

"Hmmm, yes," he mumbled. He pondered for a moment then rose from behind his desk. I watched him stroll the perimeter of the room as he spoke. He may not have displayed the imperious style typical of a man in a multimillion-dollar home, but he certainly had a big shot's love for his own voice.

"Time goes by and takes so much with it," he said, hands clasped behind his back. "The young grow old, the old grow older, the oldest die. Cherry blossoms fall then bud then fall again. Buildings are built and torn down and new ones erected in their places. One after another until you no longer recognize the street you grew up on. The old customs slip right out of existence, and so too the people who practiced them. Like the mere passing of a cloud. It is said that nothing is impervious to time, that even memories change. But I wonder if this is true. Does nothing last? Is change all that never changes?"

"If you brought me here to answer those kinds of questions, you're going to be incredibly disappointed."

For a moment Mr. Nakodo just stood there, seemingly lost in thought. Then he nodded and walked slowly back behind his desk. He sat down again, refolding his hands on the desktop.

"Forgive me," he said. "Lately, these sentimental moods seem to arise from nowhere. In any case, I only meant to say that life must certainly be different today. For young people."

From the looks of it, it wasn't a thought he relished.

"To make a long story short, when Miyuki turned twenty, I permitted her to move out. To get an apartment and go about this dream of finding herself." He inhaled deeply, his expression darkening. "It's a decision I have come to regret. Thankfully, I had people keeping an eye on her. What they reported was very troubling. Very troubling, indeed. I ordered Miyuki to return home. When I told her why, she accused me of spying."

"Sounds kinda like you were."

"What was done was for her own safety. There are a host of reasons why a man in my position would find such precautions necessary."

"Maybe," I said. "But there are a host of reasons why your daughter wouldn't like it. She's a young woman, in the prime of her youth. Probably wants a chance to make her way in the world without Daddy looking over her shoulder. Look at it that way and it's not hard to understand why she'd want to get away from . . . well, all of this."

Mr. Nakodo winced slightly, then cast his sad eyes to the desktop. "I've always envied foreigners' ability to speak their minds."

"I didn't mean—"

"Please don't apologize. Candor is a privilege too rarely enjoyed by we Japanese. But I'm afraid you don't understand, Mr. Chaka. My daughter has disappeared."

After all the preamble, there it was. I still didn't see what it had to do with me, but I wasn't about to come right out and say as much. Interview as many people as I have and you learn the less you ask for, the more they give away.

"It happened yesterday," he said. "I sent my driver to pick her up at her apartment in Minami-Aoyama, but she wasn't there. Then, at approximately five P.M., Miyuki reportedly suffered a grand mal seizure inside an establishment known as the Lucky Benten Pachinko. A hall near Ueno station. Records indicate a man named Billy Chaka made the emergency call. A few minutes later, an ambulance arrived from the Tokyo University Branch Hospital. Medics loaded her onto a stretcher. But before they even reached the ambulance,

Miyuki woke from her slumber. According to the ambulance crew, just outside the pachinko parlor she simply unstrapped herself, jumped up from the stretcher and ran off. No one has seen her since."

"That was your daughter?"

"It was. It *is*. Miyuki, my daughter."

I thought about Miyuki sprawled out, the pachinko balls slowly rolling over the floor. The bumblebee boys standing around, the manager and Gombei leering at her underwear while she slept. And of course I thought about her mole.

"You witnessed this seizure of hers, correct?"

"That's right," I said.

"I see," he replied, nodding slowly and drawing in his breath. "Tell me—was there anyone else with her?"

"Not that I saw. She was sitting alone."

"You're quite certain of this?"

I nodded.

"That correlates with what my people have gathered," he said. "Still, I was hoping you'd seen her with someone before she disappeared."

"What do you mean exactly by 'disappeared'?"

Nakodo examined his knuckles. "After the incident in the pachinko parlor, she simply vanished. Without a trace, as they say. Without so much as a puff of smoke. She's been missing ever since."

"But that was less than twenty-four hours ago."

"Nevertheless, I am concerned."

Obviously the guy had been keeping his daughter on a short leash. I could understand his concern if the girl was fifteen or sixteen, but she was twenty years old. It didn't sound like she was too anxious to come back to Papa, and given the short time I'd spent in the House of Nakodo I couldn't blame her.

"Is it the seizure that bothers you?" I asked.

"In part, yes. There is no epilepsy in her bloodlines and she has no history of experiencing seizures. I can only wonder what may have caused it."

"You been in a pachinko parlor lately?"

"Still, the seizure is but one detail in a disturbing overall portrait. I'm worried for her safety. For her well-being."

"Any particular reason why?"

"Because I am her father, Mr. Chaka."

"Mr. Nakodo," I began. "You might not like this. But from everything you've told me today, it doesn't sound like your daughter *disappeared*. It sounds like maybe she just ran away."

He thought about it, or pretended to, then shook his head.

"Maybe there's a boy," I added.

"She has no boyfriend. My people assure me of this."

"Then maybe there's something you're not telling me. You mentioned before that she'd been in some sort of trouble. Care to be more specific?"

His eyes darted up to mine for a second then dropped back down. I couldn't help thinking something is wrong with your life when you needed "people" to find out if your daughter had a sweetheart. Nakodo shook his head slowly as if he was thinking the same thing. He started to speak, then he stopped. Then he started again.

"Perhaps you're right. I suppose I am prone to jump to conclusions. Like many parents. I'm sure Miyuki can take care of herself. As you say, she is nineteen—"

"Twenty."

Nakodo gave me a puzzled look.

"You said she was twenty years old."

"Ah, yes," Nakodo said. "And indeed she is. Just turned

twenty two months ago. You see what worrying does to me. I suddenly feel terribly foolish for troubling you with my family issues. I listen to myself and can't help but think I've become a doddering old man."

Before I could offer a polite contradiction—like telling him he only sounded like a doddering middle-aged man—he was out of his chair and coming around the desk, his hand extended. "Mr. Chaka, I apologize for disturbing you. I certainly hope you understand."

I didn't, but maybe it was one of those things you couldn't understand until you had a nineteen- or twenty-year-old daughter. I stood and shook his hand anyway, vigorously, smiling as if Nakodo's worries made all the sense in the world.

"I am told you are a magazine writer, by the way."

"Journalist," I said. *Youth in Asia* magazine."

"I admit I haven't had the pleasure of reading it."

"It's for young people. Teenagers."

"Oh? Must be fascinating work."

From the way he said it I could tell he found the idea about as fascinating as the tax code. Then again, he seemed like one of those guys who got his jollies from the tax code. Whatever the case, the scene was fast becoming like one of those dates where you've both decided there will be no good-night kiss but can't seem to think of any graceful parting line.

He scratched the back of his head. I smoothed imaginary wrinkles in my pants. We exchanged a series of awkward smiles. I started to bow just as he extended his hand again. Then we switched roles and tried once more. After that we both gave up.

"It has been a pleasure meeting you, Mr. Chaka," he said. Judging from the photographs he'd had the pleasure of meeting a lot of people, but he still didn't sell the line too well. "I'm sorry it couldn't have been under less worrisome circumstances. I will have you returned to your hotel immediately. Again, I apologize for the intrusion."

He opened the door and motioned me through. As I walked out, my eyes landed on a painting at the far end of the hallway. I hadn't noticed it earlier, or maybe it simply wasn't visible from my seat in the study. The latter seemed more likely, because the painting was pretty tough to miss. It was a billboard-sized Warhol knockoff consisting of five replicated portraits of Miyuki, all done in fluorescent oranges, neon blues, foamy pinks. The artist had her face a little out of whack, but he got her standout feature right. On canvas the mole was the size of a bowling ball.

"By the way," I said, "who's the guy in the wheelchair?"

Nakodo smiled ruefully. "Apparently you've met my father. I hope he didn't give you any trouble. He can be quite a handful."

"No trouble at all."

"He's the fourth oldest person in the Minato ward, so of course we're quite proud of him. Still, you should have seen him when he was younger. Such a strong, proud man. Handsome, even, in his day." Nakodo thought for a moment, then added: "This may sound morbid, Mr. Chaka, but sometimes I believe life holds no crueler fate than simply to go on living."

"I agree," I said. "That does sound morbid."

Nakodo gave me a thin smile and bobbed his head. Just then, the butler approached from down the hall. I wanted to tell Nakodo not to worry about his daughter, that she'd probably come back, that these things usually work themselves out and most kids grow up just fine. But before I could speak, Mr. Nakodo thanked me for indulging him, turned and walked down the opposite hallway. As I watched him shuffle stoop-shouldered between two bronzed lion statues guarding the hall I was glad not to be a millionaire with an adolescent daughter. I was glad I wasn't an adolescent girl with a millionaire father, either. I wasn't over the moon to be myself, but things always could've been worse. I could've been Gombei.

5

Professor Kujima

Thinking of Gombei, I decided it wouldn't hurt to verify the origins-of-pachinko story he'd told me. It was one of those fact-checking chores I could've easily accomplished on the Internet once I got back to Cleveland, but once I got back to Cleveland I never wanted to think about pachinko again. With that in mind, I told Nakodo's driver to skip the hotel and drive me to Kanda-Jimbocho. I wanted to see Professor Kujima, an ex–history teacher from Nihon University who owned a used bookstore.

I'd met Kujima a few years ago when I was working on a story about the Homeless Aikido Initiative. HAI!, as it was called, was a government-sponsored empowerment program based on the notion that teaching aikido to the homeless would give them the self-worth and discipline needed to put their lives back together. But the program backfired when scuffles broke out in back alleys, and in a few well-publicized incidents the homeless turned the tables by assaulting youth gangs in Yoyogi Park. When a melee erupted during a pre–World Cup shantytown sweep of Shinjuku Park and some of Tokyo's finest had to be treated for broken noses, the FIFA World Cup officials posed an embarrassing question: If the Tokyo cops couldn't handle a few bums in cardboard boxes, how did they expect to control drunken hooligans armed with souvenir samurai swords? Thus ended the Homeless Aikido Initiative.

As part of my story, I wanted a historical perspective on Tokyo's treatment of its homeless. A colleague referred me to Kujima, and we hit it off immediately. That is, as much as anyone could hit it off with Kujima. Getting a conversation rolling with him was like trying to push-start a submarine, but once the subject turned to history he could talk for hours.

That is unless the history under discussion was his own. A lifelong bachelor, Kujima had once been a rising star at Nihon University, but he had suddenly left the university at the ripe old age of thirty-six—a startling move given once you got tenure at a Japanese university they all but poured concrete around you. When I asked Kujima why he left, all he would tell me was that it was very "complicated." So I'd consulted a few of my other sources and found out that Kujima had been forced into early retirement after an *enjo kosai* scandal in 1989. I couldn't imagine Kujima engaging in "compensated dating" with a young coed, but people's actions regularly outstrip my imagination. Besides, Ed's example taught me that a midlife crisis can completely rearrange someone's core personality in a matter of months. For all I knew, when mine hit I'd suddenly take up golf, start wearing khakis and docksiders and become a big fan of Ron Howard movies. It was too terrifying to think about.

I HAD THE DRIVER drop me off on Yasukuni-dori Street, a broad avenue that led up the hill to the Yasukuni Shrine, a monument built to honor Japan's war dead. In recent weeks the shrine had been getting a lot of international ink because the Japanese prime minister was planning an official visit to the site in order to fulfill a campaign promise. Both Korea and China had lodged formal protests with the Japanese government because the shrine housed the remains of executed Class-A war criminals who'd been responsible for unspeakable atrocities all over Asia. The Japanese government's official response was pretty much the same response it gave to all unspeakable matters relating to the war: it didn't speak about it except to issue vague statements heralding a new century of cooperation among all Asian nations.

It seemed appropriate somehow that Professor Kujima's bookstore was in the shadow of what was arguably Tokyo's most visible reminder of that dark chapter in the nation's history. For as long as I'd known him, Kujima had been writing and researching a book about the city during the war. His scandalous dismissal from the university all but guaranteed his life's work would never see the light of day, but that didn't stop him. In all likelihood, he was still work-

ing on his book the very moment I pushed open the door to
Hanran Books.

Uneven light filtered in from the street, struggling to make
its way past the stacks of books piled high in the display window, through the airborne dust particles and to the back of
the room, where Professor Kujima sat poring over some
arcane tome the size of a phonebook. The desk in front of him
doubled as a checkout counter, tripled as a filing cabinet and
might've quadrupled as a trash can, awash as it was in a sea
of papers. Whatever Kujima was reading it must have been
riveting, because he didn't even notice I'd walked in.

And from the looks of Hanran Books, people didn't walk
in all that often. The only light was from the street outside
and the room had that indefinable feeling common to failing
businesses the world over. An air of resignation, the ordinary,
everyday doom of numbers adding up the wrong way. It was
the kind of place that knocked your spirit down a notch the
moment you stepped in the door.

"Professor Kujima," I called. "Long time no see."

His head jerked back and for several moments stared as if
he didn't recognize me, his eyes narrowed into quizzical
slits, mouth unhinged.

"Billy Chaka," he said at length.

"You got it. How have you been?"

"What are you doing here?"

When I asked him if that was how he greeted all his customers a weak smile made its way onto his face, one that told
me more about the state of Hanran Books than his bank
records would have. Kujima looked a little older and a little
worse for it, but his hair was the only thing that had really
changed. The brambling gray mane of Einsteinian abandon
had been tamed into a short, well-mannered, thoroughly

respectable haircut. Were it not for his worn corduroy jacket, you could've mistaken him for a deputy section chief of some company listed on the Tokyo Stock Exchange.

We spent a few moments chatting about this and that, during which I carefully avoided making any mention of Nihon University. Kujima was unmarried, had lived in Tokyo his entire life and seemed to have zero interests outside of history, so he wasn't the easiest guy to engage in small talk. It was a relief when the conversation came full circle, and he asked me again why I'd come to visit him.

I relayed the story Gombei had given me, the one about pachinko being invented as a way of dealing with surplus ball bearings after World War II. Kujima nodded along while I spoke, then walked to a shelf of neatly ordered books near the front door and ran his finger along their spines, stopping at a thick, heavy bound volume with a dull green cover inscribed with gold lettering. *The Compendium of Chance,* read the title, *Survey and Analysis of the Evolution of the Gambling Subculture and Its Political, Social and Economic Ramifications from the Kamakura Era to the Present.* By the time I finished reading the title, I was ready for a nap.

"This should have your answer," he said, pulling the bulky volume from the shelf and heaving it into my arms like a sack of cement. The movement brought dormant dust particles to life.

"Great. Throw in a forklift and I'll take it."

"Forklift?"

"Never mind. How much do I owe you?"

"Consider it a gift."

"That's very kind, but I insist."

"This volume is just taking up space," Kujima said. "As are many books here, I'm afraid. People aren't much interested in the past these days, whether to do with gambling or anything else. Please, take the book off my hands. You'd be doing me a great favor."

I tried to force money on him once more, but he wouldn't have it. Kujima seemed ill at ease, had been ever since I'd walked in the door. I sensed his relief as we said our good-byes. It was a relief I shared.

But just before I left, I went ahead and asked.

"Are you still working on your book?"

With that, something flickered to life behind his eyes. "It's nearly finished," he trumpeted. Then he pointed behind his desk to an array of cardboard boxes overflowing with typed manuscript sheets. There must have been at least three thousand pages, possibly more. "I've expanded the scope of the project quite a bit since last we spoke, as you can probably tell. The book is no longer simply the history of Tokyo during the war. Rather, I've decided to explore the history of the city going all the way back to the Tokugawa period. The more I delved into recent history, the more I discovered it was impossible to understand without going much, much further into the past. At any rate, there remain but a few key elements to be put into place. The end is now in sight."

"Looking forward to buying a copy," I said. And I was, except it would never happen because no publisher was gonna touch Kujima's manuscript given his dismissal from the university. On some level, Kujima must've known this, but in order to keep getting up in the morning, brushing his teeth, eating and breathing and all that other stuff he had to pretend he didn't. For much the same reason, I doubted he'd ever actually finish his book. There would always be a few key passages to be put into place and he'd just keep expand-ing and tinkering, unspooling his time on the planet. I held a smile in place for as long as I could, then wished him good luck and headed back onto the streets. The morning haze had burned off and the temperature was rising. Only a few clouds remained, white and fluffy and as threatening as sleeping kittens.

6

The Compendium
of Chance

Forty minutes later I was fighting my way off the Yamanote line while half the people in Tokyo seemed to be fighting their way on. The words "train station" in no way conveyed the reality of the JR Shinjuku Eki. It was a train station like the Notre Dame Cathedral was a church, the Amazon a river, the Beatles a rock-and-roll band. Trains left every two or three minutes on the nose but the platforms were still constantly swarming with people. The Shinjuku area was ground zero of the most crowded city on the planet and it didn't let you forget it for a second. The collective weight of the human beings gathered within the single square mile Shinjuku covered should have been enough to permanently dent the earth's surface, throw the planet's rotation out of whack and send us all on a lopsided orbit into the sun.

I spent the afternoon knocking back iced coffees inside the air-conditioned environs of the BeBop Safari, an African jazz coffee bar insanely popular with me and about two other people that day. While there I read everything *The Compendium of Chance* had to say about pachinko, which turned out to be more than I'd ever need to know. There were ninety pages devoted to tracing pachinko's origins from an imported children's game during the Taisho period to the hi-tech $250 billion industry it had become in modern times.

Gombei's story about a country full of useless ball bearings after World War II inspiring a eureka moment in some unnamed warehouse employee was largely apocryphal. The development of pachinko, like many things in Japan, was a complex process of importing a foreign idea and wrapping it in so many layers of newness that it became unrecognizable, became something uniquely Japanese.

According to *The Compendium*, the story went like this:

A U.S.-manufactured pinball precursor called Corinthian became a popular feature of Japanese candy shops in the 1920s. In 1926, an anonymous shop owner decided to upend the *Korinto Gemu*, as it was called, placing it vertically in order to save precious space.

The inverted game became known as *gachanko*. How this same game became known as pachinko was unclear, though *The Compendium* noted that *"pachi-pachi"* was an onomatopoeic phrase used to describe the clang of hard objects coming together as well as the sizzle of fire. The first pachinko parlor was opened near Nagoya, but when the Pacific War broke out, the pachinko industry was forced to convert their factories to munitions production.

In a certain sense, Gombei was right in saying the game had its origins in defeat. Pachinko resurfaced after the war, and its popularity boomed among a people desperate for the mindless escape it offered. (Significantly, *The Compendium* noted, a Korean-born war survivor named Nakajima christened his pachinko machine manufacturing company Heiwa, after the word for "peace," a concept the Japanese embraced wholeheartedly at the time.) During the 1950s, pachinko halls began popping up first in the entertainment districts of big cities, then near train stations, and soon they were everywhere.

The Compendium contained detailed descriptions and intricate drawings of all the different types of machines and their technological evolution over the years. It painstakingly charted development of the Masamura Gauge, an arrangement of metal pins that became the standard in the Hanemono-type machines, which featured a center tulip slot. It covered the digital Deji-Pachi machines that evolved in the seventies as a reaction to video games and made higher payoffs possible by combining pachinko with a slot-machine-style LCD display, making the art of pin reading less important and thereby taking much skill out of the game. Pins were dispensed with entirely in the recently popular pachi-suro machines, which were really just slot machines that spit out pachinko balls instead of coins or tokens. Strategic-minded gamblers, according to *The Compendium*, still preferred a type of machine called the Kenrimono, which apparently allowed the player to earn better odds by continually playing.

The remaining forty pages of pachinko information dealt with the economic and legal ramifications of the game. Ever since the 1948 Act to Control Businesses Which May Affect Public Morals, pachinko had been viewed as the stuff of degenerates. From the very beginning, gangs were heavily involved in the pachinko industry, as gambling was a cash business, thus ideal for money laundering and dodging taxes. Though unstated in *The Compendium*, part of the unwholesome image of pachinko in the early days also likely had to do with racism, as many of the pachinko parlors were owned by Koreans.

On the surface, the regulatory history of pachinko was a constant tug-of-war between the National Police Agency, the pachinko parlor owners and machine manufacturing companies. The main problem was that gambling was prohibited in Japan—except for betting on the seemingly arbitrarily selected sports of bicycle racing, speedboat racing and horse racing (covered in depth elsewhere in *The Compendium*). Thus, pachinko players weren't allowed to win cash, or any prizes with a value over about one hundred dollars. Instead, they had to trade in their pachinko balls for cigarettes and magazines, neckties and cheap watches.

But of course, this being Japan, things weren't as simple as that. Near every pachinko parlor, you could find a literal hole-in-the-wall called a *ryôgae-jo*, a "gift-exchange center" where meaningless prizes like lighter flints and golf tee cleaners were traded for hard cash, then resold to the pachinko arcade in a bizarre third-party system that just goes to prove if the Japanese ever figured out how to export loopholes and middlemen, their economy would rebound in no time.

These gift-exchange centers were often run by yakuza or ethnic Chinese and Korean gangs, but the police unofficially tolerated their involvement. Since unemployed people tended to gamble more, pachinko was one of the few recession-proof industries and the pachinko trade groups knew they couldn't convince thirty million people to spend an average $325 a week without the lure of hard cash. And so over the years they'd ingeniously managed to convince the authorities to ignore the criminal elements of their business by providing members of the National Police Agency with high-paying postretirement gigs as consultants. And what did these former cops advise the pachinko industry about? How to keep the pachinko industry free of criminal elements, of course.

The Compendium closed with a brief look at the way the pachinko industry had been expanding their customer base to include women, a trend not everyone was happy about given a few highly publicized incidents in which babies had suffocated inside parked cars while their mothers were busy flipping levers. Pachinko marketers had also been trying to attract a younger, hipper crowd in recent years with smoke-free, date-friendly parlors and massive five-story arcades worlds away from the grimy pachinko caves of yesteryear. There was even a cable television station devoted entirely to pachinko—providing up-to-the-minute reports on which machines in which parlors were paying off big—and there were at least seventeen different magazines about the subject.

Like I said, it was way more information than I needed, and ultimately sifting through *The Compendium of Chance* was just a way of putting off actually writing the Gombei Fukugawa piece. I didn't feel like hauling the weighty tome all over town, so I ditched the book next to a stack of last month's manga and noticed something called *LolNet*, a magazine that billed itself as "the superfantastic handphone magazine for girls." I picked it up and thumbed through the kaleidoscopic layouts full of beaming high school girls holding their cell phones like trophies while Day-Glo typeface screamed about this month's Top 10 downloadable ring tones, where to find the best full-color cartoons for your phone screen, the best places to buy designer faceplates. Was this what kids were reading these days? Magazines about telephones? If so, *Youth in Asia* was even more out of touch than I feared.

After I left the café, I considered calling up some old Tokyo friends I hadn't seen for a while, but in the end I decided against it. Sooner or later conversation was bound to come around to what I was working on, and then the dialogue would become one of feigned interest and polite questions that none of us were really interested in knowing the answers to. I suppose I could always lie and say I was here to write about mobile phones, but that thought was even more depressing.

I thought of about fifty other things I could do in Shinjuku to put off going back to the Hotel Cerulean and writing the story, but I figured it was time to quit procrastinating. That firmly resolved, I headed to a favorite noodle shop over on Meiji-dori across from the massive Isetan department store to kill some more time.

The noodle shop was one of those places where you order from a machine outside the door. Put in your money, punch a button, out comes your ticket. Go inside, slap your ticket on the counter, wait for your food. Human interaction reduced to a bare minimum, the kind of place that proves the more people you pack into a city, the more they try to avoid each other.

Like everywhere else in Shinjuku, the place was insanely crowded. But I managed to find a seat, and threw my ticket on the counter and waited. A TV mounted above the kitchen was broadcasting the news. The Nikkei was down, unemployment was up, some prefectural official in Fukuoka got caught taking bribes. A married couple here in Tokyo had stolen thirty Big Macs from a McDonald's with the aid of a shotgun, but insisted on paying for two large Cokes. The bad loan total had climbed to thirty-three trillion yen, juvenile crime was at an all-time high, the birthrate at a postwar low. A politician speaking in Kyoto was warning that Japan must approach moderate reform with extreme caution when the proprietor of the noodle shop got fed up and switched off the volume.

When my food came the udon was a little overcooked but nothing to complain about. I ended up having three helpings. I wasn't hungry, but there are a million ways not to write, and I was determined to explore every one of them before I quit *Youth in Asia*. After I was done slurping my noodles I sipped a Kirin Lager. Drink sweating on the bar, me sweating on the bar stool, another day slipping into the past.

As I drank I thought about the night *Youth in Asia* threw a big retirement party for Ed at the Unshaven Barber, a martini bar overlooking the Cuyahoga. It's often said that a good editor is invisible, and as the evening spilled into morning, we suddenly realized that Ed had disappeared. I decided to find out where he'd wandered off to and discovered him standing alone, leaning against the patio railing and gazing wistfully across the river.

He was drunk—we all were—but with Ed it was always hard to tell just how drunk he was. I stood next to him and began reminiscing about the good old days when he was a

chain-smoking editor with a bullet-proof concept and I was a
hotshot journalist with nothing to lose. Ed didn't say a word,
he just nodded along as I tried to cheer him by waxing nostalgic about the various scoops we'd scooped, the youth
movements we'd foreseen and reseen, the strange adolescent
spectacles we'd covered and uncovered, those happenings
we'd predicted and premiered, buried and eulogized.

When I finished, Ed spoke a single word:

Hulahoops.

Then he patted me on the back, turned and stumbled back
into the bar. I sat outside for a time wondering just what the
hell to make of it. When I got back inside, the party was still
going strong, but Ed had gone home, into retirement.

But I wasn't ready to follow him just yet. Which meant
I'd be chasing "Fallen Stars" and whatever other stories
Sarah deemed important to teenagers of the world. Then one
day they'd throw me a retirement party and the next morning I'd wake up alone in my little Cleveland apartment with
a raging hangover and the rest of my life staring me in the
face, scowling.

I downed the last of the beer and stood to leave.

Then something on TV caught my eye.

Three policemen on a narrow river, maneuvering a row-
boat through large concrete pillars. Cut to a shot of a newscaster standing on a small bridge overlooking the shadowy
water. Cut back to the policemen, bathed in the glow of floodlamps, now pulling a body onto the boat. A body clothed in
a sleeveless white dress. Cut back to newscaster.

There were lots of women in Tokyo. Millions and millions. Lots who wore sleeveless white dresses. Especially in
the summer. Lots of slender women with long hair. Go stand
outside the Shinjuku station west exit, I told myself, and

you'll probably count ten or twelve girls almost exactly like her in less than a minute.

But whoever edited the piece must have screwed up, or maybe the mistake was deliberate, a ghoulish tease. Because as the police hoisted the woman's body onto the concrete embankment of the canal, her face was clearly visible. Only for an instant, before it was blurred once more by the enlarged pixels used to disguise a person's identity. Then her lifeless body was loaded onto a stretcher and wheeled from the scene. There was a final shot of the newscaster standing beneath the expressway, the canal behind him all but lost in the gloom. The volume was off so I couldn't hear what he said, but it made no difference. Only one woman could've had a mole like that.

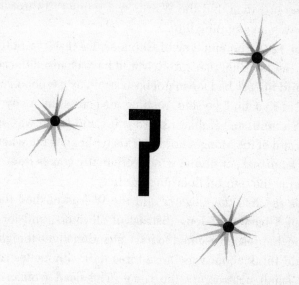

7

The Goddess Benten

I walked into the Hotel Cerulean still thinking about the girl with the mole, struggling to process what I'd just seen on TV. The Walrus greeted me, we exchanged mindless pleasantries, and before I knew what was happening he'd come around his desk and announced, "The most famous sea battle in the history of our nation was a battle never fought."

I had no idea how to react, but any reaction at all was pointless. Just like that, the Walrus had seized the initiative and launched into the hotel tour. It was about the last thing I wanted just then, but the Walrus was going full throttle and there was no stopping him.

"In 1281, the emperor of China sent a massive flotilla to Japan, an invasion that surely would have changed the course of world history had Japan not been saved by a typhoon off the coast of Kyushu," he said, rushing me across the lobby. "The storm annihilated Kublai Khan's ships and Japan was spared the wrath of the Mongol hordes. This typhoon is the where the term *kamikaze*, or divine winds, originally comes from. We'll continue the tour on floor number five."

We reached the elevator and the Walrus pushed the call button. I have a lifelong distrust of elevators, and for good reason, but reason seemed to have abandoned me tonight. All I could think about was those three dark silhouettes rowing their small boat across the canal. The dead woman being pulled from the water, her body drained of color, ghostly under the harsh glow of the floodlamps.

The elevator arrived and the Walrus beamed at me, mustache twitching on his lip as he held the door open. I took a deep breath and stepped inside. We rode in silence while the elevator hummed up to the fifth floor. Over and over I kept seeing that near subliminal cutaway shot of the woman's face. Beaded with water, pale, lifeless. And the mole. I couldn't stop picturing the mole.

The elevator doors opened with soundless efficiency to reveal the fifth-floor hallway swimming in murky green light. Plastic crustaceans ensnared in sagging fishnets were draped along the walls and ceiling. Maritime-kitsch-gothic décor, something like Count Dracula meets Red Lobster. When the Walrus spoke again his voice had dropped to a low murmur. As he talked the words seemed to ebb and flow, coming in waves and then receding.

"Shogun Tokugawa . . . a seafaring nation . . . much of our naval expertise . . . shipwrecked Dutchman . . . Captain William Adams . . ."

It took all of my concentration to follow him and I still only caught about half of what he said. Besides his subdued delivery, there was the fact that he was speaking in an arcane dialect you usually didn't hear outside the Kabuki theater. As we strode down the hall, I had the impression that I must have already fallen asleep. That I was dreaming, and had been for who knows how long, that at any moment I'd wake up and be back in Cleveland, kicking back in my office chair, wing tips planted on my desk, the evening sun slanting through the shades.

"Two hundred years of isolation . . . Admiral Perry, an American like yourself . . . Tokyo Bay in 1853 . . . Twelve Black Ships . . . in American schools?"

If I really believed the drowned woman was Miyuki Nakodo, what was I doing taking a midnight tour of a weird hotel? Shouldn't I be trying to get in touch with Mr. Nakodo? But he hadn't given me a business card, a phone number, an e-mail address, nothing. Short of scaling the concrete wall and breaking into his mansion, I had no way of contacting him. Besides, if he didn't know the bad news already, I certainly didn't want to be the one to break it to him. I doubted he was the type who'd take the death of his daughter well and I didn't want to meet the type that did.

"Mr. Chaka?"

"Huh?"

"I was asking if you were taught about Admiral Perry and his twelve black steamships in American schools?"

"Well, I had to read *Huck Finn* in college."

He cocked his head at a precise north-by-northwest angle,

an angle a lot of my Japanese hosts choose when deciding just how stupid I really am. We'd come full circle, and were now standing in front of the elevator doors again.

"Very well," the Walrus mumbled, still undecided. He punched the button and the elevator doors slid open. "That concludes the second part of our tour. If you'll kindly step inside, we'll begin part three. All aboard."

PARTS THREE, FOUR AND FIVE of the tour were more of the same. We got off on every floor in descending order and wandered the halls as the Walrus continued his hushed lecture about the history of Japanese sailing. From the intermittent parts I could make out, I learned facts so useless they were bound to stick with me forever. One day I'd be on my deathbed dazzling the hospice nurses with nonsense about the Battle of Tsushima and how Japanese submarines were named for whales while second-class destroyers were named for trees. If that didn't make them swoon, I could always quote pachinko stats from *The Compendium of Chance*.

As far as I could tell, none of the tour actually had anything to do with the hotel itself. We may just as well have been walking up the Gotemba trail on Mount Fuji or through a brewery in Sapporo. The marine lecture would've made slightly more sense if the hotel was in Odaiba's seaside park as originally conceived—but the hotel had been anchored inland for over fifteen years now. You'd think they would have time to get their land legs.

Eventually we made it to the basement. Compared to the other floors, it was pretty plain. No plastic fish, no fake seaweed. Just green-blue carpet and blue-green walls. The Walrus continued whispering but I got the feeling the tour might finally be coming to a close.

"Since the close of the Pacific War . . . we listen to the voices from the sea . . . lost under the keel nine fathoms deep . . . the transition to peace . . . Japan's navy is constitutionally forbidden to . . . yet thirty-six percent of the industrial transport vessels produced on this terraqueous globe . . . Japan remains a nation of fish lovers, fishermen, aquaculturalists . . ."

As he spoke we passed an alcove occupied by a Kirin beer vending machine, rounded a corner and stopped halfway down the corridor. A framed picture hung on the door at the end of the hall. It was an old, faded woodblock print of a woman carrying a *biwa*, a type of ancient lute. She wore a traditional red kimono and four white snakes were coiled at her feet. There was no number on the door, and as far as I could tell the picture had nothing to do with the sea. The Walrus stepped in front of me, blocking my view of the print.

"Thus concludes our humble tour, Mr. Chaka," he said in a voice suddenly grown louder. "I sincerely hope you found it educational and enjoyable. Should you have any questions about the material I have covered or the Hotel Cerulean itself, I would be most happy to address them at this time."

"What's that picture hanging down there?"

"The picture?" said the Walrus, sounding surprised. He glanced backward over his shoulder, then turned again to face me. "Oh, that picture. That's Benten. One of the *Shichi Fukujin*—the Seven Gods of Good Fortune. Did I mention that our country currently produces fully thirty-six percent of the world's industrial transport—"

"Mind if I have a closer look at it?"

The Walrus twitched his mustache from side to side, but

said nothing. Why I felt suddenly intrigued by the picture I couldn't say, but I got the feeling Admiral "the Walrus" Hideki didn't want me to see it, which of course heightened my curiosity. I strode past him and walked to the end of the hall, the carpet beneath my feet not making a sound.

The woodblock print was small, no larger than a square foot. The goddess Benten was depicted with the inscrutable look you often see in Japanese portraits, a hint of amusement playing upon her features like she knew some secret about the viewer but was intent on keeping it to herself. The white snakes seemed to be guarding a black wooden box resting at her feet, and in the background you could make out a pond brimming with lotus flowers. The Walrus walked up next to me and cleared his throat.

"Are you familiar with the Seven Lucky Gods of Japan?" he asked.

"Somewhat," I said.

"Benten was originally a Hindu goddess of fortune called Savarti. In Japan, she became the goddess of writers, musicians, geisha and gamblers. In the countryside, she is also charged with protecting natural springs, streams and ponds. The snakes are her servants, they do her bidding. She is said to be a very jealous goddess."

"What's Benten got to do with sailing?"

"Some believe she is also the goddess of the sea," said the Walrus. "And each year, she and the other Lucky Seven Gods sail upon the *Takarabune*—a treasure ship bringing in the bounty for the New Year. On New Year's Day, many people make pilgrimages to temples dedicated to each of the Seven Lucky Gods, believing it will bring them good fortune. Shall I walk you to your room now?"

Just then I noticed the welding job on the door. I'd heard

that some Japanese hotels sealed rooms where His Majesty the Emperor had lodged, but somehow I doubted the emperor had ever slept in a basement room less than a mile from his Imperial Palace.

"Why is this door welded shut?" I said.

A slight movement of his mustache gave away the uncomfortable smile beneath it. He cleared his throat again and turned his gaze to the floor. "Please accept my most regretful apology. It is the official policy of the Hotel Cerulean not to discuss this particular feature of the hotel."

"Why's that?"

"I'm deeply sorry, but Hotel Cerulean policy forbids me to discuss matters of Hotel Cerulean policy."

"Then I guess you've just violated Hotel Cerulean policy."

He thought for a moment. "It seems I have."

"So why don't you go ahead and tell me more?"

I gave him as innocent a smile as I was capable of. The Walrus considered, then let the explanation out along with a sigh. "When the building was purchased, the previous owners insisted this room remain sealed. They also insisted this picture remain hung on the door as a condition of the building's sale. This hotel, you see, has changed ownership many times during its short existence. But the empty room and the woodblock print of Benten have always remained."

"But why?"

"I'm sorry?"

"I mean, is it supposed to bring good luck or . . ."

"Yes!" the Walrus said. "Yes, exactly. As you say, it's for good luck. It's a long-standing and noble tradition, one the Hotel Cerulean is proud to be a part of."

This city never ceased finding new ways to baffle me. A hotel manager dressed up like a nineteenth-century naval commander, a goldfish where a carp should've been, a woodblock print of Benten hung on the door of an empty room forever sealed as part of a proud tradition the hotel was forbidden to discuss. Nothing about the Hotel Cerulean seemed to connect, but I just told the Walrus the secret was safe with me and thanked him for the tour.

The Walrus reached into his pocket and pulled out a watch, one of those little flip-top numbers on the end of a golden chain. He opened it for an instant, snapped it shut and returned it to his pocket. Then he executed a perfunctory bow, turned on his heel and dragged himself toward the elevator.

Something in his walk called to mind Nakodo's dejected amble after our meeting that morning. I thought about the blithe reassurances I'd given Mr. Nakodo, the way I'd all but openly dismissed his concern over his missing daughter. Of course, there was nothing I could've done for him or Miyuki. But something still felt wrong about that morning. I gazed some more at the woodblock print of Benten. Everything felt wrong.

8

The Nihonbashi River

No strange man in white filling the room with smoke the next day, so things got off to a good start. Never able to leave well enough alone, I decided to call Detective Ihara, a private dick I knew in Roppongi. Even though it was early, I knew Ihara would already be in his office. The guy was a prime candidate for *karoshi*—death from overwork—a term that only could have been invented in Japan.

"Spylens Investigations," a weary voice answered.

"Good morning, may I speak to Ihara-san?"

"Ihara speaking." He didn't sound thrilled to be Ihara or to be speaking. I didn't expect his enthusiasm to skyrocket with what I said next.

"This is Billy Chaka."

Seven seconds of indecisive static followed. I watched the goldfish turn slow circles in his tank across the room and imagined Ihara at his big desk in his chic office, peering at the phone console through his pop-bottle glasses and wishing he'd made his high-priced secretary come in early to screen calls.

"So they allowed you back in the country."

"Miss me?"

"Like I miss my tumor."

"Didn't know you had a tumor."

"Don't anymore," he said. "Don't miss it, either."

Ihara and I went way back. When we'd first met, he was just a gumshoe with a struggling business and I a clueless young reporter with too much time on my hands and too many unsown wild oats. Our paths crossed in Yokohama when his penchant for what he called "proactive surveil-lance" nearly got me shanghaied by cuckolded jarheads from the USMC. In the years since, Ihara had gone on to be a very successful private investigator, opening a swanky office in the Roppongi-Aoyama area called *Spylens!*—a name he pronounced with the kind of gusto that ended up a fine mist across your face. Ihara's biggest claim to fame was once being hired to do background checks on potential brides of Crown Prince Naruhito so the Royal Imperial Household Agency might dismiss candidates whose ancestral bloodlines showed signs of cancer, Alzheimer's, cerebral palsy, meningitis, prosopagnosia, leprosy, tooth decay or the dreaded "foreign influences."

I'd settled the Yokohama score with Ihara years ago, and I suppose we'd become reluctant allies if not exactly friends in the years since. I could never bring myself to fully trust the guy, but he knew more about the men and women that kept this city afloat than anyone had a right to. And Nakodo, with his multimillion-dollar mansion ensconced in Ark Hills, was just the type of guy Ihara was likely to have on file.

"I need some information," I said.

"Try a search engine."

"I can buy you candy and write you love poems about the moon, but I was hoping to skip all that and just get down to business. We both know I'm not looking for a handout."

"What kind of candy?" he said.

Now it was my turn to look at the phone in disbelief.

"I'm serious," he said. "What kind of candy?"

"I don't know. Pocky sticks."

"Hmmm. Chocolate or strawberry?"

"Chocolate."

"Can't eat chocolate," he said. "Doctor's orders."

"Strawberry then."

"Don't much care for strawberry."

"Look, Ihara . . ."

"Take it easy, Billy," he chuckled. "Your sense of humor wilt in the heat or what?"

I felt the blood rush to my head and tried to remain calm. If I lived to retire from *Youth in Asia* I was gonna write a book called *Zen and the Art of Dealing with Idiots*. Detective Ihara would get his own heavily footnoted chapter.

"I need information on a guy named Nakodo," I said.

Silence followed. The silence of panic. A silence of alarms going off, sirens wailing, riots in the streets. After the silent chaos died out Ihara spoke.

"I'm hanging up now."

"Ihara—"

"Are you on a cell phone? Please tell me you're not on a cell phone. You are on a cell phone, aren't you?"

"I don't even own a cell phone."

"And I'm still hanging up. Meet me in the Aoyama Cemetery. Say twelve-thirty. Bring fifty thousand yen wrapped in today's copy of *The Daily Yomiuri*. And I changed my mind— bring candy after all."

Before I could figure out which kind, he hung up.

I commiserated with the dial tone then replaced the phone on the cradle and went to take a shower. The sound of the water drumming against the tub somehow reminded me of the sound of pachinko balls spilling across the floor at the Lucky Benten. I thought about luckless Gombei, wondered what he'd be doing at this hour. Probably standing on a sidewalk somewhere, staking out a place in line along with all the housewives, pensioners and newly unemployeds hoping to get first crack at the jackpot when the pachinko parlors opened at ten A.M. I found myself wishing Gombei luck. Guy deserved a break.

AFTER MY SHOWER I threw on a white button-down, laced my wing tips and hurried off toward Tokyo station, hoping to beat at least a million people headed to the same place. The outside of the red-brick building looked charmingly nineteenth century, no different from any train station you might find in a midsize European town. Inside was a different story. Armies of commuters advanced up the escalators like products on assembly-line conveyor belts. Wednesday morning bolted to their faces, shirts pressed, ties straightened, shoes buffed to a shine you could all but see the future in. A recording urged people to watch their step as they got on the escalators and again as they got off, and unseen trains clattered overhead and rumbled underfoot as the corridors grew thick with the black- and gray-suited thousands.

I wandered through catacombed passages, past turnstiles and ticket machines, coin lockers and curry restaurants, finally stopping at a kiosk, where I picked up a paper and flipped past all the stories about the coming election and the water restrictions that would be imposed if rain didn't come soon. I read about how police had been seizing a lot of cheap Russian Tokarev handguns from the yakuza lately, saw that Sony was scrapping plans to produce a robotic cow due to an extremely-soft-verging-on-nonexistent robotic cow market, and skimmed an editorial about the need to bolster Japan's self-defense forces in light of the escalating North Korean threat.

Finally I found the article I was looking for.

WOMAN DROWNS IN NIHONBASHI RIVER

Chuo-ku, Tokyo—The body of a twenty-year-old woman was found in the Nihonbashi River under Expressway Number Five in Kanda-Nishiki-cho yesterday afternoon. Police arrived on the scene at approximately 17:21 after witnesses reported a body floating facedown in the water. The woman was taken from the river and driven to the Nihon University Hospital, where she was pronounced dead of asphyxiation by drowning at 17:53. Police are refusing to release the woman's name until her relatives have been notified. Several eyewitnesses reported seeing a woman described as "dis-traught" standing on a stone bridge under the highway hours earlier, leading some to suspect sui-cide. Police, however, refused to speculate on the cause of death.

Aside from paying a visit to Nakodo, there was no way I could know for sure if it was the same woman. But you don't survive long in teen journalism without learning how to dig for information in unusual places. And in its own way, the site of Miyuki's drowning was one of the most unusual places in the city.

THE NEIGHBORHOOD WHERE it happened wasn't far from where I'd visited Professor Kujima the day before. I got off the train at the Jimbocho station and headed southeast toward the Number 5 Expressway, an elevated highway running above the Nihonbashi River. It was an area rich in history, but much of that history had been paved over.

I was no Professor Kujima, but I knew the story of the waterways well enough. In old Edo, the smaller rivers and canals linking the inner city to the massive Sumida River on the east side were crucial links for the city's commercial life. But the waterways started losing their importance as Tokyo rushed to modernize after Admiral Perry and his famous Twelve Black Ships forced Japan to end their isolation. River traffic was already falling off by the 1920s, and after World War II the waterways were pretty much doomed. But the real death knell hadn't sounded until the 1960s, when construction in Tokyo started booming and the city shifted westward.

I wasn't certain about Expressway Number 5, but many of the big highways were built for the 1964 Olympics and were constructed as much to impress the outside world with Japan's modernity as to provide Tokyoites with new travel routes.

I walked along the canal underneath the expressway while cars and trucks thundered by some twenty feet overhead. The water was murky green under the constant shadow of the massive roadway and no grass grew along the riverbanks as they'd long ago been smothered in concrete. Stone bridges dating back to the Meiji era arched over the canals, but no tourists would be making the trek from the nearby Imperial Palace to see them. The area was dark, noisy, smelled like diesel and mold. Picture the New Jersey Turnpike looming over the Amsterdam canals and you've got the idea.

Standing there in the gloom, looking at the series of dirty white concrete support pillars reflected in the stagnant water, I found it hard to believe Miyuki Nakodo had died here of her own accord. Only the most unromantic person in the world would choose a gritty expressway underbelly as the place to spend their final earthly moments, and even the twenty-first century hadn't crushed the romance out of most twenty-year-old women.

Besides, the bridge was only about eight feet above the water, and I figure if you're gonna jump off a bridge, you might as well try to find one high enough to kill you on impact. As for the river itself, there was no way of knowing how deep it was because you couldn't see beyond its clouded surface. All in all, it seemed like dying here would be a lot of work, a job that required an ugly determination.

Unless, of course, you had a little help.

I suppose I'd come here hoping that one look at the place

would somehow ease my curiosity about Miyuki and her father, and allow me to concentrate on finishing the Gombei story and going back to Cleveland. But being in this forgotten concrete swamp in central Tokyo had the opposite effect. I was now surer than ever that there was something very wrong in the House of Nakodo. In a morbid way, maybe that's what I'd hoped to find all along.

I tried to picture Miyuki Nakodo standing on the bridge, contemplating taking her own life, but I could hardly remember what she looked like aside from the mole. Maybe what intrigued me wasn't the mole itself, but the attitude that keeping it represented. Any conventional young woman—which in Japan was to say any young woman who wanted to be married before the dreaded age of twenty-five—would've had the thing removed long ago. Keeping it spoke of stubborn independence, of indifference to years of schoolyard teasing and a lifetime of oh-so-delicate suggestions from all those well-meaning types who'd have unicorns made into horses.

Without the mole, I wouldn't have recognized Miyuki on the news. I wouldn't have read the article in the paper, wouldn't have been lurking under the expressway and wouldn't have seen the figure now standing on a bridge about a block away.

She stood absolutely still, leaning over the concrete railing, gazing at the surface of the water below, just as I'd tried to picture Miyuki doing. I watched her for several moments, waiting for her to turn away from the water and continue across the bridge. But she didn't. And just like that, I knew she was here for the same reason I was. Had I known what would happen to us both in the days ahead, I would've left her there, would've turned and walked away. Hell, I would've run away and never looked back.

Instead I moved toward her, down the street running along the bank of the river. Outside the shelter of the expressway, the heat was unbearable. It seemed to come not from the sun above but from every direction at once, like some soundless, invisible inferno. The woman never moved and I never took my eyes off of her. Her posture was unyielding, almost formal, as she stood wholly fixed on the brackish water below. And I now recognized the stone bridge as the one from the newscast. No doubt about it. This was the exact spot where they'd found Miyuki Nakodo's body.

Traffic moved across the street. A man on a bicycle passed, the river flowed sluggishly downstream. Only the woman remained motionless. I moved back into the shadows and was about twenty feet away when she suddenly turned and saw me coming toward her. She looked at me only for an instant before dropping her eyes back to the water.

The woman had short pixied hair and wore a loose-fitting turquoise tank top, prefaded denims rolled halfway up her calves and red duck-billed shoes. I walked up beside her and nodded a silent greeting. She returned the gesture, never once taking her eyes from the river. For a few moments we just stood there, both looking down at our still, silent reflections in the water. Had Miyuki gazed at her own reflection moments before she died? At night the canal would have looked black, bottomless. An abyss.

"Was she a friend of yours?" I said.

This being the big city, I was sure the girl would beat a hasty retreat as soon as I opened my mouth. But she didn't. She just nodded slightly, blinking her eyes and chewing on her lip. When she finally spoke her voice was nearly lost in the sound of cars hurtling by overhead.

"Do you believe in ghosts?" she asked.

"Ghosts?"

"Not ghosts exactly," she said. "More like demons, I guess. Or goblins. There are these things called *kappa*. They have slicked-back hair and their skin is damp and they like to drown children. Then they eat them. They also like to eat cucumbers. Go figure."

I told her I didn't believe in ghosts, demons or goblins.

"Me neither," she said. "But if there were *kappa*, this would be a good place for them. Don't you think?"

"I don't know," I said. "Not many cucumbers around."

"Miyuki believed in *kappa*. And ghosts and demons, too. She believed in all kinds of weird stuff like that."

As she spoke I watched her face in the water. Checking my own, I noticed I was doing a decent job hiding my surprise at hearing the name Miyuki. Then again, I wasn't surprised. I knew the drowned woman was Miyuki. I'd known the moment I saw it on the news, but I guess I was still holding some faint hope that it hadn't been her.

I turned away from the water to face the girl. She was thin and no taller than five feet three, a mere whisper of a girl really. Not a kid anymore, not quite an adult, either. Try as she might to don a jaded expression, her eyes were unclouded and her features hadn't yet hardened into that perplexed mask formed by years of wondering where things went wrong and if they were getting worse.

"Were the two of you close?" I asked.

Her eyes flashed up at me for a moment before returning to the water. She let her bony shoulders rise and fall in a shrug, a gesture that didn't come off as indifferent as she'd hoped. Overhead there was a honking of horns and a squealing of tires. I waited for the sound of metal on metal and glass

shattering, but the accident must have been averted. Cars just
kept going by.

"She was my best friend since junior high."

"I'd like to hear more about her," I said. "If you want to
talk. They say talking helps."

"How is talking going to help?"

"I'm not sure. But they say it does."

"They also say don't talk to strangers," she said. "I don't
know anything about you. Not even your name. You could be
some kind of pervert. I mean, you have to admit that hanging
around under the highway isn't exactly normal. I'd say it's
pretty creepy."

"I don't know what passes for normal these days. But I'm
not a pervert or even much of a creep. I'm a journalist."

"You're writing a story about Miyuki?"

"Not exactly."

"So what are you doing here?"

"I'm not one hundred percent certain," I said. "But I think
I'm here for similar reasons you are. I'm guessing you came
here because part of you can't accept that your friend is gone.
What happened is bothering you and you're searching for
some kind of answer, something to help it make sense."

"You knew Miyuki?"

"Not really," I said. "I only met her once."

"There were a lot of guys in that club," she said, reaching
into her shoulder bag—a 1970s-style swirl of vibrant pinks
and greens and oranges that looked like something from
Laugh-In. The brand was Cecil McBee. I'd have bet a million
dollars she had no idea McBee was a famous jazz bassist and
wouldn't have cared if I told her. So long as the hip boutiques
carried it, the brand name might as well have been Soupy
Sales or Albert Speer. She took out a pack of Lark Slims,

placed one between her lips and lit it with a lighter decorated with yellow flowers. A slight breeze kicked up just then. Not enough to cool me off, just enough to whisk away the diesel fumes and scatter the cigarette smoke. Tiny ripples moved across the water. The girl pushed a few errant strands of hair from her face, took another drag, and exhaled with lots of drama. She tapped her ashes and turned to face me.

"You still didn't tell me your name."

"Chaka," I said. "Billy Chaka."

"And you say you're not a creep, huh?"

I shook my head. Didn't do much to ease her skepticism.

She took one more drag from the cigarette and then tossed it in the water. Then she stepped away from the bridge and looked me in the eye. Confident, fully in control. Only much later did I realize how frightened she must have been. "All right, Mr. Billy Chaka," she sighed. "Let's get out of here. I'm totally starving."

9

Afuro-Short-for-Nothing

The two of us walked side by side, neither of us speaking. The girl was slightly pigeon-toed, moving like her knees were tied together with string. We turned off Yasukuni-dori and meandered down a side street until we came to a rack tangled with bicycles standing next to a chalkboard covered with a childish scrawl. The chalkboard advertised daily lunch specials. Welcome to the Let's Elementary Café, a sign on the door said. Class in session.

"Let's Elementary?"

"C'mon," the girl said, and yanked open the door.

Children's drawings of *anime* characters and zoo animals were tacked to the primary-colored walls, along with hiragana and katakana alphabet charts and a list of classroom rules. A surly-looking college kid with more metal in his nose than a Concorde sat smoking at one of the tiny desks in the corner and a group of young women clad in identical denim jackets were sitting around a cafeteria-style table built for children, giggling.

"Is this your first day at school?" a hostess greeted us. She had a name-tag sticker that read Hello, My Name is Sensei Maruyama! in big squiggles. The girl said something I didn't catch. The hostess nodded curtly to her then gave me one of those sympathetic smiles reserved for ugly babies and three-legged dogs.

"Don't be shy," she cooed. "No one will bite you. Everyone here is very nice. There are no free tables, so we'll have to sit you two down at desks, OK? Come come, follow me."

I shot a look at the girl to see what she was making of it, but she ignored me. The hostess guided us across the room and motioned us to take a seat under an instructive poster about proper tooth-brushing techniques. Only taking a seat wasn't that easy. The desks were about two feet off the ground, and wedging a full-grown adult into one was like trying to get a giraffe into a phone booth.

"You'll find a menu in the desk," our hostess said. "And don't worry. There are no wrong answers!"

She scurried away to greet another customer. The girl sat down and opened the flip-top desk. I did the same. Inside were a food menu and an order sheet taped to a box of pastel-colored markers. Underneath that was an early reader called *Tiki Turtle Goes to the Beach* and a small wooden abacus decorated with red ladybugs and blue butterflies.

"Isn't this place great?" the girl said. "I can't believe we lucked out and got a seat. Usually it's packed to the gills."

Truth was, I didn't know what to make of the place any more than I knew what to make of the girl. It's been said that Japanese are exceptionally nostalgic about childhood because it's the only time in their lives when they are truly free, unburdened by the heavy social pressures and endless duties of adulthood. Maybe this is true of people everywhere, but I couldn't think of another country where elementary school décor was the hottest new thing in the café biz.

I took out the order sheet and put a check mark inside the coffee box. The girl made a few marks on hers before a waitress came by and collected them. Several tables away, a bunch of students sang the chorus to some song about bean-jam cakes before they sputtered out in laughter. I studied the crude drawings tacked to the wall and thought about that giant painting of Miyuki, the one hanging in Mr. Nakodo's house. Those five grinning portraits kept projecting themselves onto my mind screen, interspersed with shots of Miyuki sitting at the pachinko machine, staring off into nothingness, Miyuki being carried out of the pachinko parlor, Miyuki being dragged from the water.

The girl took out her cigarettes and lit one.

"You shouldn't smoke, you know," I said. "Bad for your health."

"Like I don't know that."

"I have to say it anyway. Part of being an adult."

"Meaning I'm *not* an adult?"

"I don't know. How old are you?"

She rolled her eyes, took another drag and dodged my question. "Age has nothing to do with being an adult."

"Fair enough. But you could at least tell me your name."

"My name is Afuro."

"Afro? Like the hairstyle?"

"Ah-Foo-Ro," she puffed. "Like short for Afoorodeetay."

It took some untangling to figure out she was giving me the Japanese pronunciation of Aphrodite.

"Like the goddess of love Aphrodite?"

"Uh-huh," she said, zero enthusiasm.

"Very unique."

"When people say unique, they usually mean retarded."

"Not me. When I say unique I mean I like your name."

"I can't stand it," she said. "What were my parents thinking with a name like that? There's not even *kanji* for it. If I had been a boy, my dad actually wanted to name me Pythagoras. *Pythagoras*. Unbelievable."

"Big fans of the ancient Greeks, huh?"

"They went to Greece for their honeymoon, and supposedly that's where I was conceived. Which I *absolutely* don't want to think about. Anyway, I'd rather you forget all that Aphrodite nonsense and just think of me as Afuro, short for nothing."

Just then the waitress came. She gave me my coffee and deposited a chocolate-strawberry milkshake and a slice of banana crème pie on Afuro's desk. Afuro snubbed out her cigarette, took a big slurp of the shake, scooped a forkful of pie into her mouth then popped one of the strawberries in after it. If this was her idea of breakfast, her idea of lunch must've been to skip it. Judging by how skinny she was, the same must've held true with dinner.

"I wanted to ask you something about your friend," I began.

Afuro wrinkled her nose. "I don't want to discuss Miyuki

right now. She is all I've been thinking about for a long, long time. Since way before, well, before what happened. You have no idea, OK? Nobody does. But my brain needs a rest from Miyuki or I'm seriously gonna have a nervous breakdown. I'm about this close to crying. Every single second, this close, you know what I mean?"

She started blinking, then took a deep breath and looked away. For a moment I thought she was going to start crying right then and there, but instead she slowly exhaled and pushed another spoonful of pie into her mouth.

"Can you do me a favor?" she asked.

"Name it."

"Let's pretend everything is normal. We'll pretend we're just normal people eating a normal breakfast and having a normal conversation. Like we're on a date or something."

"A date at nine in the morning?"

"Just as an example," she said. "Pretend whatever you like. Pretend I'm your niece if the date thing freaks you out. I can be your niece and you can be my foreign uncle the oddball."

Pushing for information never really gets you anywhere and Afuro seemed like a pleasant enough imaginary niece, so I decided to play along. But I was getting the feeling she was a pretty strange duck, even for a duck her age. Growing up with a name like Aphrodite probably didn't help.

She took another big bite of crème pie. "So, Uncle, what are you doing in Tokyo? Do you live here?"

"I live in Cleveland, mostly."

"Where?"

"Cleveland. In the American Midwest."

"Would I have heard of Cleveland?"

"Maybe," I said. "One time the river caught fire. Anyway,

it isn't such a bad place. But I travel a lot, and I'm in Tokyo as much as anywhere else. My home away from home, so to speak."

"You said you're some kind of writer or whatever?"

"That's right. *Youth in Asia* magazine."

"Oh," she said, a trace of disapproval coloring her voice.

"You don't like *Youth in Asia*?"

"Magazines are dumb. No offense."

"None taken. What's so dumb about them?"

She put her fork down. "All that stuff about what to wear, for one thing. Which sweater goes with which skirt, which colors are for spring, which for fall. What kind of idiot has to read a magazine to dress themselves?"

"We're not that kind of magazine."

"Stupid diets, ridiculous hairstyles. Plus all that sex stuff. 'One hundred and one ways to please a man in bed, tips and tricks for mind-blowing sex.' Gimme a break. Like it's really so hard to make a guy come, you know?"

"*Youth in Asia* doesn't—"

"I mean you pretty much just have to show up, am I wrong? Moan every once in a while, wriggle around and say *oh baby baby* and stuff like that. Not the most difficult thing in the world."

"Our magazine is more about—"

"If sex was so complicated, why would all these stupid people be having babies? Or get this—there was this retarded girl who used to live down the street from me, I mean actually *retarded*, and some of the jerks in high school would pay her to get them off. Like with her mouth, right? Behind this shrine in the park. And they wouldn't even pay her *money*. They'd pay her in cat shit."

I sat there squirming, looking around to see if anyone was

listening and feeling like I needed to change the subject before I started choking and spitting coffee all over the desk like in some bad sitcom. But Afuro didn't give me a chance.

"Not actual *shit*, mind you, if that's what you're thinking. In which case you just might be a creep after all. But like cat stickers, cat key chains, stuffed cat toys—anything with a cat on it did the trick. *Really* disgusting. Those guys, I mean. Not the cat thingies or this retarded girl. Not her fault she was retarded, after all. But my point is, I'm pretty sure she wasn't reading magazines or studying sex manuals or anything else and here she was, a regular bona fide *professional* at making guys—"

"Point taken about magazines," I interrupted. "So are you in college?"

"No," she said. "And next you're gonna ask if I have a job and yes, I do, and it's so boring I don't want to waste breath even discussing it. Next, you'll ask what my dad does because that's what people always ask next so I'll just tell you and get that out of the way right now. My dad is a mathematician. He was even kind of famous for a while. Famous for a mathematician, whatever that means. Have you ever heard of Noguchi's paradox?"

I shook my head.

"That was my dad's paradox. Had to do with amicable number theory."

"Amicable number theory?"

"Don't ask me." Afuro took a noisy slurp from her shake. "Anyway, they solved it."

"Well, that's good."

"No, it isn't! After they solved his paradox he was pretty much finished. Had a total mental breakdown, lost his research grant. It was very hard on our family. Now he teaches mathematics at a cram school back in Muramura."

"Where's that?"

"Exactly," she said. "And what's worse, I knew people who went to his school. They were always telling me what a weirdo he was in class. It used to be so embarrassing."

"You have lots of friends in Muramura?"

"I lived there practically my whole life."

"You're not from Tokyo?"

"Couldn't tell, could you?" she said. "I've learned to disguise my accent. Makes life easier. A lot of Tokyo people will treat you like a *yamazaru* if they hear the Kansai in your voice. Between you and me, everyone in this city are uptight snobs."

"But you and Miyuki were friends since junior high?"

"Best friends, but—"

"So Miyuki is also from Muramura?"

"Nothing gets by you," she said. "We moved to Tokyo together. About two years ago. Only I thought we decided—"

"And Miyuki's father lives in Muramura?"

She gave me a funny look and put down her fork. "No, he doesn't. Miyuki's father is dead, all right? He died in the Kobe earthquake when Miyuki was like fourteen."

"Miyuki's from Kobe?"

"No. Her dad just took the train in for some yearly business meeting, was supposed to be there for exactly one day, and next thing you know . . . Anyway, I thought we agreed not to discuss Miyuki just yet."

"I'm not sure I *am* talking about Miyuki anymore," I mumbled. Afuro stared at me as I said it, her baffled expression giving me some idea of what my own must've looked like.

"What's that supposed to mean?"

Yeah, said my next thought. *What is that supposed to*

mean? Could there really be two Miyukis? Two Miyukis with the same mole? Did I just imagine the mole when I'd seen the news clip on television? The waitress-slash-schoolteacher strolled by and topped off my coffee. I stared down into the mug. My face stared back up at me, utterly at a loss.

"Oh my God!" Afuro suddenly said. "What time is it?"

I checked my watch. About nine twenty-five, I told her. She cursed under her breath and all but leapt out of her chair.

"I gotta run."

"Right now?"

"I'm gonna be late for work!"

Then she started rummaging through her Cecil McBee handbag, pulling items out and scattering them across the desk. Lipstick tubes, barrettes, eyeliner pencils, cigarettes, a cigarette lighter, one black sock, a losing lottery ticket, a pen, a nine-volt battery, a piece of milk candy and a pink mobile phone. Throw in a Slurpee machine and the bag would've been a regular 7-Eleven.

"If you're looking for money, breakfast is on me," I said. "What's more, I don't think you should go just yet."

"I *have* to go."

"It's not polite to run out on a date like that. You'd know if you read more magazines."

"You're not my date. You're my oddball uncle, remember?"

"This is important, Afuro. I can't explain it to you right now, but I really need to learn some things about your friend Miyuki. You'd be doing me a great favor."

She stopped rummaging through the bag. "What did you just say?"

"I said you'd be doing me a great favor."

She seemed somehow startled by my words, and I couldn't

tell whether she was intrigued or frightened or about to cry or what. I was never able to tell what girls her age were thinking, even when I was her age myself. She set aside a pen, then swept everything back into the Day-Glo Cecil McBee, zipped it up and slung it over her shoulder. A moment later, the tip of the pen was poised against her wrist.

"What's your cell number?" she said.

When I said I didn't have a cell phone she looked at me like I'd just told her I ate kittens for dinner. She asked where I was staying and I told her the Hotel Cerulean.

"I'll call you," she said. "If I feel like talking about Miyuki. If I decide it helps. But don't wait underwater. To tell you the truth, I still haven't made up my mind whether you're a creep or not."

Before I could help her decide, she went racing out of the Let's Elementary Café like the end-of-school bell had just sounded. I stared at Afuro's empty pie plate and half-finished shake in a daze. Afuro's whirlwind conversational style would've left me feeling disoriented no matter what we'd discussed, but for not talking about Miyuki she'd said plenty.

As I sat at the desk finishing my coffee I was forced to conclude that Miyuki Nakodo and Miyuki-who-died-beneath-the-expressway were two different people. I realized it was entirely possible. What I'd mistaken for a mole could simply have been mud from the canal, or maybe a fleck of dust on the camera lens. Maybe I'd just completely imagined the mole. I'd seen the woman's face for less than one full second on a small TV from a distance of some fifteen feet inside a crowded, steamy noodle shop. Even if your legal training consisted of nothing but *Perry Mason* reruns, you could've torn my eyewitness testimony to shreds. Besides, there was no other way to explain how Afuro's Miyuki could've been from some village called Muramura and been fatherless since the age of eleven.

The realization should've made me feel better. After all, if Miyuki Nakodo was still alive, it meant the whole thing had nothing to do with me. There was no need to feel any sense of responsibility for her fate, or for anything I'd said to Mr. Nakodo.

But it didn't make me feel better.

I was wondering why when I noticed something on the floor. A pocket-sized red notebook. It was the same kind I always take on interviews, but it didn't belong to me. I figured Afuro must've dropped it when she was rummaging through her handbag.

It was lying open faced, displaying a crude map consisting of three intersecting lines with the words *Miyuki—Club Kuroi Kiri, Ginza sanchome* written above an X. I picked up the notebook, examined the map for a moment, then closed it. On the cover was a photo-booth sticker about the size of a postage stamp. The type of picture you can have taken in arcades in Shibuya and Harajuku and anywhere else kids hung out. This one featured two girls flashing the peace sign, framed by a border of pink hearts and blue stars.

Not surprisingly, the first thing I noticed was the mole.

There was only one Miyuki, and she was dead.

10

Detective Ihara

Rows of tombstones rolled over the grassy slope, their crammed but orderly arrangement mirroring the tony apartment buildings huddled in the valley below. Sunlight speckled through the thick canopy of trees and the place was quiet and empty. I'd been strolling the Aoyama Cemetery for ten minutes searching for Detective Ihara, but so far I'd only come across an old couple sweeping their family grave.

I watched as they put some flowers in an urn and placed an offering of o-hagi cake and a small cup of tea at the foot of the headstone. A crow rested in the shade of a nearby tree, eyeing the mochi cake and biding his time. The old couple stood shoulder to shoulder for a time, heads bowed as if in prayer, he in a rumpled brown suit, she in a white kimono. After a while, they both turned away from the grave. The man opened an umbrella against the noontime sun, then the woman took him by the elbow and they began slowly walking down the hill, out of the cemetery. All of this was done without the two of them exchanging a single word.

The crow swooped down to claim his prize, only to find another crow hopping along the ground with the o-hagi already planted in its beak. A third crow showed up and they all started cawing, beating their wings and making a big fuss. By then the old couple had disappeared from view.

I wandered in the opposite direction, enjoying the shade and the solitude and doing a fair job of keeping Miyuki out of my mind. I was doing pretty well not thinking about Afuro, Mr. Nakodo, Gombei, or even Sarah back in Cleveland. If I could keep all these thoughts out of my mind indefinitely, I had a fair chance of becoming a well-adjusted adult with a positive outlook on life and a high opinion of myself and my fellow human beings.

The momentary peace slowly eroded as I got the nagging sensation Detective Ihara was hiding somewhere in the cemetery, watching my every movement. I can't say what gave me the impression but once it entered my head it was impossible to shake. A small breeze kicked up, bringing the trees to life and rattling the wooden prayer tablets placed in special holders near the tombstones. The chattering of the wood and the constant cawing of the crows made for an eerie sound, one that was a little unnerving even in broad daylight. That's why I almost jumped when I heard someone whisper behind me.

"Where's the candy?"

I spun to see Detective Ihara sitting on the base of a tomb-stone shaded by a willow tree, his elbows resting on his knees. I couldn't make out his face too well, but he looked to be sulking.

"No candy," I said. "If you were thinking of leaving a treat for your dead ancestors to feast on, you'll have to buy it your-self."

Ihara burst out laughing. It wasn't a pretty sound.

"You think a humble family like mine could afford to be buried in a place like this? These plots cost more than my house and office combined."

"Who are you kidding?" I said. "With what you charge for information, you could build yourself a solid-gold mau-soleum in the middle of Ginza. Equip it with state-of-the-art surveillance equipment so you could spy on all the other corpses while awaiting safe passage to Nirvana."

Detective Ihara grunted unintelligibly, rose and stepped out of the shadows. A closer look at him told me the years since we'd last met had taken their toll. His face was fleshier, the loose skin mapped by a growing network of wrinkles. No longer in his prime but too young to look distinguished. One look at his mirrored sunglasses revealed the years hadn't let me off scot-free, either. His waistline had expanded where mine hadn't though, so I figured it was safe to compliment him. I make it a rule never to compliment men better looking than me. As for women, I hadn't found a rule yet that I could live by.

"You're looking fit," I said.

"Like hell I am. Spend all day on stakeouts eating junk food and you'd look like this, too. I blame you Americans and all your fast-food chains. Did you know the average Japanese school kid is getting fatter every year? All because of American junk food."

"American kids are getting fatter, too. We blame Nintendo."

He made some subvocal noises then asked if I still wanted to talk about what I wanted to talk about. I nodded and handed him the fifty thousand yen bundled in a copy of the *Yomiuri Shimbun*. It was gonna be a tough one to explain to accountant Chuck back in Cleveland, but I could always tell him I lost the money playing pachinko in order to understand Gombei's inner demons. Ihara took a furtive glance around the cemetery then tucked the package under his arm.

"Here are my terms," he said in a hushed voice. "I'll tell you what I know about the gentleman in question. You may not interrupt. You may not ask questions. When I'm finished talking, I'm finished talking. Those are my terms. Understood?"

I nearly offered to double the payment if he'd drop the no-interruptions rule. Ihara was the type who starts a two-Chinamen-walk-into-a-bar joke and ends talking about how beer was invented by ancient Assyrians. Guy must've come out of the womb mouth-first. Still, I needed to know about Mr. Nakodo even if I was likely to learn all kinds of other nonsense in the process.

After Ihara had another suspicious look around the cemetery, we started on a zigzagging course through the headstones, never moving too close to the streets bordering the cemetery, often doubling back and making sudden turns. Ihara probably couldn't get up to take a leak at night without checking to see if he was being tailed, but by the time he finished talking I was starting to understand the roots of his paranoia.

11

The Case of Mr. Bojangles
and the Shadow Man

It's a rainy night in July 1975, and Spylens! isn't
yet Spylens! but a humble two-person operation
called Ihara Investigations situated in a modest
area of Taito-ku. It's early evening. Detective Ihara
has already sent his secretary home and is preparing to leave when he hears someone come into the
reception area. He peeks through the blinds of his

inner office to see a nervous-looking man with medium-length hair. The man is in his late twenties or early thirties perhaps, about the same age as Ihara himself, and wears a rumpled white jacket.

"Can I help you?" Ihara says, emerging from his inner office.

"Perhaps," replies the man. "I wonder—how would one go about hiring a private investigator?"

"You can call up my secretary and make an appointment. That's the way we usually do business."

The man's small eyes leap around the room like anxious birds alighting from one branch to the next. "Let us say that I have a very sensitive matter to discuss. A matter I wish to keep as secret as possible."

"My secretary will keep your name in confidence," Ihara says, wondering why clients always feel they are the exception when it comes to having sensitive cases. He'd only had two other cases so far, routine marriage investigations at that, but in each case the client liked to play it very cloak and dagger, as if it were a matter of national security.

"You can even use a fake name," Ihara tells the man. "Call yourself Yujiro Ishihara or Burt Reynolds if you want, makes no difference to me. Once you have an appointment, we can discuss the job in greater detail."

At this the man begins absentmindedly picking at a fern plant in the office, plucking dead leaves and dropping them to the floor. The sight greatly vexes Ihara, for evidently his pretty young secretary has been fatally derelict in her plant-watering duties. Perhaps he should have bought fake plants after all.

"Let us assume the matter is an urgent one," the man says at length. "One in which time is a critical factor. Would it then be possible to expedite matters by making a personal appearance, rather than contacting your secretary over the telephone?"

"Certainly," says Detective Ihara.

"Very well. If you could please direct me to your secretary, I would like to make an appointment."

"My secretary isn't here," Ihara says. "She went home."

"How incredibly unfortunate."

"I was just headed out the door myself. But you can call for an appointment tomorrow."

"How incredibly unfortunate," says the man again. "I fear tomorrow shall be too late. A pity I couldn't have come sooner. Good day."

The man turns toward the door.

Ihara checks the clock hanging over the window. The hands rest at 6:43. His young son, Hiroshi, would be getting home from cram school soon. Ihara hasn't seen the boy for nearly a week, as he's been so busy arranging his new file cabinets. Outside, the sky is growing dark, and on the rain-soaked streets below motorists are making their nightly journey homeward.

"All right," Ihara sighs. "Let's hear what you have to say."

● ● ●

IHARA GUIDES THE MAN into his inner office, though there is no need for privacy as Ihara Investigations—indeed the entire floor of the building—is empty of people. The only ones who remain are Ihara's upstairs neighbors, a shameless real estate agent and his noisome assistant. The upstairs neighbors are having an affair, and are apparently too uncivilized to rent a love hotel. Ihara often hears them making love, like animals, right above his head. He would've complained to the landlord, but as he is two months behind in his rent he is in no position to make a fuss. Ihara just hopes his upstairs neighbors won't begin one of their beastly couplings while a client is in the room.

"I should inform you that I have chosen to employ a pseudonym, as you suggested was permissible."

"That's fine," Ihara says.

"Mr. Bojangles."

"Come again?"

"I have chosen the name Mr. Bojangles as my pseudonym."

The man shifts uneasily in the chair, tears off a minute sliver of his fingernail and drops it carelessly to the floor. It is then Ihara notices the dust on his carpet—the expensive upkeep service, StarSparkle Cleaning and Reform, has clearly neglected to vacuum during their visit the night before. Ihara stares at the man's brown loafers for a moment then scratches a note to himself on a yellow legal pad. *Call StarSparkle re: vacuuming.*"

"Well, Mr. Bojangles," says Ihara. "What is this urgent business you wish to discuss?"

"I wish to stop a marriage from occurring," Mr. Bojangles says. "Between a man named Nakodo and a woman named Ame Kitazawa."

"Is the woman a relation of yours?"

The man shakes his head in a way that precludes further questions, leading Ihara to believe the man is likely a jealous suitor. Having failed to win the woman's favor, Bojangles wants to smear the name of his rival by uncovering some family scandal. Depressing business, Ihara thinks, but business nonetheless.

How far along are the wedding preparations?"

"The marriage is scheduled to occur one month from now."

"Hmmm," Ihara says, scratching his chin. He does this not for effect, but because his chin suddenly itches. "Doesn't give us much time. I'll look into the Nakodo family past and see what I can find, but I'm not in the business of stopping marriages. I merely present facts. Even if I find some skeletons in the closet, there's no guarantee that will end it. With all the so-called love marriages these days, family scandals don't mean what they once did. You might even say marriage doesn't mean what it once did."

Ihara is pleased with his speech. He knew marriage investigations would be a large part of his business initially, and he'd spent much time rehearsing the scene in his mind, crafting a response that would make him appear a seasoned professional. He looks at the man to see if his speech has had the desired effect, but the man gives no indication of even having heard him. Ihara clears his throat and speaks again.

"So tell me a little about the potential groom. What does he do for a living?"

"He recently secured a post at the Ministry of Construction."

"Impressive. And what does his father do?"

"He is vice chairman of the Oshoku Construction Group."

"What business are they in?"

Bojangles's face contorts with displeasure. "Construction."

"Of course," Ihara says, chuckling. "Of course."

"The Oshoku Group builds nothing tangible," Bojangles says. "Rather, they unofficially represent Japan's largest construction companies. The Oshoku Group manufactures harmony. They construct understanding, pave over confusion and otherwise help smooth the bidding process for large government and corporate building contracts. As vice chairman, the elder Nakodo helps insure that ball is played, or that balls are made to roll, that balls are in a certain player's court and figures in a given ballpark. Nakodo the elder is what one might call a shadow man. He's as powerful as any Diet member or company president, yet he remains unknown to the general public despite having a broad face among the business and political elite."

Ihara nods and scratches *Nakodo = shadow man (?),* constructs "understanding" on the yellow legal pad. On paper the words strike him as meaningless, nonsensical.

"But what exactly does he do?" Ihara asks.

The man shakes his head, a measure of derision in the gesture. "Isn't it obvious? The whole group is nothing more than a giant collective that rigs bids and bribes politicians to insure that government contracts are routinely and systematically doled out to Oshoku companies. From what I understand, in many other countries, his activities would be illegal."

"How interesting," Ihara sniffs, still not sure he completely understands. "Tell me, just how did Nakodo come to such a position?"

"Supposedly, he made a fortune in the black market following the war, then used this money to start his own construction company. The outfit was little more than a glorified yakuza work crew in the early days, but Nakodo knew how to make connections. By the sixties, his construction company had won a number of lucrative building projects and were making larger companies take notice. But suddenly, in 1965, in the midst of a construction boom, Nakodo sold the company to one of the massive conglomerates. There is reason to believe the transaction was a veil, and that he continues to profit handsomely from his former business. After selling, he was awarded a post in the newly created Oshoku Construction Group. By the end of the Izanagi economic boom, he was as powerful as any figure in the industry."

"Seems you know the groom's father quite well," Ihara remarks. "I almost wonder what could be left to investigate."

Bojangles ignores Ihara, examining a loose button on his shirtsleeve, turning it between his fingers until the button tears off and tumbles to the carpet. Ihara looks upon the paper where he has written *Call StarSparkle re: vacuuming* and adds an emphatic "!" to the missive.

Bojangles resumes. "It is generally expected that his son will remain at the Ministry of Construction for some time, rising in the ranks and making yet more powerful connections before stepping down to join the Oshoku Group when the time comes. On its surface, the Nakodo family looks promising, indeed, an ideal family for any woman to marry into. But there's one problem. There is no Nakodo family. The name Nakodo is completely made up. A pseudonym, not unlike my own."

"I don't follow you," Ihara says.

"I believe Nakodo the elder was born as someone else," Bojangles says. "A man named Takahashi. I believe he changed his name to hide a dark secret in his past. I believe he was a member of the military police and was involved in some very disagreeable business during the war."

"This is a shocking accusation," says Ihara. "Do you have any evidence—"

"I believe gathering evidence is your job."

"But I wonder what inspired your suspicions regarding—"

"My inspirations, like my identity, shall remain my concern," Bojangles says. "I believe I have given you sufficient information with which to decide whether or not you care to pursue the case."

The intensity of Bojangles's expression gives Detective Ihara the impression that this young man is not merely uncouth, but perhaps a touch unbalanced. Still, the case could prove interesting and Ihara needs the money. His wife hadn't been thrilled with his decision to quit his job as an insurance claims investigator, and unless he makes a success of his new business, he feels his marriage is doomed. There is nothing left to do but discuss his rates.

Upon hearing Ihara's estimate, Mr. Bojangles reaches into his pocket, withdraws a litter of crumpled bills and drops them on Ihara's desk. When he has done this four times, he's produced enough for a retainer. Next, he retrieves a business card from the pocket of his threadbare trousers.

"May I borrow a pen?" the man asks.

Ihara hands him a pen and the man makes a series of brutal strokes, as if trying to single-handedly prove the instrument mightier than the sword. Then he places the pen back on Ihara's desk, along with his business card. The card reads only,

Bojangles.

On the other side is the number of a post office box in Ochanomizu.

"You may send your findings, along with the bill, to this address when the job is complete," the man says. "There is no need to contact me personally. In fact, it will prove quite impossible for you to do so." With that, Bojangles rises, brushes off his white jacket, and makes for the door.

Ihara examines the card again. "May I ask you one question, Mr. Bojangles?"

Bojangles grudgingly halts and turns to face Ihara.

"You must realize, given the Nakodo family's prominence and the collapsed time frame we're dealing with, that the chances of stopping this marriage are pretty slim. What do you really hope to accomplish with this investigation?"

The man waits several moments before answering. When he finally speaks his voice trembles as if too much emotion is being forced through too narrow a passage.

"The captain of a doomed ship gazes across the horizon and sees a vague shape in the distance. And he wonders, 'What can that be?' The shape plays upon his imagination, and he grows daily more afraid. By the time the ships meet, this captain has already lost the battle. Do you understand?"

"Not entirely."

"I wish to be that vague shape in the distance, Detective," Bojangles says, carefully enunciating each syllable in a low voice. "I wish to be trouble on the distant horizon."

Before Ihara can say he still doesn't quite

understand, the man turns and shuffles out of the inner office. Ihara looks down at his pad of paper. Upon it he has written,

Call StarSparkle re: vacuuming! Nakodo marriage to Ame Kitazawa. Groom post @ Ministry of Construction. Father @ Oshoku Construction Group. Nakodo = shadow man (?), constructs understanding. Nakodo pseudonym, dark wartime secret as Takahashi. Captain of ship to gaze into distance, grow afraid, lose battle (?) Bojangles = vague shape, trouble on horizon

As Detective Ihara prepares to go home he hears the first gentle moans of the woman in the office above him. He wonders what would happen if he made a pass at Yumi, his own secretary. She'd probably bite his head off. But still he wonders.

TWO DAYS LATER, Detective Ihara takes off his jacket, unbuttons his shirt collar, loosens his tie and settles into the reclining chair behind his desk. He'd spent much of the day dodging the rain and being bounced from one government building to the next as he went about visiting the various bureaus and agencies that made up western Shinjuku. It has been a productive morning, and Ihara has returned with a briefcase full of photocopied land titles, family registers, bank records and business deeds—all the rudimentary information he needs to begin his investigation of the Nakodo family.

As he undoes the laces of his wet shoes, he recalls shopping with his wife in Ginza a week ago. They had just bought a Mickey Mouse watch, the same kind worn by Emperor Hirohito, as a birthday present for their son Hiroshi when Ihara's attention had been drawn to a pair of brown leather shoes displayed in a shop window on Harumi Street. They were marvelous looking, these shoes, and combined the best elements of many different styles of footwear. Just as he was considering trying them on, his wife hooked him by his elbow and reeled him into the mass of pedestrians pouring across the intersection. You have a perfectly good pair of shoes already, she told him, and until you start landing some real clients we can't afford any luxuries.

Recalling the moment, Ihara decides that once this case is complete and the invoice is paid, he will celebrate by returning to the store, trying on the shoes and—if they fit—buying them without hesitation. He snatches up his legal pad and etches the decree with his favorite pen.

Buy those shoes!

Before Ihara can delve further into this matter of Nakodo the groom and senior Nakodo the father, he needs a name for the case. Calling the case by its invoice number (#00003) simply won't do. In the insurance business, of course, it was standard to refer to a case by its claim number—but he is a detective now, a thought that suffuses him with a sudden thrill, and detectives put names to their cases. Ihara looks over his notes, and two words leap out at him.

Shadow man.

The Case of the Shadow Man?

The Case of Shadow Man and Mr. Bojangles?

The Case of Shadow Man Who Saw Trouble on the Horizon?

The Case of Nakodo and the Vague Shape?

Ihara is weighing the merits of such names when he notices the blinking light on his Casio PhoneMate 400 Telephone Answering Device. The machine's insistent nictitations dissipate his appellative brainstorm. He hits the Play button on the reel-to-reel machine, plugs in his earpiece and listens.

The message is from Yumi, his secretary.

"This message is from Yumi," she whispers. "There's this man waiting in the lobby. He's been here approximately all morning and I'm pretty sure he's bad news. As in bad news yakuza bad news. I asked him if he had an appointment, but he won't say word number one. He's just sitting there, right now, using both eyes to stare at me. I'm a little spooked here, sir. This message is ending now. Good-bye."

The message had been left for him three hours ago, but Ihara hadn't noticed anyone waiting in the lobby when he arrived. Then again, he'd rushed straight to his inner office without even glancing around. Forced now to recall his damp and hurried entrance, he remembers the vexed look upon his secretary's face as he rushed by her toward the sanctuary of his private office. He's been avoiding Yumi ever since he got the idea of making a pass at her. With such thoughts in his head, he finds it suddenly impossible to carry on even the most harmless conversations with his sole employee.

The next message is also from Yumi.

"This is another message from Yumi," she says in a nervous singsong. "Where can you be, sir? This question weighs heavily upon my mind. A second piece of bad news just walked in and took a seat next to the first. Much staring yet zero effort to communicate verbally or respond to attempted verbal communication from myself. If this continues much longer, the sitting and the staring, I'm calling the police. I'm kinda freaking out here if you can't tell, sir. OK, that's my message, now I'm hanging up."

Ihara gets a sinking feeling in the pit of his stomach. He knew it had been a bad idea to take on Mr. Bojangles. There was something off-kilter about the man. He swears that from now on he'll do background checks on all clients before agreeing to take a job. Of course, that will make two investigations of one, doubling the workload and likely making any job ultimately unprofitable. The world of private detection is perhaps more complicated than he had imagined.

Ihara listens to the third message.

"This message is from Yumi," Yumi says, her voice trembling now. "Bad things come in threes, and number three has just arrived. This I cannot abide. I'm calling the police and I'm getting out of here in a most expedient fashion, sir. I hope you understand. That's my message. Please don't—"

The message abruptly ends.

Detective Ihara takes out his earpiece and tries to dial Yumi's extension, but there is no answer. He replaces the receiver. At that moment, Ihara wishes for nothing more than to open the window and fly away like a great black crow. He would fly across the western borders of the city, past Mount Fuji and all the way across Honshu to his hometown of Kanazawa. And once he got there? Well, it didn't matter. He couldn't fly. He wasn't a crow, he was a detective, and he'd have to toughen up and think like one if he wanted to stay in business. With this in mind, he grits his teeth, rises and walks into the outer office, trying to ignore the fact that his legs are shaking.

SEVERAL MEN ARE MILLING around the reception area. Some sit on the couch, others on the coffee table and still others on the floor. These men sport loud Hawaiian shirts and unfashionable white patent-leather shoes. These men wear shirts unbuttoned to the navel, and hair slicked back with foul-smelling grease. These men all stare at him in perfect silence.

These men are surely yakuza.

Ihara counts nine of them. How could he have missed them when he came in? Nine men, he thinks incredulously. Nine men, all wearing colorful Hawaiian shirts, no less. If he is to become a successful detective, he will have to work on being more observant in the future. If Ihara Investigations has a future.

Detective Ihara glances at Yumi. Her lower lip trembles and her eyes are filled with tears, but she looks otherwise unharmed. The same cannot be said for her telephone, which lies on her desk a shattered heap. Ihara takes a deep breath, steels his nerves and speaks.

"Gentlemen, I apologize for keeping you waiting," he says. His voice sounds distant and frail, as if it has been carried in on a gust of wind. "I wonder if perhaps there is some business you wish to discuss?"

Eighteen eyes stare back at him and no one answers.

IHARA HOLDS THE DOOR OPEN, inviting them into his inner office. All at once they rise and shuffle lazily past him. Ihara has an impulse to lock the door behind them, trapping the gangsters inside. Then he will take Yumi by the hand and rush her out of the building, to safety. From that point forward she will look at him as more than merely her employer. She will see him as her rescuer, her protector. He needn't worry about making a pass at her then— she'll be falling into his arms.

Unfortunately, the door locks only from the inside.

Once the last yakuza has walked into the room, Ihara reluctantly follows them inside and closes the door behind him. As he looks around at his tastefully furnished office, he is struck by a terrible notion. Perhaps these yakuza are not at all related to the Mr. Bojangles case. Perhaps they have come to collect so-called protection money before the agency has even really gotten off the ground. Perhaps, thanks to Ihara's fine taste in office furniture, the men truly believe that Ihara Investigations is the successful, thriving business he works so hard to portray it as. Perhaps they believe it is a host organism ripe for invasion by a criminal parasite.

Ihara's horror grows with the realization that everything—the desk, the chair, his notebook, his Casio PhoneMate 400 TAD, even his hopes for new shoes and his dream to be a successful private detective—all of this can be taken away. Everything he's worked for could simply vanish, turn to nothing in the blink of an eye. The thought fills him with a panic that manifests itself in a wild, leering grin.

None of the men return Ihara's dizzy smile.

Detective Ihara struggles to maintain his composure as he reaches into his desk and withdraws a stack of newly printed business cards to distribute to the assembled yakuza. He hears the reception area door slam as Yumi scrambles out of the office. Ihara thinks surely one or more of the yakuza will chase after her, but none does. Instead they stand there, looking for all the world like they are merely waiting for a train or queuing in line outside the cinema. The smell of their hair grease is truly nauseating.

Detective Ihara tries to pass out his cards, but the men refuse to take them. Now at his wit's end, he is sure some type of violence will soon commence. He knows the particular silence that envelops the room, recognizes this soundless prelude from his unhappy youth as an awkward, sickly child. How old must one get, he wonders, to finally outgrow bullies?

A man in a yellow floral shirt steps forward. Ihara recoils, closing his eyes, awaiting the first blow. But the man does not strike him. Instead, he places a small package wrapped in gold foil on Ihara's desk. A second man then steps forward and picks up the telephone. He dials a number and hands the receiver to Ihara. Ihara's eyes move from one man to the next, but none offers any clue as to what is going to happen. Ihara puts the phone to his ear.

"Moshi moshi," he says.

The voice on the other end is warped, distorted.

"Open the package," it says.

Ihara studies the gold box for several moments. Then he carefully unwraps the package with one hand while holding the phone to his ear with the other. Inside is a black wooden box.

"Lift the lid," says the voice.

Ihara slowly lifts the lid from the box.

The box contains a child's watch.

A Mickey Mouse watch.

The same Mickey Mouse watch he had given his son for his birthday. Ihara recognizes the scuff mark on the watch's face, damage that occurred when Hiroshi fell from his bicycle two weeks ago.

"Have we reached an understanding?" says the voice.

Ihara nods, still transfixed by his son's watch.

"HAVE WE REACHED AN UNDERSTANDING?"

"Yes," Ihara manages.

"Drop the investigation."

"Yes."

"Immediately."

"Immediately," Ihara echoes.

"We've reached an understanding. Now hang up the phone."

Detective Ihara does as instructed. The moment the receiver hits the cradle the nine gangsters simultaneously turn and make their way out of the office. When they are gone, Detective Ihara lurches across the floor and slumps into his chair. His heart is racing and drops of sweat roll down his back. He stares at the watch. Mickey Mouse smiles up at him, his hands dropped between his knees to indicate six-thirty. Rain pounds against the window and Ihara hears a thin creaking noise overhead as the realtor and his assistant begin their nightly lovemaking.

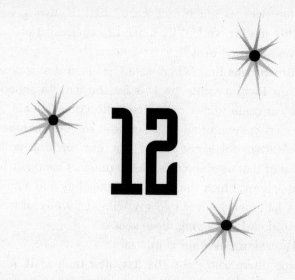

12

Descending from Heaven

Detective Ihara dabbed the sweat from his forehead with a folded cloth. We'd been walking around the cemetery for at least an hour, and from Ihara's doggish pant I got the idea it was as high as his pulse had gotten since the gangsters had shown up in his office all those years ago. I waited for him to continue speaking, but apparently he'd finished.

"So what happened?" I finally asked.

"My secretary quit," Ihara said. "I hired another one who

cost me twice as much and wasn't half as nice to look at. Probably just as well. Why make life complicated?"

"Was your son okay?"

"Hiroshi was fine," Ihara said. "He said that a nice man came up to him while he was on the way to school and offered to trade him a new electronic yo-yo for his watch. Who even knew there were electronic yo-yos? He loved that stupid thing, but every time I saw him playing with it, I thought of that terrible voice on the phone. One day when he was at school, I took the yo-yo into the alley and smashed it with a hammer. I never told my wife about any of it. And I never did end up buying those shoes."

"The yakuza ever show up again?"

"No," Ihara said. "But the day after their visit, a top-of-the-line telephone was delivered to the office. And when I tried to pay rent the next month, the building manager told me my lease had been covered for the remainder of the year. Strangest of all, the realtor and his secretary suddenly stopped screwing. At least in their office."

"Did Bojangles contact you?"

"I never heard from him again. The marriage came off, of course. About two years later I ran across an article about a woman drowning in the Sumida River. Turned out the woman was Nakodo's wife."

"How did she drown?"

"How does anyone drown?" Ihara said. "She fell in the river, couldn't swim. She sank like a rock, her lungs filled with water—"

"I mean was there evidence of foul play?"

"No. She fell off a tour boat. An accident. Plenty of witnesses, as I recall."

"So was there anything to the allegations that the older

Nakodo changed his name? To hide his wartime past or whatever?"

Ihara shook his head. "No way. His son wouldn't have made it into Nihon University, much less the Ministry of Construction, with something like that in his background. It would've surfaced somewhere down the line. Bojangles was just using me. I've seen the game a thousand times since, but I was too inexperienced back then to realize what was going on."

"What do you mean?"

"It usually goes like this," he said. "As soon as Bojangles hires me, he writes an anonymous letter to the bride's family. Something along the lines of 'you may wish to know that a future member of your family is being investigated in a very serious matter.' Gives them my number. They call, but under client privilege I can't discuss the case with them. Which makes them even more nervous. They get nervous enough, they make their own inquiries. Get someone to investigate me to see what I'm investigating. When the answer comes back 'potential identity falsification to cover up wartime past,' that's it. They freak out, call the marriage off. That's the way it's supposed to work. But Old Man Nakodo put a stop to it before Bojangles could enact his plan."

How long ago was all of this?"

"Let me think," Ihara said. "I'd just started in this business, so that would have been 1975. Amazing how time goes by. Listen, Billy. I know we've had our differences in the past. Still, I've grown to like you."

"But?"

"You're a smart guy, plenty smart, but you're still *gaijin*. Meaning you don't really understand the way things work here."

It was a variation on the standard foreigners-can-never-fathom-our-mysterious-Japanese-ways speech, one I'd heard a million times in relation to everything from aikido to zaibatsu. Of course, I often resorted to the same tactic when trying to explain monster truck rallies, personalized license plates, or the electoral college.

"What I'm saying is leave it alone. Whatever it is, if the Nakodo family is involved, just leave it be."

"You know something you're not telling me?"

"I know that Nakodo is a very big fish in this particular pond. And you, Billy, are a very small fish. Compared to Nakodo, we're all small fish—but you're one of the smallest. Plankton to a whale. Nakodo could swallow you without even noticing."

"Plankton aren't fish," I said. "Neither are whales. But just so I have this straight—we're not talking about a yakuza boss. We're not talking about the CEO of a multinational conglomerate, or even an elected official. We're talking about a civil servant? A bureaucrat with the Ministry of Construction? The son of the vice chairman of some mysterious—"

Ihara shook his head vigorously. "Don't get hung up on titles and appearances, Chaka. Nakodo has spent a lifetime building *jinmyaku*, has all the right connections, top to bottom. Maybe you don't know him, but he knows you. He went to college with your niece's husband, golfs with your dentist's accountant, goes out drinking with your lawyer's uncle. There's a reason why when people step down from the government they call it *amakudari*—descending from heaven. It's like gods coming to live among mere mortals. People like him run the country. Get in good with his crowd, life is smooth sailing. Fall out of favor, you sink to the bottom."

"You know anything about him having a daughter?"

Ihara stopped walking and turned to face me.

"His daughter? Is that what this is about? You've got your-self mixed up with his daughter?"

"Not exactly—"

"Goddamn it, Billy. Have you no self-control?"

"It's not like that."

"Nakodo's *daughter*? You might as well just stay here in the cemetery. Dig yourself a hole and get comfortable!"

"You've got the wrong idea."

"I don't want any ideas," he said, holding a hand up to silence me. "Look, take my advice. Whatever it is, just walk away. Don't get in any deeper than you are already. You're never gonna win playing with someone like Nakodo. You're never gonna know what's at stake, you're never even gonna see the cards being dealt. In fact, here—" Detective Ihara shoved the newspaper and the money into my chest. "I don't want any part of this. I mean, goddamn it, Billy, his daugh-ter? You're not a kid anymore, you know. Get married. Settle down with that woman Sarah or whoever. You'll live longer for it."

I started to say something, but Ihara clapped both hands over his ears like any reasonable four-year-old might. Then he turned on his heel and stormed away, tripping on a tomb-stone and kicking over an urn filled with chrysanthemums in the process. I didn't bother chasing after him. Even beneath the shade of the trees I could feel the temperature rising. The sun was high and angry and taking it out on everything in sight.

13

The Octopus's Garden

Back in the Octopus's Garden I sat around watching the goldfish wander his empty tank. A blank piece of paper sat on the desk in front of me. I was going to use this paper to write the Gombei Fukugawa story the moment inspiration hit. So far I'd managed to duck it.

Every once in a while I was certain Afuro was about to call, but the phone never agreed. *Don't wait underwater,* she'd said. Yet here I was in the Octopus's Garden staring at a goldfish, which seemed close enough. Pound for pound, the goldfish had bigger living quarters than most of the people in the city, but it didn't seem to make much use of its space. Mostly it hovered at the center of the tank, looking out into the room, mouthing silent O's.

Five minutes went by. Ten more followed. Twenty, half an hour, an hour. Afternoon lapsed into evening and all the while the phone just sat there, refusing to make a sound. I felt like I was fifteen again, waiting on some girl to call. How many hours had I spent this way? You'd think the universe had a finite supply I would have exhausted long ago.

I got bored watching the goldfish and flipped on the TV. The big summer Nagoya sumo tournament was on NHK and a Seattle Mariners game was on NHK2. They were showing every Mariners game this year because there was a Japanese guy on the team. There were eighteen Japanese guys on the Yomiuri Giants, but Seattle was still the country's most popular team.

On another channel, a blow-dried American guy who resembled a muppet come to life looked on with rabid enthusiasm while two adult Japanese students exchanged the following dialogue during their English language lesson:

BOY: What is your mother like?
GIRL: She is a big tree.
BOY: She is like a big tree?
GIRL: Yes, my mother is like a big tree. Do you like sports?
BOY: No.

My only escape was a wacky quiz show called *Jikokuhyo SuperGenius* on which every single question was about trains and subways. What time the last Chuo Line Special Express stopped in Yotsuya, how many JR lines met at Ueno station, which subway tunnel covered the most geographical distance. When the host asked how much a transfer from the Hibiya to the Chiyoda line cost at Asakusa station, a contestant buzzed in and shouted "Flim-flam!" The audience went nuts. The host awarded the man a bunch of money for identifying the trick question of the day and then it was time for a commercial.

I had a lot of questions myself, maybe even enough for my own game show. I turned off the TV and studied the picture of Miyuki, the one affixed to the notebook dropped by Afuro. My eyes started with the mole, but with some effort I managed to drag them over the rest of the picture.

Both the girls were smiling. Big natural smiles, the kind you smile when life sits before you like an unopened gift. Miyuki looked a bit different from when I'd seen her in the Lucky Benten Pachinko hall, but it was definitely her. Her hair was shorter, dyed reddish brown and studded into pufferfish spikes. Her face was somewhat rounder, less severe looking. Judging by her hair length, the picture must've been taken at least five or six months ago.

Miyuki wore a thick lime-green sweater offset by a bright orange scarf and a blueberry handbag draped over her left shoulder. Her fingernails were painted the metallic yellowy green of reptile eyes. Not to be outsassed, Afuro-Short-for-Nothing was wearing a tight-fitting Where's Waldo–ish red-and-white-striped sweater along with a purple stocking cap displaying a silver emblazoned logo for the J-League soccer team Nagoya Grampus Eight. I didn't know what the hell a Grampus was, but in their swirl of mismatched colors, Afuro and Miyuki looked like a box of melted crayons.

At around seven-thirty I went down the hall to get a beer

from the vending machine, stopping to gaze at the Benten portrait on the sealed door along the way. When I came back the light on the phone was blinking. *Typical*, I thought, *step out for one minute and she calls*. Guess my luck hadn't changed much since I was fifteen, but at least I could legally console myself with alcohol now. I cracked open my beer, picked up the phone and listened to the message.

"It's Gombei," a cheery voice announced. "I just wanted to see how your story was coming along. I know our interview kind of came to a premature end the other day, so if there were any other questions you wanted to ask, feel free to call me. I really enjoyed talking with you, man. Did a lot of interviews back in the day, and I can tell you're a real professional. So if you need anything more for your *Youthful Asian* article, don't hesitate to get in touch."

Enjoyed talking with me? The guy hardly said five words over two hours. Bizarre. He left three different numbers where he could be reached, the message ended and I hung up the phone.

By eight-thirty I'd finished off another vending-machine beer and Afuro still hadn't called. The goldfish looked at me with an expression that seemed to say *It ain't gonna happen, pal.* I told the fish to be patient, show some of the courage and dedication the placard proclaimed it dearest for. The goldfish responded with a look that said *You realize I'm a goldfish and not a carp, don't you?*

"You can at least humor me," I said.

You realize you're having an imaginary conversation with a fish, don't you?

And a thrilling one at that, Mr. Goldfish.

I thumbed through the notebook again, holding up blank pages to the light, looking for any indentations from writing on pages that had perhaps been torn out. But there was nothing, just the one page with the crude map and the words *Miyuki—Club Kuroi Kiri*. Gazing at the picture and the map had awakened all those questions I'd managed to more or less keep quiet that afternoon. I tried to put the questions back to sleep, but it was no use. They were like kids when their nap was cut short. Noisy, grumpy, demanding constant attention. There was nothing I could do but drag them across town and hope the excitement and all the bright lights wore them out.

14

The Black Mist Club

The cabbie scrutinized the map, turning the notebook first one way then another. I looked out at the dazzling lights of Ginza lining the wide avenue as far as the eye could see. In Tokyo the eye can never see very far, but what the cityscape lacks in depth it makes up for in surface. The building we'd pulled up next to was seven stories tall and had a series of elaborate neon signs running vertically down its side, each advertising a different hostess club or bar. Rare Disorder in the basement, Trotsky Fox on 1F, The G9 Lounge on 2F, something called Night Piggy on 3F, Chomejin Konton on 4F, and so on. On the roof a huge video billboard for Seven Stars cigarettes blinked their logo into the night. Just for fun I tried finding seven real stars in the sky, but I gave up at four.

"You sure this thing is right?" asked the cabbie.

"That's the map she gave me."

"Club Kuroi Kiri?"

I nodded. *Kuroi kiri* meant *black mist*—a popular euphemism for business and political scandals, the types that had been dominating headlines for the last decade as the country sifted through the wreckage of a collapsed economy. The club owners must've had a grim sense of humor, which was about the only kind people could afford these days.

The cabbie studied the map once more. Then he turned his attention to the building and began counting softly to himself, pointing a white-gloved finger at each story in succession. He folded up the map and handed it back to me.

"It's on the seventh floor," he said.

I craned my neck and had a look. No sign hung from the building indicating anything on the seventh floor. Not even a hint of light played at the windows. The seventh floor had no windows.

"Perhaps you'd like to go somewhere else?" he said.

"But you said it's here, on the seventh floor?"

"Yes. But perhaps—"

"How much do I owe you?"

"Yes. Well . . ." I watched his face in the rearview mirror as it went through a whole range of pained contortions.

"Is there a problem?"

"There's no problem, honorable customer. It's just that, please understand, those kinds of hostess bars are members only. And they tend to get more exclusive the higher up you go. This Kuroi Kiri place is on the seventh floor, see? The top floor. And the fact that it doesn't even have a sign, well."

By "well" he meant that I had about as much chance of getting inside the Club Kuroi Kiri as an elephant would have getting inside a coin locker.

"I know a nice hostess bar in Roppongi," he said. "A place called the Slow Club. It's not far from here and it's much cheaper. Everything here in Ginza is outrageous. I'd be happy to take you to this place in Roppongi, if it pleases you."

Any other country and I'd think I was being swindled for extra miles on the meter, but it's been my experience that if every person in the world was as considerate as your average Tokyo cab driver armies would disband, prisons would be emptied, law firms dissolve and daytime talk shows go off the air forever.

Just then a car pulled over in front of the cab. A silver Aston Martin the size of a whale. I recognized the bearish driver who hustled out to open the door and there was no mistaking the black-suited figure who emerged from behind it. His sad little stoop-shouldered amble was as distinctive as his daughter's mole. I watched him walk into the building and felt that things were finally connecting.

"Thanks for the offer," I told the cabbie as I handed him the fare. "But I think I just found a way in."

I TOOK MY TIME HEADING up the stairs, partly because I like stairwells and partly because I needed time to decide just what to say to Mr. Nakodo. If it really was his daughter who drowned, I should be preparing condolences rather than questions. But if his daughter had died the day before, what would he be doing at a swanky hostess club in Ginza?

By the time I reached the fourth floor I was reminding myself that whoever the drowned girl was, it had nothing to do with me. We'd never even spoken. She was just some woman I'd seen in a pachinko parlor. A woman having a seizure. A woman with a funny mole that I couldn't stop thinking about.

By the seventh floor none of that mattered.

I exited the stairwell and walked down a short, narrow hall. The door to Club Kuroi Kiri was wide open. There were no meaty bouncers at the entrance, no slick-looking gangster types, not even a Members Only sign. None of that was needed because everyone already knew the rules and could guess at the consequences. Calling attention to the Club Kuroi Kiri's exclusivity was like pinning a Danger sign on the nose of a shark.

A row of Japanese women in matching black dresses and white elbow-length gloves was lined up just inside the entrance. Thin bare necks, sculpted cheekbones, shimmering black hair, sparkling brown eyes. My eyes jumped from one woman to another and back again in such quick succession that I couldn't be sure how many there were, much less tell them apart. Black-stockinged legs that went on forever, lips painted heart-attack red, the kind of curves that would leave a cheap detective novelist drooling metaphors. I had to stare at my wing tips for a moment to recalibrate my vision. The women were much less impressed with me, acknowledging my presence with uneasy smiles and sidelong glances toward their boss.

"Oh! Oh! Oh!" the matron said, fluttering her hands as her high heels clicked across the floor. The *mama-san* was a middle-aged lady with too much hair stacked on her head, too much makeup caked on her face and too many pearls draped around her neck. She got halfway across the floor when she suddenly stopped and headed the other direction, hands still dancing around her face like moths orbiting a lightbulb.

I stood there by the entrance, dumb American smile on my face, and scanned the room for Nakodo. It was too dark to see much. The light was dim and the décor was black. Black walls, black floors, black tables. All the men wore black coats over starched white shirts. All the women wore black dresses, black pumps and elbow-length white gloves. I had on my usual black pants, white shirt and black wing tips, but I still belonged like an earthworm in a dragon roll.

The matron reemerged with a young blonde in tow, dragging her across the room and all but shoving her in my face. I wouldn't have minded. The blonde was about six feet tall, had long hair the color of sunlight and so many freckles you could spend days counting them. Judging by the way her body was poured into the requisite black dress, they'd likely be the most memorable days in your life.

"Sorry, mate," the blonde said in a thick Australian brogue. "This here club is members only this club here is! Bastards, eh? Lady wanted me to tell on account of she can't speak English, right? Anyway, you'd best go on a walkabout unless you want her throwing a wobbly and calling in the stand-over man. Hard luck, mate. No worries. Cheers! G'day!"

A regular Eliza Doolittle down under, this one. I smiled at the Aussie and waved to the matron anxiously watching a few feet away.

"*Sumimasen*," I called. "*Chotto matte, kudasai!*"

The matron tilted her head, surprised to hear me not only speaking Japanese but barking it. She approached cautiously, all smiles now, hands resting calmly at her sides. It did little to hide the fact that she wasn't comfortable dealing with foreign men, or maybe just nonmillionaires.

"Forgive me for bothering you," I said in Japanese.

"Yes?" said the matron.

"It's this woman here." I nodded toward the Aussie, who lit up with a big smile. No freckles on her teeth.

"Yes?" said the matron.

"I can't understand a single word she's saying. She keeps speaking English at me. At least I think it's English. See, I'm French. From France."

"France?" said the matron.

"Well, France by way of Poland, at least on my mother's side. She's actually Russian, from a little village in Istanbul, formerly Constantinople. But I don't speak English. I speak French. *Français*. And frankly, I'm a little insulted to be treated like this."

"French?" said the matron.

"I'm here to rendezvous with Mr. Nakodo. I'm a touch late and must've just missed him downstairs where we were supposed to meet. And now you and this babbling *je ne se quoi* are making me later."

"Mr. Nakodo?" said the matron.

"*Hai, si vois plais*. Tell him it's Billy Chaka."

The matron then smiled and unleashed a barrage of very fluent, unaccented, straight-outta-the-Sorbonne-type French. I had no idea what she was saying, but it hardly mattered. Seeing I was now firmly put in my place, she bowed and walked across the floor, into the dark recesses of the Black Mist Club. One or two of the five or six Japanese beauties trilled musical giggles before they followed her en masse. The blonde stuck around for a moment longer, torturing me with another smile before strolling away nice and slow to prolong the agony. And just like that, six or seven of the most beautiful women I'd met in my life walked out of it before I'd even had a chance to tell a knock-knock joke.

As soon as they'd gone I felt several eyes upon me. The place didn't fall silent, but the atmosphere of the club had undergone a subtle shift, as if a cloud had passed momentarily in front of the sun.

Suddenly Nakodo was standing right in front of me. He arrived without warning, before I'd even seen him come shuffling across the floor. Nakodo seemed to share my surprise. His mouth opened and closed and his eyebrows came together at the center of his broad forehead.

Then all at once that expression was wiped clean.

Suddenly I was no longer looking at the same man I'd met only two days ago. Nakodo the Worried Father was gone and I was facing another man entirely. The transformation was enough to jar a molar loose and before I could pinpoint just what was so different about him he walked away, gesturing me to follow. Nakodo's stoop-shouldered shuffle had been replaced by a purposeful stride of almost military bearing. I trailed him to an isolated table in the corner, feeling eyes follow us through the dark.

GROUPS OF SIX OR SEVEN sat in spacious booths, arranged like chess pieces awaiting the endgame. The women mostly looked on and smiled while men held low conversations punctuated with slow, vaguely sinister gestures. On a small stage in the corner, a thin man in a tuxedo sat plinking a piano. I wasn't familiar with the tune. No one under sixty would be.

Mr. Nakodo sat ramrod straight, spine bracing the wall, face peering out over the room, hands resting palms down on the table. Each of us waited for the other to start. I was just about to speak when a hostess came to our table and placed a drink in front of Nakodo. He tilted his head about four degrees my way and tapped the side of his glass with a forefinger, sending the hostess sprinting out of the room. I stalled for a few moments, unsure how to begin. Nakodo offered no help.

"I saw the news last night," I said.

He blinked once in reply. Before I could continue the hostess returned and placed my drink in front of me. I tried to thank her but she was already gone, so I just put the drink to my lips. Scotch and water, mostly the latter.

"*Okuyami o môshiagemasu,*" I started. All the stock formal phrases I knew sounded too cold, too pat, so I switched courses. "Look, I'm not going to pretend I know what you're feeling. I don't have the faintest clue. I know it must be difficult, and I know the word 'difficult' doesn't begin to cover it. I'm sorry."

Nakodo stared at me like you might stare at a wall or television set or into the deep reaches of outer space. His gaze unnerved me, and I found myself again at a loss for words. Nakodo took a sip of his drink without taking his eyes off me, then he spoke.

"Forgive me," he said. "But I don't understand."

I studied his face in the dark, trying to figure out how to proceed. It wasn't an easy conversation to have in any language. In Japanese, with its heavy dependence on formality, hierarchy, subtle implication, euphemisms and vague innuendo, conversations like this were riddled with linguistic land mines. I dropped my eyes to the surface of the table.

"I know your private affairs are none of my business. But ever since Miyuki had the seizure in the pachinko parlor, I feel like I'm involved. After all, when she went missing, you came to me, sought my assistance, asked . . ."

"Miyuki is fine."

"I'm sorry?"

"Miyuki is fine," he repeated. "She came home. You were right. My concern proved to be premature, for she ended up strolling in not an hour after you and I spoke. She left because she was angry with me I guess, wanted to teach me a lesson. Get some kind of revenge for my so-called spying. Whatever her motives were, it's all over now. She's come home."

"Oh," I said.

"You sound disappointed."

"Not at all."

"But something is troubling you, Mr. Chaka?"

"I'm just a little confused."

The piano player reached the end of the song. A smattering of applause. The crackle of tobacco, ice clinking in glasses. Then the piano player started another tune. This one I recognized as "Mack the Knife." Nakodo permitted himself the thinnest of smiles.

"I can see how you might be confused," he said. "I had no right to involve you in my troubles. The wrong approach, I think. It's my nature to believe every problem has a solution. And I'll admit to being a man who likes to be in control. But where daughters are concerned . . . well, it's not always possible. Their nature, I suppose, is to resist control. To create problems that lack clear resolution. At any rate, please forgive me for troubling you."

My head was buzzing so loud I could hardly digest what he was saying. Miyuki was fine. Miyuki had come home. Meaning I was supposed to believe the girl on TV wasn't Miyuki, the girl on Afuro's notebook wasn't Miyuki, Miyuki hadn't drowned, and Miyuki wasn't dead. I took another slug of my scotch and water, a big enough slug to burn going down.

"What were you saying earlier?" Nakodo asked. "Something about the news?"

"A suicide," I said. "A young woman drowned and I thought it was your daughter. I saw a clip on TV. The girl looked just like her. Exactly like her. Even had the same, uh, well, she looked exactly like Miyuki."

Nakodo downed the remainder of his drink.

"I haven't heard about this drowning you refer to, but I can assure you Miyuki is safe and sound," he said. "Not terribly happy to be back home, but certainly not ready to jump into the Nihonbashi River. Drowning, what a terrible way to go."

"Terrible . . ." I echoed.

I hadn't mentioned the Nihonbashi River.

"Breaks my heart when young people senselessly end their lives. Still, I can't help but wonder if modern existence and all its conveniences lead to a kind of emptiness," Nakodo said. "A loss of purpose."

"A loss of purpose . . ."

"Today's youth are so listless, so depressed all the time. There's no pleasing them. You write for young people, maybe you can tell me—why all this alienation?"

"It's no different than acne," I said absently. "Almost everyone gets it. For some it's a phase, but some get permanently scarred, and some, well, some never get rid of it. Others get pimples on and off for the rest of their lives and learn to live with it."

"Pimples? I don't follow you."

I shrugged. I didn't really follow me either. My thoughts were centrifuging, spinning around my head in the hopes that I could separate what I knew from what I only thought I knew. Nakodo rattled the cubes around in his glass.

"I'm pleased you came to see me just the same," he said. "Brings this whole strange episode to a close, doesn't it?"

While the question hung in the air, his eyes did everything they could to make sure I came up with the correct answer. But at the last moment, he looked away. I followed his gaze across the room, where the gorgeous hostesses were lined up by the entrance like heaven's greeting committee. For some reason, I found myself picturing Miyuki standing with them. It was an easy picture, as natural as they come. She'd fit in here the same way she stood out at the pachinko parlor. And I knew right then that everything Nakodo had told me was a lie.

Miyuki hadn't disappeared, and she hadn't come home, either. Miyuki wasn't even his daughter. She was his mistress and she'd worked here at the Club Kuroi Kiri—that's why Afuro had the map with her name written on it, that's why she'd said Miyuki's father died years ago in Kobe. And Nakodo was probably here now to tie up loose ends, maybe even to pay off the *mama-san* to keep quiet if the cops came sniffing around. Maybe I was another loose end and even as he turned his gaze back upon me he was planning ways to take care of me, too.

"Maybe this brings it to an end," I said. "But maybe not."

Nakodo made question marks of his eyebrows. "Maybe not?"

"You know what the Buddha says."

"What," he asked, "does the Buddha say?"

"To eat is to live to be hungry."

There was a smattering of applause as "Mack the Knife" came to a close. Nakodo stared at me a moment longer, making sure he understood what I was saying and making doubly sure I understood what saying it meant. There wasn't anything more to discuss, so I rose, thanked him for the whiskey and made for the door. As I walked across the floor I could feel all the eyes once again upon me, peering out from the shadows of the club. Tobacco crackled, ice clinked in glasses. In the far corner someone laughed a fat man's laugh but quit when no one laughed with him.

PART TWO

"At the bottom of this clear blue ocean
Where the seagulls play
There lurks the ghostly blue-black light of death."
—Mitsutaka Baba

15

Into the Light
of a Sun Never Seen

ack at the Hotel Cerulean I found Admiral Hideki the Walrus behind the front counter, manning the lobby. I wondered if the guy ever went home or if he just lashed himself to the desk whenever he started to nod off. This time he was standing on a ladder by the giant aquarium, holding a small net in his hand. When he turned to face me, I noticed the dead fish he'd just scooped out of the tank.

"Good evening, Mr. Chaka."

"Evening," I said. "Lose one?"

The Walrus descended the ladder. Drops of water dripped from the net, leaving a trail of small dark splotches on his uniform. The rest of the cuttlefish ignored their dead compatriot and kept charging to and fro in unison, continuing their unending pursuit of excellence.

"Gases in the belly," the Walrus announced.

"The fish died from heartburn?"

He shook his head and extended the net out across the desk, dangling the dead cuttlefish beneath my nose. "See how the poor fellow is bloated? When fish die, their internal organs start decomposing, breaking down into gases that expand inside their bodies. That's why fish float when they're dead. Gases in the belly."

Also why they stunk so badly, I bet. The Walrus kept holding the dead thing to my face as he spoke, seemingly oblivious to the fact that the thing reeked like, well, a dead fish.

"Certain deep-sea creatures never see the sun their whole lives," he said. "Light only penetrates a few hundred feet into the ocean, after all. And so their entire existence is spent in darkness. Alas, one day, the fish dies. Its carcass begins ballooning with gas and its lifeless body slowly ascends from the depths of the ocean, rising to the surface, into the light of a sun it has never living seen." He savored the image a moment. "Unless they get eaten on the way up," he added.

Just when I was about to swear off seafood for life he withdrew the cuttlefish corpse from under my nose and emptied it into a small trash can lined with a plastic bag. He sighed almost inaudibly then took the plastic liner out of the trash can and tied it into a neat little knot.

"Somebody left a package for you," the Walrus said.

"A package?"

The Walrus reached under the reception desk then put the package on the table. It was roughly the size of a shoebox, wrapped in golden foil, and had an envelope attached. Gold foil. Just like the package the yakuza had delivered to Detective Ihara all those years ago, the one containing his son's watch.

I thanked the Walrus and carried my package upstairs to the Octopus's Garden.

EVEN IF THE DELIVERY wasn't from Nakodo's goons, I had good reason to be afraid. In Japan the simple act of unwrapping a present can get you tangled in a network of social obligations from which there is virtually no escape. Every time I saw something with a bow on it I thought about escalating gift exchanges until my stomach knotted.

I shut the door behind me and set the package on the bed. Across the room, no blinking light on the telephone, meaning no message from Afuro. The knot in my stomach loosened as I opened the envelope and read a note inside scrawled with all the care and affection you'd find on your average parking ticket. *Hey Billy!* it read, *Ever since we met I'm winning like crazy. You brought me luck. You give me Hope and Hope I return! Call if you wanna talk. Our conversation the other day was the best I've had in years. Anyway, hope your article is coming along nicely. Good Luck! Gombei*

Unwrapping the gold foil, I found seven cartons of Hope Regular cigarettes. Pachinko winnings, no doubt. I didn't know what to do with seven cartons of Hope, but at $3 a pack, I was looking at about a $200 social obligation.

What could be going through the poor guy's head? Was he trying to butter me up, did he think my piece was somehow gonna jumpstart his career? Hard to say what a guy like Gombei could be thinking at any given moment.

I took a cool shower and then just sat on the bed and watched the fish. It went through the same motions over and over. Swim one direction, turn around, and swim the other. Stop, hover in the center of the tank. Open mouth, close mouth, blink. Repeat.

You're never gonna win playing with someone like Nakodo, Detective Ihara had said. *You're never gonna know what's at stake, you're never even gonna see the cards being dealt.*

Maybe I couldn't see what cards I had, but I knew they'd been dealt just the same. The grim line of Nakodo's mouth as he stared across the table at the Club Kuroi Kiri made that much unmistakably clear, but that was where clarity ended. Why had Nakodo gone through all the trouble of summoning me to his mansion on that day? What had he hoped to learn from me? Why had he lied about Miyuki being his daughter, and why had he pretended to be unaware of her death?

I was sure Miyuki had been his mistress. He'd met her at the Club Kuroi Kiri, paid her to bring him drinks, light his cigarettes and make small talk. He'd bought her expensive little presents; she'd told him he was handsome and funny. When flirting wasn't enough for him anymore, he proposed they make other, more permanent and more lucrative arrangements. Not so unusual a development in the life of a Ginza hostess.

And maybe he'd even fallen for her—hell, he'd had a big painting done of her and hung it inside his mansion. But somehow I doubted she'd fallen for him. For his yen maybe, but not for the cheerless, rotund bureaucrat more than twice her age.

My bet was that Nakodo told me she was his daughter both to arouse my sympathy and ease any misgivings I might have. He might've figured that in my puritanical country, having a mistress was still cause for scandal. He might've thought it sounded a whole lot better to my American ears that he was trying to track down a missing child than a much younger lover who'd walked out on him. And I had to admit he would've been right on that count.

When Miyuki turned up dead, he figured it was too late to go back on his lie without looking suspicious. So he made up another one, and said his daughter had come home.

But why had he been so intent on finding her in the first place? The fact that she'd drowned in a river under the expressway told me there was probably more to it than that he missed his sweetheart.

I decided to go grab another beer from the vending machine down the hall. Not to help me think, but to keep me from thinking. I passed the lucky goddess Benten gazing at me with her mix of benevolence and mischief from the sealed door, found the beer machine, deposited my four hundred yen, and was rewarded with a tall, ice-cold Kirin Lager.

When I turned around, three men were standing before me.

They were arranged like bowling pins and seemed to have appeared out of nowhere between me and the stairwell. All three wore pristine white suits that practically glowed against the deep blue lights of the hallway. All three had short white hair. All three were smoking small brown cigarettes and regarding me with the same look of hollow detachment.

"Excuse me, fellas," I said. "Beer's getting warm."

All three stood just this side of five feet tall and had the same porcelain smoothness to their features. They looked like variations of the Man in White, but none of them were actually him. I thought of the nine Hawaiian-shirted gangsters Nakodo had sent to Detective Ihara's office and felt a little insulted that I only rated three wispy runts in pressed suits and cravats.

The guy on the left inhaled smoke from his cigarette. The guy in the middle did the same. Then the guy on the right. They all exhaled one after another in the same order, each tilting his head back and aiming a stream of smoke toward the ceiling, away from my face. Conscientious smokers, I guess.

Nevertheless, I was getting the idea they weren't going to move. I knew something like this was coming sooner or later, but I was surprised Nakodo had reacted so quickly. If he was trying to send me a message, I was gonna send him three right back.

I'd take out the middle guy first, hit him with a nice backfist and then send a kick to the knee of the guy on the left. Nothing that would ever make the movies, just good old dependable working-class attacks. As for the third guy, when he saw what quick work I'd made of his buddies, hopefully he'd run. If not, I'd just play it by ear. Try to plan anything too far ahead, you wind up disappointed.

I took one step closer, making sure I was within range.

The man on the left blew smoke directly in my face. An acrid, sulfurous smell like rotting oranges filled my nose and my eyes started watering. I tried to blink the tears away and felt a hard catch in my throat, like someone had rammed a seashell down my esophagus. A jolt of electricity surged through my body and I saw my arms fly out to my sides.

The man in the middle blew some more smoke at me, as did the man on the right. The pungent, sickly sweet odor hit and my eyes burned, my throat closed down and left me gasping for breath. All the air had been sucked out of the world. Another jolt of electricity and the lights started going dim, an underwater sound pulsed in my ears.

Next thing I knew I'd toppled sideways and was jerking across the floor, my limbs flailing as if trying to break free of my body while my jaw clenched shut and my head slammed against the wall. The whole thing happened so fast it was almost funny, but I didn't have enough bodily control to laugh and suddenly everything was washed away in a flood of white.

16

The Man in the Photograph

A low wooden table sat between two antique cushions wrapped in plastic. I was sitting on one of the cushions. The Man in White was sitting on the other. A single candle flickered on the table while the rest of the room was lost in shadows. I couldn't see the other three guys, but I knew they were there. Embers from their cigarettes sporadically flared from the dark corners of the room like fireflies.

The Man in White stuck a cigarette between his thin lips and lit it with a flick of his wrist, flint and steel clicking like an ammunition cartridge being loaded into place. I held my breath as the Man in White sent a thick billow of smoke toward the ceiling. When my eyes didn't water and my throat didn't burn I decided it was safe to breathe. So I breathed, and for several moments that's all that happened. Eventually I decided if I waited for the Man in White to speak I might be there the rest of my life.

"All right," I said. "You've got my attention. I'm here. You can start by telling me where exactly here is. Then we'll get around to why Nakodo sent you. In the meantime, if you've got a throat lozenge, I wouldn't refuse it."

The Man in White held up a bony finger. One of his cronies then emerged from the darkness carrying a black lacquer box approximately the size of a lunch pail. He placed it on the table and walked away. Another white-suited drone appeared and took the burning cigarette from between the Man in White's lips. The Man in White then carefully lifted the lid from the box.

An array of small ivory tiles with hiragana characters inlaid with what looked to be carved jade glinted from inside the box. Fine craftsmanship, but I would've appreciated throat lozenges more.

"You bring me here to play mahjong?" I asked.

Somehow managing to ignore my stupendous wit, the Man in White reached into the box. Seconds later, he'd fastidiously arranged several tiles on the table.

I AM NOT PERMITTED TO SPEAK, the tiles spelled.

I grabbed for the box to spell out a reply but I never got the chance. Suddenly all three men came rushing from the shadows and the Man in White leapt to his feet and snatched the

box from the table, eyeing me with a mixture of hurt and suspicion. I held my hands up, palms out in the international
don't-shoot-me gesture. After a moment he sat back in his
chair and feverishly rearranged the tiles on the table, adding
a few more from the box.

YOU ARE NOT PERMITTED TO WRITE, he wrote. Several quick
movements changed the message to: YOU ARE PERMITTED TO
SPEAK.

I nodded. I guess I was permitted to do that, too.

"Two questions," I said. The Man in White leaned back
and let his face go blank again. The other three men slunk
back into the shadows. I couldn't decide whether the whole
scene was creepy or just amusing, but I sure could've used
my Kirin Lager just then. "Who are you, and what do you
want from me?"

The Man in White listened dispassionately then motioned
over his shoulder. One of his assistants again emerged from
the shadows and handed the Man in White a photograph.
The Man in White didn't bother looking at it before passing
it across the table to me. I had to hold the photo about four
inches from my face and squint hard to make it out in the
dark.

For several moments all I saw was the mole.

The mole acted like a trip wire, setting off all those other
images in my head in series of a linked explosions. Miyuki at
the pachinko machine, Miyuki on the arcade floor. Five
Miyukis hanging in the hall of the House of Nakodo, Miyuki
on television being pulled from the water, Miyuki on a notebook smiling next to Afuro.

And now a new image to add to the mix.

Miyuki in a red winter coat standing with Mr. Nakodo in
front of a large wooden *torii* gate. It looked to be the entrance

to the Meiji Shrine over in Yoyogi Park, but I couldn't be one hundred percent certain. The longer I stared at the photo the more it started to sink in that something was amiss. I couldn't figure out what it was until I covered Miyuki's face with my thumb and forced myself to take a closer look at Nakodo.

Even in the dim light of the lamp I could see there were all sorts of things wrong with Nakodo. No wrinkles in sight and he wore a smile I wouldn't have guessed him capable of. His hair was thicker, his posture more erect and his paunch only in its second trimester. But it was the smile that really threw me. A smile that was broad, exuberant, youthful. Nakodo must've been at least twenty years younger in the picture.

As in just about any photo taken in Tokyo—if it was in fact Tokyo—there were a lot of figures scurrying around in the background. I noticed a number of women wore perms. Big perms. Even a few women around Miyuki's age had them. Not the wanna-be black afros the *ganguro* teens and latter-day hippies wore, but serious coiffeur and feather affairs, the type that hadn't been fashionable since the days you could still find *Heibon Punch* on the newsstands.

When I'd finished inspecting the photo I put it on the table. The Man in White left it there and started in with the tiles again, his hand moving between the box and the surface of the table with incredible speed.

THE WOMAN IN THE PHOTOGRAPH JOINED US SOME TIME AGO.

The Man in White gauged my reaction for a full three seconds. I wasn't aware that I had a reaction, since I had no idea what he was talking about. Or spelling about, that is. The Man in White then crafted another message. Just a few tiles needed changing this time.

THE MAN IN THE PHOTOGRAPH WILL JOIN US SOON.

I thought about asking what he meant by the word "join" but decided maybe I already knew. But why tell me? To answer that one, I'd have to have some idea of who the Man in White actually was. I'd assumed he was one of Nakodo's goons after he'd shown up in my hotel room two days ago, but it sure didn't seem that way now.

"Look," I said. "I don't know who you are. I don't know what you've been told or who did the telling. But before you wear out your tiles, I've got some telling to do of my own."

The Man in White just sat there, face like an empty plate, waiting patiently for me to continue. He looked to be the type who did everything patiently. Chewed each bite a set number of times before swallowing, never changed lanes on the highway unless he was exiting, never fast-forwarded through the dialogue in porn movies. Looking at him sitting there under the spotlight, I found myself unable to say anything more. The Man in White methodically spelled out another message.

BENZAITEN SAYS TWO MORE WILL JOIN US.

"Benzaiten?" I asked aloud.

Then he held out both hands and brought his palms together twice in a slow, silent clapping motion. As I was watching him a burst of orange illuminated the room like a sudden flash of lightning. For a split second I could make out a half-opened door across the room. Before I could see where the door led everything was dark again.

A cigarette burned between the Man in White's lips and the melted remnants of the photograph lay on the table. Somehow he'd incinerated it and managed to light another smoke at the same time. Whoever these guys were, they must have spent a lot of time playing with matches.

"Who is Benzaiten? Who is gonna join you?"

The Man in White exhaled and the liquidy smoke

uncoiled toward my face. That acrid smell hit me again and the back of my throat lurched forward. I held my breath and covered my nose as I leapt up and stumbled toward the door I'd just seen, but it was already too late. The Man in White made no effort to stop me. Waves of nausea crashed through my head, my vision warbled and then I felt a surge through every nerve simultaneously. My lungs collapsed, my legs followed suit and there I was again, on the floor, eyes bulging, mouth opening and closing like fish dying on the beach.

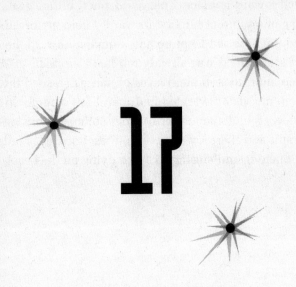

17

Chronic Fiscal Irresponsibility

No matter how hard I tried I couldn't keep my eyes open for more than half a second. Thick clouds drifted around inside my skull and two dark shapes hovered above me, haloed in the soft blue light.

"He's blinking," said one of the shapes.

"Do you think he can hear us?" said the other.

It took some effort, but I managed to bring the world into

focus. The shapes belonged to two old women. Both had bubble gum–pink lipstick smeared in the general area of their mouths and wore white paper hats and shapeless tan dresses. Each also wore thin latex gloves, and one woman was holding an orange while the other held a can of beer. I blinked several times but the picture never made any more sense. They seemed to feel the same way, and were scrutinizing me with the fascinated revulsion of little girls looking at a dead frog. All they lacked was a stick to poke me with.

"Now his eyes are open."

"Can he see us?"

"Whatever can be taking them so long?"

Their wrinkles deepened as the women traded worried glances. That's when I noticed Admiral Hideki the Walrus. He was standing several feet away, holding his flip-top watch with the gold chain attached to his navy blue uniform, shaking his head and tut-tutting his tongue.

"My watch," said the Walrus, "has stopped."

"Maybe they got in a crash."

"Don't say that!"

"It happens. My nephew drives an ambulance."

"Yes, yes. In Nagoya. We know all about your nephew."

"My nephew speaks of terrible crashes."

"Ladies, please," said the Walrus. "Let the man breathe."

And breathe I did. I inhaled and exhaled, celebrating every glorious exchange of air and vowing not to take the miracle of respiration for granted anymore. Still, the novelty soon wore off. Breathing just isn't that interesting. That's why there are no pro wrestlers called "the Exhaler" and it's a major reason competitive yoga never caught on as a spectator sport. Watching these thoughts go by, I wondered if I'd suffered some brain damage.

"I think he's awake," one of the women said.

"Do you think he can hear us?" said the other.

"I don't know why I hadn't spoken yet, but for some reason the notion just didn't come to mind. Like I was in a dream that someone else was controlling. Nothing I could do but wait for a cue from the dreamer. In the meantime, I decided to sit up. Or maybe the dreamer decided it for me.

When I rose the two women backed away—I was no longer a dead frog but a dangerous animal whose tranquilizer shots had just worn off. I took a fresh look around and realized I was back in the basement hallway of the Hotel Cerulean. The two older women must've been maids, because I saw a cart loaded with fresh towels and cleaning supplies parked just outside the elevator. At the other end of the hall, Benten and her white snakes looked over the scene with characteristic aloofness.

The Walrus walked over and knelt by my side. He looked me up and down, his expression so deadly earnest that normally I would've had a hard time keeping a straight face. As it was, I couldn't even feel my face.

"Are you all right, Mr. Chaka?" said the Walrus.

I nodded slowly. The cumulus clouds in my head shifted, rubbing up against each other, sparking lightning behind my eyes and filling my ears with distant thunder.

"You've had a seizure," said the Walrus.

A simple enough declaration, but one it took me a moment to fully comprehend. I'd only had a seizure once before in my life, back when I drank too much of some poppy wine snake-blood concoction at a fertility festival in Burma and had convulsions on and off for three days. The locals said it was a good sign, that it meant I was full of "fertile urges." But that was ages ago, and I figured I'd lost some of my fertile urges since then.

"When the maids came, you were still shaking. Then you slept. You've been sleeping for nearly half an hour. We called an ambulance and it should be arriving any moment."

Sounded familiar. All that was missing was pachinko balls.

"The ambulance should have arrived already," said one maid.

"Maybe it got in a crash," said the other.

"Don't say that!"

"What time is it?" I asked.

"My watch," said the Walrus, "has stopped."

I remembered I had my own watch and gave it a glance: 8:30 A.M.

I'd been out for nearly twelve hours.

How could that be? Simple enough. While I watched the Man in White manipulate alphabet tiles the big hand made several sweeps over the twelve and the little hand trailed from one number to the next and the world kept spinning and so twelve hours plus went by just like that. Nothing strange about it. Nothing at all.

"Would you like your beer?" one of the maids said.

"How about an orange?" said the other.

The maids seemed mildly irritated when I declined, but I got the feeling it was more or less a permanent condition with them. I struggled to my feet, swimming through waves of dizziness. The Walrus nervously tickled his mustache, the maids clutched their offerings. Then I started toward the stairs, toward the Octopus's Garden.

"You really should wait for the ambulance," said the Walrus, trailing after me. "It wouldn't hurt to let someone have a look at you."

I said I was fine, just a freak occurrence. I wasn't fine, not by a long shot, but I didn't think any doctor would be able to help, and if I told him what really happened I'd probably wind up in the psych ward with all the guys claiming to be Lord Oda Nobunaga. The Walrus shooed the maids away. They went back to their cart, clearly feeling cheated. As I walked back to my room, the Walrus followed me, renewing his pleas to let a doctor examine me. Just as I reached the door, he brought up something else.

"A man came for you last night," he said.

"What did he look like?"

"Seemed a very pleasant sort," said the Walrus. "He walked into the lobby at around midnight. I thought it a strange time to visit, and he admitted you weren't expecting him. I tried calling your room, but there was no answer. I thought you were probably sleeping and did not wish to be disturbed. At any rate, he said he would return today."

"He didn't leave his name or a card or anything?"

The Walrus shook his head. "Shall I call you if he returns?"

I was unable to do anything but move my head in a slow approximation of yes. Once inside the Octopus's Garden, I closed the door, kicked off my wing tips, turned off the lights and flopped down onto the bed. There were a million other things I should have been doing, but I was utterly exhausted, unable to focus my thoughts enough to form any coherent plan of action. The fish turned sideways and stared at me with his right eye from inside his tank. I stared back at him.

Have you ever heard of anyone having a twelve-hour seizure, Mr. Goldfish?

Your dry-world ways are a fathomless mystery to me.

You're not much help, Mr. Goldfish.

What were you expecting? It's a complicated world. Even the life of a goldfish isn't carefree, you know.

Just when Mr. Goldfish and I were reaching a real under-standing the clouds rolled in and I was out.

WHEN I WOKE THE goldfish was still staring at me, this time with his left side in profile. My watch said it was 3:48 P.M. and the phone was ringing. It took everything I had to drag myself out of bed to answer it, and I didn't have as much as I used to. A famous handicapped karate sensei had once told me that pain was only weakness leaving your body, and if it was true, I must've had a lot of weakness stored up. My body felt like it'd been taken apart at the cellular level and put back together with a few million molecules out of place.

"Billy?"

"Uhhh," I groaned into the receiver. "Afuro?"

"*Who the hell is Afuro?*"

The voice belonged to possibly the last person in the entire world I wanted to talk to at the moment. I should've let it ring after all, but it wouldn't have mattered. Sarah didn't give up that easily. One of those things I admired and despised her for.

Who the hell is Afuro? Sarah asked again.

Long story, I said.

Speaking of stories, she said, where was her Gombei story?

I told her that was also a long story.

She reminded me that "Fallen Stars" was not *Ulysses*. "Fallen Stars," she added, was not *War and Peace* and it was not *Moby-Dick*. "Fallen Stars" was a one-page feature. Three hundred fifty words and a picture. Q & A, caption, pull-quote and sidebar. This was not a biography I was writing. I was not Boswell; Gombei Fukugawa was not Samuel Johnson; our audience was not expecting Shakespeare or Marcel Proust. So, she said, she didn't want to hear it's a long story.

OK, I replied. But who is Marcel Proust?

Sarah snorted and handed over the phone to someone else.

It was Chuck, *Youth in Asia*'s long-suffering accountant. Speaking in a tremulous voice he said he was looking at a column of figures and thought maybe I should be aware of these figures. There were figures for airfare to Tokyo, there were figures for hotel accommodations, there was a figure called my per diem. Along with these figures were all the other figures from all my other ill-fated adventures in the field over the years. These figures, he explained, when considered as a whole, formed a pattern, told an epic tale, even. And the epic tale they told was one of chronic fiscal irresponsibility, of unnecessary, outrageous expenditures and—

Sarah ripped the phone away from him.

Two days, she said. What Chuck is trying to say is that she wanted me back in Cleveland in two days. She wanted the Gombei Fukugawa "Fallen Stars" story sitting on her desk, typed, double-spaced and spell checked. She said she was faxing my flight information to the Hotel Cerulean, and if I missed my plane I needn't bother coming back to Cleveland because no job would be waiting. My beloved desk would be sold on eBay and my office would be turned into a storage facility for cardboard boxes stuffed with various papers of neglible importance.

"Is this about us?" I said. "Because I thought all that was in the past. What happened happened, and I still maintain—"

Click.

Just like all of our conversations ended. If Martians came down to earth and studied me and Sarah, they'd never discover the human concept of good-bye. They'd get skewed views on all sorts of things. I imagined myself seated at a table of Martians, trying to explain that it wasn't really like this here on Earth, not for most people. They'd probably laugh and tell me all their earthly subjects said the same thing.

Replacing the phone on the cradle, I noticed the light was blinking. Meaning someone had left a message. I picked up the receiver again and punched in my password.

"Hey, Uncle, this is you-know-who," Afuro said. The words came out half garbled because she was munching on food as she spoke. Probably ate an entire meal in the time it took to leave her message. "I was thinking maybe we could meet later tonight. Say by the Hachiko statue in Shibuya. You know where that is, right? Why don't we meet there at eleven P.M. And hey, did you happen to pick up a notebook of mine at the café this morning? I called the place and they couldn't find it. Anyway, see you tonight, eleven P.M., Hachiko statue. If you need to get ahold of me, my number is—"

A beep and the message was cut off. Meaning I had no way to reach her. The time stamp told me the call was made at nine P.M., right around the time I went to grab a beer. Typical somehow. I put the phone back and sat down on the bed. Little by little, I could feel the normal world coming back together, restitching itself into something whole. It's hard to know what to do after you've been out of it for so long, but I figured taking a shower was a good start. And it was a good start. The steaming hot water felt so good it almost washed away all thoughts of Miyuki, Mr. Nakodo, Afuro and those strange men in white.

The phone rang again while I was brushing my teeth, but no one was there when I answered. And just like that, I could feel the normal world stretching at the seams again.

18

Cultivating Luck

It was nearly seven P.M. when I finally strolled down to the lobby of the Hotel Cerulean. The silvery fish were busy enacting their endless groupthink ballet inside the massive aquarium while the Walrus stood at attention behind the desk, just as he always did, head aloft, chest pushed out, the buttons on his ridiculous starched uniform polished to gold that sparkled under the lights. The only indication that something was wrong was the Walrus's mustache. It wasn't sitting snugly on his lip the way it did when he smiled, but was sagging at the edges, drooping like something left out in the rain.

"Good evening, Mr. Chaka," he said as I approached the desk to drop off my key before leaving, a standard practice in Japanese hotels. His eyes darted quickly to one side before coming back to mine. "There is somebody waiting for you. I'm afraid he's been waiting here for quite some time."

Bojangles? The Man in White? I felt a sudden surge in my stomach as I followed the Walrus's glance to the far side of the lobby.

I was momentarily stunned to see the expression on the man's face. He looked like he should be sitting poolside, fanning himself with a palm frond, sipping a margarita. Of course he always looked that way, but it was a hard look to get used to. He was dressed much flashier than when I'd seen him last—shoes gleaming like knife blades, sleek Zenga suit the color of an unripened plum, a gold watch so big it could've been one of Wonder Woman's magic bracelets. I could hardly believe it was him at first, but I got over it soon enough. "Unbelievable" wasn't such a big deal anymore.

"Gombei Fukugawa," I said. "What brings you here?"

Gombei rose unsteadily from the sofa chair and made his way across the lobby. I walked to meet him, and as he came closer I noticed someone had given him one hell of a shiner. His face was the same color as his suit and the smell on his breath told me why. Either Gombei had found a pachinko parlor that served whiskey or he'd found a new way to spend his afternoons.

"You doing all right?" I asked.

"What, this?" said Gombei, furtively gesturing to the puffed and blackened skin clinging under his eye like a leech. "Just a little misunderstanding. No big deal. You get those cigarettes?"

"Cigarettes?" Then I remembered. The gold-foiled cartons of Hope cigarettes he'd given me yesterday. Seemed like ancient history, part of another life. "Yes, I got them. Thank you very much. It was very thoughtful of you."

"You don't smoke, do you?"

"Well, never too late to start."

The normal inscrutability of Gombei's pleasant grin was exacerbated by all the alcohol coursing through his system. As he stood there swaying in the middle of the lobby, I could no more gauge his mood than I could tell what the fish in the giant aquarium were thinking.

"Is the story finished?" he said.

"I was just putting the finishing touches on it, but—"

"I knew you didn't smoke," said Gombei. "It was a dumb thing to give you. Really stupid of me. But I'd like to make it up to you."

"I greatly appreciate this kind gesture," I said, trying to decide what level of formality the occasion merited. "It is indeed an honor for such a humble person as myself to be graced with your thoughtfulness. My heart brims with one thousand regrets that I must—"

"Whoa, take it easy there, pal," Gombei said, rocking back on his heels. "I just wanted to show my appreciation a little. Stopped by last night, but I guess you were out. Anyway, whaddaya say? Can I show my appreciation?"

Gombei's permagrin was wreaking havoc with my nerves. What was the guy trying to get at? The Walrus watched us from across the room, the fish behind him darting in formation while the soothing sound of waves rolling in on the beach drifted through the lobby.

"What exactly did you have in mind?" I asked.

"Follow me and I'll show you," Gombei said. With that he

gave me what might've been a wink, then turned and began walking toward the front doors of the hotel. I glanced back over my shoulder. The Walrus gave me a short bow, his mustache resuming its normal posture upon his lip. I shrugged and followed Gombei out of the Hotel Cerulean.

FRIDAY NIGHT AND THE sun was long gone, but it had left more than enough heat behind to last until it returned. About five years ago a weathergirl I was interviewing from SkyPerfect TV had explained that in Tokyo more rain fell on Fridays than on any other day of the week. Something to do with industrial pollution buildup cycles and the emission of heat and particulate matter into the atmosphere. Living in balance and harmony with nature was a nice idea—looked good in haikus—but production quotas were a reality, and so the Friday rains. But not tonight. Not even a cloud in the sky, only a slender gray moon winking between two tower blocks in the distance, looking like it didn't really want to be there but had nowhere else to go.

Gombei guided me down a narrow side street. He'd seemed eager to talk inside the hotel, but ever since we got outside he hadn't said a word. Interview as many people as I had over the years, you learn to deal with silence on a case-by-case basis. Some people you prompt, some you cajole, some you just leave alone until they're ready to speak. In Gombei's case, it didn't take long.

"You mind if I ask you a question?" Gombei said.

I shook my head.

"Do you consider yourself lucky?"

"Never thought much about it."

"But what would you say?"

"I'd say I'm not even sure what luck is."

"I know what you mean," Gombei said. "But I think there is such a thing as good luck and bad luck. There certainly is in pachinko. And life is no different. It's a little more complicated, a little less clear-cut at times, but at its core, life is just like pachinko."

More pachinko fatalism. I fought the urge to roll my eyes.

"I mean look at this godforsaken city," Gombei said, stretching his arms wide. "It's like some giant pachinko machine. The buildings jutting from the ground like a complex pattern of pins. The never-ending noise, the giant TV screens and neon billboards blinking on an off with no real purpose but to distract. Just like pachinko. And people? We're the balls, Chaka. Bouncing from one building to the next, from one woman to the next, one job to the next, one idea to the next, whatever. We think we're in control, that we're choosing our destinations. But we're not. We're just balls propelled through a giant machine, mindlessly bouncing and rolling. Repeating the same patterns, over and over, tumbling ever downward. Some hit the big prize, but most won't. That's just the odds, and there's only one way to beat the odds. You know what that is?"

I shook my head.

"Cultivate your luck," he said. "Forget the existence of odds altogether and learn to master the most mysterious force in the universe. That's what brings me here tonight, Mr. Chaka."

"You're here to master the universe?"

"To cultivate my luck. To nurture it. Fact is, ever since I met you I've been unstoppable. I literally can't lose! See this jacket? Won it. This watch? Won it. You've put me on a lucky streak like nothing I've ever seen."

Wished I could say the same. With the enthusiasm in his voice and the bounce in his step, it was hard to believe this was the same guy who'd sulked his way through the interview back at the Lucky Benten Pachinko hall. Amazing what a little liquor and a few lucky games could do. Maybe too amazing.

"Cultivating your luck means showing gratitude," Gombei said. "Paying tribute to the source of your good fortune. I want to thank you, Mr. Chaka. By seeking me out to do this story for *Young of the Orient*, you've touched my life in ways you can't imagine. And as a token of my appreciation, I bring you this."

He suddenly stopped walking and stood beaming at me, face flushed, hands clasped behind his back in a stiff pose that would've made the Walrus proud. Then Gombei took a large, theatrical step to the side, revealing what all the buildup had been about. Parked at the edge of the narrow street, next to a crate of empty sake bottles, stood a battered yellow moped.

"It's all yours, my friend," he trumpeted. "Whaddaya think?"

I said exactly what I thought. "You shouldn't have."

"Nonsense! Gotta show respect to the source of my good fortune, right? This is a Honda Hobbit, made in 1978 and in near-mint condition. A real collector's item, still handles like a dream."

"It's beautiful," I said. Problem was, I'd no more be caught dead on a moped than the Marlboro Man would be seen riding a show pony. Especially one named Hobbit.

"Hop on. Take it for a spin."

"I wish I could take it, but I can't. Journalistic ethics forbid me from accepting gifts from my subjects."

"Subjects?" Gombei said.

"I hope you understand."

"Forget about the article! This is a man-to-man kind of thing. After everything you've done, you must take this. It's the least I can do. I'm begging you, Chaka. Please don't shame me like this."

Gombei dug into the pocket of his flashy Italian jacket, then reached out his hand and forced a set of keys into my own. Ever since I'd arrived in Tokyo events had been moving according to their own imperceptible and irresistible flow. Trying to impose my feeble will on the circumstances was like trying to fight back a tidal wave with a canoe paddle. The goldfish was right; our dry-world ways were a fathomless mystery. I closed my fist around the keys and forced myself to smile.

"OK," I said. "Thank you."

"You make me very happy."

"So how'd you get the black eye again?"

I detected the subtlest shift in his expression, but I couldn't tell which way it had shifted. Gombei scuffed the ground with the sole of his shoe. "It's no big deal. Just a little misunderstanding."

"About what?"

"Like I told you, I've been on a lucky streak. Thanks to you. Some pachinko hall owners, they get a little uptight when that happens. Anyway, some clown accused me of cheating and there was a little scuffle. Everything worked itself out though. Always does in the end, right?"

The bruised skin beneath his eye caught the moonlight, the whites of his eyes shot through with red. Add his ill-fitting grin and stringy hair to the picture and he looked certifiably insane. Maybe he was. Spend seven years watching steel balls endlessly stream down the faces of pachinko machines, your mind could slip quietly out the back exit without anyone noticing.

"Sure," I said. "Always works out in the end."

AN ANNOYING LAUGH. An angry mosquito. A never-ending fart.

The moped sounded a little bit like all three as I maneuvered it the short distance back to the Hotel Cerulean. My only consolation was that there were few people out at this hour in this area of town to witness it. Made me ponder the question, if Chaka rides a Honda Hobbit and no one is there to see him, does he really ride the Hobbit?

No. Absolutely not.

After ditching the moped in the tiny hotel parking garage I decided to take a trip to a nice little mansion on the other side of town, in Ark Hills. I didn't have time to make discreet inquiries, read newspaper clippings and do a lot of legwork. I needed to confront Nakodo, surprise him at his house and find out what had really been going on between him and Miyuki and why he lied about it. It was risky to surprise him, but given what had happened last night, it was riskier still to wait.

THE MAN IN THE PHOTOGRAPH WILL JOIN US SOON.

In the photograph, a much younger Nakodo posing with a much the same Miyuki. It made no sense. Then again, nothing about the guys in white made sense. Given that a seizure was basically an electric firestorm of the brain, I figured it was wholly possible that I could have hallucinated the entire scene. But if my brain was so overcharged with firing synapses, how could I even have remembered a hallucination? Could it all have been a dream I had as I lay in a post-convulsive heap on the basement floor? And what about Miyuki's seizure at the pachinko hall? Had she been visited by this same figure? Were convulsions contagious? Funny how there's never a neuroscientist around when you need one.

I decided to catch a ride at the cabstand outside Tokyo station. I could've just phoned one from the Hotel Cerulean, but I had to consider the possibility that any conversation I had there might be listened to. I was swimming with the big fish now. I had to be vigilant, mindful, anticipating my opponents' moves before my opponents even knew they were making them.

Why I considered tapped phones but didn't realize somebody could've been following me was an interesting question. Let's just say maybe some of those postconvulsive clouds were still wandering my brain. But when I ducked into an alley as a shortcut, right away I knew something was wrong. It wasn't a gut feeling or a hunch or an intuition, or even really a thought. Just an overall physical sensation, something I felt the way a fish in a quiet pond feels the ripples of a tossed stone.

I tried to make my spirit calm as the moon, but it didn't take. Trying to unmind my mind only made it keep minding. Preparing for death was something I wasn't prepared for, so I briefly considered employing fighting strategy number thirty-six of the famous *Thirty-six Strategies*—the one about running away.

I never got the chance.

Something hard cracked against the back of my skull.

I started to fall forward, but managed to catch myself. Ducking low, I spun around and rose with an uppercut aimed at the stars.

It caught Afuro right under her chin.

Her little body lifted off the ground and seemed to hang in the air before landing back on the pavement, hard. My hand instinctively went to the back of my head. Good news—no blood. Bad news—Afuro lay completely limp in her canary-yellow blouse and pale blue skirt, the brick she'd just tried to brain me with right next to her, while behind her stood a row of trash cans filled with empty bottles from a nearby restaurant. A horn sounded in the distance, somebody sped by on a motorcycle. The closest Tokyo got to deathly still.

I wondered if I'd killed her. Not that I've got such a killer punch anymore, but she was a small girl, and if she came down on her head, that would've been all it took. I felt sweat bead on my forehead and drip into my eyes.

Afuro groaned and propped herself up to a sitting position. She looked up at me, on the verge of tears.

"Finish it," she said.

"Are you okay?"

"I know who you are!" She grabbed for her handbag. Before I thought to stop her she'd pulled out a knife. A big knife, one that looked even bigger in her child-sized hands. The blade flashed under the moonlight like something with a life all its own.

"Go on," she said, tossing the knife at my feet. "Finish what you started."

I jumped back and the blade clattered against my wing tips.

"Do it to me," she whispered.

"Afuro—"

She ripped open her blouse and thrust her head defiantly forward, offering her neck. A thin trail of blood ran down the corner of her mouth. Then she screamed.

"Kill me!"

Good Christ, I thought, were all girls her age so melodramatic? I had no idea what was going on. I shook my head, let out a deep sigh and bent over to pick up the knife. I was just about to toss it safely in the trash can when I heard a noise behind me.

A guy in an apron and a chef's hat stood in an open doorway, holding two plastic bags stuffed with garbage. His eyes went to Afuro's exposed chest, then to me, then to the knife. Realizing how it must look, I dropped the knife, but not before he'd dropped the trash bags and scrambled back inside. I could hear him yelling for help the moment the door slammed.

Afuro gave a dull laugh.

"What the hell is going on here?" I said.

"Better do it fast, Bojangles," she said. "Better do it before the chance slips away."

Bojangles?

"I don't know what silly notion you've got in your head," I said, kicking away the knife. "But I'm not Bojangles. I'm Billy Chaka and I'm not killing anyone. Least of all you. Get up. Get on your feet."

"The cops will be here any second."

"You want the cops, I'd be happy to talk to them."

That threw her. The wild panic left her face and was replaced by a look of confusion so complete she could've learned it from me. Her chin sunk to her chest, and she seemed to realize for the first time that she was sitting in an alley, half naked, bleeding from the mouth and begging a relative stranger to kill her. With that realization, she started crying. Who wouldn't?

Suddenly the door behind me burst open and three cooks

with knives and a waiter with a steel baseball bat came charging toward me. There was lots of yelling, but I didn't move. I just stood there with my hands outstretched and let them encircle me.

"Grab his knife!" someone yelled.

Someone else picked up the knife from the ground and scuttled away. Another guy put me in a full nelson. I let him. He had arms like ham hocks and his breath smelled like kimchi. Kimchi Breath lifted me off my feet and shook me up and down, just to let me know he could.

"Call the police," he said, spitting into my ear.

The waiter dropped his baseball bat and ran inside. Such is the waiter's life—always taking orders from other people. The other two guys still held the knives in their hands and looked ready to make sashimi out of me. Afuro was sniffling and buttoning up her blouse.

"You've raped for the last time," one of the guys said.

"Wait for the cops," Kimchi Breath said.

"Fuck the cops." He took two steps forward.

"Take it easy, Sanjuro," said the other guy.

"Fuck take it easy. These cowboy fucking marines think they come into my country and do anything they want? I say fuck that."

"Marines?" Kimchi Breath said. "Sanjuro, just calm down. Everything is under control here."

"Fuck under control."

"This guy is no marine, okay, so calm down!"

"Fuck calm down."

I didn't know whether Sanjuro was upset about the recent gang rape of a young girl in Okinawa by U.S. marines or if he hated the American armed forces on general principle or if he was just a psycho looking for an excuse, but it was clear his buddies weren't gonna be able to control him. He took another step forward, his grip tightened around the knife. I weighed my options. That a guy might get killed by a stranger for refusing to kill another stranger who'd just tried to kill him would've struck me as ironic if it were happening to somebody else. But it was happening to me. The second Sanjuro lunged, I was ready to spin. Poor Kimchi Breath had done nothing but try to keep the situation under control, but he was gonna have to take a knife in the back for his efforts. Tough break, but no one said peacekeeping was easy.

The lunge came.

Only it wasn't Sanjuro the psycho. It was the guy standing next to him. And he didn't lunge at me. He lunged at Sanjuro, tackling him to the ground. The two of them rolled into the trash cans and bottles crashed down and tumbled across the alley while the men wrestled on the pavement, both still clutching knives, both screaming bloody murder. Kimchi Breath started screaming too, yelling at them to stop, yelling at them that he had everything under control.

But the one who screamed loudest was Afuro.

It was a high-pitched, inhuman scream. The two guys on the ground suddenly stopped fighting, amazed to hear such a piercing cry emanating from such a small person. Kimchi Breath unconsciously loosened his grip on me. None of the glass bottles shattered from the sound, but I wouldn't have been surprised if they had.

All eyes were fixed on Afuro.

She fell to her knees and touched her forehead to the ground.

"Forgive me," she said quietly. "Please forgive me. I'm sorry. Please forgive me. There has been a misunderstanding.

Forgive me, please, I'm sorry. It's all my fault. There has been a misunderstanding."

She glanced at me once as she raised her head before lowering it again to the ground. In that moment, I got the idea that she wasn't just trying to appease them, she was apologizing to me, too. But I could've been wrong. I'd been wrong about a lot lately and I wasn't finished making mistakes by a long shot.

19

A Creature of
Contradictory Impulses

"Sex games?" I said.

Afuro sat down on the red silken bedspread, shrugged and lit a cigarette. I fetched a red ashtray from its place upon the red nightstand. Everything in the Red Baron Suite at the Hotel Ophuls was red. Red velvet drapes, thick red carpet, a red hot tub in the corner just big enough for two. Even the overhead lights were the warm crimson of an old-fashioned

photographic darkroom. I couldn't find anything having to do
with German World War I fighter pilot Captain Manfred von
Richthofen, but you can only expect so much contextual rel-
evance in a love hotel.

It felt more than a little strange accompanying Afuro to a
place like this, but short of hanging out in a karaoke box all
night we didn't have many options. I was paranoid about
being tailed by Nakodo's people, she thought a guy called Mr.
Bojangles wanted her dead and the streets were alive with
thousands of people who looked suspicious if you were looking for suspicious people. We couldn't go to her apartment
because something terrible had happened there. We couldn't
go back to the Hotel Cerulean because terrible things went on
there, too. A love hotel was one place we knew we'd be able
to talk in private, unseen and unheard, and we had a lot of
talking to do.

"Sex games?" I repeated.

Afuro ignored me and checked her face in a compact. I
gave her another tissue. I'm not the tissue-carrying type, but
I'd picked some up from the girls constantly standing outside
Tokyo station. They were there every hour of the day and
night, passing out free packs attached to flyers advertising
i-mode phone deals and travel packages to Thailand. What
telephones and Thai trips had to do with tissue paper I didn't
know, but in Tokyo, if it's free I take it.

"Did you really have to say sex—"

"I had to say _something_."

Just then a doorbell rang. I went into the otherwise empty
hallway to retrieve the bucket of ice and two pink concoctions
so fruity Carmen Miranda could've worn them on her head.
The drinks had been discreetly delivered by an invisible waiter
and were topped off with maraschino cherries, lemon slices,

coconut shavings, peeled grapes, pineapple wedges. They cost as much as a decent meal at a Ginza sukiyaki restaurant and likely had less kick than my Honda Hobbit on a steep incline.

"Agreed," I said, handing Afuro her drink. "You had to say something. But *sex games*?"

"You could've done better? Anyway, I don't see what the big deal is. I know people who play little games like that all the time."

"Your friends pretend to rape each other in alleys?"

"All right, fine," she said. "Maybe not in alleys, but rape play is not that uncommon. Those cooks wouldn't have bought it if it were so far-fetched. I bet it made their night. I bet it turned them on. Probably even turned you on a little."

I let that slide and wrapped the ice in two red towels. One I handed to Afuro for her jaw. The other I used on the back of my skull. Getting a bump on the head wasn't that bad. What was worse was prostrating myself next to Afuro and repeating "sorry" over and over to them, just as she had done. Didn't make me feel real swell, but it had to be done. They abused us for a while, calling us both perverts and asking Afuro what her father would say if he knew she was playing sex games in a dark alley with a foreigner twice her age. I wasn't anywhere near twice her age, but I didn't say a word. Except for sorry. Over and over and over, to the point where I almost meant it. That psycho Sanjuro was the worst of them, spitting where I knelt and calling Afuro a whore and almost making me take it all back. But in the end, the cooks wandered back into the restaurant and we got the hell out of there.

And somehow we ended up in the Hotel Ophuls's Red Baron Suite.

"Tell me what happened at your apartment," I said.

She put out her cigarette, took another drink of her tropical fruit stand and started to tell me everything that had happened to her since we last met at the Let's Elementary Café. It almost explained how she'd come to think I was a character called Mr. Bojangles and why she'd felt the need to take a brick to my head. Almost.

AFURO REMINDED ME THAT she'd been friends with Miyuki ever since they met in junior high back in Muramura. They moved to Tokyo together and shared an apartment, but Miyuki had moved out about six months ago. They hadn't spoken much since. But Afuro told me she'd received a letter from Miyuki that day at work, two days after Miyuki drowned. There was no return address, but she recognized the handwriting.

"Getting it freaked me out," Afuro said. "I've been trying to just keep everything off in one corner of my mind until I can sit down and like really think about it and I know maybe that's not the best way to deal with it or whatever, but—well, she left things very complicated between us."

"Complicated how?"

"Complicated in all kinds of complicated ways. The last time I saw her we got in a fight. After she moved out she just completely changed. She just like, I don't know, shut down or something. Became this zombie. And after the fight, I was pretty sure I would never see her again. Guess I was right. But then I get this in the mail. At work. And I never get any mail at work."

With a heavy sigh, Afuro started digging through her handbag. Her hands were trembling and she looked away as she gave the envelope to me. I opened it to find a plane ticket and a letter. The ticket was for an ANA flight to Sydney, Aus-

tralia. The letter was written in black ink on plain white stationery in tiny angular characters smudged across the page
like crushed insects.

> *Dear Afuro,*
>
> *I'm sorry about the other night. I'm sorry about
the last few months, I'm sorry about everything. I
wish I could tell you what's been happening, I
really do. Maybe someday I can explain everything
to you, but I need some time and I need some distance. Please understand, my problems have nothing to do with you. I've gotten myself involved in
something that's very difficult and not a little bit
scary. I'm in a strange place right now and I don't
think I even know who I am anymore. I feel like I'm
not even me, just this empty nothing that other
people fill with their own versions of "me." Like a
mirror where people only see the "me" they want
to see, see themselves reflected in my image—does
that make any sense? Probably not. I can't tell
what makes sense and what doesn't anymore.*
>
> *But I know the way out. I've found a way to
escape, a way to become Miyuki again. Soon this
empty "me" will be dead and things will be back to
how they were before. Only better than before. You
must believe me. I know this must seem totally
crazy and not at all fair, but sometimes I think you
are all that remains of the real me. I need you to be
my friend, Afuro. I need you to help me find myself
again, to bring me back into the normal world. (I
know I'm not making sense now, but please bear
with me . . .)*

I want to get away from Tokyo, away from Japan, and I want you to come with me. I know you've always wanted to go to Australia, and I need you there with me. And don't worry—it's not gonna be all heavy heavy stuff like this sad crazy letter. We'll play on the beach and go dancing every night with surfer boys and we'll live like movie stars. And I promise I'll pay for everything— yes, for us both. Before you start preparing your standard lecture on credit cards, let me just tell you those days are over. My ship has finally come in and after tomorrow, I'll be a free woman!

So think about it. Please. I will call you the moment I get a chance, which should be very soon. Everything is coming to a close now and I think I can be happy again or at least whole, a real human being instead of this empty ghost I've become. But I'm going to need your help to forget everything, to become Miyuki again and leave this all behind me. I hope you can understand.

Take care of yourself, and whatever happens, please don't forget about your friend, the true Miyuki, the little girl from Muramura who misses and needs you so much now.

Miyuki

Lots of troubling language pointing to some kind of severe identity meltdown, but even with the remarks about the impending death of the false Miyuki it sure didn't read like a suicide note to me. I checked the ticket again. The plane would've left in two weeks' time. It still would be leaving, of course, only without Miyuki. I refolded the letter, put it back

in the envelope with the plane ticket and handed it to Afuro,
noticing how her ridiculously yellow blouse looked ridiculously orange under the red lights.

"She mentioned credit cards," I said. "Was she in debt?"

"Who isn't?"

"I thought Ginza hostesses made a mint."

"How did you know she was a hostess?"

"Just a lucky guess. Club Kuroi Kiri, right?"

"Yeah, but she didn't get that job right away," Afuro said.
"When we first moved here, she was living on credit cards.
No savings to speak of. And those first few months, she spent
like crazy. Buying all kinds of expensive dresses, going out to
fashionable restaurants on Omotesando and wherever. Places
she read about in magazines. Once she got a job, she was
totally out of control. The more she made, the more she
spent. I mean, I had to talk her out of buying a car—a car in
Tokyo!—and she didn't even have a driver's license."

Afuro jabbed her cigarette in the ashtray, angrily snubbing
it out as if trying to quell the memories the letter had brought
back. But there was an air of resignation to the gesture, an
acknowledgment that she was powerless to turn them back,
that having allowed herself to feel this much it was only a
matter of time before the dam burst and it all came flooding
forth.

"But anyway, so back to last night," she resumed with a
sigh. "This letter is why I called you. To see what you'd make
of it. I left a message for you to meet me in Shibuya at eleven.
So I went there and waited and waited, but you never showed
up. Then I took the last train to Ochanomizu and walked back
to my apartment. When I got there, I noticed that the door
was unlocked. I never leave it unlocked. *Never.* So I pushed
it open and right away I knew someone had been there."

"Something was amiss?"

"Amiss?" she huffed. "The whole place had been torn to pieces. All the books were pulled off the shelves, my CDs were all over the floor, the sheets were torn off the bed, my clothes were everywhere, all my makeup was in the bathtub. Someone had even searched the food! Ripped through the little fridge and my excuse for a pantry like they were on a search-and-destroy mission. Rice every fucking place, flour dumped out on the coffee table, just an unbelievable mess. And just like that I knew it was you."

"Me? I don't get it."

"You were the only one who knew I wouldn't be at my apartment. You knew I'd be waiting for you in Shibuya."

Of course, I hadn't known. I didn't get Afuro's message until the next morning because I was off in seizure-land watching the Man in White play with his tiles and was still there when whoever broke into Afuro's apartment was tearing through the place. None of which she would've known.

"I'm always home at that time because that's when *Panic Man Extreme* comes on," she said. "Have you ever seen *Panic Man*?"

"No."

"It's hilarious," she said.

"I'll take your word for it."

"Anyway, even if someone had been observing me all this time, casing my apartment, they wouldn't know I'd be out. And once I read the letter, I knew Miyuki hadn't killed herself. I'd always known, but the letter made me even more sure of it. I thought about that day when you just came up to me, out of the blue, under the highway. It was so creepy that even then I wondered if you were Bojangles. After my apartment got trashed, I knew Bojangles would come after me again. Try to kill me. So I decided I'd kill him first."

"That's it? That's why you attacked me?"

"Like you never made a mistake in your life."

"But I told you who I was. Billy Chaka, *Youth in A*—"

"What, and everyone tells the truth?" she said. "I've been under an emotional strain lately, all right? So maybe I went a little crazy, give me a break. Yeah, you told me your name and that you wrote for some dumb magazine, but there's a lot you didn't tell me. Like how you even knew Miyuki, for one thing. So how did you know her?"

"I saw her once in a pachinko parlor."

"Pachinko? Miyuki didn't play pachinko."

"She wasn't playing exactly. She was having a seizure."

Afuro pulled a face. "She what?"

"She was having a seizure. I put my shoes under her head, called the ambulance. That was the only time I saw her."

"You are one seriously fucked up guy, you know that?"

I didn't say anything.

"Getting all obsessed with a girl you saw exactly one time? Did you even know her? Did you ever even speak to her before or after this seizure of hers?"

"No," I said. "Like you say, it's complicated."

"Complicated is not the word," she said. "The word is fucked up, my perverted uncle. Are you even sure the girl you were stalking was Miyuki? Miyuki never had seizures!"

"I wasn't stalking her," I said. "And no, I wasn't sure at first that the woman who'd drowned and the person I saw in the pachinko parlor were one and the same. But when you dropped that notebook I knew. I recognized her in the photo-booth sticker."

"Could be mistaken identity."

I shook my head.

"Because of the mole, right?"

"Among other things."

"*Among other things,*" Afuro huffed. "Just admit it was the mole. I bet that's what set you off in the first place. Why are men so obsessed with that thing? It's always been like that, ever since we were in junior high. Draws them in like a tractor beam. Guys are just weirdos, there's no other explanation. What the hell is so fascinating about a mole?"

I shrugged. "So who is this Bojangles?"

Afuro took another puff of her cigarette. "Good question. I guess he's not you."

"But what do you know about him?"

"Nothing really. Just the name. Mr. Bojangles."

"How did you learn this name? Who told you about him?"

"Long story," she sighed.

"It's a fake name."

"Gee, you think?"

"But you know this Mr. Bojangles was somehow involved with Miyuki, and you think you have reason to fear him. Why?"

"Mr. Bojangles started the whole thing," she said. "And I'm still going to kill him if I find him. Or maybe you should kill him. I'm starting to think I'm no good at killing people. Guess you never know until you try. But you could do it. You could kill him for me. Do you carry a gun?"

Wasn't the first time I'd been asked. Thanks to Hollywood, half the world thought Americans couldn't so much as go to the dentist without being armed to the teeth. Of course, thanks to Hollywood, half of America thought the same thing.

"Hand grenades," I said. "But I left them in the glove

compartment of my tank back in Cleveland. Listen, Afuro, I need you to tell me everything you know about Bojangles and Miyuki. You said Bojangles started the whole thing. How?"

"Order me up another drink first."

"You haven't finished your last one yet."

"Guess I'd better drink up then. *Kompai!*"

She raised her glass in a toast, then wrapped her lips around the straw and drained the remaining half of the drink in three seconds flat. Suddenly a startled look came over her face, and she barely got the drink safely on the nightstand before falling back onto the bed. Her back arched for a moment and then she started thrashing.

She was going into a seizure.

I didn't know what to do. The world was going crazy and I was powerless to stop it. Afuro clutched her forehead and bicycled her black-stockinged feet in the air.

"Cold-headache cold-headache!" she yelled.

Then she sputtered out into a giggling fit.

I couldn't help but laugh along with her. One minute she's trying to kill me, the next asking me to kill someone else, the next wriggling around and giggling like some little kid having a tickle fit. Sometimes it was hard to believe Afuro was old enough to have a best friend in the hostess business, hard to believe someone like her could've gotten herself involved in the whole strange affair at all.

"Order me another drink," Afuro said. Then she got up, snatched her colorful Cecil McBee handbag, walked to the bathroom and closed the door. I heard her turn on the faucet, wondered what the hell she was up to. I picked up the red phone, ordered Afuro another Fruit Bomb. Moments later, she emerged from the bathroom, her face freshly washed. She was wearing a complimentary white cotton robe and had another lit cigarette in her hand.

"Don't get any ideas," she said. "It's just my clothes stink. I think I got fish guts or something on me when I was lying in that alley. Boy, you really popped me. Why'd you go and do that anyway? Don't you like me?"

"Sure I like you."

"But I'm not your type, huh?"

"I don't have a type."

"Everyone has a type. Maybe you'd like me more if I had a funny mole?"

"Your drink is on its way."

"Is it you think I'm not experienced enough?"

"I have no thoughts whatsoever on your experience level."

"Not even one itty-bitty little thought?"

"Didn't you just tell me not to get any ideas?"

"I'm a creature of contradictory impulses."

"I'm starting to get that impression," I said. "Try picking one and sticking with it for ten minutes. Besides, you heard what the cooks said. I'm old enough to be your father."

"You're barely old enough to be my uncle."

Just then the doorbell rang. Saved by the bell. By the time I brought Afuro her drink she'd already lost interest in me. Not surprising. MTV, video games and the whole visual trash culture her generation was weaned on had left her without an attention span. Or maybe she just wasn't that interested in the first place. Whatever the case, I was glad she was finally ready to tell me about Bojangles. Once I found out about how the shadowy Bojangles and Miyuki knew each other, I figured it would make everything much simpler. I figured exactly wrong.

20

Three Nights in
Kabuki-cho

Nine P.M. on a Sunday night in late December
finds Miyuki and Afuro at the Café Acrophobia. Above them, the blazing, labyrinthine streets
of Kabuki-cho teem with a carnival of people. Gorgeous sandy-haired guys in leather coats yap on
cell phones as they maneuver scooters through the
crowds while foreign women stroll by in fur coats

and knee-high leather boots past drunken salarymen making broad comedy of human locomotion.
Snippets of Russian, Thai, Cantonese, Vietnamese
and who knows what else mix with the music blar-
ing from pachinko parlors and the enticements
from bullhorned touts drumming up business for
the soaplands, strip clubs, massage parlors,
karaoke boxes, disco clubs, jazz bars, snack bars
and just plain old bars that make Kabuki-cho the
liveliest entertainment district in the city, the
country, the world as they know it.

Afuro and Miyuki have just been shopping for
End of the Year gifts in Shibuya and nearby Shinjuku, an experience that has left them in a state of
giddy exhaustion. All day they have been audience to a circus of neon and noise, jostled partici-
pants among the hordes of fellow shoppers turning
the streets into a mass spectacle. They've been in
Tokyo for nearly a week and have found it incredibly expensive, unbelievably crowded, mind-
blowingly overstimulating and unlike Muramura
in a million different ways. In other words, it is
everything they hoped it would be, except for the
expensive part. But Miyuki especially seems to be
taking that in stride and all day she's been flashing
her credit card like it's some magical key opening
the gate to a world she'd only dreamed about.

Afuro and Miyuki sit on stools, an open copy of
Vivi magazine and two half-finished vodka tonics
on the bar in front of them. Miyuki flips through
the magazine, pointing out different hairstyles,
what works and what doesn't. She talks about a

hair appointment she has the next day, wonders if maybe she should go short for her job hunt. Afuro lights a cigarette and shrugs. She hates magazines and doesn't even want to think about the prospect of job hunting. So far she has only picked up a single job application from a Colorado Coffee shop a block from the apartment they share, an application she has no intention of even filling out. But she's Miyuki's roommate and her best friend so she has to say something.

"Go short," she says. "It will grow back."

"You think I should?"

Miyuki seems to sense Afuro is uncomfortable, so she changes the subject and starts talking about some of the more bizarre mountain witch getups they saw on the high school girls in Shibuya that afternoon. They order two more drinks, and Miyuki asks Afuro what she thinks of the bartender. Afuro says she doesn't think much of anything about him. Miyuki says she thinks he's cute. She thinks he looks like Naoki, guitarist for Hysteric Blue. For some reason, this makes Afuro laugh.

Said bartender then approaches, carrying an envelope. He is tall, has longish, tea-colored hair and is wearing a blue Mossimo T-shirt and tan shorts in the middle of winter.

"Excuse me," he says, "but are either of you named Miyuki?"

"She's Miyuki," says Afuro. "I'm Afuro. Nice to meet you."

"Someone left this for you," the bartender tells

Miyuki, handing her the envelope. Miyuki takes it
in both hands, a gesture that strikes Afuro as verg-
ing on coquettish. The three hiragana syllables
spelling "Miyuki" are written on the front of the
envelope in a plain black hand. She looks up at the
bartender.

"What's this?" Miyuki says.

"Search me," says the bartender. "Somebody
left it on the bar. There was a note attached that
said to give this to the girl with the, uh . . ."

"Nice smile?" Afuro suggests.

"Right, the nice smile," says the bartender,
though he'd clearly meant the mole. "The nicest
smile actually."

Miyuki blushes then glances around the bar but
can't figure out who might've left the envelope.
Afuro looks too, and decides whoever left the
envelope has already gone. Another hopeless loser,
she muses, bewitched by Miyuki's little black
mole. She wonders if one of those obsessive
weirdos from Muramura has followed Miyuki all
the way to Tokyo. Of course, she's more or less followed Miyuki all the way to Tokyo herself, but
that's different. They're best friends.

"Should I open it?" Miyuki says.

"No," Afuro says. "You should turn it over to
the police. It could be a time bomb, sarin, anthrax,
nude photos of the minister of health. I'd hand it to
the authorities right away."

Miyuki is confused and in no mood for jokes.

She waits for the bartender to walk away and
then tears open the envelope. Inside is a stack of

ten-thousand-yen notes. Afuro audibly gasps, clapping her hand to her open mouth. There's a letter inside. Miyuki unfolds it and places it on the bar, where they both silently read the message written in the same unremarkable script as the envelope:

DO NOT GET YOUR HAIR CUT. IF YOU RETURN IN TWO WEEKS' TIME WITH UNCUT HAIR I WILL PAY YOU TWICE THE AMOUNT IN THIS ENVELOPE. PLEASE GIVE FULL CONSIDERATION TO THIS OFFER. YOU'D BE DOING ME A GREAT FAVOR.

The letter is signed "Bojangles."

Miyuki and Afuro read the note again, then count the money.

There are 100,000 yen inside the envelope.

NINE P.M. ON A Sunday night in March finds Miyuki and Afuro at the Café Acrophobia. The cool night air echoes with clanging sounds from the batting cage three stories above them. It's cherry blossom season and the garish maze of Kabuki-cho is awash with people celebrating the arrival of spring in ways you don't learn studying the traditional seasonal ceremonies in grade school. The atmosphere is festive, but the atmosphere is always festive in the Kabuki-cho. Festive going desperate, a party filled with too many people celebrating too much to compensate for how little they have to celebrate.

Afuro includes herself in this category. She has finally found a job and it's so boring she doesn't even want to think about it. She's already on her third vodka tonic and thinks the fourth will probably make her vomit. Which won't stop her from having a fifth, but she doesn't want to think about that, either. Afuro's chin rests atop her fist atop the bar. Miyuki flips back her hair with the back of her hand. It's past her shoulders now, inching down her back.

By this time she has received a total of 480,000 yen from Bojangles. In exchange she has done nothing but let her hair grow, purchased a certain white dress, and, just last night, worn this dress to work. She has never met Bojangles or even talked to him on the phone. He has left written messages and money for her inside of coin lockers all over town, had the keys delivered via couriers and delivery boys. These messages have come to her at work and also at the Ochanomizu flat she shares with Afuro. She has no idea who Bojangles could possibly be and her lack of curiosity both shocks and worries her roommate.

"It's not right," Afuro says, sitting up straight now and lighting a Lark Slim. "You can't keep taking the money without knowing who this guy is. I mean, he's obviously a pervert of some kind. Probably a stalker, maybe worse."

"It's a harmless game," Miyuki says.

"You don't know that," replies Afuro. "You don't know that at all. Just because he hasn't tried anything yet doesn't mean that he won't. I'm telling you, this Bojangles person, whoever he is, is fucked up. And you're fucked up for playing along with him."

Miyuki then changes the subject, talking about how some big-time client came into the Club Kuroi Kiri last night. She tells Afuro that the man chose her out of all the girls at the club, even though the girls said he usually preferred a big-breasted foreign hostess named Zoë they all called Zochichi behind her back. In fact, the moment he saw Miyuki his eyes went wide and he was hardly able to utter a sentence the whole night long. "He looked like he'd just seen a ghost," Miyuki says. At the end of the night he gave her a huge tip, and promised he would come back very soon.

Afuro is too drunk to realize until days later that Miyuki has not changed the subject after all, and so the conversation dies. A lot of their conversations have been dying lately. After a few minutes of uncomfortable silence, Miyuki tries to lighten the mood by initiating a new game she's picked up from her coworkers at the hostess bar, one which usually cheers Afuro up. Miyuki scans the bar for a moment, then says:

"To your left. Blue tie, fogged-up glasses."

Afuro looks at the man and screws up her face. "Lotus root."

"And him?" Miyuki asks, nodding toward the wanna-be Rastafarian at the other end of the bar.

"Shiitake stem."

"Really? I was thinking daikon radish. Daikon radish at least."

"Don't be fooled by the baggy pants," Afuro says. "Shiitake stem. Shriveled shiitake stem."

Miyuki laughs and the Rastafarian across the room notices they are looking at him and he smiles back. Poor idiot, Afuro thinks. He looks completely ridiculous in that big knit hat and Bob Marley shirt, probably has never even smoked marijuana and doesn't know she has just compared his penis to a small, overripe mushroom stem. Afuro feels like she may be sick before she even reaches that fourth vodka tonic.

"What about me?" says Ichiro, appearing on the other side of the counter. Ichiro is the bartender at Café Acrophobia and Afuro has developed kind of a crush on him. He is tall, has the aforementioned longish, tea-colored hair and actually does sort of look like Naoki from Hysteric Blue. Tonight he wears a T-Shirt that says "LET'S PEACEFUL" in English. Ichiro is the only reason Afuro lets Miyuki drag her into the little basement dive bar every Sunday night. Problem is, Ichiro seems to like Miyuki more than Afuro. That's always been the problem.

"You, Ichiro?" Afuro slurs. "Why don't you ask Miyuki?"

"Afuro!" Miyuki recoils in mock horror.

With Ichiro, Miyuki always plays the innocent, pretending she is some split-tongued Kansai ingénue just off the bullet train. Which may have been more or less what she was a few months ago, but a few months was a long time. Miyuki has told Afuro she's learning to read men since working at the Club Kuroi Kiri, because pouring drinks and making polite conversation with middle-aged bureaucrats is only part of the job. What a real hostess did was discover what any given man's ideal woman was and then try to become that woman, at least for the night. She told Afuro that aspect of the job was fascinating, like being an actress. Afuro thought in becoming all these dream women Miyuki was somehow losing herself. She'd changed too much since moving to Tokyo. Maybe they both had.

"Well?" Ichiro says. "How 'bout it? What've I got in my pants?"

Miyuki blushes and drops her eyes.

"Light switch," Afuro blurts. "An itsy-bitty light switch."

Miyuki's face flushes on cue and she bats Afuro's arm.

Ichiro looks momentarily dejected, but recovers soon enough and begins laughing. The girls laugh too, and then Afuro suddenly gets sick all over herself.

NINE P.M. ON A Sunday night in June finds Miyuki and Afuro at the Café Acrophobia. Driving rain pounds the hellish maze of streets above, sending the less determined touts scurrying back into their rat-hole titty bars and grimy massage parlors where undocumented Thai and Filipino women make more in a month than they could at home in a year, but still. The more desperate touts remain outside, bit players in the ejaculation industry trying to impress yakuza or triad bosses with their fortitude. They bark out prices in terms of minutes and girls through bullhorns to be heard above the sound of the rain. And there are plenty of people to hear them. Faceless armies stream down the tiny streets under oily black umbrellas that reflect the neon bursting from every visible surface. Rain or shine, in the Kabuki-cho the sad parade never ends.

Afuro doesn't know why she keeps coming here every Sunday. The whole scummy area just depresses her now. Lots of things depress her. Her love life is a joke, and her job, she doesn't even want to think about her job. But tonight she hardly even considers her own problems. Tonight she is thinking only of Miyuki.

They haven't met for Sunday-night drinks in nine weeks, indeed haven't spoken the entire time. Afuro made an effort to get in touch with her friend, even going so far as to try to visit her at work, only to learn that Miyuki had quit working at the Club Kuroi Kiri nearly two months ago.

Afuro keeps going to Café Acrophobia every Sunday night anyway, arriving alone but not always leaving the same way. But there's no reason to keep coming here, she tells herself. Especially now that the Hysteric Blue guitarist look-alike left to take a job with a small graphic design firm. Tonight, she vows, will be her last night at the Café Acrophobia. She has made this vow on four previous occasions.

And who should stroll in tonight but her old friend Miyuki.

Afuro almost doesn't recognize her at first. Miyuki is wearing a posh cocktail dress and pricey shoes and both have been all but destroyed by the rain. A string of wet pearls is draped around her neck, a silver bracelet glistens from her wrist. No umbrella, not even a raincoat. Her long hair clings to her face and hangs in a dripping black mat down her back.

Afuro forces herself to smile and waves Miyuki to the bar. Miyuki barely registers the gesture, but manages to weave her way to the stool next to Afuro, trailing water behind her like a kappa or a slug. People are staring, a Chinese girl in the corner brays like a drunken donkey.

When Miyuki first moved out two months ago, Afuro was angry with her for leaving. They'd come to Tokyo together, after all, and she was supposed to be Afuro's best friend. Best friends didn't just up and move away like that without an explanation.

Of course, Miyuki had offered an explanation of sorts.

She'd found a patron. An older someone she'd met at the hostess club, an important someone with a lot of money to blow. He'd taken her to the finest restaurants in the Ginza and put her up in a penthouse suite in Aoyama. Beyond that, Afuro couldn't get anything out of Miyuki regarding her new lover, or as Miyuki preferred, her new patron. That's all Miyuki would tell her when she moved out, but Afuro could guess what type of guy this patron was. An older man, some *oyaji* who always wore a dull suit and a smug expression and had that musty *oyaji* smell. The type who had gone to the right schools ever since kindergarten, breezed through examination hell and could trace his family tree back to the time they lived in one. Patron, Afuro sniffed, as if her friend Miyuki was a geisha or a Renaissance painter.

But now Afuro is determined to make Miyuki talk.

"Geez, look at you," she says, after Miyuki has taken a seat. "Sugar daddy wouldn't spring for an umbrella or what?"

She's smiling when she says this, but Miyuki doesn't seem to even hear it. Mascara is slopped down her cheeks, bags hang under her eyes, her lips are swollen and cracked under the lipstick and she's lost ten pounds she didn't have in the first place. This is worse than Afuro thought.

Afuro orders them both vodka tonics. The new bartender is a guy named Kenji. He wears a plain blue shirt, has short dark hair and doesn't look like anyone. As he takes their order, Afuro catches Kenji staring. He's not staring at her, but Miyuki. And he's not staring at her because she looks like something the cat dragged in—he's staring at the mole. Afuro clenches her teeth, her grip tightens around her cigarette lighter. She gets a flash image of herself suddenly flicking the lighter underneath Miyuki's mole, listening to the flesh sizzle and pop as it burns.

"You look like a drowned rat," she tells Miyuki.

A wan smile from Miyuki. "You're just jealous."

"I'm serious. You look like hell. What's going on?"

"Isn't it obvious?" Miyuki says. "Got caught in the rain."

Their drinks arrive. Afuro lights a cigarette. Miyuki reaches out and takes the cigarette from Afuro's lips, puts it between her own. Her fingers are white and pencil thin, almost indistinguishable from the cigarette itself. Since when does Miyuki smoke? Afuro says nothing, lights another cigarette.

"So just tell me this," she says. "Is it Bojangles?"

Miyuki stares vacantly across the bar, shakes her head.

"But you're still involved with Bojangles? He's still giving you money?"

Miyuki stares vacantly across the bar, nods her head.

"And your patron, he's someone else?"

Miyuki stares vacantly across the bar. "His name is Nakodo."

"Yeah? What's this Nakodo like?"

"Please."

"I'm worried about you," Afuro says.

Miyuki closes her eyes.

"You can't keep on like this," Afuro tells her. "Maybe it's none of my business, but I don't care. You can't see it. You can't see what's happened to you since we've come here. You've become some-one else, and maybe that's what you wanted. But I'm your best friend, Miyuki. I'm the only one in this whole stupid city who really gives a damn about you, you know that? Not this creep who pays you to grow your hair, not this Nakodo person you're selling yourself to. Because, whether you realize it or not, that's exactly what you're doing. And if that's what you want, fine. But take a look at yourself, Miyuki. Take a good look and ask yourself if you're happier now."

Afuro knows she's said too much, knows she wouldn't have said any of it had she not been drinking. But she doesn't care. She's glad she spoke and she meant every word of it. Strangely, Miyuki doesn't seem upset in the least.

"He wants to marry me, Afuro."

Afuro is stunned not only by the news, but by the flat, distant tone with which it's delivered. No trace of joy, no trace of irony, no trace of anything. Miyuki's eyes are still closed, she rocks to and fro on her stool like an autistic child.

"That's ridiculous."

"No, he really does."

"Miyuki, you'd be out of your mind to even consider it."

"He loves me. Poor Nakodo really and truly loves me."

"Do you love him?"

Miyuki opens her eyes. "You don't understand."

"Then make me understand," Afuro says. "Tell me what is happening to you."

But Miyuki doesn't say a word.

And for the rest of the night, Afuro doesn't say

a word either. Both of them just drink their vodka tonics and stare off into space. An hour later Miyuki rises unsteadily to her feet and makes her way out of the bar. Afuro thinks to call after her, but what would be the point? There is nothing to say.

Afuro stays behind, sitting on the bar stool. She closes her eyes and recalls a family trip to Katsurahama Beach she'd taken during Golden Week as a child. She remembers standing barefoot in the sand, the waves coming in, tickling her feet. But the moment she's recalling now is the moment the tide shifts and everything seems suspended, silent and unmoving. And then there's a tug at her heels as the tide goes back out. She remembers closing her eyes and listening to the gulls wheeling through the sky and the sound of the waves receding and feeling the whole world being pulled away little by little, the whole world being swept from beneath her feet.

Afuro stands, stumbles her way out of the bar and up the stairs to the street. Outside the rain has stopped falling. It seems to just hang suspended in the air, a damp curtain draped over the city, waiting to come down.

21

The Ghost of Captain
Manfred von Richthofen

By the time Afuro finished the clock was blinking 3:12
A.M. She lit her gazillionth cigarette of the night and I
rose from the bed, walked to the bathroom and splashed
cold water on my face. The guy that stared back at me in the
mirror was a mess. Pasty skin, hair all over the place, folds
of flesh protruding beneath his bloodshot eyes. I couldn't
have looked like that, no way. Must've been the red lights

conjuring up the ghost of Captain Manfred von Richthofen.

I poured myself a glass of water, walked back into the main room and found Afuro fast asleep. I put out her cigarette and dumped the ashes in the red garbage can. Given the events of the previous twenty-four hours, she must have been exhausted. I was exhausted, too, but I couldn't sleep so I just sat on the edge of the bed, posed like Rodin's famous sculpture and feeling about as nimble.

Everything was quiet, so quiet I could almost forget an entire world existed outside this room. Even at this hour, on Friday night Tokyo would be pulsing with chaotic life. Motorcycles darting through the electric streets, all-night discos blasting in the hip west Tokyo nightspots. But here in the Red Baron Suite only the red glow and the sound of a young girl sleeping. The scene struck me as unreal, life inside a bubble.

I thought about how Afuro's story fit in the overall picture, ordered the events, weighed the possibilities. In 1975, some guy calling himself Bojangles approaches Detective Ihara to investigate Nakodo. Twenty-six years later, a Bojangles pays Miyuki to grow her hair. Soon after, Miyuki becomes involved with Nakodo. Miyuki tells Afuro that Nakodo and Bojangles are different people, but it's not clear she's ever actually seen Bojangles. Not long after that, Miyuki turns up dead and Nakodo summons me to his Ark Hills mansion. Afuro is convinced this Bojangles character trashed her apartment, but she's also convinced for a time that I am Bojangles. Could Bojangles and Nakodo be the same person? Or could Bojangles be a flunky of Nakodo's? Not likely, unless Nakodo was somehow trying to investigate himself back in 1975.

Another possibility: Bojangles was the Man in White. The

written messages to Miyuki were certainly his style, and the anachronistic photograph I'd seen during my seizure seemed to point to a link between the Man in White and Nakodo. But what of the content of the messages themselves? Why pay someone to grow their hair a certain length, or wear a certain dress? And the payments had continued long after that initial envelope in the Café Acrophobia, presumably even up to a few days ago. What had Miyuki's letter to Afuro said? _I've got-ten myself involved in something very difficult and not a lit-tle bit scary._ I had a feeling that when Miyuki died, she was doing more for Bojangles than letting her hair down. Bojan-gles had something planned for her, something planned for Nakodo, too. _Everything is coming to a close._

I couldn't rule out Bojangles killing Miyuki. Without knowing who he was, there was no way of ruling out any-thing. But I knew he wasn't trying to kill Afuro last night. A killer wouldn't have trashed her apartment and left. He would've waited there, or left the place untouched and come back another time. Destroying her place would only arouse fear and suspicion. Maybe that's what he wanted—to scare her. But no, the job was too thorough for that. Whoever wrecked her apartment was searching for something. But what?

If it was Bojangles, he could've been making sure Miyuki had kept none of his written messages before she moved out, that there was nothing left linking him to her. Perhaps Miyuki suspected something like this even before she died, which could explain why she'd had her letter delivered to Afuro's workplace rather than the apartment they once shared. Nakodo might have been looking for similar evi-dence—trying to gather up any jewelry or other gifts he'd bought for Miyuki, lest the police start sniffing around and

asking questions. Because when the police ask questions the
weekly scandal rags are never far behind.

But then here was the thing: Nakodo had nothing to fear
scandal-wise unless he'd actually murdered her. A fiftyish
Ministry of Construction official having a relationship with a
twenty-year-old hostess just wasn't scandal material these
days. Especially since Nakodo wasn't even married. And
even if Miyuki had killed herself over him, no fingers would
be pointed at Nakodo. Miyuki's suicide would be seen as a
foolish gesture, an act of melodrama, something done by a
romantic kid who didn't understand the hard realities of the
world. To paraphrase Detective Ihara, it would be the act of
someone who didn't know what size fish they were.

But I still didn't think Miyuki had killed herself. At the
same time, I didn't think Nakodo or his people had killed
her either. I could've been wrong, but he seemed genuinely
concerned for her that day he'd summoned me to his mansion, the day he told me she'd disappeared. Though it's possible he wasn't concerned for her safety, but concerned for
his reputation.

Maybe. Somehow. Possibly.

It was all abstract, theoretical. All I knew for sure was that
Miyuki was dead, and somehow Nakodo and a guy named
Mr. Bojangles were involved. Add to that the Man in White
and someone named Benzaiten—if those two even existed
outside my seizuring mind. I needed more facts. And it
wouldn't be pretty, it wouldn't be smooth and it probably
wouldn't even be safe, but I knew one sure way to get them.
I'd have to go to the House of Nakodo, the place I'd been
headed when Afuro attacked me.

Looking at her small body now curled and sinking into
the bedspread like a flattened white question mark on an

expanse of crimson, it was hard to believe she'd been capable of it. And come to think of it, why had Afuro attacked me with a brick when she had a knife in her purse? And where did she even get a brick? Had she carried it all the way across town, through taxis and on trains, inside her handbag? No telling what went on in a mind like hers. But I knew Miyuki's death had affected her in ways she didn't yet realize, in ways she probably wouldn't fully understand for years to come. From all she'd told me, I got the impression that she and Miyuki had lived in a pretty insular world, a world bound by harmless secrets and private jokes, contained in the easy confidences and hard-won intimacies, protected by shared history they referenced in worldless glances and a cryptic vocabulary impenetrable to outsiders. It was the kind of friendship you have maybe once in your life if you're lucky, a friendship almost impossible to sustain beyond a certain age. The world has a way of seeping in, of creating small fissures in even the most sturdy and carefully constructed shelters, forming cracks that grow and spread and inevitably push people in different directions. Nothing so insidious about it, just part of growing up.

Miyuki seemed to be drifting away nearly as soon as they arrived in Tokyo, and perhaps the friendship was already doomed before Miyuki became involved with Nakodo. On purely physical terms, Miyuki and Afuro were of different worlds. I recalled the way Miyuki had immediately caught my eye inside the Lucky Benten Pachinko hall, how I'd been unable to look away. Would my eye have lingered likewise on Afuro, had she been sitting there? Probably not. There was nothing wrong with her looks. She was young, pretty, had a nice smile and a certain spindly, coltish charm. The type that could easily grow on you and probably got better with age.

But Miyuki was blessed or cursed with something else entirely. Sad fact was, at first glance men would always choose Miyuki over Afuro. And in a city like Tokyo, her stunning looks would give her access to a life forever closed to Afuro, no matter how clever Afuro was, no matter how resourceful or good a person. How long could any friendship survive that?

I lay down next to Afuro and stared at the ceiling. Thankfully, the Hotel Ophuls hadn't put a mirror up there, so I was spared further ghastly reflections of myself. But it probably would have made an odd image. Me looking older than I was, awake and staring off into space, shirtsleeves rolled up, arms folded beneath my head, legs crossed at the ankles, wing tips aimed at the ceiling. A much younger Afuro curled in profile so she appeared about half my size, her narrow back arching toward me, short hair fanned out across the pillow, hands tucked between her knees, her tiny feet pressed one atop the other. Both of us bathed in a fuzzy red glow, almost floating within it. Maybe there was nothing so odd about the image after all. Just two people together and alone, the way so many people are.

I let my mind wander and pretty soon I was asleep. Didn't think it would happen on this particular night, but I guess I got lucky. Tell me fifteen years ago that I'd consider getting lucky to be safely falling asleep next to a twenty-year-old woman without anything happening and I wouldn't have believed you. Tell me three days ago that I'd wind up in a love hotel with Miyuki's best friend and I wouldn't have believed that either. Tell me everything that would happen tomorrow, I'd have you committed.

That night I dreamt about a man mowing grass.

That was the whole dream. No drowned women, no confused girls throwing bricks at my head. No smoking men in white, no powerful middle-aged bureaucrats. No maritime hotel managers, no permagrin pachinko addicts. Just some guy pushing a lawn mower over a nice big suburban lawn. Every once in a while, he'd shut off the mower, mop the sweat from his brow and look out over the yard, admiring his work. Birds twittered, a pleasant breeze blew through the air. A phone rang in the distance. The man turned on the mower and went back to work. The dream went on and on like this, with nothing really happening.

22

The Red-and-White Carp

A furo yawned, stretched and lit a cigarette without saying so much as a word to me. When I smiled and said good morning she scowled and told me the red lights were giving her a serious headache even in her sleep and could I please just be quiet for a few minutes and let her smoke in peace. Whatever intimacy we'd established the previous night had dissipated with the morning, and we were now two strangers trapped in an unfamiliar space and facing our own problems. The fact that some of them overlapped provided little comfort.

"Sorry," Afuro said after a time. "I'm just, I don't know. I think I must be emotionally hungover or something."

I couldn't blame her. If I'd tried to kill someone, nearly had my jaw broken, then spent all night in a love hotel unloading a painful story about losing my best friend, I'd need some peace and quiet, too.

It was Saturday, and she told me she didn't have to work. She didn't tell me what she'd be doing instead, and I didn't ask. After she'd finished smoking she started searching through her handbag.

"Take this," she said, handing me a pink cell phone about the size of the complimentary soap bars back at the Hotel Cerulean. "In case I have to call you. I've got another one, anyway. Newer model. That one is like four months old."

"And it still works?"

"Ha-ha. You know how to use it, right?"

I'd told her I could probably figure out how to use a phone.

"If it starts playing 'Bye-Bye Santa' just ignore it. That only means that someone nearby programmed Handsome Tigers as one of their favorite J-POP groups. Also, if you hear 'These Boots Are Made for Walkin',' then this jerk named Juzo Kushimi is too close for comfort, or at least his phone is. He's got bright red hair and always wears the same stinky army jacket, so if you see him punch him in the nose or something for me. Here, wait a minute, that reminds me."

She snatched the phone from my hand, typed on it with her thumbs then handed it back about three seconds later.

"There," she said. "Now if we're trying to meet and can't find each other in a crowd, your phone will play a song when I'm within a twenty-five-meter radius. Watch."

She took her other phone out and hit the power button.

My phone started beeping "Strangers in the Night."

"Cute," I said.

"If the caller ID screen doesn't show my name, don't pick up the call. Please pretty please. And if I find out you listened to my voice mail or read my old e-mails I'm going to kill you."

"You already tried that once."

"Ha-ha. Will you be able to work the phone or not?"

"Sure. But where do I put the food in?"

"The what?"

"You know, if I wanna reheat some yakitori or microwave some popcorn or something. Do I just point this thing at it, or—"

She rolled her eyes and said, "After ten minutes of no activity it will go into sleep mode, so don't worry about the batteries. Just don't lose it, because I may need to get in touch with you."

We spoke little as we made our way out of the Hotel Ophuls, though Afuro did get slightly irritated when I refused to take the elevator and insisted on the stairs. We emerged on a side street, the entrance disguised by a wall of fake rocks. The morning sky was a dense block of grayish white and it looked like there might finally be some rain.

While we waited for a cab, a mother and her child stood waiting for the light to change. The kid was maybe four years old, a boy I think, with enormous eyes and an adorable little nose, and was all decked out in his orange summer jumpsuit. I caught Afuro staring at the little tyke with an expression on her face I hadn't seen before. Something close to tenderness.

"Cute kid, huh?" I said.

Her face slipped back into hard-boiled mode again, a look almost comical when juxtaposed with her exuberant canary-yellow blouse and goofy red duck-billed shoes. "Sure, he's cute now. But in a few years, he'll be another person. Some jerk jamming an umbrella in your back on the subway, or talking during the movies. Even if he turns out to be a nice guy, he'll still be just another human being using up oxygen and eating food and trying to make more little babies. Not a thing the poor little guy can do to stop it."

"You're right. Should we go ahead and kill him?"

"I'm just saying it's sad."

The kid and his mom and a few hundred other people made their way across the street and were swallowed up by the crowd. A few moments later, a green-and-yellow cab pulled up. Afuro made a polite show of resistance when I insisted on giving her cab fare, but accepted it soon enough and even managed to thank me.

"You sure you're gonna be all right?" I said before the driver pulled away. "Maybe you should get out of the city for a while. Go back to your parents' house in Muramura until things calm down a little. After all, isn't there a funeral or a wake planned for Miyuki?"

"I wouldn't go back to Muramura even for my own funeral."

"You shouldn't say things like that, even jokingly."

"Who's joking? Anyway, don't worry. I'm not gonna die. Not with my Uncle Cleveland protecting me. Meet me tonight?"

"Where and when?"

"Shibuya, at the Hachiko statue at around ten o'clock."

Then she flashed a smile and closed the door. I watched the taxi pull away and felt the day's first drops of sweat gather on my forehead. As soon as I wiped them away with the back of my hand, new ones had already formed. I gave up staying dry and waited for the next taxi to come around the bend.

• • •

THE CABBIE DROPPED ME OFF in Ark Hills, right next to the All Nippon Air Hotel. It took me a moment to get my bearings, but I remembered the way to the House of Nakodo soon enough. In seconds I was headed up the narrow road that climbed a short, steep hill lined with concrete embankments. The promised rain was still being withheld and the soles of my wing tips were ready to melt to the pavement. Never thought I'd miss the rainy season, but at least it'd been one thing in this city I could depend on year after year.

At the top of the hill I turned left, walked past the Spanish embassy and found the wrought-iron gate set in the high stone wall. On the other side of the gate, the two rows of stunted cherry trees. The House of Nakodo glinted in the space beyond, glass and steel winking beneath the dense cover of foliage.

An electronic intercom buzzer was set into the stone wall next to the gate. I pushed the button and waited. The gate didn't grind open, no voice came over the speaker. Nothing happened. There was no sound at all, not even crows or cicadas. I pushed the button one more time and looked for security cameras hidden in the high bushes and in the vines crawling over the wall. Maybe Nakodo's people were inside watching me right now, wondering if they should alert the master of the house. Maybe Nakodo's people didn't work Saturdays. Whatever the case, I didn't find any cameras.

I waited a few seconds. Then I started climbing the wall.

The large, uneven stones gave me plenty of footholds and the vines had grown thick and strong over the years. Getting over took me all of five seconds. I know because I counted. I counted because it was a good way to keep my brain from screaming to get down off the wall, go back down the hill and get the hell away from there.

I plopped down on the other side and had another look around, half expecting some Baskervillian hounds to come storming across the yard and send me back up the wall. When none did, I started toward the house. The sound of the gravel crunching beneath my feet as I walked along the cherry tree lane was amplified by the stillness of the surroundings. The driveway soon ended and I found myself moving down the short garden path to the front door. Those two empty Doric columns were there, but no butler this time. The door was partially opened. I knocked anyway. When no one answered, I pushed the door open and stepped inside.

I STOOD IN THE FOYER trying to adjust my eyes to the sudden darkness. In the room beyond feeble shafts of light trickled in from cracks in the curtains, penetrating only a few feet before being smothered in shadows. I didn't bother changing into slippers this time, but felt my way along the hall, moving toward the main room. By the time I finally reached it, my eyes had become accustomed to the darkness but they hadn't become accustomed to what was revealed inside it.

The two bronze lion statues lay toppled on the floor. All the paintings had been ripped off the walls and were scattered about the room. The vases were now nothing more than jagged ceramic teeth and the display case that housed them had been reduced to a pile of splintered wood and busted glass. It was tempting to say it looked like a bomb went off in the room, but bombs weren't that methodical. The destruction was utterly complete, hateful in its detail.

As I stared at the wreckage I became aware of a noise coming from another room. A dull, rhythmic thumping sound. Without thinking, I grabbed a shard of glass from the floor. It was about nine inches long, fit my hand like a knife. I walked through another hallway, the one that led to the study. On the way I nearly stepped on the portrait of Miyuki. The giant painting had been ripped from the wall just like all the others and now five pink-and-blue Miyuki's grinned up at me from the floor.

Only it wasn't Miyuki.

I don't know why I'd been so slow to figure it all out, even with the Man in White showing me the old photograph. The woman in the picture had looked a lot like Miyuki, but that was only one way of seeing things. I saw the other way now:

Miyuki looked a lot like the woman in the picture.

Meaning she'd been made to look like the woman in the picture, the woman on the painting beneath my feet. Bojangles had seen to that. THE WOMAN IN THIS PHOTOGRAPH JOINED US SOME TIME AGO. Bojangles had paid Miyuki to grow her hair until she looked just like Nakodo's dead wife. The one who drowned all those years ago in the accident on the Sumida.

THE MAN IN THE PHOTOGRAPH WILL JOIN US SOON.

I wondered just how soon.

The thumping sound I'd heard before grew louder as I approached the door to the study. *Thump, whir, thump.* I tightened my grip around the glass, feeling it press into my flesh, and pushed open the door.

A desk lamp tipped onto its side flickered off and on, illuminating the scene in stroboscopic bursts. The mahogany desk had been overturned and the contents of its drawers were strewn about the room. No photographs remained on the walls. The leather recliner had been shredded, its stuffing covering the floor like a new-fallen snow.

Thump, whir, thump.

I spun to the sound. In the far corner of the room a wheelchair thudded against the wall. It would hit, back up a couple feet, and hit the wall again. The old man was sitting in the wheelchair, his head bouncing on his shoulders with each impact.

"Is everything all right?" I called.

No answer, but it was a dumb question. I walked across the room to get a closer look and started wondering if Old Man Nakodo was dead. A wooden leg busted off the desk was blocking the chair's wheels. They'd struggle backward for a moment, stall out, then start spinning forward again. *Thump, whir, thump.* When I got closer to him, I realized he was indeed alive. Alive and seemingly untouched. He was wrapped in the same black-and-tan kimono, and again looked like little more than a tiny head afloat on a sea of fabric. Flecks of white clung to the corners of his mouth.

"What happened?" I asked.

"Benzaiten."

Same name the Man in White had told me.

"Benzaiten, Year of the Snake," he said again, hoarsely mouthing the words like a curse before going into the wall. I flicked a switch on the chair and it stopped. I realized then I was still gripping the glass shard and dropped it to the ground lest it frighten the old man. Then I reached down and tossed the busted desk leg out of the way. Old Man Nakodo looked up at me, but I don't think he really saw me. His eyes were gazing into an immeasurable distance.

"Where is your son?"

"Did you see the airplanes in the blue morning sky?"

"Airplanes?"

He shook his head and made a gesture I couldn't interpret.

"Who did all this?" I asked.

"Every Saturday we must endure sanitary inspections."

"What?"

"We suffer so much from inspections of every kind. Payday every tenth day. Not even enough for a sea biscuit."

"Listen, did you just say something about Benzaiten?"

"Benzaiten," he repeated, nodding his head as if he finally understood. "The monks of Benzaiten Temple are responsible. Nothing I could do to stop them. Now Benzaiten is gone, lost forever. And the temple with it."

"I don't understand."

"The commanding officer has the best job," he agreed. "Always on horseback, coming or going."

"Was the Man in White here? Did Bojangles do this?"

"We'll meet at Yasukuni."

Suddenly his frail left hand emerged from the kimono and the wheelchair lurched backward into motion. Framed photographs of Mr. Nakodo that once hung on the wall clattered beneath the wheels as the old man raced out of the room, leaving clouds of loose stuffing and scraps of paper stirring in his wake.

I stood there for a moment considering what to do and decided I didn't want to be hanging around when Mr. Nakodo arrived to find his mansion in a shambles. I started making my way out of the place, but I must've taken a wrong turn in one of the darkened hallways because I wound up in the backyard. Racing along the stone path to the front of the building, I was so blinded by the sun that I didn't even notice Nakodo before tripping over one of his outstretched legs.

He was lying facedown in a shallow pond, arms floating,

head and shoulders submerged in the water. A large white carp patterned with red markings surfaced near Nakodo's body then kicked its tail and disappeared into the murky depths. Tendrils of Nakodo's hair rippled languorously in the current. He was still wearing his gray suit, even on a Saturday. The bureaucrat's equivalent to dying with his boots on, I guess. I leaned over, grabbed a fistful of his suit and pulled. He was dead weight, and a lot of it, but I managed to heave him out of the carp pool and roll him onto his side.

Water spilled from between his rubbery blue lips. His face was a shapeless lump of gray dough, bloated and colorless, the skin looking like it would slide off at the slightest touch. There was no point in checking for a pulse because he'd obviously been dead for a long time. Sunlight danced across the surface of the pond and reflected in the beads of water on Nakodo's face.

I tried not to look at that face as I turned him over and dragged his upper torso back into the water, leaving him just as I found him. I noticed a smear of red marking the back of his jacket just between his shoulder blades, watched it hit the water and dissipate into pale inky curls. I realized all at once that the blood on his jacket was mine and looked down to see a three-inch gash in my palm. Must have been gripping that glass shard too tightly inside the house.

I washed off my hands in the pond and a few more red-and-white carp came rolling timidly to the surface, perhaps thinking it was feeding time. When they figured out I wasn't food, they slowly swam away, disappearing again to the other side of the pool. I wiped my hands on the grass and made my way back inside the house.

I could've called the cops using the cell phone Afuro had given me, but they'd trace it and I didn't want to get either of us involved. It took my eyes a moment to adjust again to the dark, but I managed to locate the study again without too many wrong turns. Old Man Nakodo was nowhere in sight, and I listened for the sound of his wheelchair but didn't hear it. Eventually I found a cordless phone lying on the floor next to the lamp. I picked it up with my good hand and dialed 119.

23

Festival of the Dead

By the time I surfaced in Nishi-Azabu the hazy white clouds had lost the battle and the sun was inflicting victor's justice. Sweat ran into my eyes, blurring my vision, making the whole world look like a watery reflection in a funhouse mirror. Sidewalks choked with pedestrians, streets packed with cars, whole glittering skyscrapers filled with strangers going about business that was none of mine. Sirens wailed in the distance but the sirens could've been for anybody. Every minute of the day there was death and disaster somewhere in the megalopolis. I should've told the dispatcher there was no reason to rush, to just send a few cops and a cleanup crew whenever they had a moment to spare. The emergency at the House of Nakodo was already over.

As soon as I'd hung up the phone I'd walked into the bathroom and found a small towel. I'd wiped my blood from the phone and wrapped the towel around my hand. After that I left the house, climbed the wall and walked back down the hill, tossing the glass shard in the bushes outside the Spanish embassy on the way. I'd done nothing wrong, but explaining that to the cops was a different story. Of course, Old Man Nakodo might mention something about my presence, but I doubted he'd be lucid enough to tell the cops anything they could use. I'm sure I'd left traces of my blood in the study and maybe on Nakodo's shirt, but there was so much evidence to sift through the cops would be busy for days. By the time they got around to analyzing the wreckage, I'd be back in Cleveland.

I'd walked through an underground pedestrian tunnel linking Ark Hills to Nishi-Azabu nearly a mile away. No use taking a chance that some cab driver would remember a guy with a wounded hand getting into his car near the scene of the crime, after all. When I figured I was far enough from Ark Hills I found a glass phone box that doubled as an oven, popped in a phone card of dubious authenticity I'd bought from an Iranian in Ameyayokocho and dialed up the offices of *Spylens!* It wouldn't be long until the word was out about Nakodo's death, and I needed to get to Ihara before his paranoia level was off the charts. Using Afuro's cell phone to call would only have raised his ire.

"Moshi moshi," squeaked Ihara's secretary. I gave my name as Mr. Bojangles. A few moments later, Ihara himself came on the line.

"Who is this?" he said in a pinched voice.

"Don't worry. Just didn't think you'd take the call if I said it was Billy Chaka."

"You got that right."

"I need some help."

"See a shrink."

"I need you to tell me the name of Nakodo's wife. Kitazawa something or other, the one you said drowned in the accident on the Sumida River."

"Tell me you're not on a cell phone."

"Pay phone."

"And you haven't taken my advice," said Detective Ihara. "Didn't think you would. But I told you once already—leave me out of whatever this is."

"Come on, Ihara," I whined. "This isn't confidential information I'm asking for. I could look up her obituary in the library if I wanted."

"Good idea."

"No time. You see the news tonight, you'll know why."

Detective Ihara grumbled. "All right, fine. Let me look it up and I'll call you back later."

"I'll stay on the line."

Ihara grumbled some more and then put me on hold. A muzak version of Louis Armstrong's "What a Wonderful World" piped through the earpiece. I pushed open the door of the phone booth to try to get some air in, but it hardly mattered. My shirt was completely soaked and my brain felt ready to boil in my skull. I watched the minutes left on my card tick away while outside the box a steady flow of people leisurely paraded down the sidewalk carrying brightly colored shopping bags, hugging close to the buildings and their protective shade. Across the street, a wooden policeman fit-

ted with robotic arms directed traffic around a road construction crew. Everywhere I looked, a constant pageant of
color and motion.

"You still there?" Ihara said.

Affirmative grunt from me.

"I've got your information. But as I was looking it up, a
troubling thought occurred to me. Detective Ihara, old buddy,
I said to myself, what's in it for Spylens!?"

"Come up with an answer?"

"I thought I'd try you first."

"Twenty thousand yen. Take it or leave it."

"I'll take it," Ihara said. "Plus an extra fifteen thousand for
the rush service. Just give me your credit card number and I'd
be happy to—"

"I'll do a wire transfer."

"Very well," Ihara snorted. "Her name was Ame
Kitazawa."

Ame was the word for "rain," a fairly common name for
Japanese women. The last name wasn't uncommon either.
"Where do her parents live?" I asked. "I need an address."

"That wasn't part of our agreement."

"Neither was the rush fee."

"Fair enough. I'll only charge you an additional ten thousand for the address," Ihara said. "Bringing our total to forty-
five thousand. Better make it fifty just to round it off."

I told him fine and he gave me an address in Yanaka, said
it was up the hill behind Nippori station, in an old neighborhood by the Tennoji Temple. I wasn't familiar with the area,
so I listened more closely than I normally would have to
Detective Ihara.

"You know where to send the money," he finished. "Don't
delay, because I really didn't need your credit card number. I

can access all your information on my computer—bank accounts, credit cards, whatever I want. In fact, I have your savings information onscreen right now. Funny, I always thought journalists made more money."

I let him have the last laugh but hung up when the laugh lasted too long. Then I popped my phone card out of the machine, scratched the Kitazawa family's address on it, and walked to a cabstand by the Nishi-Azabu station exit. It would be faster to take the train to Nippori, but there was somewhere else I wanted to go before I called on the Kitazawa family.

AS THE CAB I'D hailed fought through the congested streets I tried to push the image of Mr. Nakodo from my mind, but it wouldn't budge. It just lay there, a blank look on his bloated gray face like he was contemplating why someone would want to drown him in his own backyard.

I contemplated the same question from the back of the cab. THE MAN IN THE PHOTOGRAPH WILL JOIN US SOON. Bojangles was looking more and more like the Man in White all the time, meaning I might have to accept that the Man in White actually visited me the other night and it wasn't all some strange seizure-induced vision. BENZAITEN SAYS TWO MORE WILL JOIN US. Meaning who? Me? Afuro? Both of us? I was so preoccupied with these questions I didn't realize where we were until the cabbie pulled over and stopped.

"Wait a minute," I said. "Isn't this Ueno Park?"

"*Hai, so desu.*"

"But I wanted to go to the Benzaiten Temple."

"*Hai, hai so desu.*"

He pointed out the window. Across the street, a concrete stairwell descended to a path lined on either side by a large pond choked with lotus blossoms the size of open umbrellas. At the end of the path crouched a low building, barely visible behind the sheltering trees.

"But isn't that the *Benten* Temple?"

"Benten, Benzaiten, same thing," he laughed.

"What do you mean same thing?"

"One long way to say, one short way. Benzaiten, Benten."

"So there's no Benzaiten Temple?"

His expression grew serious. He leaned an elbow through the opening in the partition and addressed me in English. "I drive cab Tokyo twenty year. This Benten Temple for you. Good for tourist. No problem, OK, buster?"

"OK, buster," I sighed. I'd finally found the exception that proves the rule, the bad apple of the well-mannered Tokyo cab fleet. I started to hand him my fare and realized the money was spotted with small drops of blood from my palm. The cabbie noticed it too, his face crumpling in disgust. I gave him a sheepish grin and dug out a different set of bills, using my good hand this time. He made a big show of holding his breath and keeping the offending yen as far away from his person as possible.

I got out, crossed the street and headed down the path to Benten Temple. Intermittent Latin drumbeats drifted from the nearby bandshell where someone was doing a sound check. A cluster of retirees sat at picnic tables near the bank of the pond. Men in shirtsleeves, sipping beer and squinting against the sun. Women in colorful summer *yukatas*, waving accordion fans in front of their faces just like their ancestors might've done one or two hundred years ago. For the rest of the world, it was just another sweltering Saturday afternoon.

The temple itself was in the middle of the Shinobazu Pond, on an island connected to the bank by a narrow concrete path about fifty yards long. Red and blue plastic lanterns were strung along the path to the temple, emblazoned with the sacred logo for Asahi beer. Probably wouldn't be long before they put a giant Fujifilm billboard on the temple roof and installed a Mild Sevens vending machine next to the sacred incense kettle.

A twelve-foot-high wooden lute sat beside the squat red temple. As I watched a man approach the altar and say a short prayer followed by two claps of his hands, I recalled the Man in White clapping his hands twice before incinerating the photograph and my brain instinctively squirmed the way it did whenever I thought of the Man in White.

I felt a little stupid for not realizing that Benten was just an abbreviation of Benzaiten, but I wasn't really up on the Seven Lucky Gods of Japan. I never made New Years trips to temples in their honor or put a picture of the *Takarabune* treasure ship under my pillow for lucky dreams or any of that other stuff. I could only name two of them other than Benten—Ebisu and Bishamonten—and I doubted the average Japanese under the age of sixty could do much better. Besides, who would've thought the Man in White would be talking about some Buddhist goddess? I expected the Man in White to be a flunky for some yakuza clan, maybe some big company president or political rival of Nakodo's. But a flunky for one of the Seven Lucky Gods?

Somebody was obviously screwing with me, trying to send me on a wild-goose chase. That Old Man Nakodo had mentioned the monks of Benzaiten probably meant someone was screwing with him, too. Because the monks of Benten Temple were right in front of me, and as they scooted back and forth carrying armloads of paper lanterns, they impressed me as the types of guys who understood that holding someone underwater until they died was really, really bad karma.

And so I faced a familiar question. The same question that had dogged me ever since the pachinko parlor, ever since I'd taken the Gombei Fukugawa assignment, ever since I could remember: What the hell was I doing here?

"Have you come to watch the *Obon* preparations?" suggested a voice to my right. I looked down to see a short bald man in an orange robe. The temple priest. He had a gentle smile, made gentler by the fact that it only consisted of about seven teeth. What they lacked in number they made up for in radiance, shining from inside his mouth as if they were electrified.

Obon was the Festival of the Dead—a three-day Buddhist celebration during which the souls of the departed return to earth to visit their families. If I only had three days to return to the land of the living, I doubt I'd want to spend them with my relatives, but being dead must change your perspective on all kinds of things. The priest's justification of my presence was better than anything I could come up with, so I nodded. Then I thought of something else.

"I thought *Obon* was next month," I said, recalling the mass exodus from Tokyo I'd witnessed on a previous assignment. That August the bullet trains were packed to double capacity and the city was turned into a ghost town as everyone returned to their hometowns to pay respects to their ancestors. Made you realize how few people living in Tokyo actually called the place home.

The priest bobbed his head. "*Obon* occurs during the seventh month. Depending on when New Year is celebrated, the seventh month is either August or July. Big cities like Tokyo celebrate according to the Western calendar, but the country-side goes by the traditional Chinese calendar."

"Must be confusing for the dead."

He gave a small chuckle. "You really should visit the countryside to get the flavor of traditional festivals. Especially the Kansai region. Their celebrations are much livelier than those here in the city. Still, we have our own humble traditions. Tonight, for instance, we're conducting the Lighting of Lanterns ceremony."

He pointed at the young monks shuttling paper lanterns to rowboats moored on the shore of the pond. The lanterns were painted with Chinese characters, family names of the temple's supporters. No Asahi logos on them, not yet anyway.

"It's a truly beautiful sight," the priest said, eyes lighting up. "The monks row out upon the water and make a large bonfire in the center of the pond. Then they light hundreds of floating paper lanterns and release them across the water. The lanterns are meant to guide the spirits back to the nether-world."

I was tired, confused, and in no mood to chat with the kindly old priest about ancient customs. I couldn't resist wondering aloud how the dead could find a single flame with all the neon lights of Tokyo competing for their attention. A pointless question, like asking how a virgin could give birth or a fat guy fit down a chimney.

I regretted it the moment I said it, but the priest nodded earnestly and replied: "I've often wondered the same thing myself. With Tokyo as it is, it must be easy for the souls of the departed to overlook a mere flame upon the water. I imagine some hungry spirits get confused. They lose their way, per-haps, and become trapped in the city, forever seeking the path home. Perhaps you, too, are seeking something?"

I looked down to see the priest gazing up at me with a knowing look on his wizened face. A massive black crow landed on the temple eave and began cawing. Incense wafted through the air and the breeze pressed my sweat-drenched shirt against my skin, giving my spine an unexpected shiver.

"I guess I am looking for something," I said.

He blinked his eyes. "The unenlightened man believes what he seeks lies far from home. And so he pursues it to ever more distant lands, unaware that with each journey he only puts more distance between himself and that which he seeks. The enlightened seeker does not move in seeking. For he knows that which is sought is also seeking him."

"Uh-huh," I said. "But what I'm seeking is another temple. Do you know of any other Benten temples here in Tokyo? Or any other group of Benzaiten monks?"

The priest gave me a contained smile, then shook his head and squinted up at the sky. "This heat is something, isn't it?" he said. With that, he turned his tranquil gaze on me once and walked off toward the bank of the Shinobazu Pond to join his acolytes in their preparations. The crow cawed one last time and took flight across the water. Below him, rowboats laden with paper lanterns undulated on the gentle currents.

24

The Jealous Goddess

Professor Kujima put on a pair of reading glasses and shuffled leisurely through a shaggy stack of manuscript pages he'd extracted from one of six worn cardboard boxes behind his desk. Anticipation brought some measure of life to his dour face, but otherwise, the atmosphere inside Hanran Books was the same as ever. Too much dust, not enough light, too many books and not a single customer. Professor Kujima had seemed startled when I came through the door moments before, but he would have looked startled to see anyone. I should have been across town trying to talk to the Kitazawa family before the news of Nakodo's death broke, but Kujima knew the city better than anyone and I needed to find out if there was anything to this Benzaiten Temple nonsense or if it was just the shock-induced ramblings of the Minato ward's fourth-oldest man.

Upon discovering the pages he was searching for, Kujima cleared his throat and began reading in a quiet, melodic voice that probably used to make his students fall asleep at their desks.

"A city is a living history," he began. "A collective memory etched in concrete, built with glass and steel. Even in Tokyo, city of the future, the past is never really past. It seeps into the present and becomes the future. It's in the buildings we inhabit, the roads we travel, in the very air we breathe. The past is alive in the way people talk, the way they think, the way they lead their entire lives. And like our individual memories, our collective memory—our past and so our future—is not immutable. It may deteriorate over time, suffer neglect, become damaged and misshapen by trauma or tragedy. And what is history but an endless parade of trauma and tragedy? Over the centuries Edo has seen its share of horrors, perhaps more than its share, but the health of our city, the strength of our nation, depends upon remembering. We must not repress our collective memory, nor attempt to deny the past its place in our future. For in denying our history, we are denying ourselves, denying the very ground beneath our feet in this wonderful living history we call Tokyo."

Professor Kujima stopped reading and gingerly set the pages aside, a whisper of a smile beginning at the corners of his mouth and ending in the same place.

"Sounds good to me," I said.

"You flatter me."

"Not at all."

"The prose is a bit decorous, I think. Reads too much like a speech at some museum dedication," he said. Kujima drew his usual stern face, but I could tell underneath he was pleased. Sitting in the gloom of Hanran Books, I found the small joy he took in sharing his work achingly depressing. All those years of writing and research and his only audience was a gaijin who'd hit a dead end. I suppose nobody wound up in Hanran Books without hitting some kind of dead end, but I was starting to wonder if I'd come to the right place.

"In answer to your question," Kujima said, "there is, in fact, another Benzaiten Temple in Tokyo. Actually, there are many. Inokashira Park has a famous one—you may have heard the stories about young couples being warned not to visit the park together."

I hadn't heard the stories.

"You see, Benzaiten is said to be a very jealous goddess. Legend has it that a couple visiting the park together will meet a bad end. One of Japan's finest postwar novelists, Osamu Dazai, and his wife committed suicide by drowning themselves in the nearby Tama River, and some attribute their deaths to Benten's resentment of the writer's wife. But I believe the Benzaiten Temple you seek exists in a different part of the city. A different layer, so to speak. Due to our society's collective amnesia regarding certain aspects of history, most people have forgotten its existence. You can't look it up in the phone book and you won't locate it on any map. The Benzaiten Temple in Kyobashi exists in that layer of the city we call the past."

"Meaning it's gone?"

Kujima inhaled sharply, a pained look settling over his

features. "I'm sure you're familiar with the great dramatist who once said, 'The past is the prologue in all human affairs.'"

"Chikamatsu Monzaemon?"

"William Shakespeare, actually," Kujima said. "A genius of the theater, but not a very precise historian, I'm afraid. The word 'prologue' implies the past is something separate, something apart from the human drama rather than inherent in it. I believe this to be an oversimplification. I read you the introduction to my work not out of vanity, but in the hopes it might prevent you from falling prey to just such a false dichotomy. Perhaps my opening paragraphs need some revision, but my point is simply this: the past is never gone. And so, if history is ever-present, how can we say that those things which have become our past no longer exist?"

Professor Kujima may have known Tokyo on an intimate level, but the thought struck me that he and reality might barely be on speaking terms anymore. Maybe I was foolish for expecting a quick yes or no on Benzaiten Temple, because you don't get those kinds of answers from academics. Ask if they like mustard on their hot dogs, you get an earful of discourse on the semiotic presuppositions inherent in the term "hot dog."

"Let me rephrase the question," I said. "If I wanted to visit the Benzaiten Temple this afternoon, would I need a time machine or could I just take a taxi?"

Kujima chuckled. "As a historian, time travel is not really my field, except in, perhaps, the broad metaphorical sense. How, may I ask, did you learn of the Benzaiten Temple?"

"Long story."

"In a world of unending past, all stories are."

"Here's the short version," I said. "Pale guy in a white suit first said Benzaiten's name while I was having a seizure. Actually, he didn't say it, he spelled it out with ivory tiles. Then an old man crashing his wheelchair into a wall over and over said the monks of Benzaiten Temple were responsible for some very, very bad things. He also mentioned something about snakes and airplanes and horses and biscuits, so I thought the old guy might be out to sea. But the way this week is going, maybe not."

Kujima gave me a withering look from across the desk. I smiled back at him and shrugged. As a historian, he should've known I was telling the truth because the truth is almost never believable. I wasn't telling the whole truth, of course, but a historian should've known that no one ever does.

"Whatever the case," he said, "I'm glad you came to see me. I daresay the story of the Benzaiten Temple is a uniquely tragic illustration of so many of the forces at play during that dark time in my country's history. I am talking, of course, about the Fifteen Years war. The Greater East Asia War, the Pacific War, or as you say, World War Two."

"I'm guessing an American bomb destroyed the temple?"

"That would hardly make the story of Benzaiten Temple unique," Kujima said. "The 1945 firebombing raids destroyed nearly everything. It was a campaign of wholesale civilian mass murder that taught my country the United States was prepared to kill every Japanese man, woman, and child to secure victory. The atomic bombings of Nagasaki and Hiroshima, horrific as they were, were merely codas to a war already decided. I've studied enough American textbooks to know this isn't a view of the war you're probably familiar with."

I could've brought up things not typically covered in

Japanese textbooks, too—the rapes of Nanking, Hong Kong and Singapore, the Bataan Death March, Unit 731's biological warfare experiments on human guinea pigs in Manchuria, or the sexual enslavement of thousands of Koreans as "comfort women" for Japanese troops—except I wasn't there to debate who behaved worse in a war that had ended almost sixty years ago. But Professor Kujima's worldview of unending history meant the past was never over, and he was bent on demonstrating another one of his beliefs—that every story was necessarily a long one.

"Of course, I'm not blind to my country's own misdeeds," he continued, nodding his head earnestly. "Perhaps if I were more of a patriot and less of a scholar, I might still be teaching at Nihon University, soft-pedaling a sanitized, acceptable version of history."

Kujima might also still be at Nihon University if he'd kept his hands off his female students, but I kept the thought to myself. If he wanted to imagine his dismissal was political, so be it. Who was I to shatter an illusion he'd been so carefully nurturing for the last eleven years?

"The Ministry of Education doesn't recognize the existence of gray areas. They're interested only in teaching kids to be functional members of Japanese society. The university itself was no better, doing nothing to encourage freethinkers or true scholars. Their sole aim is to produce an army of privileged bureaucrats and elite businessmen to lord over an apathetic populace motivated entirely by consumerist impulses."

His tone was quiet and measured and completely shot through with contempt. I'd been around professors enough to know when a lecture was coming on and if I didn't swing the conversation back now, I might not get another chance.

"But about this Benzaiten Temple . . ."

"A uniquely tragic occurrence," he said. "An act of super-
stition motivated by rational fear but executed with irrational
force. But to fully understand the confluence of events leading up to that fateful night in July so many years ago, it is
necessary to go back a little further. . . ."

Too late. The lecture had already started.

25

The Benzaiten
Temple Incident

NOVEMBER 1707

Mount Fuji erupts, blanketing Tokyo (then known as Edo) in volcanic ash. Shortly thereafter, two children playing on the bank of the Nihonbashi River discover a glassy black figurine in the shape of Benzaiten, perhaps the most beloved of the Seven Lucky Gods of Japan. This three-inch statuette is taken to the neighborhood priest, who, after consulting local artisans, declares the obsidian figurine could not have been crafted by human hands, but has miraculously sprung from the molten depths of Mount Fuji, an especially odd occurrence given that Benzaiten is traditionally associated with water. Nevertheless, a temple is built on the site to house the sacred idol and honor the goddess Benzaiten.

During the next two hundred and thirty some years, the small Benzaiten Temple becomes a popular place to visit for geisha, musicians, writers, gamblers and ordinary people making traditional New Years pilgrimages to temples devoted to each of the Seven Lucky Gods. Mount Fuji, it should be noted, has not erupted again since.

MARCH–MAY 1943

The United States and Japan have been officially at war since the Japanese attacked Pearl Harbor in 1941, the Year of the Snake. As the war in the Pacific rages on, the United States begins testing a new incendiary bomb called the M-69, the first weapon to use a jellylike gasoline substance the world will come to know as napalm. At the Dugway Proving Ground in Utah, twelve typical two-story Japanese wooden row houses are built with painstaking attention to detail. Authentic tatami mats prove difficult to manufacture on the mainland, so the mats are requisitioned from Japanese Americans living in Hawaii. Similarly, no native tree produces wood similar to those used in Japanese residential construction, forcing the testers to import Russian spruce from Siberia.

The Dugway tests prove Japanese cities are highly susceptible to the new napalm bombs for two reasons: (1) Japanese houses are constructed mostly of wood and paper, both highly flammable materials, and (2) urban residential areas in Japan are extremely congested, with rows of homes separated by streets often no more than eight feet wide, allowing flames to spread quickly.

Meanwhile, production gets under way on the B-29 airplane, the largest, most technologically advanced bomber the world has ever seen.

NOVEMBER 1944–JANUARY 1945

On November first, a lone B-29 appears thirty-two thousand feet over the skies of Tokyo. Publicly, the Imperial Headquarters assures Tokyo residents "there is no need of caution against future action of the enemy air force." Privately, air defense organizations expect heavy raids and tear down whole blocks to create fire safety lanes and prevent the spread of flames. Many children are evacuated from the city, sent to live with relatives or in orphanages in the countryside.

Later that month, B-29s stage a series of high-altitude attacks on Japanese industrial and military targets. The results are somewhat discouraging. Flying at safe heights makes hitting precise targets nearly impossible, but when the aircraft fly any lower, they suffer heavy casualties from newly modified Japanese "Baka" fighter planes designed to suicidally ram the undersides of the giant B-29s.

In January, napalm bombs miss their intended target and land on a subway station in Tokyo, killing over one thousand civilians. Fifteen bombers unload over Ginza and Nihonbashi, destroying much of the commercial district and the geisha quarters. No bombs land within several hundred feet of the Benzaiten Temple, despite its location in this "accidentally" targeted area.

Frustrated with the precision-bombing campaign, U.S. Army Air Force commanders commit to a new strategy: indiscriminate destruction of urban Japan.

MARCH 9–10, 1945

At eleven P.M. on a windy, mild spring night the air-raid sirens start wailing. This is the first nighttime raid the country has seen and their air defenses are caught unprepared. Radio Tokyo warns of a large enemy force headed toward the city, but no one—not the citizens on the ground, not the Japanese air defense forces, not the American B-29 pilots or their commanders back at base— no one has any idea of the magnitude of that which will occur in the next few hours.

The planes come in uncharacteristically low and the first bombs begin falling around midnight, creating a ring of fire that encircles much of the northeastern section of the city. The target perimeter thus

visually established, three hundred twenty-five
B-29s spend the next three plus hours unloading
their two-thousand-ton cargo of napalm over an
area populated by roughly two million people.

The winds prove a deadly ally to the Americans. Columns of flame spread every direction at
once, hungrily sucking the oxygen from the air and
creating fiery whirlwinds that rip through the city
like burning tornados. Flames arch into the sky, are
caught and carried by high winds, then descend
like lightning hundreds of feet away, where people
racing through the streets find their escape routes
suddenly blocked. Sparks swarm through the dry
air, nesting in people's hair and clothes. Flame-
retardant jackets bought by many Tokyoites in
preparation for such attacks prove useless against
the sticky napalm jelly. People fleeing from the
inferno find themselves suddenly in flames, as if
by spontaneous human combustion; women carrying babies on their backs reach safety only to discover their children dead or on fire.

Smaller blazes grow into larger ones and those
merge with still larger fires and in no time an
inferno is sweeping through the Fukagawa and
Asakusa wards, a working-class area bisected by
the Sumida River. Within an hour, untold numbers
of people are burned to death or asphyxiated in
their houses, on the streets, in schools and temples
and in dug-out air-raid shelters. Those who survive the firestorm's initial onslaught find themselves surrounded, trapped on all sides by walls of
flame and blinding smoke.

Panic ensues, and hundreds are trampled as they seek refuge in the tiny canals and waterways. Others seek shelter inside the Asakusa Kwannon Temple, a site that miraculously escaped the fires that swept through the city following the 1923 Kanto earthquake. The miracle, however, will not be repeated, as hundreds are burned alive inside the temple devoted to the Buddhist goddess of mercy.

As the noose of flame draws tighter, both banks of the Sumida River are soon overflowing with thousands of people desperately fighting for their lives. The weak and unlucky end up being shoved into the deep river. Despite the intense heat all around, it's March and the Sumida is still near freezing. Most drown and are swept away by the icy current. Forced even from the riverbanks by ever-encroaching flames, thousands jam the bridges and hundreds are crushed to death in the ensuing frenzy.

But those who survive the mass onslaught of human bodies are still not safe. Most of the bridges across the Sumida are constructed of iron and steel, and as the fire rages on and the heat intensifies the structures begin to glow red-hot. People are forced to leap into the water below, joining the stream of burned, drowned and just plain dead bodies already filling Tokyo's mightiest river.

Virtually everything inside the target perimeter is ash by morning and for the next week Tokyo is enshrouded in a blanket of smoke so thick that American reconnaissance pilots cannot fully assess the results of their mission. When the smoke finally clears, they find a couple dozen small factories and other minor military targets have been destroyed. At least 83,000 Tokyoites are dead—though later estimates place that number nearer 200,000, three times more than will later perish in the atomic blast at Hiroshima. Sixteen square miles of the capital city are flattened, one-quarter of the buildings in Tokyo are in ruins, and over one million people are homeless.

Fires have swept the city many times in its history, so often that they became referred to as the "Flowers of Edo," but none claimed as many lives in a mere twenty-four hours. Emperor Hirohito hears muted reports of the destruction and wishes to leave his palace to see the damage for himself, but his advisors will not allow him outside the castle moat for ten days. Police, firefighters, civil defense forces and volunteers are mobilized to dispose of the dead bodies clogging the waterways and making the eastern streets impassable. Most of the dead are gathered and incinerated or dumped in mass graves.

One faint glimmer of hope emerges from the rubble: the flames have miraculously stopped outside the gates of the Benzaiten Temple in Kyobashi. A photograph from the *Mainichi Shimbun* reveals the tiny building jutting from the charred landscape, standing alone against the flattened horizon as if it had suddenly sprung from the earth. This photograph does not go unnoticed by Lieutenant General Okada, a high-ranking member of the First Imperial Guard. He cuts it from the paper and keeps it in his office as a rare symbol of hope in a war that is increasingly bleak.

APRIL 1945

Roughly two million survivors have fled the city following the March slaughter. Tokyo experiences two more raids in the middle of April, aimed at industrial and military areas toward the north, and another eleven square miles of the city are destroyed. Similar destruction is wrought on Kobe, Nagoya, and Osaka before B-29s temporarily suspend urban bombing to support the invasion of Okinawa.

Seizing on the sole positive piece of good news in the devastated capital, those Tokyo papers still operational publish several stories about the "Miracle of Benzaiten." The legend of the temple spreads throughout Tokyo and thousands flock to the temple to pray and hundreds left homeless by the air raids begin setting up camp outside the temple gates, believing Benzaiten will protect them in the event of further attacks. One such visitor is a young man named Takahashi. He comes not as a pilgrim but as a spy for the dreaded Kempeitai—the fanatical military police force responsible for ruthlessly suppressing any criticism of the war effort during the last fifteen years.

MAY 1945

On the twenty-third of May, the U.S. Army Air Force once again assaults the imperial capital, shifting their target area south to Tokyo Bay. Five hundred fifty-eight B-29s take part in the mission, the most that will fly against Japan during the war.

The B-sans return two nights later, this time over the heart of central Tokyo and the affluent suburbs to the west. Winds again conspire against the homeland, whipping up a firestorm. Though this wealthy area is not as densely packed as the neighborhoods targeted in March, thousands of lives are lost and important buildings destroyed. The War Ministry, the Navy Ministry, the Army General Staff Headquarters, the prime minister's official residence and the war minister's official residence are ruined. The Yasukuni Shrine, honoring Japan's rapidly increasing number of war dead, catches fire. Elsewhere in the city, sixty-two American POWs shot down during previous B-29 raids are left to roast alive inside their prison cells, a fate their captors must see as poetic justice.

Though American bomber pilots have been ordered to spare the Imperial Palace, even it is not safe from the surrounding blazes. As the fires spread, flames leap across the moat and land on the roof. The ancient cypress acts as kindling and in no time the front structure of the palace is aflame. Under orders from Lieutenant General Okada, Imperial Guards detonate TNT charges in the hallway linking the front structure to the rear of the palace, where the emperor and his family are bunkered underground. When that attempt to create a firebreak fails, they launch a quixotic attack on the connecting passage with sledgehammers, shovels, crowbars, their fists. Imperial troops haul out truckloads of the emperor's possessions as the flames spread and firefighters pump gallons of water into the rear palace to prevent them spreading further. Four hours later, the blaze dies out, but not before severely damaging the main palace structures and claiming the lives of thirty-four imperial retainers and members of the Imperial Guard.

Meanwhile, three M-69 napalm bombs smash through the roof of the Benzaiten Temple. All three fail to detonate.

JUNE 1945

Tokyo is effectively paralyzed. Electricity is in short supply, roadways are severely damaged and subway and train lines mostly inoperative. Travel within the city is prohibited except for those going to and from work, but despite Imperial decrees ordering them to continue their labor, many don't bother or are too weak. The population is demoralized and on the brink of starvation. The U.S. Army Air Force is greatly satisfied with its campaign and, unbeknownst to the Japanese, scratches Tokyo from its list of suitable targets; there is nothing left worth destroying.

Even widespread hunger and travel prohibitions can't staunch the flow of visitors to the Ben-

zaiten Temple. The three undetonated napalm
bombs are put on display near the front of the temple as evidence of Benzaiten's power, and offerings
of scarce foodstuffs are made before the goddess by
people who are themselves dying from malnutri-
tion.

At the Imperial Palace, a meeting among household, government and military personnel is held to
discuss whether the royal family is still safe in
Tokyo in light of the recent palace fire. Some fear
the palace itself may be the next target, as it is one
of the few important buildings in Tokyo left standing. The possibility of moving the emperor to the
old capital city of Kyoto is discussed, as Kyoto is
the sole large city that has thus far been spared
American bombing. Others worry this omission
only means Kyoto will be next.

No consensus is reached. In frustration, Lieutenant General Okada first broaches the subject of
the Benzaiten Temple and its small black idol. As
a bleak joke, he wonders aloud if the tiny figurine
could be requisitioned and placed on palace
grounds to protect the imperial family. But after fifteen years of war, no one in the room can even recognize a joke. Far from eliciting the grim chuckles
he'd expected, his proposition is taken at face
value.

It is especially favored by the head of the Kempeitai, who has brought a report on the Benzaiten
phenomenon prepared by his sharpest and most
spirited young charge, an officer named Takahashi.
In Takahashi's view, the cult of Benzaiten repre-

sents a threat from within to his Imperial Majesty's authority. The monks who run the temple should be asked to surrender the idol and, should they refuse, be executed as traitors to the imperial line unbroken over time immemorial and to His Majesty's destiny to bring the eight corners of the world under a single roof.

Though Okada will not survive the war, from his journal we know the lieutenant general is extremely careful in wording his discouragement to the head of the Kempeitai. Okada hints that taking the idol away from the temple may harm precious public sentiment needed to muster His Majesty's loyal one hundred million to fight to the death should the Americans invade. By now, anyone with a shred of sanity left realizes the war is already lost, but publicly doubting Japan's certain victory is harboring a "defeatist attitude" and is grounds for treason. Many men had been beaten, imprisoned, executed or outright murdered for less, a fact that would not be lost on the lieutenant.

After some discussion, it is decided that his Imperial Majesty shall remain on the palace grounds for the time being. A consensus between the Imperial Household authorities and the military commanders is finally reached; the idol is to remain inside the Benzaiten Temple.

JULY 1945

But as they have done countless times in the past, the Kempeitai ignores political consensus

and acts on its own volition. A second report from
Officer Takahashi says the head priest of Benzaiten
Temple is telling those gathered at the temple that
he has been visited by the goddess Benzaiten
while in meditation. Benzaiten has told him that
peace will soon be at hand, and has instructed him
to preach that his followers not fear the months
ahead.

Enraged by these reports, a general of the Kempeitai declares the idol property of His Imperial
Majesty the Emperor, and Takahashi is ordered by
his superiors to requisition the idol at all costs.
(Perhaps as a sign that some shadow of reasoning
ability still lingers amidst their general hysteria,
none of the Kempeitai consider for a moment that
Benzaiten could have been predicting peace
through victory rather than defeat.)

Accounts vary widely as to what happens next.
This much is known:

Officer Takahashi arrives at the temple with a
force of between twenty and thirty armed men
and demands to speak with the head priest. The
priest invites Takahashi into the inner hall of the
temple. They drink tea and Takahashi delivers
the ultimatum—the priest must surrender the
Benzaiten idol or face arrest. He gives the priest
one hour to decide, then goes outside the temple
to wait. Approximately forty minutes later, smoke
is seen billowing from the entrance of the temple.

Some eyewitnesses gathered outside the temple
claim the Kempeitai set fire to the structure to
flush out the priest and the three monks dwelling

within. Some even claim the three undetonated American M-69s outside the temple spontaneously exploded, showering the sacred grounds with napalm. Given what happened next, the most credible claim is that the priest and his acolytes set the fire themselves in an act of self-immolation.

Whatever the case, the Benzaiten Temple, the sacred building that miraculously survived so many American attacks, is soon in flames. The Kempeitai troops stand dumbfounded as a raving, hysterical Officer Takahashi suddenly charges inside the burning structure. A few of the braver men come to their senses or perhaps leave their senses and run in after him. They emerge from the temple moments later, gasping, choking, and carrying an unconscious Takahashi in their arms.

The temple collapses almost the instant they drag him to safety. The priest and three monks inside are burned to death or die of smoke inhalation. The next morning their charred, blackened bodies are found unmoved, sitting cross-legged on the floor, as if still in meditation. Officer Takahashi is lucky, suffering only severe burns on his right hand, which is later amputated. The Benzaiten idol is not found among the wreckage. Like so many things lost during the war, it is never to be recovered.

26

Black Skies over Tokyo

August 1945," said Kujima, wiping his glasses against the ribbed fabric of his corduroy jacket and replacing them on the bridge of his nose. Before he could resume speaking the fluorescent track lights inside Hanran Books began to flicker and then went out completely. The sudden darkness was disorienting. I hadn't glanced at my watch in hours, but it must have been nearly six judging from the fading, rust-colored sunlight trickling in through the display windows.

"Forgive the interruption," grumbled Kujima. "The lights

will be back on momentarily. Just a little reminder of sorts from the good people at the electric company. Seems there has been a misunderstanding regarding my account. The darkness shouldn't last long."

Hanran Books was even worse off than I thought. I told him to go on with his story.

"August 1945," he repeated. "Well, I suppose everybody knows what happened in August 1945. Hiroshima, Nagasaki, the atomic bomb, the emperor's famous radio broadcast and Japan's inevitable surrender. If stories must artificially conclude, this is where the tale of the Benzaiten Temple ends. For unlike many of the temples and shrines around the city, it was never rebuilt following the war. Perhaps this is because with the idol's disappearance there was no longer a purpose for the temple. But I believe it had little to do with the missing idol. I believe the memories surrounding the Benzaiten Temple's rather unique destruction were just too painful to revisit. Rebuilding the monument would only make people remember, and people wanted to forget. Just as they wished to forget so many things about Japan during the war."

"Was this Officer Takahashi ever brought to trial?" I asked.

Even through the dark I could see Kujima smirk.

"On what charges?" he said. "Crimes against humanity? Destroying a cultural treasure? Murdering innocent civilians? By the same logic, occupational forces would have had to prosecute their own generals as war criminals! No, Colonel Takahashi was never tried. In fact, no ranking member of the Kempeitai was ever indicted by the Tokyo war crimes tribunal, because their brand of terror was primarily domestic, inflicted mostly on fellow Japanese. The Kempeitai and those who systematically eradicated any resistance to the war effort would seem largely responsible for the atrocities which followed, but . . ." Kujima trailed off with a sigh long and deep enough to stir the worn papers on his desk.

"So what happened to Takahashi after the war?"

"History doesn't tell us," said Kujima. "After surrender was announced, the skies over Tokyo were black with smoke for three days. Not from American bombs this time, but from military and government officials trying to burn as many records as possible before General MacArthur and his troops arrived."

"Covering their asses."

"And their assets," Kujima said. "Untold billions in gold, platinum, diamonds, jewels were looted from the Asian continent over a period of fifteen years. To this day, no one knows how much was taken or where it all ended up. The years immediately following surrender were utterly chaotic. Six million Japanese troops and POWs were stranded overseas and had to be repatriated, a few million in the ruined cities were homeless, many thousands of children were orphaned. Some were reduced to a molelike existence, living in the underground tunnels of subway stations. The threat of starvation was very real, and the only place you could buy food was at the black markets, which were all controlled by gangs and former military types. Many survived only by eating a thin rice gruel mixed with sawdust. Bleak, despairing times."

The overhead lights suddenly blinked back on and Kujima squinted, sucking in air through his teeth. The light didn't bring much cheer into Hanran Books. Chinese acrobats, fireworks, and one of those dancing dragons might do the trick, but all electricity did was illuminate the gloom.

"At any rate," Kujima continued, "Takahashi ranks as nothing more than a footnote. A minor figure playing a minor role in a time judged best forgotten. I doubt anyone really cared what happened to the man in 1945, and certainly no one does now. Except, oddly enough, you, it seems."

I pretended not to notice the curious look he was giving me and asked another question. "What about that Okada guy?" I said. "The Imperial Guard who tried to talk them out of taking the idol. You said he didn't outlive the war?"

Kujima nodded. "Lieutenant General Okada of the First Imperial Guard was assassinated on the eve of Japan's surrender after refusing to take part in a military coup d'etat. Some of the more hysterical generals would not accept defeat and wished to overthrow the emperor and fight to the bitter end. Happily, the coup failed, and those involved protected their honor through ritual suicide."

Suicide. It took that word to fully bring me back to the present. Sitting in a stiff chair in the airless bookstore all afternoon, listening to Kujima lecture about M-69 this and B-29 that and how many square miles had been destroyed here and how many people had died there—my brain was so scrambled I'd nearly forgotten why I'd come. Could all this ugliness back in 1945 really have anything to do with a young woman found drowned under the highway three days ago and a Ministry of Construction official dead in his carp pool just this morning?

Well, let's see.

According to Detective Ihara, Bojangles had said the name Nakodo was made up. It was being used by Old Man Nakodo to disguise his wartime past as a man named Takahashi. The Man in White had mentioned Benzaiten. More importantly, Old Man Nakodo himself had said the Benzaiten monks killed his son. I'd thought he was talking nonsense. I still thought so, but not the way I had before.

The Benzaiten monks hadn't killed Old Man Nakodo's son, because they were long dead. They were dead because Old Man Nakodo had killed them sixty years ago, and somebody named Bojangles knew about it. Maybe he'd been blackmailing the family, threatening to expose their secret. But if so, how did Miyuki fit in? The key, of course, was still finding out who the mysterious Bojangles was, and whether he was in fact the Man in White. Without knowing that, guessing at a motive was like playing charades blindfolded.

"Is everything all right, Mr. Chaka?" Kujima asked.

"Just thinking, Professor," I said.

"You look troubled."

"Thinking will do that," I said. "Make my life a whole lot easier if I quit. But you know how it is. You start when you're young, don't know any better. It becomes a habit and next thing you know it's twenty years later and you can't stop."

Kujima smiled. "Wasn't it an American who said, 'the unexamined life is not worth living'?"

"Wasn't this American," I said, returning his smile. "And anyway, that was before television. Professor Kujima, who else would know about what you just told me? About the Benzaiten Temple incident and Officer Takahashi of the Kempeitai and all that jazz."

He held his chin between finger and thumb and thought for a moment. "Impossible to say," he said at length. "The stories about the incident at the time were heavily censored. Newspaper accounts make no mention of the Kempeitai, of course, only reporting that a fire had unfortunately destroyed the temple. Today, the incident isn't what you'd call general knowledge, but it's hardly a secret, either. There have been various journal articles, and I believe there may even have been a book planned about it several years ago, but a right-wing group stopped its publication."

"So you're saying the Benzaiten Temple incident is the kind of thing somebody could just find out about at the library or on the Internet or wherever?"

"I don't see why not. As a historian, you soon learn even the most obscure facts aren't so difficult to find if you're willing to work. Putting them together in a way that makes sense, that's the challenge."

Tell me about it, I thought.

The lights started flickering again and Kujima cursed under his breath. I told him I ought to be going, and he came around the desk and guided me past the piles of books and to the doorway. As he held the door open for me, I thanked him for his help. He seemed genuinely pleased, like it'd been a long time since anyone had thanked him for anything. The lights strobed for a few more seconds and then the store went dark.

27

The Six Bridges
of Recovery

A crumbling concrete staircase overrun with weeds led up the hill to the Yanaka Cemetery southwest of Nippori station. The top of the hill afforded a view out over the lattice-work of railway tracks separating the residential side of Nippori from the business and entertainment district beyond, while the darkening skyline across the sunken valley was dominated by blocky buildings and signs advertising love hotels like the Hotel Care, the Hotel Esteem and the Hotel Papion.

Strolling through the area behind the ancient hilltop graveyard was like going back in time. Traditional wooden houses slung with low tiled roofs lined the narrow streets, and after Kujima's horror story that afternoon it was easy to picture the whole area in flames. Were it not for the tangled power cables above and the satellite dishes sprouting mushroomlike from many buildings' corners, it could have been the Tokyo of one hundred years ago, before American napalm bombs leveled the city and the forces of global capitalism rebuilt it as a futuristic shopping mall run amok. Here in Yanaka, I'd walked into one of Kujima's layers of the past, a past that was never really gone.

A quick glance at the evening papers at the Nippori train station told me news of Nakodo's death hadn't hit yet, but once it did I imagined all hell would break loose. The weeklies reporters would doubtlessly descend upon the Kitazawa family, asking all kinds of questions, intimating some sort of family curse and who knows what else. I'd lost precious hours listening to Kujima's wartime history lesson, but I'd gained precious information, too. If I could beat the scandalmongers to the Kitazawa family, I might gain more.

But that was looking less likely to happen with every step I took. I wandered in circles and took so many twists and turns that within a matter of minutes I was thoroughly lost. Just when I figured I was never going to find the place, suddenly it was right in front of me, almost where I'd started. A sixtyish man in a pale green fisherman's hat, dirty undershirt and chinos was emptying a battered watering can into a potted plant out in front of the house. He looked fit for his age but his gaunt face had hardship etched into its very lines. Our eyes met and he offered me a laconic smile. I knew right then he hadn't heard about his former son-in-law's death. Not yet.

"Good afternoon, sir," I said, bowing extra low. "Forgive me for bothering you during this busy time, but are you Mr. Kitazawa?"

He looked me up and down then answered a terse yes.

"I apologize for arriving unannounced," I said. "But I have a rather urgent matter to discuss with you. It concerns your daughter."

"I have no daughter," he said in gravelly voice.

"With all due respect, sir, I believe you do," I said. "One who met with an unfortunate accident many years ago. I was hoping to speak with you about her, if it is not too much trouble. Again, I regret imposing upon you."

Mr. Kitazawa stared at me, his weathered face displaying an utter lack of emotion. Then he turned away and began watering the potted plant again. I remained on the street, head slightly bowed as if I were attending a funeral. When the pot began overflowing, Kitazawa set the can down on the pavement. A gray cat came padding through a nearby alley and threw her arched body against Mr. Kitazawa's legs. He leaned over to pet the animal, then stood upright and looked me up and down again. The cat rubbed itself against his legs a few more times then trotted off and disappeared back into the alley.

"Who are you?" Kitazawa said.

"My name is Billy Chaka. I'm a reporter for an American magazine. You probably haven't heard of it. In fact, I'm sure you've never heard of it, but I'm not really here on magazine business."

"You're here to discuss . . ." Mr. Kitazawa stared at the ground, unable to speak his daughter's name. After a moment he resumed in a throaty whisper. "I don't understand. What is it you want from me?"

For about ten seconds I racked my brain for some kind of lie I could tell him to explain why after twenty-four years an American reporter would come around asking the circumstances of his daughter's death, but nothing I could think of was plausible. Finally, I just decided to tell the truth. I told him about how I'd been summoned to Nakodo's place and had been told that Nakodo's daughter was missing. I told him how she'd turned up dead, and how it turned out she wasn't his daughter but his mistress.

I told Mr. Kitazawa how Miyuki looked a lot like his own daughter. How she'd died mysteriously, drowned just like his daughter Ame. How there were intimations that Old Man Nakodo may have been involved with some ugly business during World War II. Finally, I went ahead and told him that Nakodo had been discovered dead that very morning. I didn't say it was me who did the discovering.

He didn't so much as glance at me the whole time I was speaking, but instead let his eyes gaze into the middle distance. The sun had disappeared entirely now and the sky had grown so dark I could only see the outline of his features.

"Get out of here," he spoke in a low voice.

"Mr. Kitazawa—"

"Go away from my home and never return."

"I understand your feelings—"

No sooner had the words escaped my lips than Kitazawa snatched up his water can and emptied it across my face with a single motion. The liquid hit me with a cold blast and my head shot back involuntarily.

"You understand nothing," he said, hand shaking as he

placed his now-empty container back on the ground. "Leave before I am forced to call the authorities."

I'd had pretty much every variety of liquid thrown in my face over the years, but it was usually women doing the throwing. I was afraid something like this might happen, and all things considered it could have been much worse. On a hot night like this, the water was actually kind of refreshing.

"Good night," I said. "I'm sorry to have upset you."

I could feel Mr. Kitazawa's eyes upon me as I walked away.

THE NIGHT AIR WAS thick and the moon looked immense as it rose almost dripping above the jagged horizon. Hard to believe it was the same moon that had been running around our troubled little planet for all these years. Tonight the moon looked freshly scrubbed, radiant, optimistic. Pretty much the opposite of everything I felt. I hadn't gone twenty-five yards from the house when I heard a voice call out behind me.

"Please wait," said the voice.

I stopped to see a woman trailing after me. She was wiry, somewhere in her sixties and so small she seemed to hug the earth as she came hurrying toward me. The woman spared a single glance over her shoulder at her darkened house before latching on to my arm and pulling me into a side street bathed in shadows. Her eyes shone bright and hard through the dark.

"Forgive my husband," she said. "He becomes easily upset."

"It's all right," I said. "I can understand."

"Maybe you can't," said Mrs. Kitazawa. "If you understood, you wouldn't have come. You wouldn't have spoken about Ame. I heard everything."

"Please forgive me."

"No matter," she said. "We're not uncivilized people, my husband and I. I hope that's not the impression he's given. My husband is a good man, but perhaps he is not so strong anymore. He's been strong long enough. She was our only child, you know."

I pursed my lips and slowly nodded. Mrs. Kitazawa glanced once more in the direction of her home, wisps of silver hair showing under the moonlight. "Come with me," she said, pulling me back onto the main street, out of the shadows.

We walked in silence past the Tennoji Temple and to a nearby vest-pocket park that was mostly a patchwork of coppery dust and withered grass. It was only about the size of a basketball court, but canopied as it was by a dense thicket of trees, the park seemed somehow much larger in the failing light. Two or three fireflies danced a few feet above the ground. Used to be you saw fireflies everywhere on summer nights, but they were disappearing with the vegetation. Catching and studying them was still a popular summer-vacation assignment for elementary schoolers, though now most kids had to resort to buying them prepackaged at the store. The park was also occupied by a homeless man squatting on a piece of cardboard and listening to a baseball game through a beat-up radio, and a youngish guy on a bench across the way quietly running scales on a clarinet. Mrs. Kitazawa guided me to another bench in a corner of the park overlooking the steep grassy slope above the train station. A JR train clattered over the tracks below, its mute passengers a mass of huddled dark forms against the spectral interior lights of the trains.

"You wish to know about Ame?" she asked.

I nodded. She took a deep breath.

"Ame was very beautiful," Mrs. Kitazawa began. "Even as a little girl. And quite intelligent, too. My husband and I sensed there was something special about her, though all parents believe there is something special about their children. As it should be. We named her Ame because she was born during the rainy season. The night she was born it was pouring, just absolutely pouring. I still remember the rain drumming against the hospital windows, the sound it made. July third, 1958. She would have been forty-three years old only a few days ago."

Mrs. Kitazawa closed her eyes for a moment, then resumed.

"She met Nakodo through my elder brother," she said. "In those days, it wasn't so common for young people to meet on their own, though even then things were changing, as it seems they always are. My brother, you see, worked with Mr. Nakodo's father at his construction company, before Nakodo's father joined the Oshoku Group. Ame and Mr. Nakodo went on some dates, chaperoned of course, and we met the family. It wasn't long before Nakodo asked my husband for Ame's hand in marriage. My husband was very excited at the prospect. As was my brother. The Nakodos were a very rich family, very powerful, you understand. Frankly, we were greatly surprised the Nakodos didn't wish to solidify their position by arranging a marriage with another powerful family in the construction industry. Perhaps this should have been interpreted as a bad sign, but at the time, my family thought the marriage could be a great blessing for the Kitazawas."

"What did Ame think?"

"What did Ame think?" Mrs. Kitazawa echoed. "I often

wonder. She was, I believe, a difficult person to understand this way. There was something . . . unknowable about her. I believe she often kept her true feelings hidden even from herself. Even I, her own mother, found it difficult to discover what she was feeling much of the time. I asked her, of course, whether she was ready for marriage at the tender age of seventeen. And I let her know that in the end, no matter what her uncle and her father said, no matter what obligations she felt toward the family, in the end it was her life. I think I quite surprised her in saying that. In some respects, Ame was more old-fashioned than her mother."

Mrs. Kitazawa smiled sadly and a crow swooped down and landed on a trash can not three feet away. It cocked its head, cawed at us as if trying to chase us off. Mrs. Kitazawa curled her fist and threatened the bird with an imaginary stone, sending it beating its black wings and disappearing somewhere in the trees above.

"Did she have any other suitors?" I asked.

"There were other boys, certainly," Mrs. Kitazawa resumed. "As I said, Ame was smart, beautiful. But there were no serious rivals for her affection. If affection is really what she felt for Nakodo. But she did marry him, and for a time they seemed happy. He was very much in love with her, that much was obvious to all, and he treated her well. How he doted on that girl, showering her with the kinds of gifts she could hardly imagine growing up in a simple household like ours. I admit it made me feel very happy. Perhaps that is foolish, who can say? As for Ame's feelings, like I said, she was a difficult person to understand in such ways. But she did not seem *unhappy*, certainly. Not at first."

"Forgive my interrupting," I said. "But did you investigate the Nakodo family background before agreeing to the marriage?"

"Of course," she answered. "Of course. But maybe, I think, we didn't go about it the way we should have. Not that things would have turned out any differently, but, well, hindsight. My brother took care of the investigation. He hired a reputable firm to look into the matter. But of course, this firm also listed the Oshoku Group as one of its chief clients. I believe you understand what I'm saying?"

I nodded. Kitazawa looked away, returning her stoic gaze to the valley below.

"After about five or six months, something inside Ame began to change," said Mrs. Kitazawa. "Her energy, her spirit seemed to wane, almost imperceptibly at first. Her father and I still saw her often then, on Sundays usually, and though it took us some time to discern this subtle change, after a while there was no denying that she was different. We figured perhaps she was just getting used to married life, becoming accustomed to the duties of being a wife, the responsibility of running a household. Simply growing up, perhaps. Maybe we should have suspected the true depth of her melancholy earlier, maybe there might've been something we could have done. But we had no reason to believe she was truly suffering and were slow in realizing what was happening to her. Neither my husband's family nor my own had any history of such difficulties."

As she looked up, the moon reflected in her eyes, painting their centers a big luminous yellow like the eyes of a cat. The clarinet player across the park hit a sour note, started his scale over from the beginning.

"Ame grew sick," she resumed. "Her mind was agitated. But what could we do? We lacked the language to even discuss such things. Besides, my husband and my brother feared that her condition would cause a scandal. As did, I imagine, the Nakodos. Well, Ame visited doctors. Many doctors, very discreetly. They tried to treat her, focusing on the physical manifestations of these perturbations, but they proved no help in even stopping the fits."

"Fits," I said. "What sort of fits?"

Mrs. Kitazawa searched for the right words. "Like trembling. Convulsions, or seizures I suppose you'd call them. The poor girl. She would thrash about wildly, or simply remain locked in twisted shapes, her muscles rigid, tensed. Often these episodes would last several hours, after which she would sleep and sleep, utterly exhausted. None of the doctors had ever seen anything like it, and they worried she might even die from the physical exertion, from the stress of these prolonged fits. But what worried me was the hallucinations."

I had a horrible feeling I knew what Kitazawa was going to say next. Sweat rolled down my back and my mouth was suddenly dry and the hot night air was only partially to blame.

"My daughter said that during these episodes, she would imagine a man dressed entirely in white," Mrs. Kitazawa said. "Sometimes he would appear with other men, sometimes alone. He would never talk, she said, yet somehow he communicated with her. Unspeakable, the things this figure would tell her."

Mrs. Kitazawa literally shuddered at the memory, but she seemed determined to go on. I had the feeling she'd never told anyone exactly what had happened to her daughter, and I had the feeling she'd been waiting to for a long, long time. That it happened to be me was purely accidental, maybe, or maybe it wasn't.

"At first, this figure appeared only during the fits," continued Kitazawa. "But soon she imagined him even when she wasn't having these spells. She would see this apparition more and more regularly, and was by this point quite, well, quite confused. The doctors, the Nakodo family, my husband and I—we told her over and over that she was imagining this man, that these hallucinations were merely part of her disease. And outwardly, she would agree, would acknowledge that it was all in her mind. But looking back now, I think she said these things to placate us. I've often thought about this hallucination of hers, this man dressed in white. And I think the thought of him being imaginary was perhaps more frightening than the idea that he was real. To her, I mean. For if he were a product of her own mind, how could she ever get rid of him? By then she'd visited enough doctors to know they couldn't help. I think the more we tried to convince her that this figure was unreal, something she imagined, the more she clung to the idea that he was real. She had to believe, deep down, that he was something, someone outside of herself. But in the weeks before her death, she suddenly stopped speaking about the figure in white. In fact, she seemed to recover almost completely. She suffered no more fits, began gaining weight back. She appeared to be her old self again, if a shade paler."

Across the park, the man with the clarinet stopped playing. Mrs. Kitazawa waited as he packed up his instrument and made his way out of the tree-enclosed space and onto the dimly lit street. We were alone now save for the homeless man and his radio. Another train pulled up to the station below and Mrs. Kitazawa resumed her story.

"The boating trip was Mr. Nakodo's idea," she said. "An excursion to get her out of the house, out into the fresh air. She seemed ready, and even greeted the idea with some enthusiasm, I'm told. It was just a short sightseeing trip past the Six Bridges of Recovery—less than an hour on the Sumida, from

Asakusa to the Hamarikyu Gardens, the emperor's duck-
hunting grounds downstream. There were some sixty people
on board, mostly out-of-town tourist groups. From all reports,
Ame behaved perfectly normally in the hours before it happened, so perhaps I can't blame Mr. Nakodo for not being
watchful. And I don't, really. He loved her deeply, of that much
I am sure. And he must really have believed that she was
cured, that she had gotten better. At some point during the trip,
she wandered toward the rear of the vessel to get a picture of
the Kiyosu Bridge as the boat passed beneath it. Nakodo
looked away for just a moment. When he looked back . . ."

Mrs. Kitazawa's voice faltered, the words wavered and
stopped. I gave her a moment to compose herself. The moon
had climbed higher in the sky now and looked smaller, less
impressive and somehow less real. The fireflies glowed inter-
mittently from the far side of the park, rising and falling but
never leaving their safe corner.

"Nobody saw it happen," she resumed. "Almost everyone
was looking the other direction, toward some feature the tour
guide was talking about over the public-address system. And
maybe she didn't jump, maybe it really was an accident. For
many years I wanted to believe it was so."

"But now you think differently?"

She considered. "Now I think it makes no difference."

The massive crow landed on the trash can again, hopping
across the rim and bobbing its beady-eyed black head. Mrs.
Kitazawa ignored it this time, still staring in the distance
below. I tried shooing the crow away, but it only leapt from
the trash can and landed near my feet, cawing once and kicking up dust as it hopped across the ground.

"I have nothing against Nakodo or his father," Mrs.
Kitazawa said. "There was nothing they could have done.

Still, after the funeral my husband and I never saw them again. It was just too difficult. I am sorry to hear Mr. Nakodo has died. And I am sorry for this young woman, whoever she is. But it really has nothing to do with us any longer."

"I understand," I said. "But Nakodo's death leaves behind a lot of questions. It looks like he may have been murdered."

"Those questions are for somebody else," she said. "I am through asking questions in this life. In each other, my husband and I found the strength to carry on, to endure the unendurable. And now I've become an old woman, and my husband has become an old man and there is nothing more this world has to teach us. The time we have left we wish to spend in peace and quiet. Please respect our wishes. Do not visit us again."

"Of course," I said. "But I should warn you. Once the press gets wind of Nakodo's murder, which should be about any minute now, they're going to be looking for any angle they can find. You and your husband may want to leave town for a while until it blows over."

Mrs. Kitazawa rose slowly from the bench and looked down at me with amusement bordering on pity. "I don't imagine the press will bother us. You underestimate the influence of the Nakodo family, perhaps. I wish you a good night."

As she made her way out of the park, another crow landed at my feet, and then a third roosted on the trash can. I tried the imaginary rock trick, but it was no good. It was clear they wouldn't tolerate my presence any longer. I waited until Mrs. Kitazawa was safely out of sight then rose and headed out of the park. I passed the Yanaka Cemetery on the way down the hill to Nippori station, the loose wooden memorial tablets rattling like bones in the breeze. Which was funny, because I sure didn't feel any breeze.

28

Let's Fuzzy Logic

Outside Shibuya station kids fiddled with their hair and their cell phones while across the intersection a panorama of monstrous video screens flashed high-wattage advertisements into the night sky. The ads were inhuman in scale, so big and bright you could probably see them from distant galaxies. Maybe they weren't for promoting pop idols, Sony PSII games, Pocari Sweat soda, Fujifilm, and Kool cigarettes at all, but were secret SOS signals blinked to the deepest reaches of outer space. Sad, desperate pleas to an unseen alien race to come down and save us or enslave us or do something before we amused ourselves straight into oblivion.

I sat waiting near a statue of a dog named Hachiko. Hachiko, the story goes, would walk his master to the station every day, then wait patiently outside the station until his master returned from work. One day, Hachiko's master happened to die while at his job, but the dog remained outside the station, day after day, year after year, waiting for his master to return. Hachiko became famous, and when he died a statue was erected to commemorate his loyalty. Now it was a favored meeting place for the hip young crowd who made the glowing valley of Shibuya their nighttime playground.

I wasn't as patient as Hachiko, and I couldn't wait for Afuro to show up so I could get out of there. Shibuya had been so beautiful, so young and so lively in the old days, the days when I'd first come to Japan in search of youth trends. And now? Shibuya was still beautiful, young and lively and nothing had changed except maybe me.

Across the plaza, a cop eyed me suspiciously from his little *koban*. He kept staring at me, as if waiting for me to approach the miniskirted clusters of frosty-haired, fake-tanned teenagers and propose a little something illegal. Cop probably thought all the adults in Shibuya had Lolita complexes and all the kids were oversexed juvenile delinquents, making him and Hachiko the respectable citizens in the valley.

The Pink Panther theme started chiming from out of nowhere while two blonde girls in matching, carefully torn T-shirts that read LET'S FUZZY LOGIC sat across the bench smiling at me. I smiled back. The song kept playing, the girls' smiles grew wider and brighter. I started wondering if they were shrooming—despite Japan's tough antidrug stance a legal loophole permitted their sale and they were available in headshops all over Shibuya. Finally their grins made me uncomfortable enough to speak.

"Sure wouldn't mind a little rain, huh?" I said.

"I think your phone is ringing," one of the girls said.

I'd forgotten all about the damn thing. Sure enough. They both tried to contain their laughter as I took the little pink device from the shirt pocket and checked the digital display screen. NOGUCHI, AFURO read the caller ID. The laughter escaped from the fuzzy logic twins despite their best efforts.

"Moshi moshi," I said into the phone.

"What took you so long?"

"Hello to you, too. You're late. Where are you?"

"I thought something must've happened to you! Why didn't you answer faster?"

"I'm a big Henry Mancini fan."

"You're what?"

"Henry Mancini. Guy who wrote the Pink Panther theme."

"What are you talking about? Forget it, I don't care."

"You'll never land a guy like Henry Mancini with phone manners like that."

"Just shut up a second and listen to me," she said, her voice hushed and urgent. "Can you hear me?"

I shut up and listened.

"It's Bojangles. He's following me. I wasn't sure it was him at first but I'm pretty damn sure now."

"Where are you?"

"Where you first saw me. Under the highway where Miyuki was found. I came here because, well, don't ask me why because I don't know why but I just had to. And this guy is just standing there on the bridge, looking into the water. And he sees me looking at him and right then I *just* know. I walk away, fast, and he starts following me. Billy, can you hear me?"

Underneath her voice I heard the muffled roar of cars racing by on the expressway above the Nihonbashi River. What was she doing all the way across town? We were supposed to meet here in Shibuya fifteen minutes ago. I said the same to her but she didn't seem to hear me.

"I know it's him. God, where the hell is everybody? It's like there's just *nobody* here. Billy, can you still hear me? Please don't hang up. Just stay on the line and talk to me until I get to the train station, okay? This is totally freaking me out. Can you hear me?"

"Afuro, call the police."

"Billy?" she said. "I can't hear you."

"Hang up, call the police and run. Yell, scream, make as much noise as you possibly can. Get away from the river and head toward Kanda or anywhere there are people. I'm not trying to frighten you, but this is no time to take chances. Call the police right now."

"I'm losing you," said Afuro.

Then the connection went dead.

I dialed her number as fast as I could.

Across the plaza the stoplights changed and hundreds of pedestrians poured into the crossing, a human tidal wave flowing through the intersection in every conceivable direction while above them the endless wall of video screens bombarded the crowd with light and sound. Meanwhile, the phone just rang and rang and rang.

WHEN AFURO DIDN'T ANSWER I called the police, pretending to be an eyewitness who'd just seen a man chasing a woman underneath Expressway Number 5 by the Nihonbashi River, not far, I told the dispatcher, from where that unfortunate girl was found a few days ago. The dispatcher asked if I could describe the pursuing man. No, I didn't get a good look at him, but he may have been wearing white. How about the woman then? Thin, maybe five feet two, short hair, wears duck-billed shoes, walks kinda funny. But you said she was running? Yeah, I meant she was running kinda funny. By funny you mean . . .? Like her knees were tied together with string. She's bound in string? No, she just runs like that. And what was she wearing? Didn't get a good look at her other than the shoes, I said, but probably something very colorful. Was the man carrying a weapon of any sort? I couldn't be sure. Was he acting in an intimidating or threatening manner? Yes, definitely very threatening and intimidating. Was the woman screaming or showing any signs of distress? I hoped so.

Unimpressed, the dispatcher told me she'd send someone from the Jimbocho police box to check it out right away and hung up the phone. I sat next to Hachiko for an hour, monitoring the exit of the Shibuya JR station, hoping against hope that Afuro would come pigeon-toeing across the plaza any moment and "Strangers in the Night" would start playing over my cell phone. Everything was fast-forward, like I was living in some time-lapse clip where the world rushed by in a jittery blur, with Hachiko and me the only stationary objects in the frame.

I ran everything through my mind, hoping I could discover some vital sign I'd overlooked. Miyuki has a seizure in a pachinko parlor. The Man in White shows up in my hotel room, doesn't say a word. Nakodo the Younger summons me to Ark Hills, tells me his daughter is missing. Miyuki drowns under the expressway. Detective Ihara tells me that a man named Bojangles approached him twenty-six years ago to stop a marriage, claiming Old Man Nakodo was in fact a guy called Officer Takahashi with a dark wartime past. Afuro tells me Miyuki was born and raised in a village called Muramura, so she can't be Nakodo's daughter. Then she drops a notebook with a single entry—the word "Miyuki" and a map to a hostess club in Ginza.

At Club Kuroi Kiri, Nakodo tells me a double lie, says his daughter has come home. The Man in White's goons blow smoke in my face, I have a seizure. The Man in White shows me a photograph of Nakodo and a woman with a mole—I first mistake the woman for Miyuki, but later understand the doppelganger is Nakodo's dead wife, Ame Kitazawa. The Man in White writes THE MAN IN THIS PHOTOGRAPH WILL JOIN US SOON. Also writes BENZAITEN SAYS TWO MORE WILL JOIN US.

Afuro whacks me in the head with a brick. Tells me her place has been trashed, tells me how a mysterious character named Bojangles paid her friend to grow her hair and wear certain clothes. Tells me Miyuki had a sugar daddy named Nakodo and how she was planning on leaving him and making lots of cash in the process.

I try to visit Nakodo and make him talk only to find somebody else has made sure that he never will. Old Man Nakodo is left unharmed, and as far as I can make out blames the monks from a Benzaiten temple.

Professor Kujima tells me the temple in question was burned down nearly sixty years ago by a man named Officer Takahashi who was requisitioning a sacred idol to protect the emperor. Ame Kitazawa, who drowned twenty-four years ago, has also had seizures, has also seen the Man in White. Afuro spots a man she believes to be Bojangles, the man follows her, and then . . .

And then here I was. Nothing to do but hope. Wait and think and hope Afuro was all right. And no matter how many times I laid the facts out in my head, I couldn't get it to come together. Bojangles, I knew, had meticulously made over Miyuki to resemble the deceased Ame Kitazawa. Bojangles, I guessed, was also blackmailing Nakodo, threatening to expose his World War II family secret. How those two theories fit together I wasn't sure. But I was certain they merged at some point, and when they did, Miyuki found herself drowning in the Nihonbashi River.

But what could Bojangles want with Afuro?

The question reminded me that I still hadn't gotten any closer to figuring out what actually happened to Miyuki that night. Whether Nakodo had killed her, whether Bojangles had killed her, whether the Man in White had killed her or whether she'd killed herself just like the police had speculated. One calamity after another, the past bleeding into the present, becoming the future.

I didn't know what that future would bring, but I had to believe that Afuro wasn't dead yet, that there was still something I could do. And there was something I could do. Something so drastic and desperate I could hardly believe I was considering it. But the more I thought about it, the more I realized it had to be done. Deciding on this treacherous course of action brought some relief, for no matter what the greater future held in store, I knew more or less how the next few hours would turn out. That's one thing I liked about dealing with the boys at Shinjuku Metropolitan Police Station. You always knew just what to expect.

29

My Man in Minato

Inspector Arajiro's cigarette rested in a dirty plastic ashtray shaped like a frog's mouth. The poor frog had already eaten six or seven other smokes, which lay in a bent, ashen heap where the thing's tongue would've been. I watched the live cigarette burn and listened to the tick-tock of the clock on the wall. It'd been a while since I heard a clock that actually ticked. It wasn't a sound I'd missed.

It was after eleven P.M., Saturday night, so there weren't many cops at their desks. Most of them would either be manning the vast network of neighborhood police boxes or be out on the streets, ostensibly protecting the regular men and women watching movies, playing pachinko, hitting clubs and bars, visiting soaplands, singing karaoke and doing everything they could to escape their everyday lives for a few hours. That I was spending Saturday night retelling the same story over and over again to Inspector Arajiro made it clear that somewhere along the way my everyday life had walked off without even saying good-bye.

But I suppose it was inevitable that I'd find myself sitting across the table from my old nemesis sooner or later. Trying to imagine Tokyo without him was like trying to imagine it without crows and crowds, neon lights and beautiful women. Our encounters had become so routine over the years that some masochistic part of me even looked forward to them.

Inspector Arajiro didn't share my sentiments.

He'd been envisioning a permanently Chaka-free Tokyo ever since I'd punched out his partner. It happened years ago in the Ryogoku district after I'd seen the guy continually paw a clearly annoyed waitress at a place called the Ruined Map. Our little tussle wouldn't have amounted to much were it not for the fact that several weekly scandal-rag paparazzi happened to be staking out the bar. The Ruined Map was a favorite watering hole of Kazuhiro Yamakage, a talented but troubled young sumo wrestler with a career-threatening bulimia problem. Photographers had even hidden cameras in the bathroom, hoping to win the five-million-yen bounty for whoever got photographic evidence of Yamakage regurgitating. The sumo never showed that night, but the scandalmongers got some decent pictures and a story just the same.

GROPING COP GETS POPPED!

PAWING POLICEMAN AND FOREIGNER IN FRACAS!

GALLANT GAIJIN STOPS FEEL-COPPING COP!

Unfortunately, the incident came at the tail end of about thirty other police scandals involving everything from bribery to cover-ups to drunken off-duty officers assaulting cab drivers and hiring teenage prostitutes. Arajiro's partner was made an example of and forced to resign. Though his dismissal was due mostly to poor timing, the fact he'd allowed himself to be beaten up by a foreigner—and not just a foreigner, but a journalist, and not just a journalist, but a journalist for a teen magazine—couldn't have helped his case. Inspector Arajiro swore to avenge his humiliated partner, and ever since he'd been a constant fixture in my visits to Tokyo. Every year his face got a little fleshier, his eyes a little deader, his teeth more stained from smoking, and his attitude more bitter from Billy Chaka remaining a free man.

Right now, Arajiro was holding a big black phone to his ear, sweating the way overweight men do, and grunting about every fifteen ticks of the clock. Behind him, an ineffectual air-conditioning unit rattled in a window facing the giant Nomura Insurance building. The streets below were strangely quiet for Shinjuku, but this was the western side, home mostly to government and office buildings. All the action was on the east side of the train station, which separated the world of fun from the world of tedium as completely as anything since the Berlin Wall.

Inspector Arajiro grunted a few more times then hung up the phone. He picked a fresh pencil from his pocket, wiped his forehead with the back of his hand, then grappled with his notebook until he'd scrawled out a few words. I took a surreptitious glance at the gash in my hand and reminded myself to keep my palm out of view, lest Arajiro become suddenly interested in how I got the wound.

"Let's go over this one more time," he told me.

We'd gone over it one more time three or four times, but mentioning that to Arajiro would only mean going over it an additional five or six. So I told it to him again, leaving all the same parts out. I told him I knew Nakodo had been killed but didn't mention that I'd been in his mansion and seen the body myself only that morning. And I didn't mention anything about the monks of the Benzaiten Temple or the Man in White, lest Arajiro think I was nuts. Mostly, I focused on the fact that I knew Miyuki and Nakodo had been having an affair, and that I thought Nakodo was probably being blackmailed by a guy calling himself Mr. Bojangles. Most importantly, I was there because a woman named Aphrodite Noguchi had disappeared, was in danger at best, dead at worst, and I didn't know where else to go.

"What do you mean exactly by 'disappeared'?"

I explained, again, how I'd been on the phone with her. How she'd said a man was following her and she was sure it was Bojangles. I reminded Inspector Arajiro that Afuro was Miyuki's best friend, and look what had happened to her.

"But this girl disappeared less than two hours ago."

"True," I said. "Nevertheless, I'm concerned."

"But from everything you've told me today, it doesn't sound like this woman *disappeared*. It sounds like she just ditched you. Maybe she ran into a boy she knew."

I shook my head.

"Then maybe there's something you're not telling me."

I couldn't help but think Arajiro was trying to lay some sort of trap, though he wasn't smart enough to lay a good one. I found myself wishing I would have just gone to the *koban* in Shibuya or called the cops in Ark Hills who were investigating Nakodo's murder. Then again, it wouldn't have mattered. Arajiro had flagged my file, meaning whether I got caught slipping slugs into a beer machine in Yokohama or cracking a sake flask over the head of a yakuza boss in Ike-bukuro, all interrogations were to be handled by Tokyo's leading Billy Chaka authority, one Inspector Arajiro.

"Listen, Arajiro," I said. "Let's assume for once, just once, that I'm completely innocent. That I'm telling the truth and that I'm genuinely concerned for the safety of this kid. Let's put our pasts aside, just for one night. Tomorrow, you can go back to hating me. You can try to frame me for whatever gang-land hit goes down tonight in Kabuki-cho or have me arrested as a *chikusho* for groping girls on the Saikyo line. But tonight, let's cooperate. Let's work according to the ancient Japanese spirit of harmony."

Arajiro tilted his head, scrutinizing me. "What's this about a gangland hit going down in Kabuki-cho?"

It was hopeless. I stood up and wished Arajiro a good night.

"Where do you think you're going?"

"Last time I checked, I wasn't under arrest."

"No need to get defensive," he said, transferring the ciga-rette from the frog's mouth to his own. "Sit down, and I'll tell you what the officer I just spoke to on the phone told me about the Nakodo case."

"Why bother?"

"Because it may keep you and I from seeing each other again under different circumstances," he said. "As it is, you've got so many half-baked notions in your head, you're bound to run around and cause trouble. And then what? You'll end up right back in front of me, and I don't want that happening. So sit down."

Arajiro couldn't have surprised me more if he'd pinned an honorary badge to my shirt and handed me his gun. I sat

down, half in a trance. My dumb surprise must have regis-
tered, because Arajiro drew a sharp breath in through his
nose.

"I've settled upon a new approach," he warned me. "A
tactical change where you are concerned. Prevention. You've
proven yourself a slippery fish in the past, and if I can't catch
you, I can at least do everything in my power to keep you
from committing outrageous acts. Even cooperate with you,
repulsive as that idea is. Preventive crime-fighting may not
be as glamorous as collaring scum like yourself, but it's usually more effective in the long run."

"Glad to know you don't still hold a grudge."

"Nothing has changed between us," he said, missing my
sarcasm completely. "I'm not expecting my new approach to
work. And when you inevitably fuck up, I'll come after you
with everything I've got, rest assured. But until then, here's
what I can tell you."

WHAT HE TOLD ME was this:

The police knew all about Miyuki and Nakodo. They
learned about the affair from Mr. Nakodo himself, who'd
come to the police when Miyuki was found dead in the
Nihonbashi River. He'd told them that the woman was dis-
traught when he'd broken off their affair and that he suspected this was the reason she'd killed herself. The police
noted in their report that Nakodo seemed distraught himself
and was particularly worried that an extended investigation
of Miyuki's death might alert the tabloids to a potential scandal. He'd humbly requested that the police deal with the matter in a most expeditious and restrained manner.

Even Inspector Arajiro couldn't help noting dryly that his colleagues in the Minato ward would find this request compelling, given that Nakodo was an official of the Ministry of Construction. His indirect influence could be instrumental in winning city approval of a proposed new state-of-the-art police training facility to be built in the area.

When police responded to an emergency call from inside the house, they found Nakodo lying facedown in a small pond on the east side of his yard. Despite the odd method he'd chosen, the police were ruling the death a suicide.

"Suicide?" I couldn't help but interjecting.

Arajiro nodded forcefully.

"You're saying he just walked out into his backyard, flopped into the pond and drowned himself?"

"He had plenty of reasons to die," Arajiro said with a shrug. "You'd think a big shot like him has it made, but apparently he was plenty complicated beneath the surface. Officers on the case have already interviewed several of his colleagues, and they say Nakodo had been a broken man for years. His wife drowned, too, you know. Years ago. Officially it was ruled an accident, but that was only to spare the family embarrassment. Fact was, it was clearly a suicide. She jumped in the Sumida River after they'd been married only two years. Ever since then, outside of work Nakodo had become a grown-up *hikikomori*."

The term meant *recluse* more or less, but was usually applied to withdrawn adolescents who dropped out of school and became hermits in their parents' houses, whiling away their golden years with video games and manga characters instead of friends. With the declining birthrate and a gnawing sense that today's kids weren't just antisocial—which was normal—but flat-out asocial, the growing *hikikomori* phe-

nomenon was seen as just another sign of the country's iner-
tia. I'd never heard the term describe an adult before, but I
had to admit it seemed to match the overall impression of
Nakodo I'd had that first day in Ark Hills.

"Only recently had Nakodo shown any interest in life
outside of work," the inspector continued. "Seems the
affair with this young woman really raised his spirits,
turned him into an entirely different sort of fellow. But losing another woman the same way, it must've proved too
much for him."

"But you said Nakodo broke it off?"

"That's what he told us."

"If he was so in love, why would he do that?"

"One thing thirty years on the force has taught me—people don't know what's good for them. Men don't always act
in a rational manner, especially where women are concerned.
And women? Show me a woman who is ever rational to begin
with. Throw love in the mix, it's amazing every river in the
city isn't overflowing with corpses. You know just last week
we found three bodies in Yoyogi Park? Guy strangled two
women and hung himself in a tree. Love triangle suicide.
Strangest thing was they were all over sixty-five years old.
Can you believe it, love suicides at that age?"

"The hidden social cost of Viagra," I said absentmindedly.
My own guess was that Nakodo hadn't broken it off at all.
She'd left him, found a way to escape him, as she had put it
in her letter to Afuro. Whether Nakodo lied to the police to
cover up a blackmailing scheme, a murder, or just out of some
macho pride was an open question. I had a lot of those, but I
had to be careful which ones I aired. I hadn't seen the news
reports of Nakodo's death yet, so I didn't know what was public knowledge and what the police were keeping under

wraps. But suicide? How could that explain the way Nakodo's house had been trashed?

"When I visited Nakodo a few days ago, there were lots of servants around," I said. "Have your pals spoken to them?"

"Checked into that," he said. "Saturday is their day off."

"And I assume the fuzz grilled the old man?"

Arajiro's face was too chubby to pull off a good scowl, but I could tell he was trying. "My fellow officers of the law, Chaka, interviewed Nakodo's father. Or attempted to anyway. From what I understand, he's pretty far gone. He doesn't even remember making the emergency call."

"How do you know he did?"

"He was the only one in the house," said Arajiro. "Look, Chaka, I know you came in here all excited about your little blackmail theory, but my man in Minato says it just doesn't wash. We went to the academy together and he knows as well as I do that the first principle of investigation is this: nine times out of ten, the simplest explanation is the correct one."

"Maybe this is case number ten."

"The simple explanation is that Nakodo killed himself and we've found no evidence to contradict this conclusion. Hell, aside from this fling with the hostess, sounds like the guy has been on the verge of suicide for years. No one interviewed seemed surprised he'd offed himself. You know how people always say, 'he just didn't seem like the type'? Well, nobody said that. Not one person."

"Which should tell you right away something is fishy."

"Tell me this," Arajiro snorted. "If someone had killed Nakodo, do you think they would've left behind the old man as a witness?"

Having delivered his coup de grace, Inspector Arajiro leaned back in his chair. The corners of his mouth made a play for his earlobes before snapping back together in their usual sour pucker, but for a second you could almost call it a smile.

I didn't bother answering Arajiro's question. It'd been a matter of hours since I'd called the cops from Nakodo's house. In that scant time, they'd bagged all the evidence, questioned all relevant parties, drawn conclusions and sewn the whole thing shut. I doubted even the investigators believed Nakodo had killed himself, but what difference did it make? Besides a demented old man, the guy had no family, and apparently no real friends to speak of. He had lots of connections, but not the kind that count in the end. They'd go to the funeral then pull his card from their Rolodexes and delete his e-mail address from their contact lists, but nobody had anything to gain by raising a stink. All at once I started feeling sorry for the guy again, just like I had that first day in Ark Hills.

"As for your missing girlfriend, if you don't hear from her in twenty-four hours, come back and we'll revisit the subject," Arajiro said, making a big show of his magnanimity. "Until then, leave the investigating to us. After all, I don't show up in your little magazine office in New Jersey and suggest new zit creams for you to write about, do I?"

"Cleveland is in Ohio. Not New Jersey. Ohio."

Arajiro ignored me and rose from behind his desk. He slipped on his standard-issue bright blue jacket and pinned another smoke to the corner of his mouth. Then he struck a match like it was a substitute for striking me, lit the cigarette and spat a cloud of smoke in my face. I held my breath. After the Man in White, I always would.

"I'm catching the last train home," said Arajiro, loving every second of his theatrical annoyance. "I suggest you do the same. Oh yeah, going home reminds me—you might be happy to know I'm only three years from retirement."

"Congratulations."

"You might be happy, but you shouldn't be. Right now, I'm an official representative of the Tokyo Municipal Government. It's my loyal duty to uphold the laws of the city and keep the peace. But in less than one thousand days, I'll just be Mr. Arajiro. A private citizen whose only duty is to uphold his honor. And you? You'll still be making trips here, still writing little stories for the pimples crowd. Tokyo may be the biggest city in the world, but for me? The smallest town on earth. Wouldn't be surprised if our paths crossed in my little town, would you?"

"You really know how to drag out a good-bye."

"I wanna be sure it sticks," he said. "And if you're cooking up any other lame theories to come waste my time with tomorrow, let me save you a trip. We're sure Old Man Nakodo didn't kill his son, either, in case that was your next angle."

"Why's that?"

"Because he's only got one hand," Arajiro said, holding up five stunted fingers like an array of sausages. "Lost the other one during the war, so my guy tells me. Makes it pretty hard to hold a fella underwater, don't you think?"

Inspector Arajiro waddled across the floor, pausing in the doorway for a moment to glare at me one last time, no doubt wishing twin laser beams would come shooting out his eyes like in a Godzilla movie. Then he snorted once and flipped off the lights, leaving me in the dark. The air conditioner carried on its death rattle, the clock kept ticking.

30

Dreaming Pachinko

Old Man Nakodo was missing a hand.

I kept repeating the fact over and over to myself, as if I still needed convincing, as if I really needed more evidence that he was in fact Officer Takahashi of the Kempeitai, the man responsible for destroying the Benzaiten Temple, the man who caused the deaths of the Benzaiten monks and in so doing set some strange clockwork into motion that resulted in the deaths of Ame Kitazawa, Miyuki, his own son, and counting.

Remembering my two brief encounters with him, I realized I'd only ever seen the one hand he used to control his
wheelchair. His left hand. I guess I'd just assumed his right
hand was tucked somewhere in his lap, hidden in the folds
of his elaborate kimono. Funny, I'd noticed the flowers on
Miyuki's underwear as she lay on the floor of the pachinko
parlor—but that a guy was missing his entire hand escaped
my notice not once, but twice. So much for my journalistic
eye for detail.

Nakodo was missing a hand, I thought as cars and trucks
thundered by, one after another, on and on, rumbling over the
concrete, vibrating the metal girders on the underside of the
elevated highway. No moonlight reached the water below but
occasionally the headlights from a car passing down a nearby
side street would illuminate the black surface of the river,
only for an instant, before the water slipped back into darkness and became an invisible current slithering through the
concrete pillars that gleamed a ghostly white even in the
shadows.

What had I expected to find here? Afuro standing on the
bridge, just as she had been the first day I'd met her, forlorn
and staring at the water? Or a news crew on the scene, film-
ing the police dragging her body from the water just as they
had done with Miyuki? Was I looking for clues, hoping to
find Afuro's ever-present handbag lying on the street, her
other cell phone perhaps, or a trail of bread crumbs leading
me to Mr. Bojangles? Or maybe Mr. Bojangles himself, returning to the scene of the crime, wearing a black hat and trench
coat and twiddling his mustache in the shadows? Or Mr.
Bojangles as I thought him to be, a pale little man in a white
suit surrounded by his cigarette-puffing flunkies?

I didn't know what I'd expected to find, or whether I

really expected to find anything at all. I'd just felt compelled to visit the dreary site again, to somehow prove to myself that I hadn't given up, that I was doing everything I could think of to find Afuro, to save her from ending up like Miyuki.

Miyuki had been an attractive stranger enacting the final moments of a drama already scripted and I happened to wander onstage just as the curtain was about to fall. After everything I'd learned, I now knew there was nothing I could've done to prevent what happened to her. But Afuro was different. For better or worse, Miyuki's death had brought us together, gave us a connection. We'd been through a bizarre night together in that nameless alley and in the Red Baron Suite, the sort that engenders a sudden intimacy, an understanding you often never reach with people you've known your entire life. And I genuinely liked Afuro. She was intelligent, headstrong, impetuous and an absolute mess in a lot of ways. Everything a girl her age should be but almost never is.

And I got the sense that she was drawn to me, too, if only because I was an outsider. Someone who didn't fit in. For me, it was a matter of skin color, of nationality. A matter of being a foreigner in Japan. A matter, finally, of a chosen and flexible geography. But Afuro? She had no choice. A girl like her was never really going to fit in here, probably wouldn't fit in anywhere. She was at the age when she was starting to realize that her quirks weren't just an adolescent stage or a phase, they were who she was. What she probably didn't know was that if she had the strength to keep being who she was, she'd soon grow into a very rare and beautiful human being, the kind the world can't afford to be without yet does everything possible to crush just the same.

All of this assuming she wasn't already dead.

I'd do everything in my power to keep her in this world, but the fact that I was here showed me just how little power I really had. Just an outsider in a concrete nowhere, under the expressway in a hidden pocket of urban wasteland that only underscored the futility of believing anyone or anything could be saved from that unseen force Mr. Nakodo called change, Kujima called the past and Gombei knew as luck. One hundred years ago, merchants happily going about their business on the waterways. Sixty years ago, bodies roasting from American bombs. A few nights ago, Miyuki's corpse floating in the water. An hour ago, Afuro and Mr. Bojangles. One event after another drifting by, the world changing in big and small ways, now becoming the past, and me standing here thinking about it didn't mean anything and didn't help anybody.

But I stayed there for a while anyway, standing on the bridge, staring into the shadows at the unseen water below. I stayed and stared and thought. Because even if thinking couldn't help anyone, I couldn't help thinking. No more than the water could help flowing downstream or the moon help shining.

The old man's missing hand all but confirmed that Bojangles had been right all those years ago when he visited Detective Ihara and accused Nakodo of changing his name after the war. And if Old Man Nakodo really was Officer Takahashi, that explained why the Nakodo clan had been so quick to squelch Ihara's investigation. But if Bojangles had evidence to prove this, he wouldn't have needed Detective Ihara. He could've gone straight to the bride's family. Or he could've started blackmailing the Nakodo family years ago. And why did he want to blackmail Nakodo, aside from money? What did Bojangles hope to gain, what motivated him to hatch so complicated a plot? And more importantly, why now? What happened to change things after so many years?

The answer came so suddenly it must have been there in my head all along, crying to get out from beneath layers of marine trivia and Benzaiten mythology and World War II history and everything else people had been filling my brain with over the last few days.

Miyuki happened.

Bojangles, whoever he was, never had any hard evidence that Officer Takahashi and Old Man Nakodo were the same person. Maybe all he had was a hunch. And if he ever wanted to be more than trouble on the horizon (as he'd put it to Ihara), he needed someone to get close to Nakodo in a way he never could, which is where Miyuki came in. Had Bojangles been silently scheming against Nakodo during the intervening years? Probably not. More likely, he'd seen Miyuki at the Café Acrophobia and she reminded him of Nakodo's dead wife. The plan must've come to him in a flash. Whether he remade Miyuki into Ame Kitazawa then had her killed as some type of twisted revenge intended to drive Nakodo over the edge or if he'd simply used Miyuki as one element in a blackmail scheme was a tough question. Whatever the case, the guy was definitely patient, resourceful, and dangerous.

Bojangles had to have known Nakodo's dead wife fairly well. Well enough, at least, to recognize her doppelganger in a crowded bar years and years later. And how could he have known about Ame Kitazawa's seizures, and her disturbing visions of a man in white? My guess was that he'd somehow gleaned the information from one of her doctors, one of the many specialists Mrs. Kitazawa had told me her daughter was seeing at the time. It was possible Bojangles could even have been one of these doctors.

Tomorrow morning, I'd go back to Yanaka to visit the Kitazawas again. I'd go against their wishes, do whatever it took to overcome their reticence, get the name of every one of Ame's doctors and go from there. Real grunt work, but it was apt to be more productive than standing on a bridge in the middle of the night, hoping the answer would just come floating by on the water.

There was a slight problem with my plan, one I'd completely forgotten about. One I'd been trying to forget about ever since that first day in the pachinko parlor. Tomorrow morning, I was supposed to be on an airplane headed back to Cleveland, finished "Fallen Stars" story in hand.

And there was something else I was trying to forget about. The Man in White, or Bojangles, had visited me, too, and somehow caused me to have a seizure. Just like Ame Kitazawa, just like Miyuki, both of whom were now dead. He'd written THE MAN IN THE PHOTOGRAPH WILL JOIN US SOON and Mr. Nakodo had died. He'd written BENZAITEN SAYS TWO MORE WILL JOIN US and Afuro was missing, and as for me . . .

My head buzzed in the heat, my mouth was dry and I was six different kinds of tired. If I was next, I wished they'd just get it over with.

BACK IN THE OCTOPUS'S GARDEN, I checked my messages, but there were none. Billions of people on the planet and none of them had a thing to say to me, but it was more or less mutual. I didn't even feel like having imaginary conversations with the goldfish. Instead, I grabbed a piece of Hotel Cerulean stationery and a pen and jotted down a timeline of the events, hoping it would somehow help put my thoughts in order.

1707—Benzaiten idol discovered, Temple built
1945—Benzaiten Temple destroyed by Officer Takahashi
1945–50—Officer Takahashi disappears
1950–65—Nakodo Sr. emerges, runs Nakodo Construction
1965—Nakodo leaves construction firm to join OshokGroup
1975—"Bojangles" approaches Ihara to investigate Nakodo
1975—Nakodo Jr. marries Ame Kitazawa
1976–77—Ame Kitazawa plagued by seizures, Man in White
1977—Ame Kitazawa drowns
1999—Miyuki and Afuro move to Tokyo
2000—Miyuki is approached by "Bojangles," involved w/Nakodo
2001—

In July 2001, I show up to interview some guy at a pachinko parlor and everything goes to hell. The first day Miyuki has a seizure, the next day she dies. The day after that I have a seizure, and the following day Afuro's apartment is trashed, she tries to kill me then begs me to kill her instead. On my fifth day in Tokyo, Mr. Nakodo drowns in his back-yard and Afuro disappears.

I wondered what fun day six would bring. I crumpled up my timeline and tossed it in the trash. Trying to make sense of the past wasn't gonna stop the future from coming, and I decided I could stay up all night and torture myself with questions I couldn't answer or I could try to get some shut-eye. In the end, I did both simultaneously.

Drifting somewhere between sleep and wakefulness, I became the audience to a fevered dance of disconnected sounds and incomplete images that spilled from my con-scious mind to unconscious mind, flowing back and forth and back again until they all flooded together into something that might have been a dream, but a dream unlike any I've ever had.

Sex games, says Inspector Arajiro, speeding by on a yellow moped. Afuro-Short-for-Nothing flies through the air in a Fokker DR-1, dropping bricks over Tokyo to the tune of "Strangers in the Night." The Man in White plucks moles from his face, laying them out in a message that says *you're never gonna win playing with someone like Bojangles*. Nakodo's hair fans out over the water while paper lanterns undulate on the currents. The Benten Temple priest sits in a wheelchair, feeding sea biscuits to crows flocking all around him. *My watch has stopped*, he tells me, showing me the Mickey Mouse on his wrist, then the crows start cawing and beating their wings and he goes into a seizure. I unwrap a gold-foiled package and find a severed hand inside. Silver balls crash together, *pachi-pachi*, the sound of fire, a flood of red and white carp flopping across the floor of a pachinko arcade, Gombei digs through Miyuki's purse looking for a map to Club Kuroi Kiri and fireflies emerge. Smoke uncoiling above a river of silvery bubbles, the Walrus poised beneath the protective shade of a willow tree in a graveyard crammed with pachinko machines, the smell of fish and gasoline drifting through the air. *That which you seek is also seeking you*, Detective Ihara tells me, then slams a phone on his desk, shattering it into a million pieces. A woodblock portrait of Miyuki on the sealed door, flanked by four men in white suits, Mrs. Kitazawa handing me a Warholian portrait of Benzaiten replicated in pinks and blues, the goddess with a mole the size of a cluster bomb. Burning people screaming through the Shibuya crossing while above them a giant video screen flashes TWO MORE WILL JOIN US and a squadron of B-29s arcs overhead to the sound of the Pink Panther theme. Miyuki's limp body emerging from the water over and over again, *I'm in a strange place right now*, she says. Afuro with a black eye asking again and again *can you hear me?*, her voice getting farther and farther away until there is nothing but the sound of the waves.

And when the tumult of images and sounds washed away and I finally awoke damp and trembling the next morning, all the uncertainties that had been plaguing me coalesced into a single question that rang through my head like an angry alarm. The question stayed there long after I'd leapt out of bed, thrown on my clothes and dashed out of the Hotel Cerulean.

How could I have been so blind?

PART
THREE

"I am dead grass on the riverbank.
You are dead grass on the riverbank."
—"The Boatman's Song"

An Average Month
for Cockroaches

Sixty-six kilometers outside Tokyo, All Nippon Air flight 7006 to Cleveland via Chicago via San Francisco lifted off the runway of Narita Airport at approximately eleven o'clock under a morning sky heavy with the promise of long-awaited rain.

Of course, I wasn't on that flight.

I was on a yellow 1978 Honda Hobbit moped, racing

toward the Ameyayokocho shopping arcade and picturing my empty seat on the plane. When that image got old, I pictured someone else in the seat, some lucky someone who scored my spot on standby. I imagined him staring out the window as the plane disappeared into the clouds, eating complimentary roasted seaweed-rice crackers meant for me and thinking maybe things were finally going his way. I liked the picture. Made me feel like I was doing my part to spread good feelings throughout the world, even if I could only do it through my absence. On the other hand, there was something gratifying about the image of an empty chair, too.

I don't analyze dreams for deep meaning or psychic revelations or winning lottery numbers or other nonsense of that sort, but sometimes they can be telling just the same. Not in any overtly symbolic or visionary way, but for their ability to bring to the surface things we've forgotten. Fact was, I should have put everything together sooner. The dream made that clear. It didn't give me the missing clue or the final piece of the puzzle, but only reminded me of what was there all along, right in front of my face.

I've blamed Tokyo for a lot of my failings over the years, but in this city it's easy for the mind to become overwhelmed. Catacombed train stations to be maneuvered, mazes of streets to be negotiated, streaming masses and endless noises and countless blinking lights. The blank expressions you see on passing faces, the blank expression you wear on your own, are the outer manifestations of minds racing to filter a barrage of stimuli, minds one synaptic misfire away from being buried in an avalanche of signals and experiencing full sensory meltdown. If Tokyo was the city of the future, our brains had a lot of evolving to do.

Or maybe just my brain.

As I pulled up outside Ueno station I thought about the old Zen story in which the master admonishes his pupil for seeing the finger instead of the moon it pointed to. Which made me think of the Buddhist priest at the nearby Benten Temple—the Benten Temple in Shinobazu Pond, the Benten Temple that existed in this particular temporal reality. That I was even thinking in terms of "temporal reality" made me fear for my mental health, but if I'd gone insane at least I had a lot of company. Everyone involved in this whole affair seemed insane in one way or another.

That which you seek is also seeking you. The old priest turned out to be right, of course, but speak in vague enough terms and you're always right. It was a trick the world's religious leaders, politicians, and market analysts had been cashing in on for years. The details were left to saps like me to sort out.

The priest was right because Gombei had been seeking me. He'd left messages at the Hotel Cerulean, sent his cartons of Hope cigarettes, brought me the Honda Hobbit as a gift for changing his luck. That I had resorted to riding the thing was testament to just how desperately I was now seeking him right back.

I should have realized what had happened when Gombei showed up in a flashy Italian suit when only days ago he'd been dressed in a tattered trench coat. That he'd given me an expensive, vintage moped when he couldn't afford another one-thousand-yen prepaid pachinko card a few days previous only underscored my new realization. Gombei had come into money at a pachinko parlor all right, but it wasn't from playing.

Thousands of balls spilling over the floor. Miyuki going into a seizure. Gombei handing me his cell phone, telling me to call the authorities. Gombei rifling through Miyuki's Luis Vuitton handbag looking for identification, not finding any.

But he'd discovered something, all right. Something else entirely.

As I parked the moped around the corner from the JR tracks and walked through the hectic, narrow pedestrian thoroughfare of the Ameyayokocho shopping bazaar, my thoughts centered on one question. Was Gombei part of the blackmail scheme all along, or had he just innocently stumbled on the huge cash blackmail payment Miyuki was carrying from Nakodo to Bojangles?

AMEYAYOKOCHO WAS FULL OF shouting. Shouting about the cheapest leather coats in town, real Chanel perfume at unreal prices, deep discounts on the latest video games from Sony and Nintendo, eel and octopus fresh this morning from Tsukiji, licensed, high-quality replica soccer jerseys from Serie A, i-mode phones, Arnold Palmer golf clubs, DVD players and a million other things I didn't want. I managed to filter all the yelling as I wound my way through the crowds toward the pachinko hall, concentrating on the past that was prologue imbedded in everything that followed my first visit to Lucky Benten Pachinko.

In her letter to Afuro, Miyuki said that she'd found a way to break free of her circumstances, to pay off her credit cards. The day of her impending freedom would have been the same day I'd seen her in the pachinko arcade. My first impression was that she looked out of place in the seedy pachinko parlor, and now I knew why. She'd only come there to make her payoff to Bojangles. Why he'd chosen that particular location was tough to say, but maybe he was a sucker for the cheesy symbolism inherent in picking a pachinko hall devoted to the same goddess as the destroyed temple. And a pachinko hall wasn't a bad place to make a drop—there was only one door to the Lucky Benten Pachinko, so it was easy to see who was going in and out, and all the customers would be focused on the silver balls cascading one foot in front of their faces, so anything short of a major earthquake would escape their notice, as Miyuki's seizure proved.

Miyuki's presence at Lucky Benten Pachinko was clearly by design, but Gombei's placement there was trickier. As a pachinko nut, he may just happen to have been there making the rounds. After all, it was his former agent who had pointed me in the direction of Ueno station. On the other hand, if he was a regular there, his presence wouldn't arouse any suspicion whatsoever, making it an ideal drop site for him, too.

Whatever the case, I knew Gombei wasn't the mysterious Bojangles. He was too young for one thing, and I didn't think he had the brains to mastermind a blackmail scheme. But I hoped he was an accomplice, because that was the only shot I had at finding Bojangles, and thus finding Afuro before it was too late.

But if Gombei was Bojangles's accomplice, the whole scheme should have ended right there in the Lucky Benten, and it didn't. Miyuki had drowned, most likely with some help. Nakodo had been killed, his place trashed. Afuro's place had been trashed and now she had disappeared. I figured whoever Bojangles was, he never received his money that first day. That pissed him off, but he wasn't ready to give up after all those years of waiting. He figured maybe Miyuki stashed the money at her old place, the one she shared with Afuro. When he didn't find it there, he figured maybe

Nakodo had never made the payment. He threatened him, killed him, and tore apart the house looking for the bundle of cash. Or maybe he even had Gombei do it—there was the matter of Gombei's black eye. Could there have been a struggle inside the House of Nakodo? Whatever the case, Nakodo's payment was never found because it was in Gombei's possession.

There was one obvious problem with all this: If Gombei had double-crossed Bojangles and made off with the money, how come Bojangles hadn't come after him? As an accomplice, he would have been the obvious suspect.

So I was back to my Gombei-as-innocent-bystander theory.

But if he was innocent in finding the money, by keeping it he was an unwitting accomplice in the crimes that followed. It was time to stop asking myself questions and start putting them to Gombei Fukugawa. Funny to think putting questions to him was the whole reason I'd come to Tokyo in the first place.

THE ENTRANCE TO LUCKY BENTEN PACHINKO was decorated with stiff plastic blossoms in saturated shades of yellow and blue sprouting from an overgrowth of thickly coiled vines and vinyl leaves. I wouldn't have been surprised to find even fake flowers shriveled and wilted from the heat, but these were holding their shapes. Beside the faux floral arch stood the "Benten's Showcase," a sandwich board pasted with snapshots of pachinko winners, jackpot figures written underneath in numbers pink enough to make you wince. All the winners were grinning in a slightly dazed way, but none looked more pleasantly bewildered than Gombei Fukugawa, who took his place at the top of the board as this week's "Benten's Weekly Favorite Number One."

The glass doors whisked open and I was hit with a blast of cool air carrying the smell of nicotine and the sound of cookie-cutter techno. Every machine in the house was occupied but one. The glass face was removed from the unplayed machine and two kids in bumblebee vests were examining the arrangement of metal pins and arguing with each other. I squeezed my way through the rows of machines until I was behind them and cleared my throat. When that proved futile, I tapped one of the kids on the shoulder.

"Irasshaimase," he greeted me. "Welcome to Lucky Benten Pachinko. Sorry, but all our machines are currently occupied. If it pleases you, I could—"

"Do you have a customer named Gombei Fukugawa?"

"I wouldn't know, sir."

"His picture is on the board. Benten's Favorite Number One."

"Guy that smiles all the time?"

"That's him."

The two kids stopped looking at the machine and looked at each other. After a moment of silent communication, the skinnier kid bowed slightly to me and said, "We're not allowed to talk about our customers. You understand."

"Is your boss allowed to talk?"

While the kids mind-melded over the question my eyes wandered around the pachinko hall. Mostly slouching middle-aged men occupied the fifty or so machines, along with one tough-looking old crone who was making a killing judging from the four baskets of balls resting at her feet. Besides the bumblebee twins, there were no young people in sight. Miyuki clearly wouldn't have come here of her own volition.

"Please follow me," the skinny bee said at last.

We shuffled sideways through the machines toward the back of the parlor to an unmarked door the size of a coffin lid. The kid knocked quietly and the response was a trollish grunt. A few moments later, the tiny door swung open and I half expected to see a hobgoblin emerging, but instead it was just the manager with his rolled-up sleeves and failed comb over.

"Don't tell me he caught a boomerang," the manager snapped.

The kid indicated my presence with a tilt of his head.

"Oh," said the manager, visibly relieved. "Excuse me, didn't see you there, buddy. Hey, wait a sec. I know you. Weren't you here the other day when that raggle went spastic? Yeah, you were, I remember. You were here with honorable Bright Root."

"Who?"

"*O-neaka-san*. Mr. Happy-Go-Lucky. Guy Smiley."

"Yeah," I said. "I wanted to ask you about him."

With a troubled look he beckoned me into a room the size of a cat's forehead and shut the door behind us. The tiny office was in marked contrast to the game floor outside. No bright lights, no mirrored paneling. The thin walls provided just enough soundproofing so you could almost hear yourself think, while a ceiling fan dangling too low for comfort rotated in the air above as I sat in the folding chair offered by the pachinko manager. He'd started to take a seat on the other side of the desk when suddenly he stopped, his expression gone sour. He rifled through a desk drawer then slammed it closed and gave me a look of unmasked contempt. The theme music from *Rocky* bled through the walls. It was a pachinko hall standard.

"Don't move a goddamned muscle," the manager growled.

Before I knew what was happening, he'd leapt from his chair, raced around the desk and shot a fist out. At the last moment I managed to dodge the blow, and his knuckles rapped weakly against the top of my shoulder. I leapt out of the chair and readied my counterattack, assuming the drunken monkey stance.

"What the hell are you doing?" the manager asked.

"I might ask you the same thing."

He gave me a funny look but didn't answer. Instead, still holding his fist closed, he marched across the room to a chart hanging on the wall. The chart was about the size of a tatami mat and was spotted with misshapen brown dots. He pinned something to its surface and stood for a moment admiring his work.

"Number forty-two," he said.

I relaxed my stance and stepped in for a closer look.

The chart was a large calendar.

The brown dots were dead cockroaches.

There were dozens of them, clustered together in the squares that marked the days. The one he'd just grabbed from my shoulder scuttled its feet over the paper with a dull scratching sound. Six others shared today's square, but they'd long since stopped struggling.

The manager wiped his hands on his trousers and turned to face me, looking pleased. Judging from the rest of the calendar, he was having a good day.

"Interesting hobby," I said.

"Some Aum Shinrikyo freaks used to have a recruiting office on the floor above us. Idiots were forbidden from killing a kitchen cockroach, but somehow gassing human beings on the subway was yippy skippy. They were thrown out years ago, but the cockroaches weren't so easy to get rid of. I get one hundred yen knocked off my rent for every one of the things I kill."

"Looks like a good month," I said.

"It's about average. Rainy season usually brings the little buggers out in droves—hell, last July I was tin mittens. But no rain this year. Anyway, grab a seat and let's punch the guff."

The cockroach kept struggling, but its movements were slower now, like a toy winding down. I sat back in the folding chair and got ready to punch the guff, whatever that meant. The manager handed me one of his business cards, which I studied with the overawed expression etiquette dictated while apologizing profusely for the lamentable fact I had no cards of my own. The card identified the pachinko manager as Song Lee. Lee sat down behind the desk, leaned back in his chair and crossed his arms over his chest.

"I know why you're here, so let's skip all the cackle bladder," he began, speaking in an accent I couldn't quite place. "Your buddy has been a fantastic customer over the years and we value his esteemed patronage and yakity yak, but he's gotta lay off the squeeze. Meaning or else someone is gonna lop off his topknot. I just became a grandfather, which makes me easygoing, makes me a sentimental old happy pappy, but not everybody shares my weakness for compassion. Bright Root keeps it up, he's gonna find himself dusted."

"I don't understand what you're saying. Literally."

"Looky here, I don't know how your buddy hash-housed it for you, but we had no choice but to shake his buttons. Could've played the hinge, but I don't like calling the cops unless. Who needs them probiscifying and ranking the joint? Customers see that, the whole place curdles. But your pally-pal, he can't go on cheating like this."

"Cheating?"

"There's no other explanation," Lee said matter-of-factly. "I don't know his squeeze—we buy only the best machines and it ain't like the old days when any lop-eared goldbricker with a magnet could try to slickbox us. But you can only beat the odds so many times until people start noticing. And it's not just me noticing. Frankly, Mr. Bright Root is getting a reputation as quite the hopscotch with the major ball-and-pin boys."

I studied Lee's stern expression and wondered if what Gombei had been saying was true. Could his sudden wealth really just be from pachinko winnings? If he had no role in the Miyuki-Bojangles drama, pretty much all my theories were shot to hell.

"I know, I know," Lee said, apparently misreading my confusion. "*No evidence*, you're thinking, *show me the bent nail, produce the coiled copper*. But I don't have to. We don't operate in a court of law. Bright Root knows this. That's why he sent you here to pad his nuts. So you can go back to room number 412 in Rikkyu Apartments in nine-chome, Komagome, and tell your buddy this."

Had Lee just given me Gombei's address?

Lee smiled, unsheathing his nicotine-stained teeth. "Surprised we know the coordinates of his tatami box? Like I said, some of my pals have taken an interest in this lucky streak of his. He keeps getting so fortunate, they might just pay him a visit. Which would be unfortunate. Again—not my idea, and I'm trying to put the chill on it, but I can only keep it cool so long. Tell your friend he is welcome to play at the Lucky Benten Pachinko if he agrees to be a square paper. I like him, like seeing his dippy smile, you know?"

"I'll tell him," I said. By giving me Gombei's address, Song

Lee had saved me from driving the moped from one pachinko hall to the next in search of Gombei. I could've kissed him, his yellow teeth and all.

"You'll tell him," Lee echoed. "But he won't listen. Guys think they have a sneeze-proof squeeze, they lose their hearing. If he can't quit, tell him to at least light a rag for a while. Take a vacation, hit some pachinko halls in Hawaii or something."

"They have pachinko in Hawaii?"

"How do I know? It's your country."

"Right," I said, standing to leave. "Thanks for your understanding in this unfortunate matter. And good luck with the roaches."

Lee rapped his knuckles against the metal desk. "I've been in this business too long to believe in luck. You tell Mr. Bright Root I said that."

The manager showed me his yellow smile again while across the room the dying cockroach began scuttling against the calendar in a final attempt to escape. Cockroaches and human beings alike, some of us just don't know when we're licked.

32

The Chinese Farmer and the Wild Cows

Komagome used to be famous for its cherry trees back when Tokyo was known as Edo, but now it wasn't famous for much of anything. Eventually I gave up trying to find the address the manager had given me, parked the moped at the top of the hill near the JR station and asked a cop for directions. As most streets in Tokyo don't have names, giving and following directions were arts unto themselves, urban survival skills that required near photographic recall, precise mapping ability and not a little imagination. In about three seconds, the cop had drawn me a map that utilized a bicycle repair shop, a row of vending machines and an outdated campaign poster of the prime minister as navigational aides.

By Tokyo standards, Komagome was a ghost town. No giant department stores, no armies of high school kids, shoppers or salarymen, no dazzling jungles of love hotels, soaplands, pachinko halls and karaoke parlors. After passing the poster of Prime Minister Koizumi with his unduly optimistic smile and flowing gray hair, I walked down a long, narrow street lined with shuttered discount stores. Hundreds of plastic flowers were strung overhead in an attempt at seasonal festivity, but on this Sunday morning there wasn't much to be festive about.

Though unusual, the directions proved to be incredibly precise. Inspector Arajiro and his boys in blue may have been clueless about cracking complicated cases like the deaths of Nakodo and Miyuki, but if all there was to working a crime scene was knowing how to find it, the Tokyo cops would be the finest police force in the world, hands down.

Komagome wasn't the kind of place I'd expect someone like Gombei Fukugawa to call home, but then again I had a hard time picturing him anywhere but plopped in front of a pachinko machine. Turning off the shopping lane, I encountered a network of residential streets. Crowded racks of unlocked bicycles stood outside the small apartment complexes, while mobiles of drying laundry hung from the patios above.

Rikkyu Gardens was a modest five-story aquamarine-colored apartment complex with an exterior constructed out of what appeared to be bathroom tiles. I checked the mail-boxes to confirm his apartment number, then made my way up an exposed staircase so narrow it precluded two-way traffic. I imagined a man and a woman trying to pass on the stairs, getting stuck, being wedged in the stairwell for the rest of their lives. They fall in love, get married, have little stairway children, grow old together. A real urban romance for the twenty-first century.

I stopped outside Gombei's apartment and listened at the door. No sounds from the other side. I knocked, softly at first and then louder. Nothing. I took a cautious glance at my surroundings. Across the street, a solitary crow perched on a sagging telephone wire, observing me with an air of superiority. The crow was the only witness to what would happen next.

I took out my Cleveland YMCA membership card and slid it in the crack between the door and the frame. Easing the bolt backward, I had the door just about jimmied when suddenly it swung open. I stood upright and shoved both hands in my pockets, trying to pretend I'd just been innocently standing there all along.

Feigning innocence was never my specialty.

And had I not done it, my hands would have been free. Had my hands been free, I might've been able to block the five iron arcing toward the crown of my head. At the very least, I would have been able to break my fall with something other than the side of my face. As it happened, I was able to do neither.

It wasn't a powerful blow, but it was accurate enough. The club hit me, I hit the floor. Despite being stunned, I was able to dig my hands out of my pockets and crab backward against the railing of the landing. I didn't know if I was moving fast enough to escape the next swing of the club and all I could see were stars splashed across a suspiciously blood-red sky.

But the second blow never came.

"Billy Chaka?" Gombei said. "Shit! Are you all right?"

I stood up and wiped my forehead with my palm. One wound bleeding into another. Did that make me my own blood brother? Useless question number eight hundred and twelve. I clutched my head and tried to assess the damage. There was a lot of blood, but with head wounds there always is.

"What are you doing here?" Gombei said. He was standing in the doorway, still holding the golf club, smiling but not looking at all happy.

THE INSIDE OF GOMBEI'S single-room apartment looked like a one-hundred-yen shop after an earthquake. Sample-sized vials of Gatsby cologne, cartoned tubes of Jenet toothpaste, unopened packages of Naive wetwipes and pocket-sized retractable chopsticks, and back issues of out-of-print men's magazines littered the floor. On the futon couch were a collection of garishly patterned neckties and boxed rice cookers and medicinal bottles with the Chinese characters for "strength" and "longevity" splashed over illustrations of comically ferocious tigers and bears. Kitschy digital alarm clocks, stuffed toys of canceled anime characters, cheap ceramic tea sets, tiny stereo speakers molded in the shapes of classic cars, bottles of off-brand *shochu*. Gombei needn't have hit me over the head with a golf club—one glance at his claustrophobic apartment would have left me with the same dizzy nausea.

I held a towel to my head while Gombei hacked his way across the room and put the five iron in the bag with the other clubs. After that he offered me a beer, at which point I noticed there was in fact a small refrigerator and even a tiny stove buried underneath baskets of pachinko balls. I declined his offer and nodded toward the baskets.

"Isn't it illegal to take pachinko balls?" I asked.

"Place refused to trade them in," Gombei said. "They claim I've been cheating. So to hell with them, I said. They won't give me what's mine, I'll just take the balls."

"Have you been cheating?"

Gombei's smile twisted into an enigmatic new shape.

"What do you think?" he said.

"Looks like you've been winning an awful lot."

"Just good luck."

"Maybe."

"Maybe? Look at all this stuff!"

"There's an old Chinese story," I began. "A farmer's cow runs away. All the neighbors gather around, consoling him, telling him what an unlucky turn of events it is. 'Maybe,' says the farmer. The next day, his cow returns with eight wild cows that have followed him home."

"Wild cows?"

"Maybe it was horses," I said. "So okay, let's say it's a horse returning with eight wild horses. Then the neighbors all tell the farmer what a lucky guy he is, because he's now got nine horses. 'Maybe,' says the farmer. The next day, his eldest son is tending the horses when one of them charges him. Tramples the kid, breaks his leg. So the villagers all come to visit, and they tell the farmer, 'How unlucky that one of those renegade horses broke your son's leg. He'll be crippled for life, such a dreadful turn of events.' The farmer just says, 'Maybe.' The very next day, an army recruiter comes through town and forces all the eldest children to join him and battle the Mongol hordes to the north. But they're forced to leave the horse farmer's son behind, on account of his broken leg. All the villagers come to the old farmer and say, 'What a lucky guy you are, that your son broke his leg and can stay at home while our eldest children must fight in the war.' Old farmer just smiles. 'Maybe,' he says."

Gombei shook his head. "You know what I always wondered? If the Chinese are so wise, how come they never learned to wash their feet? You ever had a good look at a Chinaman's feet?"

"What happened at Lucky Benten Pachinko?"

"Nothing I can't take care of."

"If you piss them off enough, they're gonna—"

"Thanks," Gombei interrupted. "But I live here. I've lived here all my life. When you go back to America, I'll still live here. I've been playing pachinko for a long time, and I know how things work."

"Then you know that if the yakuza come, you're gonna need more than golf clubs," I said. "But I'm not here to talk about your alleged cheating. Frankly, I'm half inclined to believe you. Everyone has a lucky streak now and then and maybe you were about due. But remember the Chinese farmer."

"So what are you here to talk about?"

"I want to talk about what happened the day I met you for our interview. You said that meeting me changed your luck. But I had nothing to do with it. See, Gombei—I don't think you won all this stuff playing pachinko. Maybe the low-grade rice liquor and the cigarettes and the neckties—but not that fancy suit and the new watch. And not the Honda Hobbit, thanks again, by the way."

"How's she running?"

"She's running. Gombei, I think you bought all this stuff with money you stole from the woman having the seizure. I think when no one was looking, you took an envelope full of yen from her purse and stuffed it in that shabby raincoat of yours."

Gombei glanced around the room but said nothing. I gave him some time to let the accusation settle in. That he wasn't flat-out denying it told me I had it nailed. But I didn't want to press him right away and come off like a cop, because I still had to find out if he was in it with Bojangles. I doubted it, but I wasn't gonna jump to any conclusions. After a moment, he put his hands to his face and turned his back. His shoulders heaved and shuddered. Was he crying? That I didn't expect. If he and Bojangles weren't in cahoots, he probably had no idea how much violence his opportunistic pickpocketing had caused. If he was, he had plenty of reasons to start bawling.

"How much did you take?" I said at last. "A million yen? Two million maybe? I suppose there could have been more than one envelope. Hell, your raincoat had deep pockets and her handbag was large enough. How much did you get away with?"

Gombei turned to face me again and lowered his hands. He wasn't crying and he wasn't just smiling either. Strange as it seemed, he was laughing. It wasn't the cartoonish evil laugh of some B-movie villain, nor the desperate laugh of a man with nothing else left. It was just a laugh. A laugh of genuine amusement, tinged perhaps with relief. Which almost made me want to start crying myself.

"You amaze me," Gombei said, catching his breath. "How in the world did you ever get a notion like that in your head?"

"You tell me."

"OK, I took something," he said. "But it wasn't money! You think if I stumbled onto a couple million yen I'd risk letting on? You think I'd make it obvious by donning nice threads and buying you gifts? You think I'd even stick around Tokyo and risk getting busted? Funny, ever since I got this face, people don't credit me with much intelligence. Believe me, if I found that kind of money, you'd never see or hear from Gombei Fukugawa again."

"So what did you take?"

"Nothing anyone would be liable to miss much."

"What was it?" My voice tightened.

"You really want to know?" said Gombei. "A good-luck charm. Just some worthless little figurine thingy, like the kind you might find at a temple flea market. One of the Seven Lucky Gods."

It took a moment for what he said to sink in. And once it started sinking, it didn't stop. It sank all the way to the bottom and then it sank some more.

"I don't even know why I took it," Gombei said, amused at the memory. "Just caught my eye. I got an impulse and went with it. It happens. So what?"

"A figurine," I mumbled.

"Yep. Dopey little statue. About this big." Gombei held his thumb and forefinger about three inches apart.

"Let me guess," I said. "It's black and glassy. Made from some kind of igneous rock and carved in the shape of Benzaiten."

His surprise was evident only in the way his eyes receded, pulling back as if they were trying to retreat deeper into his skull. "What's igneous rock?"

"So I'm right."

"Yeah. But how did you know?"

"Lucky guess," I said.

Gombei wasn't the only one who couldn't resist stealing the Benzaiten idol. I realized all at once that the same thing must have happened way back in 1945, when Officer Taka- hashi and his goons raided the Benzaiten Temple. The mira- cle statue supposedly belched from Mount Fuji hadn't been lost in the fire at all. It had been with Officer Takahashi for the last fifty-six years. Until Miyuki stole it from the House of Nakodo and stuffed it in her handbag.

"So what are you gonna do?" said Gombei. "Call the cops on me? Tell all the readers of *Young Oriental* that I'm a petty thief?"

I ignored Gombei and tried to think it through. It was no use. I'd done so much thinking during the last few days that I simply didn't have any left.

"You still with us, Chaka?" said Gombei.

"You're going to give me the idol. Right now."

"Give it to you? What do you want with it?"

"I could talk all day and never explain it. Let's just say that a young woman's life is at stake. Maybe mine is, too, and maybe even yours."

"You're serious?"

The look on my face was the best answer I could give.

"All right," Gombei said. "Hell, I've got no use for the thing. No use for any of this junk, come to think of it. Take a couple tubes of toothpaste if you want, maybe some sham- poo, too. I figure a traveling journalist like yourself could always use some extra—"

"Where is it?"

"All right, easy, man," Gombei said, holding his palms out to me. "It's in that closet OK? The one right behind you. Just step aside, and I'll walk over and get it for you."

There was a new quality to Gombei's speech, a raw, pinched sound I didn't much care for. For all I knew, he was in it with Bojangles, or with the Man in White, or he had a gun stashed in the closet, or a pit viper or an M-69 napalm bomb. Paranoia moved in on all sides, squeezing my head like a vise, but if it kept me breathing, I didn't care. Besides, you don't have to be paranoid to know you should never trust a guy who smiles all the time, even if it's a surgical condition.

"Forget it," I said, shooting a hand out to block Gombei as he passed. "I'll get it myself."

"Fine," Gombei sighed. "Get it yourself. This is crazy."

No arguing with that. I edged toward the closet without taking my eyes off Gombei. He just stood there in his new Zenga suit, half bemused, half irritated. Probably had no idea what he was getting himself in for when he agreed to do the "Fallen Stars" story. Neither did I, but I guess none of us ever knows what's really gonna happen. Not Ame Kitazawa, not Nakodo, not Miyuki. Not Bojangles, Afuro, Gombei, not even the Chinese horse farmer.

I tried the door of the closet, but it wouldn't budge.

"You gotta push first," Gombei said, clearly annoyed. "Lean into it, then turn the knob. The doorjamb is too tight. Here, let me get it—"

"Stay where you are!" I barked.

Gombei threw up his hands in disgust.

Had I been paying less attention to Gombei and more to the door itself, I might have noticed the four-inch round hole that had been drilled in its upper corner. But I didn't notice the hole until much later.

I leaned against the door and turned the knob until I heard a click. Then the door sprung back, thumping against my body and sending me stumbling across the room. I heard the sound before I could even see them coming, before I could try to scramble out of the way. It was a sound I'd heard only once before, back that first day at the Lucky Benten Pachinko parlor. Only it was much, much louder now.

The wave of pachinko balls spilled out of the closet and across the floor with a deafening noise, like a huge metallic wave crashing against the shore. The swell hit me about halfway between my ankle and my knee, but it still had enough force to knock me slightly off balance.

I regained my footing just in time to catch that second blow to the head. As I fell I got one final blurred image of Gombei grinning and hoisting the golf club for a third swing, but I have no idea whether it connected or not. Sometime much later I woke up with a terrible headache to find the room completely dark, awash in pachinko balls. Gombei was long gone.

33

Three Is the
Magic Number

Outside a family clad in light summer *yukatas* splashed with purple and gold made their way past the window, up the hill toward the Yasukuni Shrine, whose massive *torii* gate was illuminated by two giant searchlights burning a giant X into the darkening sky. The thirtysomething parents and their little tyke were headed to the *Mitama Matsuri*, the summer festival. I'd seen posters for it on the train. Nightly *bon-odori* dances meant to placate the spirits of the dead, some martial arts demonstrations, broiled eel and yakitori stands, carnival games, a spook house, cotton candy, beer. I wished I was headed up the hill with them. Instead, I was sitting in Hanran Books, breathing air so heavy and stale it felt like it'd been breathed a hundred times before.

"Did you actually see the Benzaiten idol?" asked Kujima.

I shook my head. My head didn't like it much. I'd just told Professor Kujima everything that had happened, starting with the Lucky Benten Pachinko hall and ending with me collapsing in a pool of pachinko balls on the floor of Gombei's overstuffed apartment. I gave him all my theories, including everything I understood and some of the stuff I didn't. Had I told him everything I didn't understand, I would've been there until next year's summer festival.

"I don't know," Professor Kujima mumbled. "It may be possible. It's certainly not *impossible*. But without the proper historical data, I can't give a definitive answer one way or another. Implausible, but not impossible."

"I don't think it's so implausible," I said. "Here's how I see it. The monks of Benzaiten Temple willfully surrendered the idol when Officer Takahashi was invited in for tea that afternoon back in 1945. Only Officer Takahashi decides maybe he'd rather not hand over the idol to the Imperial Household Agency. But in order to make it look good, he has to make the thing disappear. He does this by burning the temple, starting with the priest and the monks inside it."

"It's not impossible," Kujima said. "But why, if he already had the idol, would Takahashi wait outside while the fire burned? Why would he later try to run back into the burning building? I believe the eyewitness accounts are fairly consistent on this aspect of the Benzaiten Temple incident."

"Because he had to pretend he was awaiting the monks' decision," I said. "He couldn't let on that the monks had already surrendered the idol. Running into the flaming temple was a way of thwarting any suspicion that might come his way when the idol wasn't found. He had to do it to show he was absolutely committed to the emperor and his sacred mission—'seven lives to serve the nation' and all that nonsense. And no one would suspect him of stealing the Benzaiten idol if he was willing to risk his life by charging into a burning building."

"An interesting interpretation of the events," said Kujima. "You might have made a first-rate historian. The trouble is, from what you've told me, your interpretation of the incident is not entirely unprecedented."

"Bojangles thought of it a long time ago," I agreed. "From what the Kitazawa family told me, my guess is that he might have tried a version of what he's doing now years ago, with Nakodo's first wife. She also mentioned a Man in White, though frankly, I don't know how she drowned back in 1977. But I think I know what happened during the last few days. Bojangles used Miyuki to steal the idol from the House of Nakodo, but before she could hand it over to him, my pachinko-addicted, and, as it turns out, kleptomaniacal 'Fallen Stars' subject, Gombei Fukugawa, stole the thing from her purse. Bojangles didn't know this. That's why he trashed Afuro's place, that's why he wrecked Nakodo's house before killing him. After all the work he'd put into it, he's increasingly desperate to find this stupid little statue. Increasingly desperate, increasingly reckless, and increasingly dangerous."

Kujima wrinkled his brow in consternation. "And you think this odd figure dressed in white was Bojangles?"

"Right," I said. "Say he showed up at Lucky Benten Pachinko right after Miyuki had the seizure—he could have seen me there. Or he could simply have found out I'd made the emergency call the same way Nakodo did before summoning me to his mansion in Ark Hills."

"And you think he broke into your hotel room to search for the missing Benzaiten idol?"

I nodded. Slowly, to ease the pain.

"But did he actually search your room?"

"He didn't tear it to pieces, like he did with Nakodo and Afuro's places, but he could have searched it almost anytime during the last few days. He obviously had no problem breaking in."

Kujima furrowed his brow. "But why the second visit? The three men in the hall, the spelled messages—what could he have hoped to accomplish with such theatrics?"

"I don't know," I said. "Maybe he wanted to spook me, show me who was boss. I don't know."

"And why go after the other young woman—Afuro, I believe?"

"I can't figure that part, either."

"And you have no idea who this Bojangles could possibly be, aside from his proclivity for dressing in white and his ability to, ahem, cause sudden seizures?"

"You think I don't know how ridiculous it sounds?"

"Have you gone to the police?"

"See previous comment."

Professor Kujima let out a long breath and rubbed his eyes. I'd hoped confirming the historical possibility that Takahashi had stolen the idol back in 1945 would bring me closer to making it all come together. But all talking with Professor Kujima did was make me realize how far I was from solving anything. Every time I tried to put the puzzle together I was left with pieces that didn't fit. Maybe I knew what happened to the Benzaiten monks in 1945, but I still couldn't figure how it meshed with Ame Kitazawa's death in 1977, or Miyuki's in 2001. But they had to be related.

Or not. I had experienced a twelve-hour seizure and suffered a nasty blow to the head recently, and maybe those events effectively ended my days as a rational, mentally stable human being. Maybe I'd spend the rest of my life raving about a Man in White and how he was responsible for the drowning deaths of every man, woman and child from the Tokugawa era to the present, as well as every grand mal seizure not caused by Pokémon cartoons.

"What do you propose we do?" Kujima asked.

Wished to hell I knew. I glanced around at all the books surrounding me, not a single one of any help. Why hadn't anyone written *Unraveling Blackmail for Dummies*? Where was an *Idiot's Guide to Lucky Gods and Seizures* when you needed one?

"Wait a sec," I mumbled. "That's it. A book."

"A book?"

"Didn't you tell me that someone once tried to write a book about the Benzaiten Temple incident? A book that never made it into print."

Kujima raised an eyebrow and pushed his glasses up the bridge of his nose. "Correct. From what I understand, the publisher came under pressure from certain right-wing groups and decided releasing the book was more trouble than it was worth."

"Pressure meaning what exactly?"

"I don't recall the specifics, but they likely employed the usual tactics. Parking a sound truck outside the publisher's office and blasting slanderous accusations day and night. If that doesn't work, they've been known to break in, trash the place and threaten their employees. But like I said, I don't remember the specifics in this case."

"Could the Oshoku Group have right-wing affiliates?"

"Certainly. The construction industry has a long history of using right-wing toughs and yakuza when necessary, whether for breaking strikes or—"

"Do you remember the name of the publisher?"

Kujima shook his head. "I wonder where this direction of inquiry is headed."

"Consider this," I began, trying to lay it all out in my head. "Let's say the book in question not only covered the Benzaiten incident—an incident you said had been written about before, though wasn't widely known. Let's say this new book was going to out Old Man Nakodo as Officer Takahashi. Someone tipped the Nakodos off about this book, and the Nakodo clan used their connections to make sure it never hit the streets. My guess is that the right-wing groups had nothing against the book from an ideological or historical standpoint or whatever—they were just being used by the Nakodos."

"Again, it's possible, but . . ."

"But our censored author didn't just forget about the book and go on with his life," I said. "He became more determined than ever to ruin Nakodo. Made it his life's work. Or, maybe it wasn't the author at all, just someone who had seen the book prior to publication. An editor maybe, or, hell, I don't know, but someone. My guess is, we look at the people involved with this book, we've got our Bojangles. Professor Kujima, can I use your phone?"

"Of course," Kujima said. His bemused tone told me he

found my latest theory totally crazy, but there was no time to waste convincing him. Professor Kujima plopped a big black phone down on top of his desk. I picked up the receiver and started to punch in Detective Ihara's number when I suddenly stopped.

"There's no dial tone," I said.

"No?" Kujima said, feigning surprise to cover his embarrassment. "Ah, yes. I'm afraid perhaps there has been, how shall we say, a slight misunderstanding regarding my account with the phone company."

"No matter," I said, remembering I still had the little pink cell phone Afuro had given me. I dug it out of my pocket and hit the power button. And after all my endless running around and useless worrying and far-flung theorizing, the whole thing suddenly fell into place. Just like that, with the simple push of a button.

My heart didn't skip a beat, I didn't feel the need to shout for joy or anything else. There was no elation in it, no relief. Just a sense of disappointment. Disappointment with myself, mostly, and disappointment with the man sitting across from me.

As soon as I turned it on, the phone started ringing. I was about to answer it when I realized there was no incoming call. The phone wasn't playing the incoming-call song. It was playing a nice little jingle called "Strangers in the Night." Meaning Afuro was within a twenty-five-meter radius. Meaning Afuro was here, inside Hanran Books.

I switched the phone off and stuck it back in my pocket. Kujima cocked his head. "Is something the matter?"

I didn't say anything. There wasn't anything to say.

Professor Kujima stared across the desk, eyebrows lowered, mouth twisting in anticipation of words that refused to come. We just sat there staring at each other in the dimly lit dusty room for what felt like several minutes. In reality, it was probably less than four or five seconds. Then time lurched forward and several things happened almost simultaneously.

The overhead lights suddenly went dead. I heard a drawer open. I jumped up from my chair. There was a burst of light across the desk and something hot slammed into my shoulder. My ears rang, I spun around and the next thing I knew I was on the floor and Kujima was standing over me, invisible but for his glasses reflecting the streetlights outside. I could also just make out the shape of a gun in his hand, the metal barrel gleaming through the dark. I was wondering if Afuro was still alive when the second flash came. Searing pain tore through my gut, my eyes rolled into the back of my skull as if looking for a way out, a way to escape witnessing what was about to happen. But when that third shot came, I saw everything.

34

The Thousand Faces
of Benzaiten

Thousands of bombs drop from the sky, obliterating an entire city, and yet some buildings are miraculously left standing. Thousands of silver balls plummet down the face of a pachinko machine, but a lucky few never hit bottom. Billions of people are born into a complex game of chance, a game in which the rules are hidden and ever-changing, a game in which there is no winning, only slower ways to lose.

And yet, some of us manage temporary victory. Some of us manage to keep playing long after the odds say we should've been finished. Some of us get lucky.

Gombei once asked me if I considered myself lucky, and I said I didn't know what luck was. Now I had a working definition. Luck was when someone holds a gun not four feet from your nose, aims this gun and fires and you still don't die. Luck is when not only don't you die, you don't even get hit. Luck is when the shot that should've killed you jams the gun. Luck is when the gun then explodes, and blows off the hand of the man holding it.

Unless, of course, you're the man holding the gun.

When the lights flickered back on, Professor Kujima was scrutinizing what remained of his hand with the mute fascination of the truly misfortunate, as if he just couldn't for the life of him figure out how this once functional and ordinary body part had suddenly transformed into a pulp of torn flesh, blood and bone, a useless mass recognizable as having once been a hand only by the thumb and pinkie still twitching at the end of the stump like the antennae on a lobster.

I tried to pick myself up from the ground and felt a raw jolt of pain pierce through the general burning sensation. A red stain was creeping over my shoulder and down my chest, merging with the red stain spreading over my abdomen, coloring my shirt in a pattern that reminded me of the *kohaku* carp in Nakodo's pool. I hadn't been lucky enough to avoid Kujima's first two shots, but I guess you can't win them all.

My movement jarred Kujima from contemplating his missing hand. Before I could get to my feet, he sprung forward and aimed a kick to the side of my head. The blow connected and it was by far the hardest kick I'd ever taken from a historian. The impact sent me rolling onto my wounded shoulder, and I let out a scream. My luck must've pretty much run out by then, because he managed to land two more kicks to my kidneys and another one to the back of my head. After that I stopped counting. After that I stopped doing pretty much everything.

But I remained conscious long enough to see Kujima stumble across the room and attempt to shove a bookcase out of the way. It was awkward going with only one hand, but he put his shoulder into it and eventually managed to nudge the bookcase far enough aside to open the door behind it. Then he lumbered back over to me, grabbed the back of my collar with his good hand and pulled. I had a dim notion that the bleeding guy being dragged across the floor should try to put up some resistance before Kujima finished him off. A good idea, but trying to get my body to follow instructions was like screaming at characters onscreen during a horror movie.

My head lolled from side to side and I heard myself groan and shriek as my body thumped backward down the stairs, but I couldn't feel much of anything. I just stared at my wing tips above me and noted in an abstract kind of way that judging from the slug trail of blood smeared in my wake, the guy being dragged down the stairs was losing an unhealthy amount of precious bodily fluids.

We must've arrived at the bottom of the stairs because I noticed I wasn't moving anymore. Kujima turned on the lights and suddenly hundreds of eyes were staring at me from every corner of the room. Some the size of silver dollars, some no bigger than the head of a pin, some shiny, some dull, all of them belonging to the same woman and none of them terribly impressed. I suppose after all Benzaiten had witnessed over the centuries, it would take more than a gaijin dying of gunshot wounds to get the goddess's eyebrows up.

Kujima had assembled an amazing collection here in the basement of Hanran Books, from three-foot-high concrete statues, to carved wooden dolls, to little golden Benzaitens you could fit on the end of a key chain. Every incarnation of Benzaiten you could imagine, but still, apparently, none of them quite the Benzaiten he was looking for.

Besides the idols, the basement was empty but for a few scattered cardboard boxes. Whether they contained books, more Benten figurines or pages from the professor's unfinished manuscript, I couldn't say. All at once Kujima came thumping back into my field of vision carrying a large, squarish aluminum container. He calmly placed the can on the ground, took two steps forward and leaned over to have a closer look at me. His face was contorted with pain and rivulets of sweat beaded over his waxy flesh like water rung from a towel, but his eyes were hard and alert, fully focused on the task ahead. Now, I thought, would be a good time for the guy on the floor to send a powerful kick into the back of Kujima's knee. Now, I thought, might be the last chance the guy on the floor is gonna get.

The guy on the floor didn't hear me, but the guy standing over me seemed to. As if punishing me for my thoughts, Kujima swung a foot into my stomach and followed up with one to my face. I heard a thin crunching sound but felt only a tingling sensation and a distant sense of displeasure. The guy on the ground was simply beyond reach.

Kujima's blows rearranged my body so that I was staring up at the wall behind me. New sets of eyes stared back at me now. Above a small desk in the corner, an array of photographs and yellowing newspaper clippings was pinned to the wall. Ame Kitazawa was there, posed next to Nakodo in front of the massive wooden *torii* gate, he wearing an ear-to-ear grin, she looking demure, camera shy. The photos of Miyuki were mostly dark, blurry, hidden-camera-type snapshots, likely taken with one of those tiny cameras they sold in Akihabara specialist stores. Afuro was in some of the photos, sitting next to Miyuki at what I guessed was the bar of the Café Acrophobia. All the people on the board were smiling, it struck me, and all the people on the board were dead.

Next came a splashing noise and the unmistakable scent of gasoline. I struggled to keep my eyes open, watching Kujima haphazardly douse the room, liberally soaking the army of Benzaitens. Much of the remaining gasoline ended up on me. I could smell it, could hear it splattering over my body, but didn't feel a thing. I took that as a good sign. If I couldn't feel gasoline being poured over my open wounds, maybe I wouldn't be able to feel myself being burned alive in a few moments. Maybe I had exactly that much luck left.

Kujima dropped the empty can to the floor, then walked back to his desk and rifled through a drawer. Some of his self-control was slipping, because he suddenly yelped like a dog whose tail was stepped on. When he returned, he was holding a small box of wooden kitchen matches, whimpering. Opening them with one hand presented a challenge, one Kujima overcame by placing the box between his teeth. He withdrew a single match, then opened his mouth wider and let the box tumble to the floor. The matches spilled out with a dry clatter and he took a couple steps backward and surveyed the room one final time, as if checking to see if he'd forgotten anything.

Apparently he had, because he dropped the match, leaned over and began going through my pockets. He barked again and sputtered into a series of half-choked cries, but I didn't think he could even hear himself by now. Kujima's ugly stump was silhouetted in the light above me, drops of blood falling from it and splattering against my forehead like some sick version of the Chinese water torture. The wrecked mess of flesh had to hurt like hell and I was just starting to feel a little sympathy for Kujima when some distant corner of my brain sent a reminder that he'd shot me, beaten me and was about to light me on fire.

Kujima found what he was looking for. The pink cell phone. He hit the power button with his thumb and "Strangers in the Night" filled the basement. Across the room, a second phone chimed in, echoing about half a beat behind. Kujima retrieved Afuro's phone from her kaleido-scopic Cecil McBee handbag, turned them both off and shoved them into the pocket of his corduroy jacket.

Then it was back to the matches.

He picked one up off the ground, placed the sulfured end against the bottom of his front teeth and jerked it forward. There was a spark, then a flame. Then a thick cloud of smoke passed across his face and the match went dead. Kujima barked, flecks of white spittle burst from his mouth. He picked up another match from the floor.

That's when I noticed the Man in White was sitting atop the cardboard box. He had one leg crossed with geometric precision over the other and was holding a short brown ciga-rette between his pale, elongated fingers. The Man in White said nothing and wore no expression whatsoever.

And somehow, Professor Kujima didn't even notice him. Kujima flicked the match against his teeth, and again the match sparked to life before being doused in a cloud of smoke from the Man in White. And still Kujima didn't see the dapper little man only a couple feet away, but just stared at the blackened stick of wood with the same bafflement he'd given his exploded hand.

This strange pantomime was enacted three more times. By his final attempt, Kujima's face was knotted with hurt, frustration and disbelief. The whimpering was constant now and the intervals between yelps of pain were growing shorter. All at once Kujima went hulking up the stairs, one arm dangling uselessly at his side and trailing blood. The door slammed behind him and he was gone.

The Man in White glanced down at me, then extinguished his cigarette on the bottom of his shoe and dropped it delicately to the floor. He placed another one between his thin lips, then produced a gunmetal lighter and lit the cigarette with a birdlike movement of his wrist. I was starting to wish Kujima had set fire to the place, because it was suddenly freezing cold. For a while my body trembled and my teeth chattered and then everything gradually grew warmer, as if the sun had slowly emerged from behind a bank of clouds. I closed my eyes and my body felt like it was floating on a gentle current, being silently swept along on a deep, dark river. Somewhere in the distance I heard the sound of a door opening, footsteps descending stairs. I heard my name and saw Afuro standing over me, her eyes wide in the dark. Behind her, the Man in White sat atop the cardboard box, cocooning himself in smoke, but she never saw him.

35

The Pachinko Funeral

When the rain finally came it didn't let up for days. It just poured and poured, an endless slanting sheet of gray draped over the muddled horizon. I spent a lot of those days just sitting there, watching the rain trail down the window, watching it flood the pavement below as hundreds of umbrellas flowed down the street, swirling and merging in the zebraed crosswalks like leaves caught in the eddy of a stream. And at night I would listen to the steadying drumming of the rain against the glass, a sound at once lonely and soothing, a sound that said pretty much everything there was to say.

I could've spent my entire convalescence listening to the rain, but there were a lot of visitors coming and going and all of them had questions. Some I chose to answer, some I chose not to, some I couldn't answer and still can't to this day.

Inspector Arajiro had the most questions. The first time he came, he was alone, and the questions were about why Professor Kujima had shot me and where I thought he might be hiding. I gave Inspector Arajiro all the answers I thought he was capable of understanding, and told him that Kujima was going to go after Gombei Fukugawa if he hadn't already, because now he knew that Gombei had the Benzaiten idol. Arajiro got a funny look on his face and didn't ask me any more questions. He made a big show of concern for my well-being whenever nurses were in the room, but there was an unmistakable gleam of satisfaction in his eyes at seeing me laid up with two bullet wounds, two broken ribs, a fractured nose, a split lip, and sixteen stitches in my forehead.

"I'm amazed that old relic was even able to fire once, let alone twice," Arajiro chuckled. Turned out the gun Kujima had shot me with was a Taisho 14 Nambu, a Luger-style pistol used by Japanese military officers during World War II. "Museum pieces like that almost always jam the first shot, especially if they've been sitting around for fifty some years. Guess you're just unlucky."

"Maybe," I said.

"On the other hand, you survived two gunshot wounds and a lot of blood loss. So perhaps you're luckier than you think."

"Maybe," I said.

Just before leaving, Arajiro tossed me a newspaper.

After he'd gone, I read about how Gombei Fukugawa had

been found bludgeoned to death inside his apartment in Nippori. There was no mention of Kujima or the Benzaiten idol. No mention about how Gombei's death was tied to those of Miyuki and Mr. Nakodo. The article said only that police were interviewing owners of pachinko halls the victim frequented. According to sources in the Tokyo Metropolitan Police, Gombei had apparently discovered some new, undetectable form of cheating and had recently made a lot of enemies in the pachinko world. They suspected this was the motive behind his killing.

Of course, Gombei hadn't been cheating, not really, but it didn't surprise me that the cops settled on the pachinko angle. Inspector Arajiro and his ilk avoided complicated scenarios by nature, the way cats avoided water or vampires avoided the sun.

The article closed by noting that the seventh anniversary of the death of his singing partner, Aiko Shimato, a.k.a. Lime, had just passed. Turned out the anniversary was on the very afternoon I'd met Gombei at the Lucky Benten Pachinko, a fact I regretted not realizing earlier. If I'd done my homework, I probably would've been a little more sensitive and waited until at least the next day to interview Gombei. Meaning I never would've witnessed Miyuki's seizure, and without me noticing it, I doubt Gombei would've either. Which meant he wouldn't have stolen the idol, which meant he'd probably still be sitting in front of some pachinko machine today. But you can only take this line of thinking so far. The world is hopelessly complex and you never have all the facts until it's too late. I'd tried to do what I thought was right, and that's all you can do.

A few media outlets got wind that I'd conducted the last Gombei interview and offered to buy my story, but no matter how many baskets of oranges they sent—and baskets of oranges were what they always sent—I told them they'd just have to read it in the next issue of *Youth in Asia*. The gambit worked because Sarah called to tell me that even though I'd missed my flight and my deadline, there would still be a job waiting for me back in Cleveland. Fact was, *Youth in Asia* headquarters was getting inundated with so many calls from the Japanese media that they had no choice but to expand the scope of the Gombei piece from a three-hundred-and-fifty-word "Fallen Stars" snippet to a seven-thousand-word feature article to be serialized in Japan by the highest bidder. Stranger still, before hanging up the phone, Sarah actually said good-bye. By the time I overcame my shock enough to respond in kind she'd hung up.

I'd have to start thinking about actually putting pen to paper and writing the Gombei piece soon, but the funny part was, even after everything that had happened I still didn't have much to say about the guy. Gombei liked his pachinko, had some funny ideas about luck, was a bit of a klepto and stole the wrong thing at the wrong time and caused a lot of people a lot of harm in the process. How many words was that?

Inspector Arajiro paid me one more visit. He showed up in the middle of the night, dripping like a drowned rat. Professor Kujima, he told me, had finally been found. He'd been discovered by a hotel manager in Kyobashi who was making the rounds and noticed a sealed room in the basement had been broken into. They found Kujima's body inside and four things about the discovery were making Inspector Arajiro's sciatica act up.

One—the autopsy revealed water in Kujima's lungs, meaning he'd apparently drowned then somehow been transported across town and dumped in an empty hotel room. Two—surveillance tapes revealed no one coming or going from the hotel during the time the incident was to have occurred. Three—the sealed room was broken out of, rather than into, and four—this same hotel was the one I had been staying at, a place called the Hotel Cerulean, which made Inspector Arajiro furious even if he couldn't say why.

Once he told me all this, he showed me a photograph from the crime scene. Kujima's body was slumped forward over a low wooden table that sat between two ornate floor cushions wrapped in plastic. There was a half-opened door on the other side of the room, a room I recognized as one I'd visited during a twelve-hour seizure. Inspector Arajiro rubbed his bloodshot eyes and asked me what I made of all of it. I told him I had only lame theories and half-baked notions and none of them were simple and nine times out of ten the simple answer is the correct one. So unless he wanted to show up in my office in Cleveland with new zit creams for me to write about, I'd leave the investigating to him and the rest of the police.

Inspector Arajiro glared at me for a good ten minutes before pulling his fat face into a sneer and reminding me of his impending retirement. Then he waddled across the room, pinned an unlit cigarette to the corner of his mouth and flipped off the lights, leaving me in the dark, alone with the sound of the rain.

That was the last night I spent alone, because the next day I got a roommate. Admiral the Walrus Hideki arrived in the afternoon still dressed in his fancy uniform, carrying a basket of oranges and a small goldfish bowl that contained my pal from the Octopus's Garden. I apologized for any trouble I might have caused the Hotel Cerulean, but he insisted that it was he who should be apologizing. Funny thing was, he could never tell me exactly what he should be apologizing for. When I pressed, he made vague statements about how perhaps maybe he hadn't told me exactly everything about the hotel, particularly about the Benzaiten painting hanging in the basement, and about the unwanted guests it sometimes attracted. When I asked if he meant the Man in White and his three cohorts, he merely said that hotel policy forbade him to discuss matters of the supernatural.

"The supernatural?" I said.

His mustache twitched once in reply, then he consulted his flip-top watch, wished me a speedy recovery and made a speedy exit. The fish turned slow circles in his bowl and looked out over the hospital room, mouthing silent O's.

The Walrus wasn't the only well-wisher I received. Detective Ihara took time out of his busy peephole-gazing schedule to drop by and personally deliver some information I'd requested, along with yet another basket of oranges. He was even kind enough to give me a 50 percent discount on the info, what he called his invalid rate. Had I known Detective Ihara could be so bighearted, I would've gotten myself shot years ago.

Both pieces of information bore out my theory on what exactly had led Professor Kujima to become so obsessed that he'd enact a bizarre revenge scheme that eventually led to me nearly bleeding to death in the basement of a used bookstore.

The first had to do with an unpublished manuscript called "Burning the Benzaiten Temple: An Historical Account of the Confluence of Events Leading to Tokyo's Darkest Hour and Its Present-Day Aftermath." The book was to be printed in 1989 by Sufosha Ltd., but they stopped the presses after being pressured by a group of right-wing fanatics. As you might suspect from the long-winded title, Kujima himself was the author. And as you might suspect, the right-wing group responsible had rumored ties to the Oshoku Group.

And the second piece of info told me that the Nakodo family hadn't been content with stopping the book; they needed to thoroughly discredit Kujima to make sure their dirty little secret never came to light. Detective Ihara had discovered the identity of the student who alleged that Kujima had paid her for sexual favors. I forget her name, but her name wasn't important. That she owned a home in the wealthy suburb of Setagaya and was currently employed as an independent consultant of the Oshoku Group told me everything I needed to know about how Professor Kujima was forced out of Nihon University.

I never understood how Kujima learned about Old Man Nakodo's true identity, but maybe it was like he told me— even the most obscure facts aren't so hard to find if you're willing to work at it; the hard part was putting them together. The way I put them together, somewhere along the line Kujima had transferred his obsession with Officer Takahashi and the Nakodo family to an obsession with the Benzaiten idol itself. Maybe he thought possessing the thing would prove once and for all that he'd been right all those years ago about Nakodo/Takahashi, but maybe it was even more complicated than that. Maybe he believed the idol actually had magical properties, believed that whosoever owned it would be protected by the goddess Benzaiten.

If so, he was sorely mistaken about the nature of those magical properties, because everyone who'd come into possession of the thing was now dead. Everyone except dreaded Kempeitai Officer Takahashi, who'd set the whole bizarre plot in motion almost sixty years ago and was now just a harmless

old man whizzing about in a wheelchair. He'd outlive everyone in the Minato ward and probably the rest of us, too.

How do you explain that, Mr. Goldfish?

Your dry-world ways are a fathomless mystery to me.

You're not much help, Mr. Goldfish.

Still, you can't say I'm not a good listener.

THE CONVERSATIONS I HAD with Afuro were much livelier. She
never brought oranges but she visited every night, timing her
arrivals to mysteriously coincide with dinner. No matter
what we talked about, and we talked about any number of
things, at some point in the conversation we always had the
following exchange.

"This stuff tastes gross," she would say. "How can they
expect you to get better eating crap like this?"

"I'm not eating it," I would say. "You are."

"Yeah," she would respond. "But still."

Looking back on our conversations, I'm struck by how
ignorant I was to the reality that she needed these visits as
much as I did. It gradually dawned on me that Afuro never
mentioned any friends besides Miyuki, that she absolutely
refused to talk about her job and subtly avoided questions
about her family back in Muramura. Despite her slangy
speech and girlish façade, she revealed herself as smart and
thoroughly unconventional, a lot like Sarah was when she
joined *Youth in Asia* all those years ago. Afuro was that rare
duck who never tried to be quirky, but was what she was just
the same. Which meant she had a tough life ahead of her, and
was probably already getting used to the idea that she'd never
escape a certain type of innate loneliness.

And although I was the one in the hospital bed, it felt like she was the one regaining her strength during the hours we spent together. I think having someone there to listen helped give her a reason to keep getting up and blindly stumbling alone out into the world, which, no matter what sophisticated delusions we comfort ourselves with, is the way we all face a universe where change is all that never changes.

But during her first visit, I spent most of the time trying to figure out how both of us were still alive to be having these conversations in the first place. It took her a while to explain what had happened, but basically it went like this: the night Bojangles was following her under the expressway, she'd taken off running, just like I'd urged her to do. Bojangles—Professor Kujima—tried to tackle her but was only able to wrench away her handbag before she fled to the safety of Jimbocho station.

I figured Kujima was going after her because, at that point, he still may have thought she knew what Miyuki had done with the idol. But why, I asked, hadn't Afuro called me once she got away from him? Because, she explained, her cell phone was in the handbag. Ever heard of a pay phone, I asked. She rolled her eyes and said that she'd thought of that, but all her money and her phone cards were in the handbag Kujima had stolen. So why didn't she go home and at least leave a message for me at the Hotel Cerulean? Because she had all the hotel info programmed into her cell phone, which Bojangles/Kujima was now in possession of. When I asked her why she didn't just call information, she told me she couldn't remember the name of the hotel.

"You couldn't remember the name of the hotel?"

"Like you've never made a mistake in your life," she huffed.

I reminded her that she'd followed me from the Hotel Cerulean the night she tried to kill me with a brick, so she had to know where it was. Couldn't she have come by that night to let me know she was OK? She said that without the maps feature on her cell phone she'd never be able to find the place again. Even after two years in Tokyo, she still didn't know where she was half the time.

"You ever think maybe you're a little too dependent on your cell phone?" I asked.

"If I wasn't you'd probably be dead," she replied.

Because, she explained, the only reason she located me was that she located Bojangles, and she only did that by locating her missing phone. She did this by contacting the phone's manufacturer, who, for a small fee of twenty-five hundred yen, were able to find any of their phones lost in the greater Tokyo Metropolitan area as they'd been implanted with a special global positioning chip. I was just lucky, Afuro said, that she happened to read about the service in *LolNet* magazine.

"*LolNet* magazine?"

"The superfantastic handphone magazine for girls."

"You're kidding."

"There are lots of magazines about cell phones."

"I thought you didn't read magazines."

"I said they're dumb. I didn't say I don't read them."

After having located her phone, she spent the afternoon staking out Hanran Books. She saw me walk in, but waited, still harboring some gnawing suspicion that maybe I was a creep after all, maybe I'd been in this thing with Bojangles all along. But when she heard the gunshots and later saw Professor Kujima emerge looking panicked and with a towel wrapped around his hand, she knew something was wrong.

When I didn't come out, she decided to go in. Kujima had been in such a hurry to find Gombei and the precious Benzaiten idol he'd neglected to lock the front door.

"I actually saw one of his fingers," she said, spooning raspberry Jell-O into her mouth. "When I walked in, it was just like, *lying* there in the middle of the floor. The little one, I think. Not the pinkie, but the ring finger. The blood didn't freak me out as much as the way the skin looked. It was kind of shiny, like polished or waxy almost, and at the exploded end there were these little whitish chunks of—"

"Some of us are trying to eat dinner here," I said.

"You're not eating," she said. "I am."

"Yeah," I said. "But still."

I spent a lot of time unraveling the whole story as I knew it. I told Afuro a lot more than I'd told the police, but then she was better equipped to deal with the information. I was surprised to find she knew even less than me about the Benzaiten, but maybe I shouldn't have been. After all, she said, nobody she knew paid attention to the Seven Lucky Gods anymore except maybe her grandma. Afuro asked a lot of questions I couldn't answer and came up with some angles I'd never thought of, and in the end we couldn't even agree on how Miyuki had died. I maintained that after all the psychological weirdness Miyuki had endured while playing at being Nakodo's mistress, losing the idol and seeing her chance to pay off her debts had proven too much. I'd come around to believing Miyuki really had drowned herself in the miserable water beneath the expressway—it was the only way she believed she'd be able to extricate herself from the whole mess.

Afuro liked the supernatural angle. She thought the Man in White definitely sounded like a ghost, and had been responsible for drowning not only Professor Kujima, but for drowning Miyuki and Mr. Nakodo as well. She also did some research at the library and found a couple of old newspaper photographs of the original Benzaiten Temple. One of these showed the head priest of the temple posing in front of it in 1945. The picture had been photocopied from the original article in the *Mainichi Shimbun*, microfiched and rephotocopied, so the image had degenerated into little more than a blurry smudge of black on white. Even so, the priest's small, delicate features couldn't help but remind me of the Man in White.

"I thought you didn't believe in ghosts," Afuro said.

"I'm a creature of contradictory impulses," I said.

And I couldn't help but think of another priest at another holy site devoted to Benten, the old guy I'd met at the Benten Temple in Ueno Park, the one who'd talked about *Obon* and the dead visiting the earth. How he'd said some souls lose their way and become trapped in the city.

Of course, nothing Afuro found in old newspapers and nothing the priest told me could explain everything. The seizures, the smoke, the white suits, the fact that the Man in White had shown up in time to save me from being roasted alive inside the basement of Hanran Books. But I knew no matter how much I pondered, I'd never be able to answer these questions. It's hard enough to figure out why living people act the way they do, much less ghosts or supernatural emissaries of the goddess Benzaiten or whatever the hell the Man in White and his three helpers really were.

The second-to-last time I saw Afuro, most of our conversation centered on Miyuki. She talked a lot about growing up together, and how Miyuki was already drifting away long before she finally slipped into the dark waters of the Nihonbashi River. She could never fully understand Miyuki's reasons for going along with Kujima's plan, except to say that Miyuki's motivation couldn't have been simply the money. Miyuki had always wanted to become someone else, had always dreamed of living as one of those beautiful, charmed creatures orbiting the bright lights of Tokyo, a universe far removed from the humdrum existence of Muramura. Miyuki, Afuro thought, had been in such a giddy rush to throw herself headlong into the big-city excitement that she probably saw her relationship with Mr. Nakodo as nothing more than a training exercise in seduction, a sophisticated game, the type of game a mysterious big-city woman might play. Miyuki's letter hinted that in the end, she realized it wasn't all just harmless fun, that it was taking a toll on her. But by then it was already too late.

Afuro suddenly stopped talking and I listened to the rain filling the silence as we both sat there, two strangers in a drab hospital room, a long way from home. Except that we weren't strangers anymore, which was I guess the silver lining. Four people were lost, but two had found each other. Uneven math, but I was happy with my place in the lopsided equation.

"You know what the worst part is?" Afuro said. "I'm already forgetting her. Every day, a few details disappear. Like one day I can picture her eyes, but not her hair. And the next I can see her smile, but can't remember exactly what her voice sounded like. It feels like I'm losing her all over again, little by little. Before long, everything will be gone and I won't be able to recall her at all. All I'll remember is that stupid mole."

It began slowly, but once she got going, Afuro cried for quite a while. She cried and cried as the rain came down and it felt like the whole world was filling up with water. I didn't know what to say, but I figured this was the part where I should say something. I told her that she did the best she could for her friend, that there was nothing more she could have done to save Miyuki. I told her she had no way of know- ing what was happening, that Miyuki herself couldn't have known. I told Afuro that she was safe now and that nobody was going to hurt her. She was never going to forget her friend, not completely, but we all need to forget a little to keep from going crazy. You have to forget and you have to have faith that things will turn out all right in the end. Even when you know they probably won't. Even when you know they never do, not all the way.

THE DAY I GOT released from the Nihon University Hospital the rain had stopped and the sun was back, beating down on me from above just like old times. I was so glad to finally get some non-hospital air that I didn't even care how hot that air was. Everything smelled fresh and clean, almost like spring- time save for the indeterminate Tokyo miasma that hung over the city day or night, rain or shine.

Before I started finally writing the story, there was just one more piece of research I wanted to do, so I went straight from the hospital to a public library in Shinjuku. It didn't take me long to locate an old map of Tokyo, circa 1941. The city had changed so much since that it might as well have been a map of Cleveland, but I found what I was looking for. The original 1707 Benzaiten Temple was situated on the banks of a canal in Kyobashi, in Chuo-ku, central Tokyo. The canals were long gone, but there were just enough landmarks left to indicate the temple site as the current location of the Hotel Cerulean. The past bleeding into the present. It made a certain kind of sense, and just proved that you never know what you'll find in the basements of strange Japanese hotels.

I made a few photocopies, then went outside to wait for Afuro by the east exit of Shinjuku station. She came motoring up on the Honda Hobbit about fifteen minutes later. In her rolled-up jeans and flowing red windbreaker, Afuro didn't look quite as ridiculous as I imagined I did on the yellow moped, but even she seemed eager to distance herself from the thing as fast as possible, illegally parking it across the street and pigeon-toeing toward me without so much as a glance over her shoulder.

"How was work?" I asked.

She rolled her eyes.

Then she handed me a newspaper clipping she said I might find interesting. It was a story about funeral services being held at the Sensoji Temple in Asakusa for the fifty thousand pachinko machines being taken out of circulation this year by Heiwa Manufacturing. A photo showed a Buddhist priest in orange robes giving last rites in front of an altar bedecked with flowers and burning incense. Instead of a picture of the deceased, there was a golden pachinko machine, which the article said was meant to represent not just the retired machines, but the souls of all the deceased who found joy in playing them, making them, or working with them. With fifty thousand machines being retired from over seventeen thousand pachinko halls, it was tough to say what the odds were that Gombei Fukugawa had played one of them, but I liked to think somebody was praying for him, if only vicariously, if only through the machine that provided him a crude metaphor for his luckless existence.

I folded the clipping and tucked it in my shirt pocket. A few minutes later, Afuro and I got in a cab and took a wandering route southeast. It would've been quicker and cheaper to take the trains, but I'd already blown my per diem days ago and there was no point in trying to be fiscally responsible now. As the sun began to drop, the multicolored lights coming to life upon the wide, pulsing avenues of Ginza streaked by like comets. Soon we were traveling along the expressway on the coast of Tokyo Bay. To the west, a cutaway landscape of half-illuminated tower blocks rising above a mangled geometry of low apartment buildings. To the east, deep waters reflecting the lights from industrial shipyards and seaside factories glinting in the distance beyond. From this vantage point, Tokyo looked like a peaceful, half-slumbering seaside city no different from countless other urban coastal areas the world over. A postcard metropolis totally alien to the one I loved despite it all, that churning, unrelenting pageant of the new century, the Tokyo you experienced from the inside.

We were headed to Odaiba, the man-made island in the middle of Tokyo Bay, to watch the annual summer fireworks display. Apparently a lot of people had the same idea, because traffic slowed to a crawl before we'd even reached the Hinode pier.

The towers of the Rainbow Bridge shone in the near distance, rising up from the dark water a glowing red. The Rainbow Bridge got its name because the colors of the columns changed all the time in true twenty-first-century fashion, and from the pace of traffic I figured I'd be able to see it go through the full spectrum before we made it to the other side.

"I've decided to go to Australia," Afuro announced.

"By yourself?"

She nodded. "I've got the ticket, so I might as well use it.

Besides, I need to get away for a while. I'm just sick of being here. I thought Tokyo would be different from Muramura, and it is, but I don't know. Even with all the people, sometimes being here feels like being stuck on some island."

"Japan is an island," I said. "So is Australia."

"That's not what I mean," Afuro said. The sky had grown almost totally dark now, and the fireworks would probably start any time. I watched Afuro's face as she looked out the window. The taxi moved slowly up the steep entrance to the Rainbow Bridge and the world fell away beneath us.

"Maybe I guess it feels more like being on a boat," Afuro resumed. "This huge boat you can't get off of. One that just keeps sailing and sailing and never reaches land. I mean, you travel a lot for work, right? So you get away all the time. Does traveling make you happy?"

"It's like they say. Wherever you go, there you are."

"But I'm asking are you happy."

"I survived being shot, not once but twice, thanks to a beautiful and intelligent young woman coming to my rescue, and—"

"I'm not kidding."

"Neither am I. It's a beautiful evening, I've got a beautiful and intelligent young woman in the cab beside me and I'm headed to an island built out of trash to go watch some fireworks. What's not to be happy about?"

"Be serious," said Afuro. "Are you really *happy*?"

We were about in the middle of the bridge now, suspended between water and sky. From the expression on Afuro's face, I could tell how I answered the question meant a lot to her, but how could I answer? That one minute you're a young hotshot journalist ready to conquer the world, the next you're just trying to stick around long enough to see how it all ends. That you can't decide if happiness is something you find in other people or something wholly your own. That you begin to suspect happiness is something innate, like having perfect pitch or good taste in neckties, something you can't learn or strive toward, something no one else can give you. That eventually you accept that maybe this happiness business is best left to other people to fuss over. That, in a funny way, this makes you feel happy. And that, finally, nothing I tell her can answer the question she's really asking. She'll have to find out for herself and in the end she might just discover a conclusion wholly different from my own.

But before I can say any of this, there's a loud pop.

"It's starting!" Afuro gasps. She smiles and clutches my arm, looking out the window of the cab, across the water. Her eyes go wide as fireworks explode across the night sky.

"Isaac Adamson paints an ultramodern Tokyo that contrasts with its enigmatic history like neon against a dark sky. The characters resonate, the mystery engages, and the rich narrative takes us on a vivid tour through a culture that few of us will ever see. You can't ask for more than that from a storyteller."

—CHRISTOPHER MOORE, author of
Fluke: Or, I Know Why the Winged Whale Sings and
Bloodsucking Fiends: A Love Story

Additional praise for
Isaac Adamson and Billy Chaka

"Adamson . . . evokes an animated Tokyo-as-Toontown that is simultaneously vivid, vibrant, gaudy, and in glorious decline. . . . A big adventure."   —*Time* magazine (Asian edition)

"Billy Chaka's adventures are as vibrantly hypnotic as the best Japanese *anime*. Adamson's wild, witty whodunit deftly sends up the genre while providing extreme doses of excitement."
—*Publishers Weekly*

"If you crossbred *The Big Sleep* with *Memoirs of a Geisha* and then took its offspring and crossed it with *Chinatown* you'd end up with *Tokyo Suckerpunch*—a tongue-in-bloody-cheek quasi-punk-noir tale of death and deception in the superfantastic Far East."
—BILL FITZHUGH, author of *Cross Dressing* and *Pest Control*

"Danger lurks in the well-lit corners of Tokyo's immaculately clean streets, and it takes a teen-mag journalist to unravel the mysteries of this inscrutable world. . . . [*Hokkaido Popsicle*] is a good tale with a nice slant on geography and the pop scene."
—*Kirkus Reviews*

"[*Hokkaido Popsicle*] is rock solid; the punny dialogue sounds like a noir version of screwball comedy, and the atmosphere is pure fun. Billy meets a lot of weird people (including a Tokyo kid hooked on Willa Cather), smart-mouths himself into a lot of trouble, and somehow manages to emerge victorious. An entertaining blend of mystery and mischief."   —*Booklist*

"Astonishing. Simply astonishing. Mind-blowing, in fact. Isaac Adamson makes those other Isaacs—Newton, Deutscher, and Asimov—look like the slow-witted primates they doubtless were. *Tokyo Suckerpunch* will bitch-slap you down and dare you to get up. Do."

—DENNIS PERRIN, author of *American Fan: Sports Mania and the Culture That Feeds It* and *Mr. Mike*

Jason Trock

About the Author

ISAAC ADAMSON was born in Fort Collins, Colorado, during the Year of the Pig. He plays soccer well, guitar poorly, and is currently living in Chicago. He doesn't know his blood type. Find out more at www.billychaka.com.

Acknowledgments

I'd like to thank Dan Hooker for keeping me focused on the big picture. I'm also hugely indebted to Krista Stroever for believing in the novel and helping make it a much better one. A big thank you to Calvin Chu, whose great design work makes sure the books get seen. Props to Jason Trock for the photograph and hats off to Chumpot Ratanawong for the website.

I'm grateful to Mimi LeClair and everyone at the Mercy Home for Boys and Girls for allowing me the time to complete this work. Thanks also to Mr. Tetsuki Ijichi for suggesting Tokyo sites to visit, Caroline Bouffard and Shane and Yumi Stiles for answering my sometimes off-the-wall questions, and to Eiko Izumi Gallwas for her translation work.

And finally, thanks again to all of you who frequent www.billychaka.com.

MANY WORKS were useful in researching this book, but the following deserve special mention:

Tokyo Underworld by Robert Whiting

Flames Over Tokyo by E. Bartlett Kerr

The Pacific War 1931–1945 by Saburo Ienaga

Japan's War by Edwin P. Hoyt

Winning Pachinko by Eric Sedensky

Low City, High City by Edward Seidensticker

Listen to the Voices from the Sea by Midori Yamanouchi

♨ Perennial

Books by Isaac Adamson:

TOKYO SUCKERPUNCH

ISBN 0-380-81291-6 (paperback)

Raymond Chandler meets John Woo when an outrageously cool American reporter tries to track down the killer of Japan's worst movie director AND find the elusive geisha who has stolen his heart, all in the super-heated labyrinth of the Tokyo streets. No doubt about it: this is a pop culture potpourri of epic proportions.

"This pop romp through the Tokyo of martial arts, yakuza, and legendary geishas has more sly smarts than a Hong Kong gangster shoot-em-up. . . . Fast action, clever dialogue and all-over atmosphere." —*Publishers Weekly*

HOKKAIDO POPSICLE

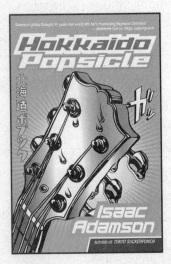

ISBN 0-380-81292-4 (paperback)

An altercation between journalist Billy Chaka and the director of a movie loosely based on his life places Chaka in Hokkaido on mandatory vacation. Here, at the Hotel Kitty, the elderly night manager stumbles into Billy's room one night and dies. Meanwhile, in Tokyo, the lead singer of Japan's most popular rock band is found dead in a sleazy love hotel. When Chaka goes to Tokyo to cover the story, he soon finds out there's more to the rocker's apparent drug overdose than meets the eye. Could it be that the rock star and the night manager share a very strange link?